SHIFT

JEFF POVEY

SIMON AND SCHUSTER

First published in Great Britain in 2014 by Simon and Schuster UK Ltd
A CBS COMPANY

Copyright © 2014 Jeff Povey

The right of Jeff Povey to be identified as the author of this work has been
asserted by him in accordance with sections 77 and 78 of the Copyright,
Designs and Patents Act, 1988.

1 3 5 7 9 10 8 6 4 2

Simon & Schuster UK Ltd
1st Floor, 222 Gray's Inn Road
London
WC1X 8HB

Simon & Schuster Australia, Sydney

Simon & Schuster India, New Delhi

A CIP catalogue record for this book is available from the British Library.

PB ISBN: 978-1-4711-1868-5
EBook ISBN: 978-1-4711-1869-2

Printed and bound by CPI Group (UK) Ltd, Croydon, CR0 4YY

www.simonandschuster.co.uk
www.simonandschuster.com.au

SHIFT

This book is for my amazing mum and dad, Brian and Beryl Povey. A brief escape in uncertain times. And how we could do with that.

It's also dedicated to my lovely Jules; love still comes in at the eye, and that's a fact. And to Rachel, Alexa, Naomi and Milo for telling me exactly where I went wrong and, exactly how to make it right.

ALARMING

There's an ape staring at me.

It's sitting in the stale musty classroom and it keeps looking at me.

I'm trying to ignore it. But it won't stop staring.

'What?' I ask it, but it doesn't reply.

I'm supposed to be meeting my boyfriend Kyle and could have done without getting an after-school detention. I won't even have time to get home and get changed out of my school uniform now.

'What?' I hiss at the Ape again. 'Like, seriously, what?'

The Ape doesn't even blink – just carries on gazing at me from halfway across the classroom.

'What d'you want?' Billie, my all-time best friend, asks the Ape. She is sitting at the school desk nearest to mine. Because of her supermodel height, her long slender legs are bent awkwardly under the desk.

The Ape doesn't reply but the teacher, Mr Allwell, clears his throat – his way of telling us to stop talking without actually bothering to speak himself.

1

Which acts as a cue for the Ape to *start* talking.

'What you in for?' It's only taken five minutes for the words to travel from his empty brain to his mouth.

'What are we *in* for?' Billie screws up her face. 'This isn't a prison.'

The Ape's eyes drop down to my chest. Many a boy has done this, but never so blatantly.

'What you in for?' I think he's expecting my boobs to speak.

'If we tell you, will you stop staring?' Billie asks the Ape.

'What?' he says transfixed.

Billie sighs hard enough to make her point. 'I got thrown out of rehearsals for *Hamlet*.'

'What's Hamlet?'

'Seriously?' Billie rolls her eyes.

'I dyed my hair pink. Didn't know it wasn't allowed.'

The Ape's eyes wrench themselves from my chest and wander up to my hair, which is dyed a hot pink. Kyle's going to either love it or hate it.

'That not real then?'

Allwell clears his throat again, only louder this time. Good, I think. Excruciating conversation over.

'Ask me what I'm in for,' the Ape says, continuing to ignore Allwell.

The Ape is bigger and wider and hairier than anyone at the school – hence the nickname – and I swear all of the staff are praying that he finally leaves this year. Holding him back to retake Year Eleven for the third time wasn't the best idea they ever had.

'Sykes caught me stealing petrol from his car.' The Ape points to a petrol stain on his red T-shirt that depicts a

2

bikini-clad woman from the Fifties posing amongst faded playing cards. I don't think he's ever worn a uniform. The Ape is wearing the stain like a badge of honour.

'That's amazing, really – awesome,' Billie tells him with a straight face.

We look away from the Ape and hope he gets the message that we seriously don't want to talk to him. But as soon as we do, Carrie sticks her brittle-boned middle finger up at me.

'What are you looking at?' she snipes at me, her icy blue eyes staring right through me, and I wish she didn't hate me so much. She is a size minus, as in her weight is somewhere in the negative, and which ever way you look at her, her bony body always comes to a point.

Being in detention is bad enough without having a gorilla and a human knitting needle for company. The only bright spot is the eternally sunny GG, who is sitting at the desk between me and Carrie, painting his fingernails canary yellow.

'What's your problem?' I hiss at Carrie.

'You know what!' She looks at me with complete hatred. 'You *so* know what.'

'Ooh. Girl war. Handbags are locked and loaded.' GG talks without taking his eyes off his nails.

'Who asked you?' Carrie gives GG a sneer, which bounces straight off him. Getting his nails right is all that matters.

Still seated, the Ape grabs his desk in one meaty paw and then kangaroos it and his chair across the classroom, straight towards Billie and me. We look up at Allwell, expecting him to tell him to stop, but like most of the staff here, he prefers to avoid direct confrontation with the Ape.

He edges loudly across the floor, in his weird chair and table caravan, and it's like the Ape's decided we're in his circle now, or he's in ours, because he's grinning hopefully at us. 'I got a question.'

Billie gives me a wary look and I know she's thinking the same thing I am. The Ape is trying to make friends with us, but that is most definitely not going to happen. He's barely the same species as us.

He drags the chair and table right up to mine.

'What you doing after?'

'Oh, good God,' Billie mutters. Thankfully the door opens and distracts the Ape.

Lucas stands in the doorway waiting for the Moth, who motors in in his wheelchair. Lucas is a straight-A student and doesn't do anything wrong *ever*, so coming to after-school detention is the equivalent of getting twenty years for armed robbery for him, and his anxious face shows that's exactly how he feels. Lucas is clever, athletic, and talented at everything he tries – at our school he's like the boy who would be King, a beautiful, caramel-skinned god.

The Moth is Lucas's best friend. A paraplegic with glasses, acne and a flat boneless nose that means his glasses keep sliding down it. No one could be physically further from Lucas than the Moth, but on other levels they are closer than brothers. Whenever you find one of them, the other isn't far away.

Lucas doesn't know where to sit at first. He looks at the permanently scowling Carrie and then gets a delicate little wave from GG.

'There's a lap going free here,' he suggests to Lucas with a smile.

Not that GG really knows Lucas. None of us here apart from the Moth have ever reached that rarefied height.

Lucas turns to Allwell, hesitant in case he does anything

4

else wrong. Allwell points to a vacant chair at the front. Lucas nods, sits down and the Moth parks his wheelchair beside him.

The Ape immediately scrapes his desk and chair in Lucas's direction, manoeuvring himself as close to him as he can manage. He can't believe Lucas is in detention either.

'What you in for?'

'Oh, I was—' the Moth begins.

'Wasn't talking to you, Hawkings.'

The Moth sometimes gets called Hawkings because everyone thinks he must have a brilliant space-brain to balance out his broken, twisted body. He is cleverer than most so it's not completely inaccurate. Usually though, he goes by the Moth, which is short for his real name, Timothy.

'How many times do I have to say this? It's Hawking,' says the Moth. 'Haw-king, not Haw-kings.'

'What you in for?' The Ape grins eagerly at Lucas.

'Nothing,' says Lucas quietly. It's hard to tell if he's blushing because his Caribbean skin gives little away.

'Tell me.'

In truth we all want to know what happened to bring the school god to this room, even Allwell, so he lets the Ape grill Lucas some more.

'Be a pal. What you in for?'

The Moth nods to Lucas as if to say it's OK. He also knows that everyone is now looking at Lucas, who will hate the scrutiny. Lucas may be the boy that everyone wants to be, but he's also painfully keen to do the right thing. He puts constant pressure on himself and one slip, or in this case, one detention, and Lucas is approaching total meltdown.

'I kicked a football at my games teacher.'

'It hit him in the nuts,' adds the Moth.

Lucas gets a big hefty slap on the back from the Ape. 'Yowza!'

But Lucas just folds in on himself, looking like his whole, entire life is ruined now.

The Ape turns to the Moth. 'Your turn, Hawkings.'

'Daz, it's Haw-king,' the Moth replies.

'You in for?'

'Doesn't he know any other words?' Billie says to me.

'Brakes failed on my chair and I ploughed into that parents' night presentation, the one in the hall – brought the whole lot down.'

'Yowza!' The Ape leans over and high-fives the Moth.

'They keep doing that. Malfunctioning.'

GG puts up his hand. 'Can I go to the bathroom please, sir?'

The Ape snorts, puts his hand up and does the worst impression of GG ever. 'Can I go and do a big dump, sir?' The Ape laughs loudly while staring at Lucas, willing him to laugh along with him because then he could fantasise that they were best friends.

GG is the world's happiest person. Happy and gay. Run the two together and you get happy gay, and gay used to mean happy, so someone said it was like he was double gay or Gay Gay, and the name kind of stuck. Rake thin and with eyeliner to match his dyed blond quiff, GG revels in his total campness. He's completely OK with who he is, and because of that everyone likes him. Apart from Billie, he's probably the only other person in detention that I actually talk to.

'Sir,' he says again, 'may I have a tinkle, please? I'll be

very quick. Barely time for an unzip and drip.' GG told us earlier that he's here because he was flirting 'inappropriately' with the new maths teacher. I'm so not surprised.

Before Allwell can respond, a match strikes and we all turn to the back of the classroom. Johnson holds the match and watches it burn before blowing it out.

That's it. That's all he does. One simple act that gets everyone's attention.

He is sitting with his feet up on the desk gazing out of the window, long thin legs stretched out in front of him. His wild dark curls fall over his eyes and I'm so glad I'm half facing away from him because there's nothing like a bad boy to turn a girl's head. Not that Johnson is bad like the Ape is – he just does his own thing and makes his own rules.

'That's Johnson,' whispers Billie, barely keeping the thrill out of her voice. As if I needed telling anyway. 'Johnson,' she repeats. No one knows if that's his first name or surname, or if in fact it's his *only* name. I've certainly never managed to get close enough to ask.

Johnson flicks the dead match across the room and as soon as it lands on the floor the fire alarm goes off in the hall outside. It's loud and piercing. Panicked voices join in with the alarm and Allwell gets to his feet, worriedly raising his hands to us. 'Stay there.' He has to speak loudly to be heard above the alarm and the shouting. Something is happening in the corridor outside. More people are joining in, footsteps charge up and down.

'Sir?' Carrie calls out, looking worried.

Allwell opens the door, and the voices and the fire alarm immediately fill the classroom. 'Good God!' he shouts.

I don't know what Allwell has seen, but after the door closes behind him there's a flash of light that seems to illuminate the whole room. Carrie jumps in her seat, letting out an involuntary scream. It's like someone's put million-watt bulbs in all the light sockets, and the flash all but blinds me.

The light goes as quickly as it came and the Ape kangaroos his chair and desk towards the door. 'Did you see that?'

'Don't open the door!' yells Lucas, panicked.

The Ape ignores him and yanks it open. We wait with bated breath as he gets to his feet and leans over the desk so he can peer out.

'Well?' asks Billie.

The Ape turns his big head left and then right, checking the hallway. It seems to take him forever.

'Tell us then!' urges Carrie.

'Nothing,' he says, eventually.

'It can't be nothing!' Lucas wails.

'Wait. The alarm's stopped,' says GG. 'And the shouting.'

We take a moment to listen and it's true, there's just silence now.

'Where's Mr Allwell?' asks the Moth.

'Who's Allwell?' says the Ape.

I get to my feet. The Ape is clearly the last person you'd send on a fact-finding mission.

'Rev, what you doing?' Billie looks worried.

'I've got to see.'

I edge over to the Ape at the doorway and dare to peer out.

'Well?' the Moth asks.

All I can see is an empty hallway. The Ape is right. There is nothing out there. Nothing at all.

'No one's out there,' I add.

'There must be,' GG argues.

'No.'

'Is the school on fire or what?' snaps Carrie.

The Moth can see that she is tense and tries to calm her. 'It doesn't feel like it's on fire.'

'And you know what that feels like do you, Hawkings? You've been in hundreds of fires, have you?' she snaps back at him, and I can see it hurts him a little.

'There'd be sirens by now, people would be spilling out into the car park,' he says in his strange little nasally voice.

I turn back to the others and find that Johnson is looking straight at me. The surprise of it makes my heart skip a beat. 'There's no fire,' I tell the room.

'Later, losers.' The Ape shoves the desk out into the hall, then gets up and lumbers into the corridor.

'I'm not staying either.' Carrie brushes past me, jabbing me with her bony elbow on purpose as she leaves. 'And you *so* know what.'

Lucas is now in a total panic. I can see his brain overloading as he tries to decide whether to stay or not. 'What if the teacher comes back and none of us are here?' he says.

'I shouldn't even be here anyway. I was wrongly accused,' the Moth says as he whirrs his way towards the door.

'But you can't all just disappear.' Lucas looks seriously worried. 'Moth, wait.'

The Moth stops and turns to his best friend with a pretty good stab at irony. 'C'mon, live on the edge, Luke, just like I do.'

Lucas wrestles with his conscience and then, with a low, ominous groan, he follows the Moth out into the corridor,

9

giving himself an excuse as he does. 'If anyone asks, I've got football practice and I need to get changed.'

Before I leave, I sneak one last glance at Johnson who remains seated with his feet up on the desk, looking to be in no particular hurry to leave.

His eyes meet mine and he gives me a lazy salute, touching his index finger to his temple and then gently cocking it my way.

'Don't get burned out there.'

Billie drags me away before I can respond. Not that I had any idea what to say to him.

L8ERS

Billie and I are walking down the steep grassy hill that leads from the school to the centre of town. I have become a little anxious about my hair colour now and wonder if I've gone too far. Billie, with her spectacular half-Indian, half-Irish colouring that translates into dark lush hair and blue eyes, has never needed to improve on that, and I'm still not sure what possessed me to do something so crazy. Did I need to be noticed that much? There's got to be something psychological going on here but I have no idea what.

'D'you think Johnson has a special pass that allows him to wear tight jeans?' Billie asks.

I'm not sure why Billie's talking about Johnson. She's rarely, if ever, mentioned him before.

'Was he wearing jeans?' I ask innocently.

'Like you didn't notice.'

'I wasn't really looking,' I lie.

'Must've seen the way he saluted me.'

I know for a fact that he saluted me, but I let it go.

'Did he?'

Billie smiles to herself at the thought. 'Oh yeah.'

We carry on to the bottom of the hill and take a short cut through the car park and over the tiny river that snakes its way through the town.

'You really have to meet Kyle?' Billie asks.

'I promised.'

'My bus isn't for another twenty minutes.' Billie looks at me hopefully. 'I'll buy you an Americano.'

Her big beseeching blue eyes are too much for me and I quickly text Kyle: **Still in detention.** We both giggle like little kids and then I feel bad. I should really be racing round to see Kyle.

We have been so busy chatting we haven't noticed that the town is unusually quiet. We're halfway to Costa before Billie comments on it.

'Look at that,' she says.

'What?'

'The high street.'

I take a moment to register the emptiness.

'Never seen it like this before,' she adds.

There are no cars or buses driving past, no people walking around.

'Bank holiday?' I ask.

'We wouldn't have been at school.' Billie continues to scan the usually packed high street. 'And people would still be out and about. Wouldn't they?'

She's right, but there doesn't appear to be another single human being anywhere. Billie gently pushes open the nearest shop door, a health food shop run by the unhealthiest-looking man I have ever seen. The door creaks a little as Billie peers in.

I wait for her to look around before she pulls the door shut again.

'Empty.'

'What d'you mean?'

'What d'you think I mean?'

I squeeze past her and take a look for myself. The health food shop is completely deserted.

'They shouldn't leave it unlocked,' I tell her before backing out. 'Someone should tell them about that – they'll get robbed.'

We move to the next shop, a key cutter and shoe repairer. Billie opens the door. Again it's unlocked and again it's empty.

'Let's try another shop,' I tell her.

We head into the travel agent. There are computer terminals at small desks, a bureau de change at the far end and stacks of travel brochures lying neatly on shelves. But no people.

'Maybe everyone booked themselves a holiday,' Billie jokes.

We enter the phone shop next door, which is nearly always packed with people wanting an upgrade on a phone they've had less than a week, and the result is the same. No one home.

We emerge from the phone shop and look up and down the empty high street again. I even scan the second- and third-floor windows of the offices above the shops, but there's no sign of movement behind any of them.

Billie heads into the next shop along, Boots. I follow her through the automatic doors.

My heart is starting to quicken and I'm getting a tingling sensation in my arms and shoulders.

'Gas leak?' I ask. 'Chemical spill?'

Billie isn't listening because usually the first thing you see in Boots are the women on the make-up counter who have applied so much product on their faces you're always surprised there's any left to sell. But the painted ladies aren't there today. No one is.

'Where is everyone?' Billie asks, but it's not a question I'm likely to have an answer for. 'Hey!' she calls out.

'What are you doing?'

'HEY!' she shouts louder this time.

'Shh, they'll throw us out.'

'Who? Who exactly is going to throw us out?' Billie is enjoying the emptiness less and less. She breaks into a fast walk, hurrying down the aisles looking for a sign of life.

I try to keep up with her as she moves quickly from aisle to aisle.

'Hey! Hello!' Billie looks at me, her eyes wide. I know her heart is pumping as hard as mine is.

Billie hurries out of Boots and I chase after her as we race into more high street shops, calling out, hoping that someone is there. But each one is the same. Empty.

There is absolutely no one to be found. Everything looks the same, it feels the same and even smells the same, but without actual people it just isn't the same.

'Terrorists? It's got to be terrorists.'

Billie's eyes grow even wider. 'God, Rev.'

'I'm just saying.'

'You think there's been an evacuation? Like they've found a bomb or something?'

'What else could it be?'

'So where are the soldiers? The police?' she says, looking more freaked out by the second.

'Let me try my mum.' I grab my phone and call home, but it goes straight to answering machine. I try to act cool and casual. 'Mum, you there? Something going on that I've missed? Call me . . .' I try to say the last bit in a sort of happy-clappy, sing-song voice – as if I haven't a care in the world – but my voice cracks halfway through and that's when I hear my heart pounding in my ears, like it has a sixth sense or something. That it's beating out a warning. I look at Billie and she's also on her phone.

'Dad, just saying hi. Uh, where . . . Uh, well there doesn't seem to be anyone around. Could you maybe . . . well, yeah, could you call me back? Please.'

The pounding is reaching deep into my brain and giving me a splitting headache.

We head for the town square and Billie cranes her neck to study the sky. 'There aren't even any birds.' It's as empty as the streets below it. A few clouds, but no birds or planes.

'Do they evacuate birds?' she asks.

'They do now.' It's a bad joke – weak. But I'm trying not to freak out completely.

'Let's keep looking.'

'We've been looking.'

Billie looks me straight in the eye. 'OK. Here's what I think. There's been a mass evacuation. There's a war or something breaking out, and a missile is heading our way. Only they forgot to tell us.'

'Mum wouldn't forget me. Your dad wouldn't forget you either. Neither of them have called us.'

'What about Kyle – has he texted back?'

15

'No. Not yet.'

'So text him again.'

My fingers jab at the touchscreen. **Where is every1?**

We wait, staring at my phone. Seconds turn into minutes, but no response comes.

'Call him,' Billie snaps.

I do but a voice tells me that '*no connection is possible at this present time*'. I hang up and look at Billie and she's as spooked as I am.

'Why am I not enjoying this?' she asks.

'Why would you?'

'Well, this is a dream right? Having a town all of your own. We can do anything, go shopping, choose the best clothes.'

'That's called looting,' I say.

We carry on towards the town square and Billie slips her hand into mine. It feels cold, like it's lacking blood, but I hold on tightly as we emerge on to the cobbled square. It's usually packed with people. You can sit there all day and watch half the world pass by. But not today. A children's roundabout, giant cups and saucers, sits idly in the middle. The sign reads *Five years and under* and I know we're both wondering where all the five-years-and-unders have gone.

'What about the church?' Billie says suddenly. 'People go to churches in times of panic.'

There's an ancient church that dominates the centre of town and if panicked, scared people are going to gather, that's where they're going to go.

We run down the cobbled side road, charge past the war memorial decorated with the names of people who were also here once but aren't now, then burst into the church grounds.

16

I know even before we open the great wooden door that it is empty. It just has that feeling.

Billie's eyes dart everywhere but the nearest thing to a human being is a large porcelain statue of Jesus, and even he has his head bowed and won't acknowledge our presence.

'Jesus,' says Billie.

On the way home I phone Mum again, this time not cool, but totally frantic.

'Mum? *Where are you?* I'm scared. Mum! Mum, pick up! You there? Mum!'

Billie and I aren't talking. We are locked in our own dark thoughts as the fear spreads through us. No cars pass by – there's no movement anywhere.

We walk towards an empty bus, parked at a bus stop. Its door is wide open and for some reason it looks almost inviting. Before I know it, I've crossed the road to take a closer look.

'Rev!' Billie hurries to catch up with me. 'Stay close.'

I stop at the open door and I'm sure I can hear voices.

'You hear that?' I whisper to Billie.

'Hear what?'

'Voices . . .'

Billie takes a moment. 'Voices? Seriously?'

I take a step forward, listen harder. The voices are there, I'm sure of it, but they're too faint and I can't quite make them out.

'Rev, don't get too close.'

I hold up a hand to get Billie to be quiet and take another step towards the open door. There's a strange heat emanating from inside. 'You feel that?' I ask her.

Billie remains static – doesn't come any closer.

'Wait, it's not voices. It's *a* voice. There's someone on the bus,' I say. 'They're saying my name – I think.'

Billie takes hold of my arm to pull me back. 'Rev, please, this isn't funny.'

I shake Billie off and start to step aboard, but the second I do the bus doors slam shut.

Billie screams and my heart nearly breaks a rib it leaps so hard in my chest.

'Christ!' I yell.

I look at the shut door and realise that the heat and the voice have disappeared. I peer inside trying to see who closed the doors, but I can't see anyone. I jog along the side of the bus, jumping up to get a better look. But I can't see anyone on board.

'You sure you didn't hear a voice?' I ask her.

'Let's get to your mum's. Like now.'

My mum doesn't trust me to not lose my front-door key, so she always hides it under one of eight plant pots that sit in full bloom on our window sill – it's the closest we've got to a garden. I lift the third pot along and retrieve the key. But when I try the door, I can't get the key to fit. It won't go in.

'What is this?! She's changed the lock!'

'Let me try.' Billie takes the key from my trembling hand and shoves it hard into the lock. It turns easily. 'You had it upside down.'

We burst inside and I start calling for Mum as Billie goes from room to room in the tiny two-bedroom council flat.

'Mum! *Mum!*' She should be home because she works evenings, waitressing in a restaurant. Money is tight, so I know it'd be unusual for her to go out shopping or to see a friend. Most days she stays in and watches telly.

'She's not in,' Billie says, coming back to where I'm standing, having searched the entire flat.

I stop in the hallway and don't know what to do next. Our ancient answerphone on the table flashes with messages and I hit *play*. My voice echoes down the hallway '*Mum? Where are you? I'm scared . . .*'

'Dad, could you call me? *Please*.' Billie is back on her mobile calling her dad's office again as I look around, hoping that Billie may have missed something.

The lounge is pretty much as I left it this morning. The tiny kitchen is the same. Even the bathroom is the same.

But when I look closer I can see that the bath has been filled recently. I put my hand into it and the water is still hot so Mum must have been running herself a bath. Which makes me think she must have been in the flat very recently.

'Dad's not picking up,' says Billie. 'There's no service for his mobile either.'

'It looks like Mum was going to have a bath,' I offer quietly. 'She was here. Can't have been more than five minutes ago.'

'So why didn't she answer the phone?'

I have no idea, I think.

'You tried Kyle?' Billie asks.

'I already did. You suggested it, remember, when we were on the high street?'

'I did?' Billie puts a hand to her forehead. 'I'm losing it.'

I phone Kyle again anyway, but get the same '*no connection possible*' message. I try it once more just in case, but it still won't put me through.

Billie sits down beside me on the edge of the bath. She's

in most of the top sets at school and right now we need her brains.

'The TV!' she exclaims.

It seems so obvious – why didn't we think of it before? I jump up and charge into the lounge. Billie is right behind me as I grab the remote and switch it on.

Nothing. I flick through the channels, but there is nothing but static.

Billie has already started the battered computer that sits on a tiny second-hand table in the corner of the room under the window.

'Anything?' I ask her.

'It's still booting. How old is this thing?'

'Was my dad's.'

'That makes it over twelve years old!'

'Mum can't afford a new one.'

Billie watches the screen come to life and we wait for it to make the Internet connection. I managed to hook up the Wi-Fi all by myself. Mum told me that Dad would have been very proud.

But there is nothing on the Internet either. In fact there is no Internet. The connection just fails and fails and fails again.

Billie tries connecting to the Internet using the 4G on her phone, but the same thing happens. No Internet connectivity.

'The radio!' I sprint into the kitchen, banging the 'on' button on the old radio Mum listens to every morning. We wait for it to come to life but it doesn't. It just sits there spraying static into the room.

Billie slumps down at the formica kitchen table.

'It's not your birthday, is it?' she tries to joke. 'Maybe everyone's waiting to jump out and shout "Surprise!"'

My phone beeps loudly with a text. After the amount of silence we've just endured it makes us both jump. I grab for the phone, manage to drop it and watch it land on the floor. The casing springs off and the battery spills out.

'Christ, Rev!!'

'Sorry, sorry, sorry.'

We get down on our hands and knees, both of us crawling under the kitchen table to retrieve the scattered phone parts. But every time I pick a piece up, it seems to slip from my jittery hands.

'Jesus, get a grip,' Billie mutters.

'Like you're Mrs Calm,' I snap back.

Billie snatches the battery from me, slams it into the back of the phone and switches it back on. I never knew that waiting for a phone to reboot could take so long. It feels like we are under the table for hours before the phone finally lights up.

The text message flashes up.

Seen any1 l8ly?

We both stare at the phone, reading and re-reading the text.

'Who's that from?' Billie asks me.

'No idea,' I say. The number isn't one I recognise.

'Text back,' she says.

'Saying what?'

'That, no, we haven't seen anyone lately.'

I try to compose myself. My hands don't seem to be trembling so much any more. This sign of life seems to have brought a slight sense of calm.

No. Have u? I write.

We wait for the reply and almost give up when the phone pings with a response.

Duh!

'Duh?' I say to Billie. '*Duh?* What does that mean?'

'Ask them who they are,' she tells me.

Who r u

The text comes back quicker this time.

Dazza.

Billie and I hesitate at this.

'Who's Dazza?' she asks me.

Who's Dazza I text.

FFS! is the abrupt reply. We leave it for a few more moments, putting the onus on 'Dazza' to text again. A few seconds later the phone beeps.

Stupid ho

'That's nice,' says Billie. 'We've found Prince Charming.'

FU I text back.

'What are you doing?! You've just told the only person we've had any contact with to F off!'

'Well, he didn't need to call me that,' I say. I don't care if the whole world has vanished. I don't need some psycho I don't even know texting me abuse.

FU 2 he fires back.

I'm about to get into a text war when Billie snatches the phone from me. 'Everyone's gone who knows where and you've got anger issues?' she says, still glaring.

This is Billie Evitt. I'm with Reva Marsalis. Who and where r u? Billie texts, her thumbs moving like lightning across the tiny virtual keyboard.

Told ya. I'm Dazza

22

'We must know a Dazza, otherwise how would he have your number?' Billie starts to rack her brain. 'Dazza, Dazza, Dazza.'

I'm in Tesco. A new text from Dazza pings across to us.

'He's shopping?' Billie looks completely bemused now.

U the only 1 there? I text back.

☺

'He texted a smile? Who texts a smile at a time like this?' I say. Then it dawns on me. 'It's the Ape!'

'The Ape?'

My spirits are already plummeting. 'Yes, someone in detention called him Daz, I'm sure they did.'

Billie looks at the smile on the text and slowly shakes her head. 'How come he has your number? You been seeing him behind Kyle's back?' Even if the only sign of life is some gross primate, it appears to have lifted her spirits.

'Excuse me if I don't laugh,' I tell her.

'Text him back. Tell him we're coming.'

'Seriously?'

'Who else is there? We don't have a choice.'

We'll be there in 10 I write.

Then for good measure I add, ☺

SUPERDUPERMARKET

The Ape is sitting on one of the wheelie chairs the assistants use at the checkout. He's pulling himself along the aisles, trying to build up as much speed as he can. He's going so fast that by the time we walk through the automatic doors of the very empty Tesco supermarket, he nearly knocks us off our feet. I grab Billie and drag her out of the way as the Ape shoots past us.

'Loving this!' he yells on his way past, clutching a can of beer.

While we wait for him to slow down and then drag himself back towards us, we can see that the Ape has been making himself at home while he waited for us. Half-eaten bars of chocolate and empty bags of sweets lie scattered on the floor. It's like he's opened one packet, taken a bite and then discarded it so he can take a bite out of a new bar.

'That is so wasteful,' Billie says, her eyes scanning the huge supermarket looking for more signs of life, but so far there aren't any. 'Looks like it's just him.'

My heart sinks. Even though the Ape had already texted that he was the only one, I was half hoping he was either joking or just too stupid to notice. He wheels himself back towards us and, in trying to stop the chair, topples over and crashes at our feet. His beer goes flying and soaks the tobacco kiosk. He lies on the floor laughing.

'Love, love, loving it!'

Billie and I look down at him as he belches then belches again.

'So where is everyone?' he eventually asks.

'You don't know? No one told you?' Billie can barely disguise her contempt for the Ape. 'They got sucked up by aliens.'

'Yowza!' the Ape responds, delighted.

'Yowza?' Billie is clearly thrown.

'Yow-*zaaa*.' He drags the word out and then climbs slowly to his feet. We are given a flash of the top of his fleshy, hairy buttocks as he gets on all fours before standing. He then belches again and Billie and I both grimace.

'Where they sucked them off to?' he grins.

'Mars,' Billie offers.

'That's a lot of sucking off,' he says, milking his sad little joke.

'Jesus!' Billie turns to me, and I can tell she's as deflated as I am to realise that the Ape is the sole person we have met in the last hour or so.

'She was kidding with you,' I say. 'We have no idea where everyone is.'

'Oh well.' The Ape truly doesn't seem to care.

I am staggered. 'That's all you can say?'

'Hey, I've got to show you this.' He lumbers over to one of the tills and searches for a small bag that he has stashed in a cupboard under the till. 'Look what I got!' He grins as he takes some money out of the bag, showing us maybe a thousand pounds in cash. 'I found it in a bank.'

Billie and I look at him like he's crazy. Seriously, what is wrong with this boy?

'You *stole* that?' Billie asks.

'It was just lying there. Finders keepers.'

'And?' she prods.

'So, I'm rich. Want to go see a film?'

I swear I can feel my eyes bulging with incredulity. The Ape picks up a bottle of cider, unscrews the cap and takes a healthy swig. 'I've got plenty of time, cos I can't get into my flat. Mum hasn't showed up to let me in.'

'That's the point, idiot, *no one* has "showed up"!' Billie's practically yelling at him now. 'Haven't you noticed the lack of people?!'

'Well, yeah, but I thought maybe something was going on and I hadn't been invited.'

'So why did you go to a bank?'

'Door was open. Walked in. Looked around and now I've got enough green for a hundred movies plus popcorn. You coming?'

The Ape is so insanely stupid that I truly wish he'd disappeared along with everyone else.

'D'you have any idea what's happening here?' I say

'Not really. And here's a question for you. Do I care?'

'But everyone seems to have disappeared.'

'So?'

'SO!?' Billie screams at him.

'Anyway, not everyone has gone,' he counters.

'You've seen others?' Billie's instant stab of hope matches my own.

26

'Yeah,' the Ape says.

'Where? Where are they?' I say. I want to shake the great oaf.

'They're right here.'

Billie and I hesitate and watch the Ape laugh at us.

'It's you two. I've seen you two.'

Our hopes crash and burn and I know Billie feels like slapping the Ape.

'That wasn't funny,' I say.

'So was. Should have seen your faces.' His casual, uncaring tone is wretched. There is no other word for it. It is plain wretched. 'Look, I'm here. You're here. We don't need anyone else.' He takes another swig of cider.

'But your family, your mum—' I start

'She's never home,' he interrupts.

'Your friends . . .'

'Who needs them?'

'Aren't you scared?' Billie looks tired and drawn now. Fighting back our panic and fear has completely worn us out.

The Ape thinks for a moment, then comes to an outstanding thought. 'I don't do scared. So who's coming to see a film?'

I'm ready to grab the cider bottle and bash him over the head with it when we hear movement in another aisle. We immediately fall silent, even the Ape, but I think it's only because he's following our lead.

The movement sounds slow and sludgy, like something being dragged. Something wet.

'What is that?' Billie whispers.

'You said there was no one around.' I keep my voice low as I look at the Ape.

27

'There isn't.'

The movement is getting closer. 'I'd say it sounds like there is,' I tell him.

'Urgh, what's that stink?' he whispers, screwing up his face.

Then I smell it too. A strong odour that attacks my eyes, making them sting.

'Was that you, Rev? You let one go?' laughs the Ape.

'Shut up, it's getting closer,' I whisper.

The Ape weighs us up, then takes my arm in his big rough hand and nodding to Billie he moves us quietly behind the fresh vegetable aisle. 'Move.'

We edge quietly down the aisle, but whatever is moving towards us seems to sense that we have crept away and changes direction.

'It's still coming,' Billie whispers.

The slow, sludge movement continues to suck at the floor.

'I've got this,' the Ape says and turns the cider bottle upside down, brandishing it as a weapon. His large body looms like a wall in front of us. I am amazed that he is even thinking of protecting us and it almost makes me feel grateful that he's here.

The sucking, creeping sound is still coming towards us.

'Get back.' The Ape ushers us further into the heart of the supermarket. We go as quietly as we can while he scans the area around us, awaiting an attack. He is clearly better equipped to deal with terrifying sludge movements than Billie or me, and his big hulking presence and weird instinct for violence and self-preservation suddenly feels like a warm blanket thrown around our shoulders.

'What d'you think it is?' he whispers.

'How would we know?' I hiss back.

'Whatever it is, it seriously stinks,' says Billie.

'Thought that was you getting scared,' the Ape sniggers. He's clearly a master at milking the same lame joke over and over.

The sludge movement is getting closer and the smell is becoming horrendous, burning my eyes and throat.

The Ape has managed to get us all the way into the drink aisle, but in doing so he has also cut us off from escape. There's nothing but a wall of wine and spirits behind us now. And still the thing – whatever it is – keeps coming.

'Jesus, Rev!' Billie grips my hand tight.

The Ape whispers. 'I've got this.'

'You've *got* nothing!' I hiss at him.

The thing sounds like it's moving quicker now, and the noise is getting louder. It's closing in on us. The Ape pulls a zippo lighter out of his pocket. A lighter that, legend has it, he beat up a gym teacher for.

'Cod four,' he whispers.

We both look at him.

'Cod four,' he repeats.

'What?' I ask.

'*Call of Duty 4.*' He grabs a bottle of brandy and starts unscrewing it. 'I'm going to Molotov it.'

He sounds pretty sure of himself, even if we have no idea what he's talking about. He goes quickly to the nearest clothing aisle, grabs a shirt, then comes back to us and tears off a strip of material; he feeds half of the fabric into the brandy and gets ready to light it.

'Stay back,' he instructs, ushering us back even further. The thing is almost upon us and I can't believe how much I

29

love the Ape right now. It's like having a big, stupid, vicious dog to protect you.

Billie pulls her top over her nose and mouth to try and combat the stench as the Ape lets out a roar and lights the Molotov cocktail.

'Come on then!' he yells, and charges out from our hiding place. He hurls the Molotov.

And misses. Completely. He dives back into our hiding place.

'I missed!'

And I hate him. I hate him like you hate a big, stupid, vicious dog that's just bitten you.

'Could you tell what it is?' Billie asks breathlessly.

'I dunno, didn't look!' he says, while he makes another Molotov.

'Let me have that,' I say.

'My plan, my Molotov.'

'Give me it!' I snap at him.

The squelching is louder than ever and the thing totally knows where we are thanks to the Ape and his ludicrous aim. And it's coming quicker now. Much faster. I grab the Molotov.

'Make more, as many as you can!' I yell at him, then leap out, rag burning in the brandy, and I see it, the thing, the foul smelling, lurching creature. It's like nothing I've ever set eyes on before – it's not human, it's not an animal, it's just a black burned thing.

I am ready to hurl the Molotov, but when I look closer I swear the thing actually *is* human – or was. It's a person. God alone knows what happened, but it's a man, I'm sure of it. The arms are almost shredded completely to the bone, little more than blistered charcoal; the stench we've been smelling is burned skin and flesh. Its mouth is opening and closing. It wants to speak. *He* wants to speak.

I stand in silence, my heart thudding in my chest, with the Molotov cocktail ready to blow any second if I don't take the burning rag out.

'What happened?' is all I can think to ask. 'What happened? Where did everyone go?'

The man, the thing, the burned human, stares at me and I think he's probably blind because he has no pupils left. He opens his mouth and his tongue is black and prune-like. I want to scream but I also want him to sense that I care, so I do the best I can to stifle my fear. There's something about him, some sort of presence or aura that draws me in. It's almost as if I know him.

I manage to yank the burning cloth from the Molotov and even though I burn my fingers doing so I know that my pain is nothing compared to what this poor man is enduring.

He tries to speak, but words won't ever come out of a mouth like that.

The Ape's first Molotov cocktail has set fire to the magazine aisle and suddenly the rising smoke causes the automatic sprinklers to turn on. It's weird but I like the wetness, and it soothes the burned man, like an ointment on his blackened, blistered skin. I watch him and he almost smiles – maybe it's just an agonised grimace, I don't know, but the rain makes his skin steam. I can't help but wonder why the sprinklers didn't go off before if he was on fire? And then I wonder how far he must have crawled in this state. How far did he come and how much did it take for him to seek out help. Because I'm sure that's why he's here, he wants someone to save him.

31

His ears must be working, because he could hear us moving around the shop, so I squat down beside him.

'What do you want me to do?' I ask.

I'm sure that he's beyond saving and it breaks my heart. Soaking wet, I reach out and touch what I think might have been a hand once. I try to squeeze it to offer some sort of comfort but my fingers go right through what's left of his hot flesh and hit bone. I want to jump away, to recoil, but there's no way he's going to die without me touching him and being there for him.

'What can I do?' I ask, knowing it's futile.

'What the hell?' Billie has edged out of hiding to see what's happening.

I ignore her, too mesmerised by the burned man. There is a connection between us, I can sense it and I think he can sense it too.

'*Rev,*' Billie hisses.

'It's OK,' I tell her. 'Just give me a moment. What happened to everyone?' I whisper to the man.

He raises what's left of his face towards me, but before he can open his mouth again the last of his life goes out and he gently lowers his head to the floor and falls still.

Which is when the Ape leaps out wielding two more Molotovs – one in each hand – and yells, 'Come on then!'

He only just manages to stop himself hurling them straight at me. Then, possibly because I'm just sitting here in my wet school blouse that's now clinging to my chest, he douses the Molotovs and comes over and asks me if he should fetch a towel and maybe rub me dry. I don't respond because I'm sitting with a carcass, a human carcass, and I can't think for the life of me how any of this can really be happening when everything was so normal just a few hours ago.

32

Billie can't help herself and starts to cry at the sight of the dead man, and it's left to the Ape to lift me under my armpits and pull me away from the poor burned soul. His BO is overpowering, but kudos to him for showing some sign of humanity and caring.

'C'mon,' he says, 'you can't do nothing.'

'It's a man,' I say.

'*Was* a man,' he replies.

'But . . .'

'Dead, Rev. He's dead.'

I sit back and can't tell if I'm crying or if it's just the sprinkler water running down my face. I look at Billie who is equally as confused and lost.

'I wish it was still yesterday,' she says quietly.

'We're out of here,' says the Ape.

'No,' I say.

'No?'

'No,' I repeat. I don't know where it's coming from, but I have a new strength in me now. Maybe it's come from the burned man – maybe by touching him he somehow added his life force to mine. 'He heard us and he came looking for us for a reason,' I add.

'Yeah, he was on fire. Wanted someone to help.' The Ape reduces everything to the bluntest logic.

I look at Billie. 'You understand, don't you?'

She nods, but then adds, 'Not really.'

'He came from somewhere,' I say.

'So? What does that matter?' Billie asks.

'So,' I tell her, my voice as calm as I can manage, 'somewhere is *somewhere*. Right?'

'I s'pose,' she says, straightening and wiping her eyes

33

with the back of her hand. 'But I'm thinking . . . I'm think-ing that . . .' She trails off.

'What?' I ask her.

'The light. It was the light.'

The Ape looks totally lost. 'What light?'

'Have you actually got a memory?' I snap at him.

'You're the ones who didn't remember my name,' he snaps back.

'There was a light when the classroom door got opened. Bright and blinding,' Billie continues, ignoring our bicker-ing. 'Ever since then we've not seen another person.'

The Ape gets an idea and incredibly enough looks excited by it. 'Maybe the light fried everyone!'

Billie shudders. 'Don't, please.'

'Something fried that guy.'

'I'm going to follow the man's trail,' I say suddenly.

'Seriously?' Billie looks worried.

'He came from somewhere. He may have been left behind or he may have got out from wherever everyone else is.'

'I don't want you to go anywhere, Rev,' she says to me.

'I have to. We need to do something,' I tell her.

'If he came from somewhere that burned him that badly then that's not a place anyone should go,' she replies.

'I need a beer.' The Ape is already bored by the discussion.

'That light,' I persist. 'It might've fried everyone, like the Ape said.'

'You just call me an ape?'

'Everyone does,' I say, impatiently. Is he so dense that he's not heard people call him that at school?

'I'm Dazza.'

'No, you're not. OK? You're the Ape.'

The Ape almost looks hurt and walks off, muttering something about getting crisps too. For a split second I almost feel sorry for him, but I've got bigger things to worry about than his feelings.

'If everyone got burned, where's their ashes, Rev? Or their squelchy, burned bodies?' Billie asks. She's looking directly at me and I know she's doing her level best to keep a grip on reality. 'That can't be what happened, it just can't.'

'That's why I need to go and find out. Because despite what that man was going through, he was trying to tell us something, I'm sure of it.'

The Ape returns with a six-pack of Buds and a family-size bag of crisps. 'We could live for years in here,' he says with a big grin on his face.

'Keep Billie safe,' I tell him.

'Me?'

'You're the best we've got right now,' I say, realising with a sinking feeling that sadly that's true.

The Ape looks proud. 'Yep, that's me.'

'Cod four,' I say to him.

He salutes me and I haven't the heart to tell him I'm only saying that because I'm scared I won't come back and that someone will need to look after Billie.

After unpacking and laying a large cotton tablecloth over the burned man, I pick up his trail and follow it all the way to the back of the supermarket.

THE TRAIL YOU SHOULDN'T FOLLOW

A body doesn't just burn, it sort of melts too. At least that's what I learn, because the dead man's dark gooey trail isn't hard to pick up. I follow it down the soaking wet aisles, through to a storeroom and on through two wide-open delivery doors, then on towards a massive articulated lorry. The trail stops at the open door of the lorry. I take a guess that whatever burned the man, burned him in the driver's cabin and he tried to escape before the flames engulfed him completely.

I head towards the door of the cabin with the feeling that whatever I do in the next ten seconds I really shouldn't climb up into the cabin. The one thing anyone in my position should *not* do is that. But I also have this other feeling that unless I do the one thing I'm not supposed to, I won't find out what has happened. And I need to know. Me, Billie and the Ape need to know.

I reach up and pull myself onto the steps leading up to the driver's cabin.

'Hello?' I call out.

I climb a step higher.

'Anyone?'

I take another step and the higher I climb, the warmer it seems to get. My head draws level with the inside of the cabin and I can see signs of the fire that must have engulfed the burned man. The melted seats and steering wheel are pretty damning proof of that. God alone knows how hot it must've been in there. That poor man, I think.

I'm not sure what I hope to find and the cabin is in such a state that I don't think anything is going to help me discover what actually happened. But I'm here now so I climb further in and as I do I spot pieces of the burned man's skin stuck to the interior. The air starts to get hotter around me and at first I like the heat, it's like a hot bath that I want to sink into. But it keeps getting hotter and the heat is doing something to me, making me dizzy and lose focus. My clothes that had been soaking wet from the sprinklers in the shop are now dry as a bone and I realise that their dampness must have shielded me from the onslaught of heat.

I look at my arm and there are already blisters forming and my fingers are starting to clench up, not because I want them to, but of their own accord. I try to get out of the cabin, but I can't seem to move. The heat won't let me. I can't find any air that isn't going to burn the hell out of my throat and I don't have any strength in my overheated limbs. I'm willing myself to move but my brain is cloudy and can't send the right signals. My limbs continue to curl involuntarily from the heat, and it's like I'm curling up to die. *Why the hell did I come up here*, I think.

From nowhere someone grabs my ankles and yanks them hard and I crash down onto the tarmac. I land so awkwardly that for a second I think I've broken my spine.

'You're on fire,' a voice says, as I'm dragged away from the boiling lorry. I'm actually smouldering. I can see steam coming off me as I'm shoved through the delivery doors at the rear of the supermarket. I get a glimpse of wild dark locks as my rescuer grabs a shopping trolley, dumps me into it and wheels me back into the supermarket aisle at a thousand miles an hour till we hit the freezer section where we skid to a halt. Bags of ice are torn open and suddenly ice cubes are raining down on me, hundreds of them, pouring down onto my superheated body.

'You alone?' a voice asks.

'No . . .' I whisper hoarsely. 'Billie's around somewhere.'

'Wait there.'

The rescuer takes off, calling at the top of his voice. 'Hey! Billie! Hey!'

I listen as Billie comes running.

'Johnson??' She sounds shocked.

Did she say Johnson?

'Quick.'

They hurry towards me and I do everything I can to not black out from the searing pain.

'Rev, can you hear me?'

I look up and see Johnson looking down at me.

'Told you not to get burned.'

THE CHEMISTRY OF CHEMISTRY

Most supermarkets have a chemist's section and Johnson proves to be a doctor in the making when he breaks open packs of bandages and ointments and gives me painkillers washed down with a bottle of mineral water he's grabbed from the shelves. I'm screaming inside with agony, but he hands Billie the ointments and bandages and then reads out the instructions so that she knows what to do.

'What the hell happened?' she asks.

'I found her halfway inside a lorry,' Johnson offers.

'It's where the man came from,' I whisper, my throat red raw from the heat.

'Why did you go in if it was on fire? Was it on fire?'

'No. I mean yes. I don't really know . . .'

Billie keeps gently applying ointment onto my burns, and whatever Johnson found it is working miracles.

Johnson sticks a thermometer into my mouth and takes a reading. I don't really know what he thinks he is going to do with the information but he seems to think it's important.

'Did you see anyone out there?' Billie asks Johnson.

'You're the first people I've seen since I left school.'

'Didn't see anyone at all?' I ask him.

He gives a rueful smile and I notice he has deep dimples that make him look like he is smiling twice. 'No. Sorry.'

Johnson gets side-tracked by the Ape coming down the aisle with a homemade weapon. It's a broom with carving knives taped to the end of it. Nice.

'I did a sweep out back. There's no one there,' he says.

Billie leans towards me and takes a second reading from the thermometer.

'It's coming down.'

Johnson turns to the Ape and Billie. 'I thought I was the only one left.'

'Yeah, it's getting a bit crowded now,' says the Ape and from the smell on his breath I can tell he's downed another beer and eaten a packet of cheese and onion crisps.

Johnson looks back at me. 'The painkillers kicking in yet?'

'Must be. I feel a bit light-headed.'

'Light-headed is good.'

'It is?'

'Oh, yeah,' he smiles. 'Though I can break open the pharmacy and get the real stuff if you need it – there's got to be some kind of morphine in there.'

'What's that?' asks the Ape.

'A drug.'

'Break it open, Jonno. Let's par-tay.'

We ignore him.

'I owe you,' I tell Johnson.

'Was nothing. Just happened to be there.'

But it was much more than that, I want to tell him. He probably saved my life.

'What d'you think's happened?' interrupts Billie.

'Until I met you three I didn't have a clue. But now I'm starting to wonder.'

'How d'you mean?' I ask him.

'Well. The last people I saw are also the first people I saw, if you get my drift. So maybe we've been singled out, or we're linked in some way.'

'But singled out by who?' asks Billie.

No one even attempts to answer that.

CAR TROUBLE

The smell coming from the burned man has made Johnson think that we should either move him or move out. He tells the Ape and Billie to gather blankets, clothes and food and drink. He also doesn't think the Ape should drink any more alcohol.

'You'll end up stabbing yourself with that broom,' he tells him.

Billie laughs at this but the Ape scowls. 'You'll be glad of this when they come.'

'When who come?' I say.

'Whatever's out there.'

'I don't think there's anyone out there. Isn't that the point?'

'There's always someone out there,' he says. 'Always.'

It doesn't take long for Billie and the Ape to fill a trolley with food and drink from the shelves.

I watch Johnson head for the cigarette kiosk. He finds the brand he wants, slides a packet out of the shelf, opens it and then slips a fresh cigarette into the corner of his mouth. He strikes a match that seemingly appears like magic in his hand and takes a long slow draw. He holds the smoke in his mouth then blows a smoke circle. For some reason, I'm guessing all the painkillers making me light-headed, I can't stop gazing at him. It's not that I haven't noticed him before, of course I have, but there was never a reason for our paths to cross. His world doesn't touch mine, like I'd ever be cool enough anyway, and yet suddenly here we both are. He senses me staring at him and when he turns I blush and look away.

The Ape is riding the back of a packed trolley and comes hurtling towards me. 'Chicken!' he booms.

'So what's the plan?' I ask Johnson as he returns.

'We need to try another town.'

We live in commuter belt heaven. We're thirty-eight miles directly north of London and, with its famed Tuesday and Saturday market, this town is seen as desirable living. Mum and Dad had plans to move out of our tiny flat into one of the sought-after tree-lined avenues but those plans went up in smoke after my dad upped and left us when I was four years old.

'You think it's just this town that's empty?' I say.

Johnson thinks for a moment, obviously weighing up whether to worry me unduly or not. 'No. Not really,' he says finally. 'I phoned my cousin who lives in Scotland and no one picked up there either.'

'So why are we trying another town?' I ask quietly.

'Because I want to be wrong,' he says, equally as quietly.

Billie walks back, looking calmer than earlier.

'I laid another tablecloth on the man. D'you think it's all right just to leave him?'

'There's not a lot else we can do,' I tell her.

'Still, doesn't feel right. But we could maybe come back for him when we've found someone who knows what to do.'

'I was thinking the same thing,' Johnson replies.

Billie grins at this. 'Great minds.'

We hear a loud crash and for a second my heart misses a beat, until I realise the Ape has fallen off the trolley and brought it down on top of him.

'I broke my leg! Need morphine!' he yells, but we ignore him.

'Rev and I were thinking we should try another town, see if it's the same,' Johnson explains to Billie.

'I need drugs!' The Ape's voice echoes around the supermarket.

'How are we going to get there?' Billie asks.

'I was hoping one of you could drive,' Johnson says.

'You can't drive?' I'm a little surprised.

'Motorbikes,' he says and in the same breath blows smoke towards the floor.

'I can drive.' The Ape limps back towards us, with a chicken leg gripped in one hand. 'I stole my first car when I was ten years old. And crashed it,' he says proudly.

'Say we could get a car, where would we go?' I look at the others.

'The seaside!' the Ape suggests.

'We could drive to my house. I'm sure my dad wouldn't have gone without leaving a message.'

'Alton Towers!' the Ape cries, but we continue to ignore him.

'My dad would find a way to leave something. He's always worrying about me.'

44

'Was worrying,' says the Ape.

'What?' Billie turns to him.

'*Was*. He isn't there now.'

His lack of tact angers Billie. 'But his note might be,' she insists angrily. 'He'll have left me a note and that will still be there.'

'You fit enough to move?' Johnson asks me.

'Long as I take a ton of painkillers with me.'

'Madame Tussauds! They're people!'

'They're made of *wax*.' How can one person be so annoying?

'But they still look like people'.

'Better find you something to wear,' Johnson says to me.

I'd forgotten that half of my school uniform was burned or scorched. There's a clothing section three aisles away and I'm ready to go with Johnson when Billie gets in first.

'Wait there, Rev. End of the world or not, you can't keep a girl from the clothes rack.'

But you can, I think, *because you just did*.

'The zoo!' the Ape shouts. 'We could live with monkeys.'

I don't have the energy to tell him to please stop.

We push a second trolley of food and drink out into the supermarket car park and the Ape stops to look around at a sea of parked vehicles. Even though it's the second week of July and summer is trying its best to look like it means it, dark clouds have gathered and turned the early evening into the beginnings of night. Back in the supermarket Billie and Johnson raided the clothing section and found me a pair of jeans, a light cotton green top and a fake worn-look leather jacket that is a size too big. But as Johnson explained, it has deep pockets for painkillers and bottles of water to wash them down with. Billie swapped her school uniform for a short white summer dress and a silvery cardigan but couldn't find a jacket with sleeves long enough for her elegant arms. Johnson then left an IOU for everything we had taken and said he'd pay it back somehow.

'What colour car d'you want?' the Ape says to us.

'Is that really important?' I ask.

'What make then?'

'What does it matter?'

'Saloon or estate?'

'Just find us a car!' Billie flashes an angry look at the Ape that shows she is clearly not frightened of him. Lots of people at school are, but Billie is in no mood to give him an inch.

'One with a big enough boot for the food,' Johnson reminds him.

As the Ape lumbers into the car park I realise he's taken a heavy iron poker from the home and domestic aisle. I can't figure out why until he uses it to smash the driver's window of the first car he comes to and then sticks his head inside.

'No good,' he says, as he pulls his head back out.

'How come?' asks Johnson.

'It's got gears. I can only drive an automatic.'

'Couldn't you see that from outside the car?' Billie asks, and I can tell she's beyond losing her patience with him.

Another window gets smashed and the Ape peers into another car.

'Nope, no good either.'

Billie is beside herself. 'I hate him! Why couldn't he have disappeared with the rest of humanity! Not that he is human.'

46

Another loud smash. This time a car alarm goes off.

Johnson turns and heads back into the supermarket. 'Be right back.'

Another smash. Another alarm joins the first one.

'Come on!' the Ape yells out in frustration.

Billie can't bear to watch. 'He's just doing that because he likes smashing things,' she says.

More glass shatters. A third alarm rings in our ears. 'This is mental!' he yells.

It is mental – he's so right there.

More windows shatter. There are car alarms going off everywhere. It's the loudest, shrillest cacophony of noise I have ever experienced.

Johnson reappears with about fifteen sets of car keys and starts dishing them out. 'Got them from the staff room. They were in people's coat pockets. Press them and see what cars they unlock. Then look for an automatic.'

'What does an automatic look like?' I ask, wishing I didn't have to, so that Johnson would think I'm cool and car savvy rather than an idiot.

'It's got two pedals instead of three.'

More alarms are sounding and Billie covers her ears. 'That makes no sense at all. If he hasn't got a key how's he going to drive a car, even if he does find the right one?'

'I don't think he thinks that far ahead,' I tell her as we spread out into the loud flashing mass of disturbed metal.

I am so relieved that I'm the one who finds the automatic. It takes me three attempts to aim car keys around the car park before I hear a beep from a few metres away, and sitting there is the smallest car I have ever seen. I think it's a Fiat and when I reach it I see that it only has two pedals. I yell as

47

loudly as I can. I have to because the Ape has set off practically every alarm in the car park.

'Got one!'

Johnson reaches me first and smiles. 'Nice one, Rev.'

I smile back, but it's awkward because as soon as he turned that smile on me my mind went blank and I couldn't think of anything to say. Those damn painkillers.

Billie comes to a sudden stop when she sees the tiny car.

'That's it?' Billie asks.

'I didn't choose it,' I say defensively.

We can barely hear each other over the raging car alarms and don't notice the Ape shoving past us and heading for the little Fiat.

'I've got this,' he says.

'No!' I scream at him. But it's too late and he smashes the passenger window and sets off yet another alarm.

'Rev's got the key! It was already open!' Billie screeches at the Ape. 'You utter utter idiot!'

The Ape turns and looks at me in disgust. 'You could've said.' He holds out his hand and I dump the key in his giant paw. As I do he closes his meaty hand around mine and looks directly into my eyes rather than at my chest for a change. 'You'll be glad of me,' he says, before letting go of my hand.

Johnson wheels the packed shopping trolley over and starts filling the tiny boot of the car. I make to help him but Billie beats me to it and I have to look on as they work briskly in an easy harmony. I can feel the Ape's breath on the top of my head. He is standing literally two inches behind me and I realise I don't even come up to his chin.

'I'm hungry.' He talks straight over my head.

'Later. Let's just get going,' Johnson replies.

The Ape gives a low quiet burp above me. 'I love chicken,' he says to himself before turning back to the Fiat.

We pile into the car. Johnson sits in the front with the Ape, and Billie and I get into the back. To get comfortable in the driver's seat the Ape pushes the chair all the way back as far as it will go and nearly breaks my legs into the bargain.

'Ow!'

'I need leg room.'

'And I need legs!'

Billie is squeezed up beside me in the back and Johnson is polite enough to endure some discomfort so she can at least ride in the car without becoming a paraplegic. He moves his seat forward for her while bunching up his long legs.

'Such a gent,' Billie whispers to me, and I can tell from the way she quietly swoons that she really likes him.

'Hang on,' says the Ape, and extricates his bulk from the tiny car.

'What's he doing now?' Billie looks totally sick and tired of the Ape.

Johnson glances back at me, sees how cramped I am and releases the catch under the driver's seat to give me a few more inches of leg room.

'Thanks,' I say.

'Got your water and pills and stuff?' he asks.

'Yeah. Right here.' I pat the pockets of the oversized faux leather jacket that he chose for me. 'Locked and loaded.'

'Good.' He smiles.

I swear his eyes linger on mine for a fraction of a second longer than they should. But I can't tell for sure. Between the dying summer light and the painkillers it's probably just my imagination.

The Ape climbs back into the Fiat and shoves his home-made weapon my way.

'What are you bringing *that* for?' Billie asks.

'Cos.'

'Cos?' Billie imitates his big deep dopey voice.

'Someone's going to be out there,' says the Ape.

'And the first thing you're going to do is attack them?' I ask, rubbing the blood back into my shins.

'I didn't say they'd be human,' says the Ape looking at his weapon like he's in love with it.

'What else are they going to be?' Billie is at a complete loss with the Ape.

'Only things we're going to meet from now on are monsters.'

We fall silent for a while. Johnson peers out into the setting sun and I wonder if he's trying not to laugh.

'Aliens, werewolves, vampires, that's what's out there,' finishes the Ape.

'And you know this because?' Billie's eyes are like narrow slits as she regards the back of the Ape's huge block-like head.

'Cos, that's the way it always is.'

'What – in the many situations like this that you've been in before? You are so deluded! All we're going to meet are people. Everyday people like you and— Well, not like *you* because you're not actually a person,' says Billie with true malice in her voice.

'Let's just drive,' Johnson says gently.

'You'll be glad I've brought my weapon. You will. You'll

50

see.' The Ape starts the tiny car and at last we head into the gathering night.

There are traffic lights at the top of the junction leading on to a short dual carriageway. They turn green and the Ape immediately slams on the brakes. We are thrown forward and back inside.

'What the hell are you doing? It's green,' barks Billie. 'Green means go.'

The Ape falls silent, eyes fixed on the traffic lights.

Billie reaches across me and jabs the Ape's shoulder. 'C'mon, move it!'

The light cycles to amber and the Ape revs the engine.

'Idiot!' Billie looks ready to explode but the lights turn red and the Ape floors the accelerator. He drives clean through the red light and sounds the horn a few times.

'Yowza!' The Ape looks insanely proud of himself. 'New world, new rules.'

He pumps the horn a few times and I wonder if he will ever truly grasp the horror of what we are going through right now.

ZOMBIES!!

The Ape drives way too fast and Billie and I cling on in the back as he takes corners almost on two wheels. Johnson seems determined not to be impressed, as if he knows that appearing scared or worried will only make the Ape drive even faster.

We speed through the eerily empty town and quickly reach a roundabout that leads five different ways into the darkening countryside between this town and the nearest village. The Ape decides that running red lights won't be his only thrill today, so he takes the roundabout the wrong way. And at speed.

Billie is furious with him. 'If people are out there and you keep driving this fast, we won't spot them. You'll zoom right past them.'

The Ape's eyes find Billie's in the rear-view. 'And if I slow down, vampires will catch us.'

'There's no such thing.'

'There's no such thing as an empty world either,' the Ape argues and takes the third exit on the roundabout. Billie lives in a village five miles away and I'm surprised the Ape knows which road to take without being told. It's like how he knew my phone number. How did he come by this knowledge? I make a mental note to ask him if he's been stalking us. Then I think better of it. I'm not sure I want to know the answer.

'I've been thinking,' Johnson says, his voice calm. 'Given that the four of us are still here and that we were all in the same detention, then isn't it possible that the others who were in detention with us, survived as well?'

'No,' says the Ape emphatically.

'No?' Johnson says.

'No.'

'Why not?' asks Billie.

'I don't know, just wanted to say no.' He laughs, but no one else joins in.

'Maybe we should try and find the others who were with us in that classroom,' says Johnson.

'I dunno, I like this double-date thing we've got going on.' The Ape glances in the rear-view at Billie again. She sees this and all but retches.

'No. No way did he just say that,' she spits.

'Jonno can have Rev and I'll have Billie.'

Billie is flat out appalled by the Ape. But I find myself quite enjoying the thought that he coupled me with Johnson. For a few seconds anyway, before I remember that I've got a boyfriend.

'We need to turn back.' Johnson has made up his mind.

The Ape glances at him and I'm not sure if I'm imagining it or not but there might be a tiny flicker of respect from the Ape for Johnson, and he eases off the accelerator.

'Back into town?'

53

'That is where we just came from,' Billie hisses at the Ape.

'We need to at least look,' Johnson explains to the Ape. There's a moment between them while Johnson waits for the Ape to fully grasp what he's saying.

'If we don't find them then we'll go back to Billie's plan.'

It takes the Ape longer than it should to process the thought and the little Fiat keeps motoring into the dark countryside.

'Let's think about who was in detention with us,' I say.

'The walking stick,' the Ape says.

'Carrie,' I correct.

'The homo.'

'GG,' Johnson corrects.

'And Lucas,' adds Billie.

The Ape racks his brains. 'Swear there was someone else.'

'There wasn't,' I say, thinking about who else could have been in the classroom with us.

'Swear there was.'

'Does anyone know where any of them live?' asks Johnson. No one does.

'What about phone numbers?'

'We only really spoke to GG at school,' says Billie. 'And Carrie is not someone you want to talk to, like ever.'

'Lucas would never give his number to anyone,' I add.

'Hawkings!' the Ape suddenly shouts. 'He was there!'

The Moth. I had forgotten he was in detention and I feel awful about it. Lucas is about his only real friend and even then he never comes out much. But now I'm wondering if that's because he was never invited.

'Timothy,' I say, finally remembering. 'His name's Timothy.'

'So who's Hawkings?' The Ape's brow furrows.

54

'Anyone know where he lives?' asks Johnson.

Again none of us do.

'All we need to do is find one of them, and maybe they'll know about the others,' says Johnson.

'GG is a good bet. I know roughly where he lives,' I add, trying my best to help.

'But how roughly is roughly?' Billie sighs and looks into the gathering darkness. And suddenly screams, 'ZOMBIE!!'

The Ape's foot jams down on the brakes and the car starts going into a skid. Johnson and I are trying to look to where Billie is now pointing, but it's too dark outside for us to see properly.

'A zombie? Are you sure?' I can't believe this is happening. What is going on?

'Told you!' The Ape sounds more excited than scared. 'Give me my weapon.' He tries to reach in the back, but his hand lands on one of my boobs and I slap it off.

'Perv!' I shout and shove the stupid broom/knife concoction at him.

'You sure that's what you saw, Billie?' Johnson asks.

The car slews to a halt and everything falls silent apart from the quiet ticking of the engine as the Ape plants the car in park mode.

We're halfway along a country road that has open fields on one side and a small wood running along the other. There are no street lamps and our only real light is provided by the last remains of the day.

'I knew there was monsters,' the Ape says, so proud of himself.

'It's not going to be that,' says Johnson, sure of it.

'But I definitely saw something,' says Billie, but nothing is moving outside.

'Why did you think it was a zombie?' I ask her.

'Cos it was pale and thin and angry-looking.'

'I can't see nothing.' The Ape is peering into the gloom.

Johnson sticks his head through the passenger window, the one the Ape smashed. When I see him do this it's all I can do not to drag him back inside. If there is a zombie then that is not the best thing to do.

'Maybe you shouldn't do that,' says Billie and it's another indication that she definitely likes Johnson.

'There's nothing out there.' He withdraws his head, which makes Billie sigh quietly with relief.

'Yeah. False alarm,' I say, regaining my composure, when a face suddenly looms up at my window. It's pale, the eyes are grey and mascara runs down its white colour-drained cheeks. 'ZOMBIE!!' I scream.

'Drive!' Billie yells at the Ape, who slams his foot on the accelerator. But the little Fiat doesn't move.

The zombie is banging on the window and I cower, unable to bring myself to look at it.

'Hurry!' I scream.

'Put it in drive!' Johnson screams at the Ape.

The zombie is banging so hard I'm sure the window is about to cave in. The Ape slams the car into drive and it lurches forward, the wheels spinning and taking an age to find traction.

'OhmyGod. OhmyGod!' Billie is hunched over, head in her hands, not wanting to see anything. 'Is it gone?'

The car careers forward, but almost immediately hits a patch of oil and we start going into a skid. The car lurches towards the deep muddy ditch that runs between the road and the wood.

The Ape pumps the brake over and over but to no effect. 'Hold tight!' he booms.

The car is starting to tip over. We're going to roll straight down into the ditch.

'OhmyGod. OhmyGod!' Billie is still crying out.

The Ape yanks the steering wheel and himself towards Johnson and the tiny car bows to the weight of his massive bulk and slams back down on all four wheels. Johnson is half crushed under the sweaty behemoth and he's probably become even skinnier as the car comes to a spinning twisting halt. Billie's forehead bashes hard against her window and I can see that a lump is already forming above her brow. The Ape turns the engine over, but it groans, ticks and then dies. Its dry whine echoes into the darkness.

'Go, go, go!' Billie screams as I check around, knowing the zombie will come at us again.

'The head! Take the head off and we'll be fine,' the Ape says with the authority of someone who has watched one too many horror films.

'I'm not doing that,' yells Billie.

'Well someone's going to have to cos it's coming.' The Ape angles the rear-view mirror so we can see the zombie sprinting towards us. 'I've got this,' he says, opening his door, ready for battle. But because Johnson moved the seat forward to make space for me, he can open his door but he can't seem to climb out of the tiny car. 'I'm stuck!' he says.

'What!?' Billie cries.

'I can't get out!'

The zombie is almost upon us.

'Take the weapon!' The Ape shoves the broom/knife towards Johnson and almost takes his eye out with it.

'Careful!' I call out.

'Where is it?' Johnson is trying to see past me and Billie, straining his neck in the tiny space.

'Too late!' Billie's eyes have gone wide as saucers as a haze of white rushes towards the car, an angry vicious malnourished heap of hatred, bearing down on us.

'I've got this,' the Ape says again, clearly having decided that it's now his brilliant catchphrase.

'Stop saying that, you've *got* nothing! So far you've got absolutely zilch!' Billie screams.

The Ape may not have much of a brain, but what little he does possess is used for violence and destruction. The feeling of sheer relief that I had in the supermarket comes back to me, making me warm towards him all over again. He tries the engine again and this time it bursts into life and he grinds the car into reverse.

'What the hell!' Billie screams as we plough back towards, and not away from, the zombie.

'Watch this!' The Ape builds up as much speed as he can.

'Wait! That's not a zombie!' Johnson calls out.

'What?' I say confused.

'It's a girl!' Johnson shoots out a hand and wrenches the gear stick back into Park.

We look through the rear window as the car kangaroos to a neck-jarring halt. But Johnson's not quick enough and the car knocks the emaciated girl coming towards us clean off her feet, sending her tumbling backwards.

It takes at least a minute before the heavy dull echo of anorexic-on-car-metal fades into the night and another full minute or so before anyone says anything.

Billie speaks first. 'Jesus.'

'I know,' I agree.

'One of us needs to get out and take a look.' Johnson looks at the Ape.

The Ape shrugs. 'I've done my bit.'

'What, knocking some innocent person over?'

'You told me it was a zombie.'

'I said it was a girl,' Johnson counters.

'*I* said it was a zombie,' says Billie.

'So you should get out,' the Ape says to her.

'I'm not getting out. It might still be a zombie.'

'It was definitely a girl,' Johnson says.

'But it might be a zombie now – she might've turned,' Billie argues and the Ape nods. It's the first – and probably only – time they agree with each other.

'Did you have to go and say that?' I shudder inwardly.

'Why don't they just eat each other?' asks the Ape.

'What are you talking about, you moron?' Billie shouts. Her frustration at Ape's idiotic comments has clearly reached breaking point.

'Zombies. Why don't they eat other zombies – that would solve a lot of their problems. If I was one I'd eat other zombies.'

I bang my hand on the low roof to get everyone's attention. 'There's a girl out there and we need to check she's OK!'

'It might be playing dead. Waiting for one of us to do exactly that,' Billie says. I can't believe that she still believes it is a zombie.

'They should eat each other, they really should.' The Ape seems to be on another planet.

'They don't exist,' I say. 'They absolutely don't.'

'Rev's right,' Johnson says looking at the Ape. 'You ran a girl down. We have to do something.'

'Hang on.' Billie is craning her neck to look out of the rear window.

'What?' I ask her.

'It's gone.'

I turn and look and Billie is right. The girl has disappeared. There is too much happening today for me to be able to take it all in. I feel numb now, numb and completely lost. Four hours into what feels like the end of the world and all sense and logic is disappearing at an alarming rate.

'Can't we just drive off?' Billie whispers.

'That works for me,' says the Ape, who delicately slips the car back into drive. But the minute he turns the ignition the engine dies again.

'Great,' moans Billie.

'Let's think about this,' I say. 'I mean, let's be logical. Zombies don't exist. So there's a girl out there . . .'

'And we know there was one other girl in detention.' Johnson picks up my line of thought.

I peer out the window but can barely see anything. The darkness feels suffocating it's so thick. I press up against the glass to get a better look.

Which is when Carrie's face appears at the window and scares all forms of bejesus out of me.

'I'm bloody brittle you know!' she shouts at me before fainting.

THE DARKER SIDE OF DAY

The Ape is giving Carrie a piggyback into town because luckily, or not, depending on how you look at it, the car glanced off her rather than hitting her full on. Her fragile body has been badly bruised though and she claims she can't feel her legs. So Carrie is being carried and it all seems to make some sort of weird and strange sense. She hasn't stopped whining ever since the Ape hoisted her onto his large flabby back.

'Five people left in the entire world and you try and kill one of them. Well thank you, you monstrously stupid morons.'

I wish the car hadn't packed up on us because the burns on my legs are drying out my skin and making them feel like they're cracking every time I take a step. But I don't want to tell anyone because they'll think I'm just as big a whinger as Carrie is.

Meeting – and running down – Carrie has confirmed Johnson's theory that the only people left are the ones in detention. It can't be a coincidence and we have decided that we have to track down the others. I'm not sure what good it will ultimately do – they'll be just as scared and shaken as we are – but someone, somewhere will know why this has happened. So the more people we find, the more chance we have of finding an answer. I hope.

'You could've killed me!' Carrie says for what must be the hundredth time.

'There's still time,' offers the Ape, which makes me laugh to myself. He sees this and under the low glow of the half-moon our eyes meet, and for that split second we somehow connect with each other. Just a mutual something or other, but for one single split second I am glad of him and he seems glad of me.

'I bet you told him to run me over, Reva, because that's exactly what you're like. You're evil and a bitch.' Carrie still won't get off my case, but no one is listening to her. It's not as if her hating me is all that important any more. Although if there are only a few people left in the world it would be nice if one of them rose above their petty vendettas.

Billie is carrying the Ape's weapon and she keeps scanning the dark evening because I know deep down she still believes there are monsters out there.

'Where were you going?' Johnson asks Carrie. He has salvaged as much of the supplies from the boot of the Fiat as he could manage. His long sinewy arms are laden with plastic bags.

'To the next village.'

'Same idea we had.'

'Aren't you the smart one.'

The world might have disappeared, but apparently Carrie isn't going to let that soften her or turn her into a better person.

'Any idea what's happened to everyone?' Johnson asks.

'Why would I know any better than you?'

'You've been crying,' I tell her, the dark tracks on her face obvious. 'Maybe you learned something that upset you.'

'I haven't been crying,' she denies.

'Your mascara says otherwise,' Billie says, backing me up.

Carrie looks away as the Ape strides on with her clinging on to his back. Even a queen bitch with no heart or soul is going to struggle when she suddenly finds herself alone in a completely empty world.

Johnson draws alongside me and lowers his voice so no one else can hear. 'What do you really think has happened?'

I'm caught off guard by the fact that he wants to talk intimately with me. I stammer a little. 'Well, uh, well – I just don't know. How about you?'

Johnson takes a moment to weigh up his answer. 'Still working on it.' I know he won't show it but he's as scared as I am. 'But I've got a feeling it's not going to be good.'

We walk past a row of silent empty houses that stand on the edge of town. On the street opposite is a half-built block of retirement flats. All they ever do in this town is build blocks of retirement flats. I think they're banking on old people living longer and longer. Which doesn't look like the case now.

The Ape scans the rooftops, eyes piercing the gloom.

'What are you looking for?' I ask him.

'Vampires like heights,' he says as if he's an expert.

'I don't think there'll be vampires,' I tell him.

'You didn't think there would be zombies.'

'Yeah and we *didn't* find one.'

63

'We almost did,' he says simply.

I watch Johnson walking ahead of me, carrying the heavy bags of supplies. He moves easily and even though he's stick thin there's a roll to his gait that defines the term snake hips.

Billie joins me. She's still carrying the Ape's weapon. 'I almost didn't go to detention,' she says. I glance at her, surprised. 'Was seriously thinking of giving it a miss.' The gravity behind her words is evident.

'Well, I'm glad you did because I wouldn't want to be going through this without you. We can be scared to death together.' We share a smile.

'You hungry?'

'Starving.' I didn't feel much like eating until Billie brought it up, but it's close on ten o' clock now and I don't think I've eaten anything since lunchtime

'Can we stop and break out some of that food?' Billie asks Johnson.

'Someone mention chicken?' The Ape stops and casually lets Carrie drop to the ground with a thud.

'What the hell?' wails Carrie. 'How can anyone be hungry? People have disappeared. We've lost our friends, our family, everyone.' Carrie is incredulous.

The Ape shrugs. 'So what? It's good no one's around.'

'You're sick,' Carrie snorts. 'Only the stupidest oaf in the world would be enjoying this. Oh hang on. That *is* you.'

I want to tell the Ape not to listen to Carrie, that she is like this with everyone, but I also can't help but silently agree with her. The real problem is the Ape just doesn't fit. He never has really. Not at school and not now. The situation is already stressful enough without his oafishness adding to it.

64

Johnson seems to know how to handle him though. At least for now.

'We're tired, we're hungry, let's find somewhere to sit and eat,' Johnson says.

'Oh goody, we're having a picnic now,' sneers Carrie.

Johnson ignores her and I go back to watching his snake hips when a toe-curling scream erupts into the night. It's coming from a tall block of nineteen-fifties flats sitting directly across the road from us. As ever the Ape is the first to react.

'Weapon! Now!' he yells at Billie, but she's too shocked by the noise to react so he yanks it from her hand.

Johnson instinctively gets in front of Billie and me. 'Stay behind me,' he says and I don't know whether to swoon or panic and sort of get stuck between the two as Billie yanks Carrie to her feet.

'Get up!'

'Careful!' Carrie moans.

The Ape holds up a giant meaty paw to tell us to be quiet as he scans the block of flats. Someone or some *thing* is racing down the stairway inside. It's moving quickly and we see it flashing past the lit stairwell windows that line every floor.

'Told you. Vampire.'

'Did you have to say that?' Carrie whimpers.

The Ape glances at Johnson. 'Get ready.'

'Born ready.' Johnson tries to sound relaxed but I see him tense and grow a little stiffer, knowing for certain that something is about to explode from the entrance door to the flats.

The footsteps reach the bottom landing and hurtle towards the main entrance.

I glance at Billie and she looks worried and dry-mouthed. Carrie has finally shut up and I can see that despite her attitude to the Ape, she has moved herself into a favourable position behind his giant back.

The door is flung open.

Here it comes, I think, *here it comes*.

The Ape doesn't hesitate and starts charging at the figure that emerges from the door. Everyone else is holding back, but his gut instinct is to take the fight to whatever is coming for us.

'Let's have it!' he yells.

But as the Ape charges into the dark we hear another scream, and this one is even louder than the first. But it's a scream of holy terror as the figure slides to the ground, sinking to its knees, ducking as fast as it can.

'It's me! GG!'

The Ape swings mightily and his homemade weapon whooshes a couple of inches above GG's head and chops the top of his blond quiff off.

'Ape! No!' I yell, as I see him swinging again.

'Stop, you silly brute!' GG whimpers.

Incredibly the Ape stops three inches from ruining GG's blemish-free face by taking his head off.

GG is all heaving breath and trembling limbs as he gets to his feet and staggers towards us, like a man finding an oasis after a day in the desert. He opens his arms wide to us. 'I'm not alone,' he wails. 'I'm not alone.' He collapses into Johnson's arms and hugs him as tight as he can. 'I've been staring out of that window for hours. Oh, poor GG. Stranded. Abandoned. Cast adrift from humanity.'

Johnson holds the overwrought wreck. 'It's OK, we're here.'

GG raises his head and takes in the rest of us. 'My saviours.' He goes to me first and hugs me tight. I have to fight back the pain as he squeezes my burns. My eyes water and I try and ease away from him.

'People! At last.' He looks like he doesn't know whether to cry or laugh.

He grabs Billie and hugs her as well. 'When I saw you I just screamed. I didn't know what else to do.'

He turns his focus on Carrie but she quickly puts up a hand to ward him off.

'Don't touch me, I'm bruised all over,' she says.

GG turns to the Ape.

'No, homo,' the Ape says simply.

GG can't stop babbling. 'Where is everyone else? I mean this is the weirdest day of my life. I trot through town, thinking: do I really like this yellow on my nails? I get home and I think: yes, yes I do like it. But then no one else comes home. I start phoning round—'

'D'you have Lucas's number?' Johnson cuts in.

'Lucas? Oh, I wish. How cute is that boy? But really – do any of you know what's happened?' GG looks at us, hoping for an answer.

'No one has a clue, GG,' I say with a heavy intent.

Apart from the Ape, this is scaring us big time. Finding GG has made everything seem even weirder, not better. Is Johnson right? Have we all been selected? Chosen? And if so, for what?

Carrie lowers herself gingerly to the kerbside. 'I'm exhausted. Everything aches and I'm not taking another step.'

'You didn't take any, anyway. The Ape was carrying you,' Billie reminds her.

'I'm not moving. All right?'

'OK, see you around.' Billie makes to walk off.

But Johnson catches Billie's arm, gently stopping her in her tracks. 'GG, can we go up to your place?' he asks.

'Come up, come up. Chez GG awaits you.'

'We should take some time out.' Johnson studies us and knows that we are at breaking point. 'It's getting late and we're all strung out, but we need to work out how to find the others.'

'There's others?' GG asks hopefully.

'Lucas and the Moth. Least we're pretty sure of it.'

'Let me go up first – have a quick tidy round.'

'That doesn't really matter.'

'It always matters,' GG says as he hurries back towards the block of flats. 'Flat ninety-eight,' he calls back. 'Wipe your feet on the mat.'

GET REAL

Carrie is taking up the entire sofa by lying stretched out across it. She is looking at her twisted ankle which it turns out isn't at all twisted. The Ape is flicking through television channels but there is only static.

'Nope,' he says. 'Not that one either. Nope. Nope. Nope.'

GG's flat is immaculate and I have no idea why he thought it needed tidying. There are three bedrooms. His parents' room, his twin sisters' room where there are bunk beds, and then there's GG's room. He has a dressing table with a huge mirror and, sitting on it in neat little rows, is more make-up than Billie and I own put together.

He has a double bed and a great little sound system plugged into his Mac. His wardrobe is bursting with clothes and right now he is busy searching through it.

'I'm going for that end-of-the-world look,' he jokes.

'It's not the end of the world,' Billie says.

'It will be if I don't find the right jacket.'

He grins, then finds a combat jacket, which I would never have thought he'd have owned in a million years, but when he turns it round I can see that it's fur lined and there are large golden glittering letters on the back.

WAR(M) it states.

'Sergeant GG reporting for duty.'

I turn and Johnson is leaning in the doorway. His eyes flit to mine even though he's talking to GG.

'Got a telephone directory?'

'FOR GOD'S SAKES, STOP DOING THAT!!' For a brittle person, Carrie can make a lot of noise when she wants to.

Johnson and I head back into the lounge and find that the Ape is still steadily flicking through a hundred channels of static.

'Nope. Not that one. Nope.'

The sound is up loud on the television and Carrie leaps up and snatches the remote out of his giant paw and hurls it across the room.

'Get the picture, there is no picture!' she yells at him, and I realise that she can move pretty well for someone with a sprained this and a broken that.

The television's static continues to fizz and I hate the noise so much that I go over and pull the plug on the television.

The Ape sits back in a big leather chair with his weapon lying across his knees. He is totally unfazed by Carrie. 'You have issues.'

GG and Billie walk through with a barely used telephone directory. GG holds it up as if it's a relic from a bygone age.

'It's a little passé but we can only try.'

'We going to find them right now?' Carrie seems reluctant.

'We have to,' says GG. 'I was a quivering mess thinking it was just me that was left.'

'Wuss,' the Ape says.

'Yeah, that's me. Mr Wuss. But you know what? We can pretend we're calm and that we can deal with this. But my little guess is we can't. There. I've said it. It's out there now. We should all be scared. Amen.'

Johnson looks around the room at us. We're all still hungry, tired and shell-shocked. 'What about looking first thing in the morning?' he offers. 'We can eat now, shower and whatever, work out who's sleeping where, then soon as it's light we get going. Sound like a plan?'

GG holds up his hand as if he's still in school.

'Yes, GG?'

'I like that plan, but I'm not sleeping alone.'

'Me neither,' echoes Carrie. 'That was horrible out there.'

'So you *were* crying,' says Billie triumphantly. Carrie gives her the middle finger treatment.

'OK, let's get the mattresses and duvets and drag them all in here,' says Johnson.

'Orgy!' is the Ape's predictable response.

'Maybe you could take first watch,' says Johnson to the Ape. The Ape couldn't look more delighted and grabs his weapon.

'First shift is eight hours long,' Carrie tells the Ape. She follows it with a cruel giggle and the Ape doesn't quite get what she is really saying.

'Eight hours. No problem,' he says with a deep pride, then leaves the room.

'What an idiot,' Carrie mutters to herself.

I'd usually agree with her, but as infuriating as the Ape can be, she shouldn't be making fun of him like that.

'I'll go relieve him in a couple of hours,' I tell the room.

'Already on it,' says Johnson, and once again his eyes meet mine.

HANGING AROUND AND AROUND AND AROUND

The night passed without an attack from monsters. I took over the watch from Johnson at around two in the morning and he stayed to talk for a moment.

'We'll be all right,' he told me.

'That a promise?'

'I'll do my best to make it one.'

Johnson and I seem to have got in sync without any real effort. I always thought he'd be unapproachable, that someone like me would never get picked up on his radar, but it's a pleasant surprise to find that, for now at least, he's making sure I know we're in this together.

I watched him walk back to the lounge where everyone was sleeping and when he opened the door I heard the Ape fart loudly in his sleep. Then someone got up and opened a window and muttered something about too much chicken.

'Lucas's surname is Lopez,' Billie says.

GG turns to L in the telephone directory. 'It's like a treasure hunt,' he says. It's just gone six in the morning and everyone is up, fed and dressed.

'We can rule out any of the addresses that aren't in the school catchment area.' Johnson looks over GG's shoulder as he flicks through the pages of the telephone directory. GG senses Johnson's breath on his ear and giggles.

Johnson, unlit cigarette in his mouth, scans the page with the surname Lopez on it. 'There's only three possible Lopezes it could be.'

'Mr Sherlock, meet Mr Holmes,' says GG, impressed.

Billie peers at the telephone directory but I can't get a look in with them all crowded around, so I stand to one side with Carrie who makes a big point of stepping away from me.

'*So* not going to be your friend, not even with all of this going on,' she whispers.

The Ape walks into the lounge to the accompanying flush of the toilet next door. 'That's better. Got to lighten the load.' No one can bring themselves to comment.

'We're going to have to split up,' Johnson announces. 'Three addresses, three couples.'

'What about the Moth?' I ask. 'Where does he live?'

'Does anyone know his surname?' Johnson asks.

'I did know it, but I can't remember,' says Carrie.

'I barely knew him,' admits Billie.

'I just sort of said "hi" now and then,' I offer weakly.

'Scratch one Moth,' says the Ape bluntly.

We all feel pretty bad about this, but I try to make excuses. 'He never came out much, never really made himself known.'

'Yeah, it's all his fault,' says the Ape even more bluntly.

'Let's find Lucas first – he'll definitely know where the Moth lives.' Johnson knows we need to keep focused. 'Who wants to pair up with me?'

'I will,' Billie says before I can even take a breath.

Johnson glances at me, and I wonder for a moment if he'd hoped I'd step forward, but when I stay rooted to the spot he turns to Billie. 'Cool. We'll take the one on Turing Avenue.'

'Me and Rev'll team up. We've been pretty good so far,' the Ape says.

'We have?' I respond.

'Yeah, we took down the burned man.'

'He was already down.'

'But we made sure he stayed down.'

'What burned man?' asks GG. 'No one mentioned a burned man.'

'It was just this man we, uh, we *met*, at Tesco,' I say.

'That's pretty big news to keep to yourselves,' says Carrie, glaring at me. 'Are you saying there's someone else?'

'Not any more,' replies the Ape.

'He died,' I explain.

'So where did he come from? What happened to him?' Carrie is all over this, getting in my face.

'We don't know.'

'But someone else survived?' GG says, getting involved in the interrogation.

'No. No he didn't. He died. In front of us,' I tell them.

'He was all burned up,' says the Ape.

'Really badly,' adds Billie.

'And I sort of got burned as well,' I tell them.

'They're burns?' asks Carrie. 'I thought you had some disgusting skin disease.'

My burns are beginning to sting again and I'm wondering if Johnson will take note and rub more of his magic ointment into them. Maybe if I start grimacing more he might get the message.

'He's gone, so forget it.' The Ape looms over Carrie and GG as if he wants them to back away from me.

'But you don't know who he is or where he came from?'

Johnson has had enough. 'The burned man isn't the issue. We don't know anything about him right now. So let's concentrate on Lucas.'

Carrie keeps staring at me. 'Anything else we should know?'

Before I can reply the Ape takes my arm and steers me away. 'We've got Jenner Avenue.'

'We've all swapped phone numbers, right?' asks GG who is fast becoming Johnson's second-in-command and rather enjoying it. He made us Bluetooth all our phone numbers to each other last night. 'We're all logged into one another, yes? Is that a yes for GG? I can't hear you.'

'Yes,' we all echo.

'Thank you, ladies and gentlemen. We're logged and blogged.'

GG turns to Carrie and gives her the sweetest smile in the world. 'You and I are going to have just the best time ever.'

'You are so annoying.'

'I know. Isn't it wonderful?' He beams at her.

Johnson glances out of the flat window, casting his eyes over a town that has turned completely alien. It doesn't matter that I know it inside out, every street and building, it's really not the same town any more. I know he senses it too.

'We should stick to texting,' he says. 'Put your phones on vibrate.'

'There's no one around to hear them ring, stupid,' Carrie says.

'You don't know that,' he replies.

'I think I do, all the evidence is there. And anyway, we want to attract attention, don't we?'

Billie has also stepped over to the window to gaze at the strangeness. 'But do we?'

Everyone knows what she means apart from Carrie and the Ape, who is scratching his hairy belly and yawning.

GG produces his phone with a flourish, delicate fingers tapping rapidly. 'I've just gone to vibrate, better to be safe than sorry.'

'There's nothing out there.' Carrie is adamant but no one listens.

We're too busy changing our phone settings.

When we get outside, the morning has yet to heat up and Billie shivers. As soon as Johnson sees this he drapes his jacket round her shoulders. 'Here.'

Underneath he's now wearing a faded black Palma Violets T-shirt and I watch Billie wrap herself into his jacket, like it's the cosiest thing in the world, and the smile she gives Johnson is wide and too warm.

'Thank you.'

'Anytime.'

For some reason I feel a stab of jealousy and have to turn away in case I wrench the jacket off her. I'm not sure what to make of my reaction, after all I have a boyfriend so why should I care if Billie and Johnson like each other? And why am I even thinking about them when the end of the world is upon at us. I try and ignore my feelings and hurry to catch up with the Ape.

The Ape really needs a shower but I don't know how to tell him. Jenner Avenue is at the top of a steep hill and the climb is making him sweat and breathe heavily. There are small houses lined up on one side and a grass-covered hill on the other. When it snows, half the town gather here with sledges and zoom down it. Everywhere I look I'm reminded of how empty the town is now. My mind is willing me to spot someone, but as hard as I try I can't see anything but an empty silent world.

The Ape takes a long moment to grope for words that are probably way beyond him. 'You know. This is weird.' He's only just noticed? 'Not your average day, is it?'

Finally it seems to have sunk in and he looks ever so faintly troubled. I fight every instinct to reach out and try and offer him comfort. If I did, he'd think that I was deeply in love with him and try to grope me or something.

'No,' I agree. 'It's not even close.'

He stays silent for a long time and I try and force the pace a little because having nothing to say is awkward and embarrassing. And I admit I want to get back to Johnson – and everyone else of course – as soon as possible.

'I'm going to be a boxer,' he suddenly says. 'I am. Heavyweight division. King of the ring.'

'Right,' I say, not really knowing why he's sharing this with me.

'I like fighting.'

You don't say, I think. But I'm not really listening

because I've started scanning the area in case there is someone, or some *thing* out there. It should come as a relief to see someone else, it really should, but my instincts, for what they are, are telling me that if there is someone then they'd be only too keen to make contact with us. So why haven't they?

The Ape has brought his weapon with him and he grips it in both hands. 'I'll fight anyone or anything. Bring it on. I'll smash them all.'

'Can we talk about something else?' I stare ahead, trying not to think about how quickly Billie latched on to Johnson. I don't understand why it's bugging me so much. We used to talk about him sometimes, and wonder what we'd do if he ever noticed either of us, but other than that I have never really given him much thought. Least I don't think I have.

'Like what?' the Ape asks.

'Mm?' I have completely lost track of our conversation. 'What d'you want to talk about?'

'Anything but fighting.'

The Ape takes a long time to try and dredge up another subject. But fails. 'I will. I'll smash them.'

It's clearly down to me to change the subject. 'What would you have now if you could have anything?'

Like say our family, friends and relatives, I think.

'I'd get an escalator,' says the Ape after a moment.

'An escalator?'

'This hill is steep.'

The Lopez house is locked up tight. No one answers when we knock. We look in a few ground-floor windows but there's no movement and no sign of anyone.

'No one home.' As is his way, the Ape states the obvious.

I fish for my phone so I can tell the others that this isn't the house when glass shatters behind me. I turn and see that the Ape has picked up a white stone garden statue – Eros holding a birdbath, as if he was always washing birds in mythology – and hurled it through the glass patio door.

'What the hell are you doing!?'

'Going inside.'

'You did that just because you wanted to.'

'What if he's stuck?'

'Stuck? How could he be stuck? You just wanted to smash that door. Admit it. You couldn't resist. There's nothing you don't want to break. Give it a week and you'll have broken the entire world.'

But the Ape is already stepping over the smashed glass and calling out. 'Luke?'

I hang back, not wanting to cut myself on the broken glass. This wanton destruction is really getting to me now.

'Rev!' The Ape bellows louder than anyone I have ever heard. Already he is charging out of the house, almost tripping over the fallen stone bird feeder in his haste.

'Man, it's not good!'

He drags me into the house, not caring that my jacket catches on some glass, and leads me into the kitchen where I come face to groin with Lucas.

'Look!'

Lucas is hanging from the ceiling. It isn't a high ceiling but it is enough to keep Lucas's dangling feet from touching the linoleum floor. He's tied a dog lead to a light fitting and then hanged himself. A stool lies on its side under his feet.

It's the worst thing I have ever seen in my life and I groan inside and out, the breath leaving me and not coming back. Lucas is wearing his school football kit. Football boots with metal studs, shin guards under yellow socks. White shorts with yellow trim and a yellow top, short-sleeved.

'Oh my God.'

I refuse to believe this is happening. Any of it. It's just some nightmare, that's what it is, some weird stupid joke nightmare. Tears are in my eyes and I don't know how I'm not screaming.

The Ape takes a photo of Lucas on his phone camera.

I am stunned. 'What the hell are you doing?'

'I'm going to text the others, show them what's happened.'

'What?? I mean, my God. No. NO! That's a picture of a hanged boy. And you think you can Instagram him? Don't you dare. You hear me. Don't. You. Dare.'

As I rail at the Ape I spot a note that Lucas has left and pick it up. It's short and simple and full of dread and sorrow. He doesn't know where everyone has gone and he's scared and doesn't want it to be like this. My tears hit the ink and make it run. I knew Lucas was fragile and highly strung, no pun intended, I swear, but I never thought he was capable of this.

'We need to get him down,' I say to the Ape, wiping my eyes.

'I'm not touching him.'

'C'mon, he can't just . . . We can't . . . C'mon Ape, please. We need to get him down.' I don't know what I think I'll achieve by getting Lucas down but I know we can't leave him up there. 'Get the stool,' I instruct.

'I'm not going anywhere near him.' The Ape backs away.

'For goodness sake!' I grab the stool and climb up onto it

so I can cut the dog lead with a knife I grab from a kitchen drawer. 'Get ready to catch him at least.'

'I told you, no way.'

I almost fall off the chair as I try desperately to cut him down and reach for his muscular arm to try and steady myself.

'He's still warm!' I can barely believe it.

'So?'

'We must've been so close to getting to him. Minutes away. If we'd found him earlier, kept on looking last night . . .' My voice trails away. Lucas, the boy who had more than all of us put together, didn't know what else to do other than end it.

'Please just catch him. Please,' I beg.

The Ape finally takes up position so that he can help me.

'What are you going to do once you've got him down?'

'I don't know!'

But while I hesitate, the dog lead, which I've half sliced through, gives way and Lucas's body crashes to the floor in a heavy and undignified heap. The Ape and I hear a bone crack and we both wince at each other.

'Think that was his ankle,' the Ape says.

I stand on the chair wondering if we could possibly make this any worse for Lucas when a text message comes through from Johnson on the Ape's phone. **We r coming now!**

I'm stunned and turn on the Ape. 'You sent the photo?'

'You don't know what to do, I don't either, so maybe one of them will.'

I step off the stool and reel away from the Ape. He is right but he's also so very wrong.

'Rev.'

'Don't. I can't talk to you right now.'

I head deeper into the house and find a blanket to cover Lucas's body with. That's two bodies I've covered over and I truly hope I never have to again.

The Ape has found a packet of ham in the fridge and is rolling it up and stuffing it into his mouth. 'Dead is dead,' he says quietly. I think it's his stab at an apology but I don't know for sure.

'I know,' I say sadly. 'I get it. OK.'

The Ape ambles over to me, stepping around Lucas as he does. I can smell the ham on his breath and see that his prehistoric brain is working overtime to try and put the right words into his mouth. He is frowning hard and being concerned is clearly taking it out of him.

'I'm still here, Rev.'

I look into his deep-brown cow eyes and again get the sense that he cares about me. But he's also talking to my boobs so maybe it's really them he cares about.

We meet the others outside Lucas's house. They have hurried as fast as they can up the hill and all of them except Johnson are trying to catch their breath. The Ape is drinking from a can of lager he found in the fridge and, as much as I would love to get drunk and forget all of this, I remain sitting huddled and numb on the small garden wall. Johnson comes over and sits beside me. Carrie makes as if to go inside Lucas's house but the Ape bars her way.

'You don't want to do that,' he says.

'Is he really dead?' she asks.

'Yep.'

'You're absolutely sure?'

'Take a look but you won't like it.'

Carrie sucks in air and turns away as GG sits down on the wall.

'He was wearing his football kit,' I tell them quietly.

'I love that colour,' says GG. 'It's like sunshine.' But he's speaking quietly for once, without innuendo.

'We got him down, put a blanket over him. There was a note.' I peel it out of my pocket and hand it to Johnson who reads it and then hands it to Billie who has sat down next to him, which seems to be her preferred place now. She reads it and then hands it to GG.

'He gave up?' she says to no one in particular. 'Lucas Lopez gave up.' Her words drift away on the breeze and no one speaks for a good five minutes.

'I didn't really know him,' says Billie eventually.

'I heard he had scouts from Arsenal looking at him,' Carrie adds. 'He could've gone places.' Her voice sounds so much softer than usual.

'What are we going to do? With Lucas. I mean with Lucas's body,' GG asks.

'Bury him?' Johnson asks.

'Maybe it's best just to leave him,' Billie says quietly.

'What, just lying in his kitchen?' Carrie asks.

'We can't drag him around with us,' says GG.

'We need to find the Moth,' I say, getting to my feet. 'We can't have him doing the same thing.'

'That's it? We just walk away?' Carrie gets in my way. 'Leave Lucas to rot?'

'Tell you what, you stay here with him.' I'm getting sick of Carrie. 'If you're that worried, go lie down with Lucas, keep him company.' I push past her and carry on walking. The Ape sees me go and jogs to catch up.

'Where we going now?'

'To find the Moth.'

The Ape and I head off back down the steep hill that leads into town. I think that if I keep on moving then none of what is happening will actually ever catch up with me or sink in. I will always be one step ahead of this nightmare.

I hear Johnson call to the others. 'Rev's right, let's go.'

I don't need to turn around to know that they've listened to him and are following us down the hill. I make myself believe that Johnson is watching me, that he has his eyes on me the whole way into town. It gives me the smallest of comforts.

WHEN I SAY ALIENS, WHAT'S THE FIRST THING YOU THINK OF?

No one speaks as we head into town. We troop back to the high street, looking around, checking for any sign of life, but the shops remain empty and even though the sun is starting to heat up the morning, I can't shake the chill that's trapped inside me.

Billie sniffles, wipes her nose and eyes with a hanky, then sniffles some more. Johnson has his arm around her shoulders for comfort. 'Sorry, I'm usually tougher than this,' she says.

GG is still in his own little world of shock and has taken to changing the ringtones on his pink smartphone. 'So much choice, so little time,' he says quietly to no one in particular. His campness is fading away by the minute.

'I spoke to him once. Lucas. We ended up on a bus together. Nowhere else to sit so he slid in beside me,' Carrie says. 'I can't remember what we talked about but I remember one thing, he was interested in buildings. He said he could fall back on a career in architecture if football didn't work out.'

The Ape sticks close to me, his eyes scanning for danger.

'I could build a house,' he says.

'You reckon?'

'Yeah. Easy.'

'People! Hey! People!' A voice echoes up and down the high street and we come to a sudden, lurching stop.

The Ape looks up to the sky.

'What are you doing?' Johnson asks him.

'I heard a voice.'

'We all heard a voice,' I say.

'And it's not coming from the sky,' says Carrie.

'HEY!!! IT'S ME!!!'

We turn and try to work out where the voice is coming from.

'The alleyway.'

We look in the direction of a tiny alleyway that you would barely know is there. It's sandwiched between a shoe shop and a gift and card shop.

'Hey!' the voice calls again.

'It could be a trick, to make us go into the alley,' warns Billie.

'Why would anyone do that?' Carrie twists her mouth into a cynical grin. 'I mean it's not much of a trick, is it?'

'It's me!' the voice yells. 'Tim!' The voice sounds exasperated. 'I was with you in detention!'

'Moth?' I call.

'Yes!' The voice sounds relieved. 'It's me! The Moth.'

'So come on out!' the Ape yells.

'I can't.'

'Told you it was a trick.' Billie looks quietly vindicated.

'Batteries are dead on my chair.'

'Maybe not.' Billie shrugs.

'Wheel yourself out,' orders Johnson.

'Have you any idea how much this thing weighs? I've got the arms of an old lady.'

The Ape edges towards the alley. We wait an age while he weighs up whatever is lurking in there. It's the classroom all over again.

'Well??' Carrie snaps.

'Yeah,' he finally shouts. 'It's him!'

We find the Moth sitting trapped in his dead wheelchair. He beams at us as if we are long lost friends.

'I thought I was trapped here forever.'

'Ugh!' The Ape cups his face with his hand. 'Ugh! Yuck!' He turns away and fakes some big retching sounds. 'He stinks. We should've kept on walking.'

The Moth blushes. 'Yeah, well I've been stuck here all night.'

'He's wet himself.' Carrie points to his stained trousers and the drying puddle on his chair.

'What was I meant to do?' The Moth looks hurt and embarrassed. 'I couldn't move. I went up and down looking for a sign of life until the battery died on me.'

'That is serious stench.' The Ape backs out of the alleyway.

'I was in a panic.' The Moth is doing his best to convince us, but he really hasn't any need to – Carrie and the Ape are just being ridiculous. It's not like he had a choice.

'That's still no excuse, Hawkings,' Carrie says, clearly trying to reach some high moral ground.

'I'd like to see the state you'd be in if you were stuck in

an alley for a night on your own. Actually. Correction. I wouldn't because it would be too gross,' I tell Carrie.

'Where is everyone?' he asks us, half hoping we will forget about the smell.

'Maybe you drove them away with that stink,' gripes Carrie.

'We need to get you charged up.' Johnson takes a grip on the Moth's wheelchair.

'And decontaminated,' adds Carrie.

'Does that mean one of us has to dress him?' GG looks excited, returning to his old self. 'Can I choose the clothes? Say yes, go on, say yes to GG.'

'I can do that myself. But I could really do with something to eat and drink.'

'So you can wet yourself some more?' Carrie says and totters away on her impractical high heels.

Johnson manoeuvres Moth's wheelchair out of the alley while the Moth fires questions at us.

'Is this all there is? Just you lot?'

'We think it's just everyone who was in detention yesterday,' I offer.

'So where's Lucas?'

We all fall silent. I doubt any of us have ever had to break the news of someone's death before. I certainly haven't. The closest I've ever been to it was when my mum told me my dad had upped and left us.

'I know where he lives, if that helps.'

The Moth can sense our hesitation.

'It's not too far from here.'

'Yeah uh – we went there,' Johnson says finally.

'Wasn't he in?'

'Yeah. He was in,' Johnson says.

'So where is he?'

Again we fall silent. Johnson is searching for the right words.

'Thing is—'

'He topped himself.' The Ape wades in with his horrendous lack of tact.

'What!?' The Moth's mouth drops open. 'No. That's a joke, right?'

'We didn't find him in time,' I say, fighting a sadness that keeps creeping up on me. 'He thought he was all alone.'

'That's . . . That's not possible,' says the Moth, rocked to the core. 'It's not. No way. You've got to take me to him.'

'It's too late,' says Billie.

Tears well in the Moth's eyes as Johnson takes the note Lucas left from his pocket and hands it gently to the Moth. 'He left this.'

The Moth takes the note, but his hand is trembling so much he can't hold it still enough to read. Johnson lays a hand on the Moth's wrist, steadying him.

We wait in respectful silence for the Moth to read the note. Tears roll down his cheeks and he keeps wiping them away before they spill onto the note.

'Lucas,' the Moth says to no one in particular. He then remembers his phone and shows us that it's dead, out of battery. 'I would've called him. I would have.' He's now thinking we're going to blame him in some way.

'It's not your fault,' Johnson tells him.

'It's no one's,' I add.

Moth reads the note again, as if he's missed something vital, a clue or a hint that would prove his best friend hasn't taken his life.

'Why would he . . .?' The Moth is bewildered and lost. 'I mean . . . No. No this can't be. No . . .'

'Uh, hello, but who is that?' Billie says.

I turn to where she's pointing and literally stop breathing.

Crouching at the far end of the high street is a person.

'We've got company,' GG says, then squeals in delight. 'My God I've always wanted to say that!' But then he looks at the stricken Moth and checks himself. 'Sorry,' he whispers in embarrassment.

'Hey!' Carrie waves to the distant figure. 'Hey!'

'Told you we weren't alone.' The Ape moves his weapon into both hands, gripping it tight. He's not speaking as if he's pleased or excited. He's talking as if this is not good news.

Johnson peers at the person crouching ahead of us. 'Why isn't he moving?' he says.

'Hello!' Carrie takes a few steps towards the figure.

Billie waves behind her. 'Hey!' she shouts.

'Billie!' I hiss a warning to her.

'Rev, it's someone! There's other people, we're not alone. Hey, over here!'

The Ape glares at Billie. 'Stop waving!'

Billie ignores him and pushes past us. 'Hello!'

'He looks familiar.' Carrie is still walking forward, but Billie is moving faster and quickly passes her.

The person remains still – in fact he hasn't moved since we spotted him.

'It's Lucas!' Billie yells and increases her speed. 'My God! It's Lucas! Hey, Lucas!'

I am stunned into silence.

'It can't be. It just can't be.' My voice is tiny and hollow.

'Did we miss something?' asks the Ape turning to me.

90

'Lucas!' Billie calls out.

'You cruel bitch,' the Moth sneers back at me. 'So not funny.'

'But he was dead,' I tell the stricken Moth, desperately hoping he will believe me. 'Lucas was dead. Tell them, Ape!'

'Dead as dead,' he agrees.

The Moth looks at me with a barely controlled scorn. 'What kind of a joke is that?'

'He was hanging from the ceiling. Ape sent a photo.'

'A photo!?' The Moth recoils in disgust.

'The three of you faked it, right?' Johnson says, and I can tell that he's disappointed in me.

Even the Ape can't change Johnson's mind. 'He was dead, Jonno.'

Johnson doesn't bother responding and I hate the way he looks at me now.

Billie is about two hundred metres away from the figure, with Carrie hurrying to catch her up.

I don't understand what's happening, but the harder I squint the more it looks like it really is Lucas. He rises to his feet, watching as GG sets off to join Billie and Carrie.

'Well, hello, you hunk of hunks,' he calls out.

'I touched him, there wasn't a pulse.'

The Moth ignores me completely. 'Johnson, can you wheel me over there?'

I turn away, mouth dry and brain unable to differentiate between what I saw at Lucas's house and what I'm seeing now.

Billie is closing the ground on Lucas when he backs up a step or two, and then without warning springs forward, using

91

his powerful footballer legs to leap at least forty metres through the air.

Everyone stops.

Lucas lands then leaps again, propelling himself forward, closing the ground on Billie in seconds.

GG comes to a screeching, frozen halt. 'I didn't know Lucas was *that* athletic,' he says, but there's no comprehension in what he is saying.

Lucas jumps again, soaring through the air past the health food shop, the phone shop, the cake shop and the shoe repairer's, and lands right beside Billie.

He beams at her. 'Hi, Billie.'

The Ape has his homemade weapon at the ready. 'No wonder Chelsea want to sign him.'

'It's Arsenal,' I correct, but it's just an automatic response because every part of me is trying to rationalise what I just saw Lucas do.

Lucas looks past Billie and takes in the rest of us as we catch up with her. Lucas isn't remotely out of breath from the massive jumps he has just done and I'm half thinking that maybe he's a ghost, that perhaps he wasn't leaping but flying. It seems far-fetched, but who knows any more.

'Where's everyone else gone?' Lucas asks us.

No one speaks – they can't get the image of him leaping through the air out of their heads.

'I thought I was alone.' He grins out of relief and I catch sight of something in his mouth, a glint of metal. It could be a tongue stud. Which I don't think squeaky clean Lucas would ever have.

'We all thought that at first.' I try and play along, trying to keep as calm as I can, considering. 'It's uh, it's good to see you.'

'You too.'

Lucas seeks out the Moth and does a double take when he sees him.

'Tim?'

'Hey, Lucas.' The Moth offers a wary smile.

'Why are you in that wheelchair?'

'What d'you mean?'

Beside me I can feel the Ape tensing.

'We found you. Earlier,' Johnson tells Lucas, remaining calm and keeping any level of surprise or shock out of his voice.

Lucas hesitates. 'You found me?' He frowns. 'I don't understand, I haven't seen a single person since detention.'

'Tell him, Rev,' Johnson says.

'Me and the Ape, we, uh, we came to your house earlier.' I point lamely at the Ape and shrug. I don't know what's going on, but I know it's not good.

Lucas looks confused. 'That's the Ape?'

'Dazza,' the Ape corrects.

Lucas leans closer, scrutinising us. 'You look like him but . . . where's the rest of you?'

No one knows what he means. I can feel the tingling in my shoulders returning. My personal alarm bell is ringing very loudly.

'So how did you – *find me* – exactly?' There's another glint of metal in his mouth as Lucas asks questions of his own.

I sense GG take a subtle, involuntary step back from Lucas.

Lucas is coiling inside – I can feel the tension emanating from him. 'Tim, get out of that thing.'

'I can't.'

'C'mon, get up. We're out of here.' Lucas has lost any sense of calm or approachability. He's starting to panic.

'His little legs don't work, remember?' says GG.

'Since when?' he asks.

'Since – well – you know, I've never asked. I mean it's a little rude,' says GG whose voice has gone an octave higher. There's a tremble in it now.

Billie reaches for Lucas and I see her hand closing on his arm. 'Lucas?' she says quietly. 'It is you, right?'

Lucas glances at Billie and appraises her for a moment. 'It's me. But is it you?' he says.

Lucas's whole body is tensing now and there's something about his skin. It's as if it's hardening by the second, thickening. It ripples – it actually ripples like a tiny wave.

Lucas steps back from Billie, out of her reach. 'Don't touch,' he says, becoming increasingly agitated.

But Billie reaches for him again, speaks softly. 'We're all scared, but we just need to work a few things out here.'

'Billie,' I warn her.

Billie's hand touches Lucas's arm again. 'Like, how can you jump like that?'

'I warned you!' The freaked out Lucas lashes out at Billie, sending her tumbling backwards.

'Whoa!' The Ape instinctively raises his weapon.

'Who are you people?' Lucas goes into a semi-defensive crouch and the metal glints in his mouth again.

I go to Billie but GG gets to her before me. 'Billie, you OK?'

'I told her to back off. And that goes for all of you.' Lucas is becoming more threatening by the second.

'Please, we just want to talk,' I offer, keeping one eye on him while desperately searching my pockets for something to stem the bleeding.

'Rev?' Billie sounds dazed, almost numb.

'I said, who are you?' Lucas seems more like an animal now as he takes a few more steps back, head lowered, ready for fight or flight. I'm seriously praying that it will be flight.

With GG's help Billie gets to her knees. Her face is bleeding badly. She has gashes running down her cheek from where Lucas's nails have gouged her. I find a tissue and press it hard into the cuts, but the bleeding won't stop.

'It's OK,' I lie to her. 'It's OK.'

She looks at me blankly, clearly woozy and bewildered. But at least she seems able to stand up.

'Are you on steroids?' GG is trying to find a logical way through the growing anxiety that is emanating from all of us. 'That it? You all souped up? That why you're hitting girls, you've got some chemical rage going on?'

'It's not the real Lucas,' mumbles Carrie, completely bewildered.

'Oh I'm the real Lucas.' It's as if he's appraised us now and there's a newfound confidence emerging from behind a broadening grin that I know I won't forget in a hurry. All of his teeth are sharpened to a point. And the metal I glimpsed in his mouth earlier is their tips. His skin has turned thicker than leather, and I get it now – it's some sort of armour. I look down to Lucas's fingers. They are more like talons and the tips glint like steel, just like his teeth do. Some of Billie's blood drips from them.

The Ape has fallen very silent as he moves around Lucas, eyeing him, weapon clutched tight in his hands.

'I've got this,' he says.

Lucas turns and watches him, tracking the Ape's movements. 'You've got what exactly?'

'This.'

'You think?'

'Oh, yeah.'

We're all backing away now.

'Who are you?' asks Johnson.

'Who are *you*?' responds Lucas.

I try to bring some sense to the confusion. 'We need to talk about this, we won't get anywhere otherwise—'

Before I can finish the Ape swings his makeshift weapon as hard as he can at Lucas. 'You can talk to this,' he says.

Lucas is knocked backwards by the fierce blow and crashes to the ground.

'Ape!' I yell.

'What the hell?' Johnson can't believe what the Ape has just done.

The Ape is proud of himself though. 'That is not Lucas!' he bellows, like his brain has finally caught up with the rest of us.

Lucas, or whoever it is, springs to his feet. 'You shouldn't have done that,' he snarls.

Lucas leaps for the Ape, but the Ape smashes him with his weapon again, sending him arching through the air. Lucas slashes at GG with his talons as he sails over him and GG screams and ducks out of the way.

'OhmyGod!' Carrie yells.

Lucas rights himself as soon as he touches the ground and

goes for the Ape again, talons glinting in the rising sunlight, but the Ape's ready and hits Lucas in the side of the face with his broom weapon, knocking his entire head to a crazy, impossible angle. A blow like that should break his neck, but Lucas gathers himself and then cricks his head and neck back into place. The bones pop loudly as he does this.

'No way!' The Ape is momentarily frozen by Lucas's near superhuman display.

Lucas is in his element now, skin as hard as diamond, coupled with an astonishing athletic ability. 'That the best you got?' He leaps for the Ape again.

'Ape!!' I scream. 'Hit him!' It isn't lost on me how I've gone from peacemaker to warmonger in practically three seconds flat.

The Ape raises his weapon just in time and bats Lucas back. Then he hits him again and I'm not sure if he's very brave or very demented, but either way the Ape goes to war with Lucas, swinging and stabbing. He hits him over and over, smashing and lashing at him.

'Come on then!' he yells, cutting and slashing as he drives Lucas back. The blows rain down, but Lucas takes them all with a horrible ease. His eyes are trained on the Ape and I sense that he is biding his time, waiting for a moment or an opening to attack.

'Ape!' I call out. 'Ape, be careful.'

Johnson grabs my arm. 'Move.'

'What?'

'GO, REV!'

I turn and see that the others are starting to run.

'What are you doing?' I yell at them.

'That's not real, Rev, that's so not real,' Billie calls out to

97

me as she runs, blood still pouring from her face. Her fear is the only thing keeping her on her feet right now.

I look back at Johnson. 'We can't leave the Ape.'

'Get the Moth out of here.'

'You're staying?' I ask him.

'Take the Moth, Rev.'

I turn back to the fight and see the Ape smash Lucas with a bone-crushing blow that sends him tumbling backwards. 'I so got this!' He wades forward, swinging and heaving, bashing Lucas again and again. But it's futile as Lucas keeps snapping his rubbery bones back into place.

'Rev, you've got to go.' Johnson still has his hand on my arm. I can see GG racing for all he's worth, while herding Billie and Carrie along.

'Would someone please get me out of here!' screeches the Moth as politely as he can, even though he's in a total panic.

The Ape sends Lucas crashing back into a tailor's shop window and the glass shatters down around him. Lucas instinctively covers his face and neck as shards plummet onto him. Some actually embed in his skin, which makes me think he's not totally invulnerable, but then he quickly shakes them out with a lizard-like wriggle.

'Go,' the Ape urges as he waits for Lucas to right himself once more. 'I'll catch up.'

It's not what I want to hear but together Johnson and I take hold of the Moth's wheelchair and start pushing him as fast as we can. I glance back and watch Lucas spring out of the shop front and arc clear over the Ape's head. The Ape swivels and whacks Lucas over and over, battering him with all of his might, unleashing even more hell upon him.

'Don't look back,' Johnson tells me as we push the Moth

as fast as we can. I realise he's telling me that he doesn't believe the Ape will beat Lucas, or whatever that Lucas-thing is. 'There's nothing we can do.'

Which makes me turn back and immediately regret it.

The Ape swings his makeshift weapon and looks stunned as it breaks in half on Lucas's back.

I come to an abrupt halt.

'He's doing it for us, Rev,' Johnson says, trying to urge me forward. 'Buying us time, don't let that go to waste.'

'But—'

'Rev, that is not Lucas, and whatever it is, it's going to come for all of us.'

And as if to underline Johnson's words I watch Lucas leap onto the Ape and take him down.

'The train station! There's a train there!' GG has raced back to offer at least some hope. 'C'mon, Rev, run. Move, move, move!'

All I really know is that a little bit of my heart has just died for the Ape and I barely feel the road under my pounding feet. I can taste iron in my mouth and my lungs ache horribly but I don't care. All I can think about is the Ape being leaped on by Lucas and it makes me want to weep.

'Pump those pins.' GG is now half pushing me while Johnson pushes the Moth. We don't stop running until we reach the station at the edge of the town. It's half a mile from the town square and I can't fathom how we got here without the Lucas-thing hunting us down.

The others are waiting beside a four-carriage train on platform one and I don't really get why GG is so excited. But he babbles at ten to the dozen, breathlessly explaining.

'My dad's a train driver. He used to sneak me on some-times, late at night. Totally illegal, but if you'd seen how excited I was.'

'You can drive a train?' Carrie is almost impressed. '*You?*'

GG is in his element. 'I wasn't there just to look good. Though obviously I did.'

'Can you drive this one?' Johnson yells at him and GG grins.

'Buckle up, it's going to be a bumpy ride.'

TO BE FAIR, HE DID SAY BUMPY

GG darts towards the driver's cab at the front of the train. The station is a small suburban two-platform affair that doesn't afford much in the way of a hiding place and Johnson scans the small car park outside, expecting to see Lucas any second. Billie is breathing hard.

'What the hell was that? I mean what the hell!' she says to me.

Johnson bangs on the side of the train. 'Get these doors open, GG!'

Carrie must have discarded her impractical shoes on the way to the station and the soles of her feet are bleeding. 'You're kidding me!' Carrie is staring back towards the car park. I spin around and spot the Moth heading straight towards us.

Except of course it can't be the Moth because he's sitting in his wheelchair right beside me.

'That's me,' says the Moth, as Moth Two heads our way. Strong and sinewy and upright. 'That's me with proper legs.'

'The doors, GG!' Johnson bellows.

'Oh my God!' Carrie starts jabbing hard at the buttons to try and open the train doors but they remain stubbornly closed.

'GG!' Johnson bellows again and Carrie and Billie join him, yelling as loud as they can.

Moth Two is getting closer and we don't have a single weapon between us. Not that it would do much good after seeing the Ape fall to the Lucas-thing.

The others look terrified so I step forward, bracing myself. 'I've got this,' I say, echoing the Ape.

'Rev, no,' Billie says.

'I can talk to him, explain.'

'Not if he's like the other one you can't,' she says.

'The Ape's not around to ruin everything this time.' The words catch in my throat as I think of the Ape and his desperate, hopeless fight.

'What if he doesn't want to talk?' asks Carrie.

'Then he's going to have to come through me.'

'Rev!' Billie is tugging on my arm now, but I shake her free.

'Soon as the doors open, get on the train.' I take up what I hope looks like a come-and-get-me stance. I don't know where this strength – or is it madness? – is coming from. I'm thinking about the Ape, about the sacrifice he made, and it's somehow filling me with a newfound sense of determination.

Moth Two arrives at the entrance to the station. He stops and then smiles at me and I can see he has the same pointed teeth as the non-Lucas.

'Rev.' He looks relieved. 'Been looking all over for a sign of life.'

102

Moth Two stops as his eyes settle on the Moth sitting beside me. I can almost see his brain working overtime to process what he is seeing.

'I know this looks a bit awkward,' I say, trying to keep as calm as I possibly can.

'GG, c'mon!' Billie is still urging him to get the carriage doors open.

'There's two of me?'

'Trust me, we're as confused as you are,' I tell him.

The train doors open behind me with a shrill beep. GG's panicky voice echoes over the train tannoy. 'Sorry, the stupid thing wouldn't start.'

'Rev, come on,' Johnson says, helping Billie drag the Moth and his wheelchair onto the train.

'You should try the high street,' I tell Moth Two. 'Lucas is there.'

'He is?' Moth Two brightens.

'Shut the doors! Shut the doors!' Carrie urges behind me.

'Rev!' Johnson calls.

There's something in their panicked tones that stirs Moth Two on a deeper level. Chances are he's probably going to be smart like our Moth is, and his brain is making connections and calculations, taking in all he knows and measuring it against whatever he has just learned. He rapidly comes to pretty much the same damning conclusion that the Lucas-thing came to.

'You're not you, are you?'

'It's you that's not you,' I tell him.

'What are you running from?'

'We're not running,' I lie.

'Have you done something to Lucas?'

103

Even though we haven't done anything I avert my eyes from Moth Two's gaze. I look away and it's the one thing I really shouldn't have done.

'That'll be a yes then.'

'He sort of started it,' I say weakly.

'I don't know what's going on, or even who you all are, but I will tell you this. No one touches my best friend.' Moth Two coils and then springs forward. He has the same talons, the same deadly stare as the Lucas-thing.

'No one!' He comes straight for me, his mouth opening incredibly wide. He's within inches of landing on me when I feel a tug on the back of my collar and I tumble backwards into the train carriage. Moth Two hits the closing carriage doors face first. His features go flat, billowing out in a wide spreading mess of rubbery skin. For a split second his eyes turn black and lock on to mine through the toughened glass but GG floors the accelerator and leaves Moth Two behind.

The real Moth is lying on the floor, his glasses having been knocked several feet away. 'Did you see that? You did see that? Yes?' He keeps repeating it over and over until I hand his glasses back to him. He puts them on and blinks his eyes, only they aren't like eyes – they are swollen and bulging and look ready to explode from his face. He is beyond bewilderment.

'Yes? That actually happened? Rev, talk to me!'

'It happened, is happening, whatever.' I nod.

'Everyone OK?' Johnson is standing over us as he sways in time with the accelerating train.

'OK? What's OK?' the Moth all but screams. 'How can you even ask that?'

'I guess you're not then,' says Johnson wryly.

He turns to Carrie and Billie who have taken a seat in the first-class carriage. Billie has her face in her hands and Carrie is staring blankly into space.

'How's your face, Billie?' Johnson asks.

She looks up and the bleeding has stopped, but I know from the deep ugly wounds that she's going to have scars for the rest of her life.

'Where we going?' I ask Johnson as he helps me to my feet.

'Away from here,' is all he can offer.

GG's voice comes over the intercom. 'Uh, guys, sorry to have to tell you this. But it's chasing us.'

My stomach lurches. Johnson tries to get a look, but even pressed up against the window he can't see anything.

'It's OK though, we're pulling away.' GG's words ring throughout the carriage and I feel myself finally start to relax.

'What were they?' Billie asks. She winces as she talks and it's clear that she's in pain from the deep gashes on the side of her face. 'Has anyone ever seen anything like that before?'

'Oh, yeah, I see weird super-versions of us all the time,' Carrie sneers.

'I was just saying.'

'Uh-oh.' GG's voice breaks through again. Carrie instinctively grips the edges of her seat. 'Wow, look at it go,' he says. Johnson bangs hard on the locked driver's door – we need more information than GG is giving us.

'Moth Two is gaining.' GG is trying to sound calm for our sakes as he pours on the speed. 'But he's not going to catch this little locomotive.'

105

The train starts to shudder and vibrate with the increasing speed. The countryside flashes by, but somehow I know that we're going to be caught. The tingling in my shoulders is telling me as much. It's like I've developed a spider sense.

'That is one fast Moth.' GG's voice has again gone high-pitched with fear.

I get to my feet and start towards the end of the train.

'Rev?' Billie looks worried.

'I've got an idea,' I tell her. I'm still thinking about the Ape. A little of me even wants to head back and find him, even if I know it is futile and stupid. I hurry as fast as I can from swaying carriage to swaying carriage with GG's commentary accompanying me.

'No one moves that fast.'

I plough onwards.

'It's got to get tired soon.'

The train picks up even more speed.

'Oh my, it's still closing on us.'

I reach the third carriage. The automatic doors hiss open and then shut behind me. The train is rocking dangerously now as it hits full speed.

'Oh my giddy God!'

The train hurtles onwards and I have to hold on tight as I manoeuvre all the way to the back of the train. There's a security door that blocks the entrance to the driver's cubicle at the far end of the train. But when I try it, it opens. It's as if someone wants me to see Moth Two again.

I peer out of the reinforced window and can see Moth Two catching us. He has turned into some sort of animal – it has the Moth's face but the body is now hunched over and running. Its strides are bewilderingly fast, a blur of limbs, and there's something beautiful about its movement as its body adapts and then readapts itself for speed. It's a mesmerising mixture of grace and power. No wonder the Ape couldn't stop the non-Lucas. I doubt anything could stop creatures this powerful.

'Rev, where are you?' GG's voice comes over the tannoy.

I stab at buttons until a whine erupts around me and then make contact with GG over the tannoy system. 'I'm at the other end of the train – I can see it,' I say.

'You got a plan, right?'

'Uh . . .'

'Better do what you got to, girl – it's going to catch us any second.'

The beast's flattened face at the window springs into my mind. I see its black eyes staring at me – into me.

'Stop the train,' I say to GG.

'What?'

'Do it, GG.'

'I'm not stopping for that thing.'

'Please, GG, trust me.'

'It hasn't bought a ticket.' GG is trying to joke but his voice is still high-pitched and strained.

'Do it!' I repeat. I've never felt so in command. 'NOW!' I scream at him.

GG announces to everyone to hold tight and brace themselves, then slams on the brakes. A train doesn't stop immediately. But it does lock up and it does shudder and it does squeal and the smell of train brakes is overpowering – but more than all of those things, this train is well built and made to withstand severe physical forces. It's made of metal, it's heavy, it's solid and if you're running at over seventy miles an hour and you slam into it, you are not going to be a happy beast. The thing chasing us is in mid-bound and can't stop or veer away as it sees the train suddenly loom up in its vision. At first I think that it's going to come through the window at me and I instinctively duck, but its arc takes it full pelt into the undercarriage. The impact nearly rocks me off my feet.

'Reverse, reverse!' I scream at GG.

I'd clung on for dear life during the teeth-wrenching stop and I can only hope that GG has done the same. But I don't hear anything from him.

'GG!'

Nothing.

'Back up! Reverse! GG, are you there? GG!'

'*Ding ding* – this is your captain speaking.'

The train shunts backwards and crunches the life out of the stricken concussed monster. I feel the jolt and hear the crunch and it is a moment of unparalleled joy. I've never hurt anything in my life but this – this is for the Ape.

A GOD AWAITS US SOME DAY

I make my way back through the carriages as GG reverses the train far enough until he can see the remains of Moth Two out of the front window.

'Ooh. Shouldn't have done that. My tummy feels funny now,' he announces weakly and I get the impression that whatever happened to Moth Two is not a pretty sight.

Billie thinks she has sprained her right wrist when she lost her grip during the monumental braking manoeuvre and slammed into a table. It's really not her day because the deep gouges in her cheek have started bleeding again and Johnson is now applying some of the bandages he was probably going to use on my burns.

'I'm going to look like a mummy,' she tells him.

'You will if you don't hold still.' He grins, which I can see she enjoys.

I decide to leave them to it and climb down from the train. I head warily for what's left of Moth Two. It has been decapitated and most of its powerful limbs are severed or broken many times over. It lies squished, half on and half off the track. I get up as close as I dare. I have no idea what it is, what it is doing here, or why it even existed.

GG joins me, looking like he is about to throw up. 'There's itsy bits of him everywhere.'

'GG, we just killed someone.'

'Some*thing*,' Johnson corrects and I'm pleased to see him jump down from the train and head towards us.

'But it's still murder, isn't it?'

'What do you think he was planning on doing to us?' Johnson is determined to keep my spirits up. 'You made a call and you did what you had to.'

'And thank the Lord,' adds GG. 'Because I was all out of speed.'

'What d'you think it is?' Johnson can't resist touching a piece of Moth Two with the pointed toe of his oh-so-cool shoes.

'An alien?' GG suggests.

'Looks like a . . . Actually I dunno what it looks like.' Johnson frowns hard and then shakes his head. 'I have no idea. No idea at all. It's the Moth but it isn't the Moth.'

'Should we keep it?' GG bends to take a closer look.

'You're sick, GG,' I say.

'They might want to study it.'

'They?'

'Scientists. Zoologists. McDonald's. Who knows?'

'Did you say McDonald's?'

'I don't know! Did I? Oh God, I'm falling apart.' GG holds his hand to his mouth and his eyes bulge. 'I don't even like McDonald's.'

'It's got to be an experiment.' Johnson can't take his eyes off Moth Two. 'Maybe these things got out of a lab or something and they had to evacuate everyone. That's what it has to be. This is something man-made and they screwed it up and everyone was told to run.'

It's a good theory. They'd spliced a cheetah with our genes and somehow come up with this.

'Why do they look like us though?'

There is what looks like blood congealing around the wounds, but it's too oily and thick to be human. Johnson is about to touch it when I drag his hand away. 'I wouldn't,' I say and he nods his appreciation and steps away.

'Hawkings'll have an idea,' Carrie's voice interrupts. I turn to see her limping along the track on her cut feet towards us. 'Show him. He's clever. He's in all the top sets.'

'We can't show the Moth,' says GG. 'We can't show him his own decapitated head.'

'Maybe we should get moving. That Lucas-thing is still out there.' Johnson looks down the track as if the non-Lucas is going to be haring down it any second.

Which makes me think immediately of the Ape and what happened to him. I wince inwardly. He was a big boorish lout, but he still stepped up when he had to.

'Think that Lucas-thing knows where we went?' Carrie looks panicked.

'I was sort of yelling my head off about finding a train,' says GG meekly. 'He could have super-hearing.'

'It's not a he,' I say quickly. 'It's an *it*. Just like Moth Two was an *it*. We can't think of them as people.'

'So what do we do now?' GG asks.

'Don't care about you, but I'm getting back on the train,' Carrie says.

'Where does this line lead to? London?' Johnson asks GG.

'Ah, well, that depends on the signalling and what track goes where. My dad did sort of explain it all but I was too busy sounding the horn to listen.'

'You don't even know where we'll end up?' Carrie is scornful of GG.

'I know we're heading south and that usually means London. But only if the tracks are lined up that way.'

'Whatever,' Carrie says as she takes another watchful look along the railway line. 'I'll go anywhere as long as it's as far away as possible from that other Lucas.'

We board the train and GG dusts the Moth down after he went sprawling along the floor. He still smells strongly of urine and Carrie makes a point of opening all the windows.

'Where is he?' asks the Moth. 'The other me, has he gone?'

'I wouldn't worry, Moth,' says GG. 'Half of him is pointed south and the other half is pointing west.'

'Oh.' The Moth swallows grimly and decides against asking any more questions.

'Where's the Ape?' asks Billie, her cheek taped over with a bandage. The shock of everything that's just happened means she's only now realised that he's missing.

I feel a lump swell in my throat. I can't actually get the words out, but luckily Johnson answers for me. 'He bought us time to get away,' he says. The words are laden with a profound sadness. Even Carrie falls silent out of respect.

'It got him, then?' says Billie quietly.

I nod. 'Yeah. He's uh . . . He's gone.' My voice is small and I turn away as tears fill my eyes.

GG takes a moment. 'I never minded him that much,' he says simply. 'The Ape was what he was.'

Everyone appreciates the simple sentiment but I know we're all secretly thinking, who's going to be next? We're already down two people and I can't see things getting much better.

Johnson lets the silence grow for a respectable amount of time before turning to GG.

'Time to go.'

Before GG can head for the driver's cabin, a tinny, electronic tune fills the air.

I realise it's my phone and scramble to find it in my pocket. I almost drop it, I am so stunned. I open my phone and right there, before my eyes, is a message from the Ape.

Where is every1?

We look at one another, stupefied.

'It's the Ape!' I can't believe it. I've gone from despair to elation in half a second flat.

'He's OK? I mean he's not dead?' Johnson says.

'That can't be – can it?' Billie's words trail off.

'Answer him then!' snaps Carrie.

I text as quickly as my trembling fingers will allow. **Where r u?**

In town.

What about Lucas?

Offed him :) One-nil to the Dazman!

'He killed it?' Billie asks. 'Is that what he means? He killed it?'

Where r u? he texts again.

'It's a trap.' Carrie says this with a huge amount of conviction. 'It's not him. Can't be.'

'They can use phones?' Billie says.

'With those talons?' quips GG. 'That's touchscreen hell.'

'Test him,' urges Johnson. 'Ask him something only he would know.'

'But he knows nothing,' Billie says. She sounds weak, not herself.

I tap a message as quick as I can. **What do u want to be?**

'Apart from an idiot,' Carrie says.

I ignore her as we wait for an answer.

Time seems to crawl to a stop and it's taking an age for the Ape to answer the question.

'Just like in school,' the Moth says. 'He never knows the answer to anything.'

The silence expands.

'Text another question, something easier,' Carrie says.

I rack my brains trying to come up with something the Ape might be able to answer when a text pings back.

King of the ring

Finally, I think.

'It's him,' I say.

W8 there. I text back.

Carrie looks alarmed. 'Why are you telling him that?'

'We're going back for him,' I say.

The look on the others' faces tell me they aren't so convinced.

'We can't leave him twice. He bought us time. Saved us.'

'No one asked him to.' Carrie's voice is emotionless.

I can't believe we're even debating this.

'We have to think this through, Rev.' Billie's voice is barely audible. 'If there are these weird copies of us, then it stands to reason there's still five of them out there. Maybe in town, prowling around . . .' I know Billie isn't being cowardly and that she is just applying a calm logic, but even

114

so I'm a little shocked she'd abandon the Ape after what he did for us. 'We can't run them all over,' she adds simply.

Another text comes through. **Rev?**

'Should I answer?' I look at the others but no one speaks.

REV? The text pings again. I stare at the small screen on the phone.

'He bought us time to escape. Which is what we've got to do now. Escape,' Carrie says finally.

'But we don't know there are other versions of us,' I counter, just as another text comes through.

I've seen Billie

My heart hits my boots.

She aint seen me tho

'See? They're out there.' Carrie is already heading back to the train.

Before I know it, I text back. **Hang on. We r coming.**

The others see me do this and Billie is aghast. 'What the hell are you doing?'

'We can't leave him – we can't.'

'Look at my face. Look at it! How am I ever going to get over this? I'm going to look like this for the rest of my life but I'd still take it over going back there any day.'

'I know how you feel, I know that but—'

'Rev, you have no idea what to do, or how to do it. I say we stay on the train and we ride around until we find someone who can help us. There's got to be people out there. Hopefully we're already heading towards London and it's going to be packed with people. Once we find them then we can go back for the Ape.'

'Yeah, tell him to stay hidden, to lie as low as low,' adds GG. 'But we will, we absolutely will, come back for him.'

'Rev,' says Johnson, speaking for the first time in ages. 'I don't want to leave him either, but we need help.'

'No!' I shout. 'I'm going back. And you are too. All of you.'

Carrie looks at me with venom. 'You are such an idiot.'

'We beat one of them. The Ape beat one of them. How tough are these things? I'll tell you. They're not.' I'm not going to give ground on this.

I look to Johnson and I wonder if I have swayed him. He takes a moment to weigh his options then gives the faintest of shrugs. 'OK.'

'OK?' snaps Carrie.

'Rev's got a point,' he says staring right into me. Our eyes lock and I'm sure something unspoken has just sparked between us.

'Now we have two idiots. Great,' Carrie sighs. 'Well, you two can go back and the rest of us will go find someone sane to help us.'

I look to Billie who, despite the chill in the air, looks hot and feverish. 'Billie, I know this is right,' I tell her. 'We can't leave the Ape. He's one of us.'

As if to underline that sentiment another text comes through. **Hey!**

Billie ponders for a long moment, then gathers herself.

'As much as I'd like to, we'd better not abandon him, had we?'

I turn back to Carrie. 'You can always stay here. Wait on the track. Out in the open.'

She glares at me.

I get another text from the Ape as I take a seat. **U coming?**
☻ I text back.

☺

I smile at his smile, then feel the train move off. It doesn't dawn on me at first but when I look out of the window I realise we are heading south again, away from town, not back towards it. I sit bolt upright but Johnson is already on his feet and hammering on the locked driver's door.

'GG! What the hell? GG!'

The train gathers pace as it takes us further and further away from the Ape.

'I'm sorry,' GG's voice comes over the tannoy. 'But we'll find someone in London, I know we will. The Ape's tough, he'll be OK. We can't go waltzing back into town, you know we can't. We'd never get out alive.'

Johnson is hammering on the door, kicking it. 'Open the door, GG!'

'I'm a lover, not a fighter.'

'GG!!'

I start kicking and hammering and shouting alongside Johnson, but the train isn't going to stop anytime soon. Billie, now drenched in sweat, joins us. She smiles weakly at me.

'Rev, I don't feel so good.'

Before I can react, her body goes limp and she pitches forward, collapsing at my feet in a big deathly heap of stillness. It's pretty wimpy I know, but after all we've been through in the last day or so, I feel it's OK to scream.

EVERYTHING TURNS

Billie is unconscious and I can't get her to wake up.

'Billie, hey, Billie . . .'

'The hammer, Rev, the hammer,' Johnson calls over to me.

'What hammer? What are you talking about?' Does he want to hit her on the head?

'The emergency hammer.'

I spot the hammer. It's above the door Billie is now lying beside. But I can't seem to move. I'm stuck, paralysed. Billie is just lying there and I'm scared out of my wits.

Carrie steps past us and starts hitting the small plastic security box the hammer is encased in. Then she stops, takes dead aim and punches the perspex as hard as she can. Her fist goes straight through the perspex. *So much for her being brittle*, I think. The girl is harder than diamond.

She grabs the hammer and tosses it to Johnson. He rushes to the locked train driver's door and starts hacking at it.

'Is she OK?' Carrie looks down at us.

I look back at Billie, whose eyes suddenly open and are

now as black as Moth Two's eyes. I gasp, but after a split second she blinks and they return to normal.

Johnson chops savagely at the door until it swings open. GG yelps when he sees Johnson. Yes. Yelps. Like one of those little yappy dogs women in Los Angeles carry inside their purses.

'Want to put the brakes on?' he tells, rather than asks, GG.

'It's for the best – I know it, you know it,' GG says, his voice small but controlled.

Johnson stares hard at GG and he buckles within a heartbeat. 'All right, all right . . . I'm stopping the train, I'm doing it now.'

Within a few seconds the train is easing to a halt.

I help Billie into a sitting position and she takes a moment to collect herself.

'You OK?'

'Yeah, brilliant,' she pants.

'What about me?' asks the Moth who has fallen on the floor again without any of us noticing. 'Hey, hello, hey!'

'It's all me, me, me with you, isn't it?' Carrie aims a venomous look his way, but helps him up anyway.

A text comes from the Ape. **Hey!**

Followed by another. **Rev.**

And another. **In Tesco makin more weapons.**

Together Johnson and I manoeuvre Billie gently into a seat.

Rev?

Hey!

FU!

No one can face the relentless messages echoing tinnily around the carriage and I turn my phone to silent.

119

Carrie sits down opposite the Moth. 'It's time you used your big space brain, Hawkings.'

The Moth looks surprised. 'Me? And it's Hawking!'

'You're the best we've got.' Carrie stares straight into the Moth, challenging him. 'So come on. Tell us what's happening.'

The Moth realises that we are watching and waiting for him to do just that. He looks back to Carrie and I sense that he sees this as a chance to impress her. 'OK, OK, OK. Let me think. Right. The only way out of this is to work out exactly what has happened, and is currently happening.'

'We know that bit, doofus,' Carrie says scornfully.

The Moth tries again, more determined this time. 'We need to break it down into its component parts and attack each part with logic and sense. Don't forget that everything that happens has a reason for happening.'

'You lost me at "the",' says GG.

The Moth sits up taller as, willed on by his desire to impress Carrie, he becomes more dominant. 'I know that you want to help the Ape, Rev, but I don't think going back is going to achieve anything. Sorry.' He can see I'm ready to respond but cuts me off. 'It's clear we can't talk to these – these doppelgangers – because they're more savage and brutal than we are. And it doesn't seem like they know any more than we do. So going back is ultimately futile. Not to mention extremely dangerous.'

The words leave an ominous feel in the air and I can see I'm not going to get things my way. The Ape is going to be left behind and I'm already debating how to tell him. It won't be with a ☺ that's for certain.

Johnson gazes at the floor. His lips are pursed and his eyes have narrowed in thought.

'I can't do it,' he says eventually.

'Can't do what?' asks Carrie.

'Leave him.'

I sit up straighter.

'We're going back,' declares Johnson.

'Are you insane?' Carrie is wide-eyed.

'You did hear what I said?' The Moth is as stunned as Carrie is.

'We're going back.' Johnson is adamant. 'GG, get us moving. We're not leaving the Ape.' He gives me the tiniest of smiles as he speaks.

I am so taken by his declaration that I instinctively touch my finger to my forehead, copying the Johnson salute.

As I do so, the small smile on his face grows, and *right now*, I think, *right now is a moment we're going to remember.*

INVASION EVASION

We're heading slowly back to town, hoping that a slow-moving train will attract less attention. GG explained that trains can push and pull, so basically we are reversing. We have moved to the far end of the train now, so we can at least see if anything is lying in wait for us.

The Moth still smells and Carrie is now waving her hand in front of her nose and making a big show of it. 'Thanks for ponging out first class.'

'You have issues,' responds the Moth. 'Deep, deep issues, you know that? All this aggression, there's a reason for it.'

'What I have is a gag reflex.' Carrie kisses her teeth at him and waves more of his smell away. Despite the savage comments she has thrown his way, the Moth refuses to buckle.

'No one is like that on purpose,' he says, quietly confident. I am starting to marvel at the Moth. Everyone at school thought that Lucas was just his friend because he felt sorry for the Moth, but I'm starting to see how resilient and capable the Moth truly is. Lucas was fragile and paper thin underneath the near God-like exterior – he proved he didn't have it in him to cope, but the Moth has had his best friend die and he hasn't crumbled. Maybe it was him who felt sorry for Lucas and not the other way round.

I switch my phone from silent to normal and it immediately beeps with more texts from the Ape.

Rev U R here.

Not u tho.

I don't think.

Knowing there's another me, and that she's living and breathing less than five miles away, is the scariest most confused feeling I'll ever have. I want to go and see her but I also don't want to, as in ever. *I'm* Reva Marsalis, not her.

She found the burned man.

'What's he been texting?' asks Billie, who sits across from me.

'I'm in the supermarket,' I say. 'Well Me Two is,' I clarify.

'Tell him to stay out of sight,' Johnson says.

I text exactly that.

I'm sick of hiding ☺

My heart lurches.

I can take these things.

New weapon is awesome.

I read the last text out loud to the others.

'Text him no. Tell him not to fight them,' Carrie says, revealing more concern in that one statement than she has in the last four years we've been at school together. She aims a look at the Moth. 'C'mon, what are you doing? You should have all of this worked out by now.'

'Why d'you think I'm so clever? Because I'm in a wheelchair? Is that it? Being in a wheelchair turns you into a scientist?' he snaps. They share a look of mutual scorn before the Moth backs down and softens. 'I wish I was, I really do,' he tells Carrie rather than the rest of us. 'Then I'd be able to get you safe . . .'

It's a tiny moment, but something flickers across Carrie's face as she registers that the Moth might actually care about her.

The Ape phones and already he has forgotten to stay quiet. 'Yowza!'

'Get off the phone!' I urge him. 'They'll hear you.'

'I snuck into the manager's office. Got a row of screens in front of me – can see the whole shop.'

'I'm hanging up,' I tell him. 'Stick to texting,' I hiss.

'This other Rev's boobs look bigger than yours. Just going to zoom in to check.'

'How can he not understand what's going on?' asks the Moth.

'Well, you don't!' Carrie snaps.

'I'm not Stephen Hawking!' he squeaks shrilly.

'So stop making out that you are and that the rest of us are stupid.'

'But I'm not!'

Carrie looks totally disgusted and the Moth, to his credit, doesn't flinch. He's probably too used to liking girls and not getting anywhere with them.

'I'll think of something,' he promises. 'Just give me time. But I will come good, I will.' He says all of this to Carrie and it seems that despite her unwavering hostility towards him, he's going to keep trying to prove his worth to her.

Johnson talks to the Ape. 'Try and keep your voice down, but what's the other Rev doing?'

'Hang on, I'm still zooming.'

'Ape!' I say impatiently.

'OK, OK, I'm now unzooming. Coming away, coming away, coming away some more.' The Ape pauses. 'Still coming away, still unzooming. Ah.' He pauses again and we wait what feels like an excruciating eternity.

'You're crying,' he says eventually.

'Why's she crying?' I ask him.

'I stole all the chocolate,' he jokes. No one laughs.

'Is she still with the burned man?'

'She's sitting beside him. Whole body's shaking. Yow-za! She is shaking 'em!'

Billie mouths 'shaking 'em?' to me, then she gets what the Ape is looking at. 'Oh, that's just crude.'

'Who sits around with a burned dead person?' asks Carrie. 'What sort of freak does that?'

'I touched him,' I say to her.

'Ugh, you're both freaks.'

'I had to.'

'Freak squared.'

'What I mean is, I wanted to – like, I felt compelled to.'

'Why was that?' asks the Moth.

'I dunno, I just felt – and I know how this'll sound – but it was like I knew him.'

Johnson gets slowly to his feet. He pulls his jeans a little higher on his snake hips. 'So you think you knew this burned guy?'

I nod.

'OK.' Johnson eases back against the edge of the table and his long legs stretch out in front of him.

'Where'd the burned man come from?' the Moth asks.

'A lorry. Out back of the supermarket. It's where he got burned. In the driver's cabin.' I show them some of my burns. 'I got these climbing up there.'

The burns are really sore now and I have been ignoring them as best I can. But, looking down at my arms, I can see they are raw and peeling and need attention.

'So Rev Two knows the man,' says the Moth.

'But *our* Rev also knows him,' adds Billie.

'I only think I do,' I say.

'Yeah, but if that Rev is getting the same feeling you had . . .' the Moth says and then trails off to give this some more thought. 'Only hers is stronger, her feeling is much more potent.' The Moth becomes more animated. 'She's crying because she knows him. She's holding him because . . . Because—'

'She loves him,' finishes Johnson.

We take a moment to digest this.

'So who do you love, Rev?' asks Carrie instantly. 'If you can tell us that, then we can work out who he is, and maybe where he came from.'

Everyone's eyes are on me.

'Who do you love, Rev?' Johnson asks.

'Well . . .'

I look at Johnson and realise I can't bring myself to say. It's the last thing I want to tell him.

'Kyle,' I say in a really tiny weak voice, as if that's going to stop the sound travelling far enough to reach Johnson. But it does and he hears it all too clearly because I see him shift slightly. It's the tiniest movement, but it still says too much. *Oh my God*, I think. *It wasn't just the painkillers making me giddy. It was him. Johnson.*

'Her boyfriend,' Billie explains a little louder than I'd have liked.

Johnson has fallen silent and I don't know if it's my imagination or not but I swear he looks disappointed. I can feel the rapport between us disintegrating.

'So, that's Kyle lying there.' Carrie's voice breaks as she says this. 'Kyle,' she repeats for good measure.

Johnson isn't even looking at me any more and turns his focus entirely on Billie now.

'Do you think it was Kyle?'

'It could be—'

'But I wouldn't cry like that,' I butt in. 'I wouldn't. In fact I didn't.' I don't know if this outburst makes it ten times better or ten times worse. Johnson probably thinks I'm the most heartless unfeeling cow in the world now. 'What I mean is, I don't know if I do love Kyle.'

'What a bitch,' sneers Carrie. 'Burns himself to death and all you can do is wonder about your feelings for him.'

'It wasn't him!' I say. 'It wasn't!'

'So if it's not Kyle, who else do you love?' the Moth asks.

My eyes flick straight to Johnson but he is pretending to be deep in thought.

'Brother, father?' the Moth presses.

'There's my dad. But I never really knew him.' To my surprise that simple statement brings a croak in my voice. A memory comes with it. A four-year-old version of me sitting in my dad's lap while he typed on a computer. My father's arms had to reach past me, and I could feel his chin resting on the top of my head as he typed. His fingers were long and thin and I used to imagine that we were playing a piano together. He walked out on Mum and me over twelve years

127

ago. No word, no letter, just a man who never came back. A man I've still never forgiven.

'So process of elimination says that if it's anyone, it's your dad,' the Moth concludes.

Everyone falls quiet.

'No,' I say, 'I told you, I don't even know him.'

'But what if it's *her* dad?' says Billie. 'Rev Two's dad.'

'How could that even be possible?'

'How's it possible the entire population have gone missing?' shrugs the Moth.

'Good point, Hawkings,' says Carrie and the Moth lets a small smile escape from his lips.

Johnson stands, mind made up. 'It's Rev Two's dad. Has to be,' he says calmly and then speaks to the Ape. 'You can't kill her, Ape.'

'But I've got this great weapon.'

'Listen to me.' There's steel in Johnson's voice now. 'We're coming back. We need to talk to Rev Two. She knows the burned guy's her dad and if she knows that, then she might know a whole load of other stuff, including how we get out of this mess. Talking to her is our only chance. Everyone agreed?'

Everyone murmurs a yes, though equally no one's that crazy about confronting a possibly violent supercharged version of me.

'Zoom back in on her and we'll be right there,' says Johnson.

'Zooming now,' comes the response.

Johnson ends the call and there is a palpable sense of unease in the carriage. It seems we can't run, we can't hide and, for good or bad, we're destined to always return to a small market town in Hertfordshire.

128

Johnson looks at me for the first time in what seems like ages. 'You OK?'

'No.' Which is the absolute truth on so many levels now.

The slow reversal into town is made in a stunted silence. Sometimes words just won't come, and this goes for all of us until the Moth, his brow burrowed deep in thought, speaks.

'Who was your dad, Rev?' he asks.

'What do you mean?'

'What did he do? What was his job? Only if they are copies of us, then maybe their families are the same as the ones we have.'

'So?' Carrie stifles a yawn. As soon as she does, it reminds me of how strung out and battered we are. I have run out of painkillers and still don't know how to tell Johnson that I could really do with his medical touch.

'*Ding ding*, this is your captain speaking.' GG's voice echoes through the carriages. 'We'll be arriving at our desti-nation in the next couple of minutes, please collect all your belongings, failure to do so will result in a million-pound fine.' GG's sing-song voice makes me smile and Billie follows suit.

'He is such a nut,' she says.

'D'you know anything about your dad at all?' the Moth persists.

'He was a scientist,' I shrug.

'A scientist?' The Moth straightens up at this. 'What field?'

'She said a scientist, not a farmer.' Carrie yawns again and her joke is as tired as she is.

'I dunno. He wrote a scientific thesis though. About space and stuff. I don't really know much about it.'

The Moth seems to have come alive now. 'Is it well known?'

'I don't think anyone read it. Apparently he was on the verge of publishing this amazing paper but my mum said it was suddenly withdrawn. That's what sent my dad off the rails, or so she said. The fact that he put all his life's work into it and then it was just gone. Snatched away.'

'You have a copy?'

'Somewhere in our flat, I think.'

Johnson regards the Moth. 'What are you thinking?'

'If Rev's dad is a scientist then wouldn't Rev Two's dad be one as well?'

We're all thinking about this when the train stops its gentle movement. But we're not at the train station yet.

'*Ding ding.* I just popped my head out of the window and I'm afraid there's something rather large on the line.' GG's voice is barely a whisper.

Everyone instantly freezes at this and even Carrie shrugs off her fatigue and sits bolt upright. Johnson moves quickly into the empty driver's cabin at the front. He is peering down the track and when I join him I see the last thing in the world I ever want to set eyes on.

It's the Ape. Only it's not the Ape. It's Non-Ape and he is big. Huge. A rhino walking upright. And he's heading straight towards our train.

'Everyone get down!' Johnson urges.

Carrie hits the deck and I come face to face with her under a table as Billie slips out of sight under her table.

'People!' The Moth's whiny petrified voice breaks through and I realise that he can't get down from his seat without help. I can't believe we keep forgetting about him.

Johnson gets back up into a crouch and unceremoniously drags the Moth to the floor just as the Non-Ape's face peers through one of the windows.

The sunlight and grime on the window makes it difficult for the Non-Ape to see clearly so he cups his massive hands around his face and screws up his empty soulless eyes to try to get a better look.

'Anyone there?' His voice is a deep rumble that I swear makes the window vibrate.

I am holding my breath as tight as tight.

A slab of meaty hand thumps on the train window. 'Anyone?'

He sounds as slow and dense as our Ape and I hope to God that his brain can compute that because there is no response, there might not be anyone on the train. I glance across the aisle at Johnson and he puts a finger to his lips.

'Hey!' The Non-Ape is so strong that he shakes the train carriage and I am about to fly out into the open aisle when Carrie catches my wrist and hauls me back. I'm amazed at how strong she is and that she actually helped me.

'He sees you, he'll see us all,' she whispers coldly.

The Non-Ape shakes the carriage again. 'Anyone?' It's taking him an eternity to work out that no response means that nobody is home.

Billie is wide-eyed with fear and the Moth grips the metal leg of the table Johnson has shoved him under as the carriage rattles back and forth.

'Anyone home?' He shakes the carriage again. 'Anyone?'

After a long silence the Non-Ape heads off to the next carriage.

No one moves.

Carrie makes as if to speak, but the Moth stretches over and stops her, clamping his hand over her mouth and shaking his head vehemently.

Billie looks at me, paralysed with fear.

'It's OK,' I mouth to her 'It'll be OK.'

We hear the lumbering footsteps of the Non-Ape as he walks all around the train and I hope to God GG is well hidden in the driver's cabin. The footsteps then stop at the window above where I'm hiding. He is trying to look in the carriage again.

'Anyone?'

I want desperately to breathe, but I'm scared he'll have super-hearing or something.

The world falls silent as the Non-Ape waits for a response. It's hard to believe but I think he might be even stupider than our Ape. Surely he should have got the message by now. But his face squashes up against the window as his eyes continue to search the carriage. I can see the shadow of his massive head blocking out the sunlight. He is right above me now and I don't know if I can hold my breath much longer. The shadow stays over me until the Non-Ape finally steps away from the window and I dare to let myself breathe.

The Moth lets his hand slip from Carrie's mouth and Johnson dares to move his leg, which is curled up and cramped under him.

'Has he gone?' whispers Carrie.

The Non-Ape suddenly punches the train and the indentation he makes erupts towards me. The side of the carriage caves inwards under the massive blow and, as the metal screeches under the impact, I am propelled into the aisle. I quickly scurry across it and hide under the table opposite me. I go as fast as I can but have no idea if the Non-Ape has seen me.

'Hey!' he bellows.

I am mute with terror now.

Johnson tries to signal to me to stay hidden, but the carriage is shaken violently again and this time it's harder than ever to hold on. The Non-Ape punches the carriage again and there's another screech of metal as the carriage bows inwards. He's the same destroyer that our Ape is, not caring if anyone is here or not, just wanting to break something. His great fist comes clean through one of the windows and showers Carrie and the Moth in glass. I can see she's on the verge of screaming and the Moth has to launch himself on top of her to stop her, which is a considerable feat considering he can't use his legs. He manages to shield her under him as another window is punched clean out.

More glass spills into the carriage and it rains down on Billie this time – she tries her best to squirm out of sight as the Non-Ape laughs above her head. He sounds just like the real Ape, only deeper and more earth trembling. Another window is punched clean out and I scramble under the chairs now. It's nigh on impossible, but I stretch as thin as I can.

The Non-Ape's head thrusts through one of the broken windows. 'Tickets please,' he says.

I almost squeal when I realise he must be able to see us. Johnson quietly takes the emergency hammer from his back pocket. I didn't even know he had kept it. The Non-Ape's head is almost directly over Johnson and he must be thinking of smashing him in the face with the hammer. I start shaking my head. *Please don't do that*, I think, *please don't think you can fight him. No*, I try and tell him telepathically, *no*.

133

Johnson silently manoeuvres the hammer into his hand, taking a tight grip.

'Tickets!' The Non-Ape's voice booms around the carriage. He follows it with a laugh and it starts to dawn on me that he hasn't spotted us at all – he's just saying words for his own amusement.

But Johnson is unfolding himself from his hiding place. He's going to try and hit the Non-Ape, which I absolutely know won't have any effect.

'Tickets!' The Non-Ape is still bellowing with laughter at his infantile joke.

Johnson is ready to launch himself at the Non-Ape's big fat stupid head and I am caving in on myself because I need Johnson to survive, to be there for us so that he can make all of this somehow better. He's the only one who can. I know it. I so, so know it.

Before Johnson can move, the Non-Ape withdraws his head from the window. He punches the carriage one last time and then lumbers away, heading back down the railway line.

'Where is everyone?' he bellows at the top of his great voice.

I can't believe it. He's gone. We survived.

It's Carrie who speaks first, whispering to the Moth. 'Want to get off me?'

'I can't,' he says equally as quietly.

But I'm not interested in them. All I want to do is escape from under these seats, but when I try to move I realise I am stuck fast. I managed to squeeze myself into the tiny cramped space on fear and adrenaline alone, but the relief has ballooned through my body and it's like I've gained an extra inch around my waist. My jeans are caught on the underside of the seat I am under.

Johnson is already moving quietly towards me.

'It's OK, I got you.' He is reaching for me when my phone rings.

Loudly.

It has to be the Ape. He must have got bored, or something has happened in the supermarket. The ringing spirals through the air and, even though he's probably forty metres away by now, there's no way the Non-Ape hasn't heard it.

BRB - WELL, MAYBE NOT

We hear lumbering footsteps coming back down the track towards the train. The Non-Ape isn't in a hurry, but that's because wherever he's from he's probably unstoppable. He is a juggernaut that can walk through any wall or a mountain if he needs to, so why hurry?

'Turn it off! Turn it off!' hisses Carrie.

'I can't reach it. I'm stuck!' I say, desperately.

'He's coming back,' the Moth says, stating the obvious.

'Like we don't know that!' Carrie snipes.

Johnson is tugging at me, trying his best to drag me free.

'Leave me.' The words are out before I know I have even said them.

'Shut up,' he says back.

'I mean it.'

'Not going to happen.'

'Go.'

'She's right,' Carrie says, too quickly for my liking. 'We really need to go.'

'I'm not leaving Rev,' snaps Billie under her breath. 'None of us are.'

'You kidding? You seen that Ape out there?' Carrie is terrified. 'We have to go.'

'Like where?' Billie says.

'Anywhere!'

Johnson tugs hard at me but he can't budge me. 'Take your jeans off.'

'Forget it, just go.'

'Take them off. Slide out of them.'

'I can't move.'

'C'mon, Rev,' urges Billie. 'You can do this.'

The Non-Ape's heavy thunderous footsteps have put him within twenty metres of us. My phone has stopped ringing, but it's already far too late and we all know it.

'What about me?' wails the Moth. 'What am I going to do?' He is trying to drag himself along the carriage by his arms, but they are weak and spindly and he's already used up what little strength he had trying to shield Carrie earlier.

The door flies open from the first-class carriage and GG appears. 'C'mon, let's go, let's go.' He grabs the Moth by the arms and starts dragging him into first class.

'Ow, my arms!'

'You shush now.'

Carrie shuffles, bent double, along the floor after them.

'Hide,' I tell Johnson. 'I'll tell the Non-Ape it's just me here. There's no one else. He's stupid, he'll believe it. Maybe.'

Johnson tries to lift up the chair that I'm trapped under but it is bolted to the floor. He squats down in front of me, grabs my shoulders and heaves again. I move all of a centimetre.

We hear a shrill beep of doors opening on the front carriage. The Non-Ape has just boarded the train. He's two carriages away now.

Billie joins Johnson and together they try their level best to wrench the chair from its bolts. It barely moves.

'Please, just go,' I beg them.

Billie is beside herself as she and Johnson heave again. They lift it maybe all of two centimetres. 'You're just caught, it's your jeans.'

The Non-Ape has reached the end of the front carriage. 'Hello?' His voice booms out.

Johnson heaves again. I move some more but not enough. 'Kick, Rev, kick,' he whispers.

'C'mon, Rev,' Billie urges.

I try my best as I feel the train shaken by the Non-Ape's approach. 'Someone phone?' He is already in the carriage next to this one.

Johnson drags me as hard as he can and the loop on my jeans snaps. I work myself free just as the door opens at the front of our carriage and the Non-Ape stomps through. Billie throws herself behind the last set of seats and Johnson and I huddle together, trying to be as small as possible. Johnson again produces the hammer, though we both know it's futile.

'Got to try something, right?' he whispers with a hint of a grin that is almost a grimace.

We hear the Non-Ape heading towards us down the train aisle. His footsteps are more like a rumble.

'Who's there?' he asks.

Johnson looks at me, whispers as quietly as he can, 'When I say run, you run.'

I shake my head at him.

'Take Billie and I'll hold him off as best I can.'

I keep shaking my head. 'No.'

'You've got to. I'll try and stop him getting to you.'

'Anyone?' The Non-Ape is bearing down on us, his foot-falls making the carriage rise and fall under his mountainous weight.

'You're a fool, Rev,' whispers Johnson.

I shrug at him. 'So are you. You could've run.'

We share a look that spells the end of the line for us. But we're not going to go quietly, we're going to— My phone rings again and I can't believe the Ape is calling me. I seriously cannot believe that monstrous idiot. I can't believe that I didn't think to turn it off either, so maybe I'm a monstrous idiot too.

But then I realise the ringing isn't coming from my pocket. My phone must have fallen out when Johnson pulled me free.

The carriage trembles with each of the Non-Ape's steps as he zeroes in on the ringing phone. He stops a foot away from where we are hiding, so close I can smell his heavy odour. Johnson's grip tightens on the hammer. *This is it*, I think. *This is where the story ends.* I look back and can just about see Billie who has huddled into a tight ball. I'm sure that any second now she's going to start screaming. I know that because I'll be screaming with her.

The Non-Ape's breathing is chesty and laboured. We hear his knees crack as he gets down to try and locate the ringing phone.

I move closer into Johnson as Non-Ape's hand starts to reach under the seat. Johnson tries his best to pull me tightly to him as thick stubby fingers come towards us. The

Non-Ape doesn't have the Non-Lucas's talons – he has fingers like fat sausages with dirty nails and I momentarily wonder if he's a whole other breed of being. What if there is more than just *one* other version of ourselves? I look down and the ringing phone is right beside his hand. All he needs to do is sweep to his left and he'll find it. But being a Non-Ape he sweeps his great chubby hand right and is about to touch my thigh when Johnson pulls me onto his lap. Johnson raises the hammer and is ready to smash down on the Non-Ape's fingers when the hand withdraws and in doing so knocks the ringing phone with a thick hairy wrist. The Non-Ape's giant paw closes around the phone and then slips out of sight.

Johnson and I wait, not daring to move a muscle.

The ringing stops.

'Yowza!' says the Non-Ape, answering the phone in typical Ape fashion.

My phone is still on speakerphone, and the Ape's voice echoes around the carriage. 'Yowza!'

'Who's this?' Non-Ape asks.

'You first.'

'You first!'

'No, you first!'

'Don't act tough with me.'

'Ain't an act.'

'Where is everyone?' The voices are blurring into each other, but I can just about make out that this is the Non-Ape speaking. His voice is a good octave lower than the Ape's.

'Don't know. Don't care.'

'Me neither.'

'So why you asking?' asks the Ape.

'So why you answering?' replies the Non-Ape.

Their mutual level of aggression and ignorance is astounding.

'Why you got Rev's phone?' the Ape asks.

'This is Rev's?'

'I just said. What are you, deaf?'

'What?'

'I said are you deaf?'

'Ha! Gotcha!'

'Who are you anyway?'

'You first.'

'No, you first!'

They both fall silent and I can feel the Non-Ape's aggressive aura filling the carriage.

'I found it,' Non-Ape says finally.

'Found what?'

'Huh?'

'What did you find? People?' God, talking to one Ape is hard enough but hearing two of them trying to hold a conversation with each other is beyond bewildering.

'The phone. I found the phone.'

'Found it where?'

'On a train.'

'They're still on the train? Rev said they were coming back for me.'

My heart skips a beat. The Ape is going to blow it for us. He's going to lead the Non-Ape right to us.

'Who's they?' Non-Ape asks.

'The others.'

'Ain't seen no others. Just seen this phone.'

I can feel Johnson's heart beating rapidly. He's still

141

clutching me tightly to him and his quiet breath on the back of my neck is sending me crazy despite the situation we're in.

Non-Ape gives himself a moment to try and work things through in his massively empty brain. 'So where are you?' he says.

'Who wants to know?'

'I do.'

'Who's I?'

'Who's you first?'

'No, you first.'

'No, you first!'

'You second!'

'What?'

'Ha! Gotcha!'

'You third then!'

'What?'

'Double ha, double gotcha!'

Again the Apes fall silent. It's like they only have so many words in their heads and once they're done they need to wait a moment or two before their brains fill up with more words.

'Is that Johnson?'

'Nope. And don't ever say that name to me again,' the Non-Ape warns.

'Can't be the homo.'

'You calling me a homo?' The Non-Ape stamps his great foot and sends a ripple along the carriage that nearly shakes us out of our hiding places. It's like riding a metal wave.

'What if I am?'

'You'll die for that.'

'You'd die first.'

'You'd die second!'

'What?'

'Gotcha again!'

'You can't be Lucas,' says our Ape.

'I'm not.'

'Cos he's dead.'

The Non-Ape hesitates. 'Dodo dead?

'Dodo dead.'

'How come?' There isn't a trace of emotion or concern in the Non-Ape's voice.

'Stuff happened. To both of them.'

'Both of who?'

'Them. The Lucases.'

'There's two Lucases?'

'There was. Now there's none.'

'Never knew he had a twin called Lucas too.' The Non-Ape seems to have less idea about what's going on than even the Ape does.

'Where are you?' asks the Non-Ape.

'I'm in Tesco's.'

My heart sinks at this. The Ape is as stupid as stupid gets.

'You alone?'

'Rev's here.'

'Boob Girl is there?'

'Yeah,' sniggers the Ape. 'Got her on film.'

'I've got to see that.'

'Come up to the office.'

Johnson shifts uncomfortably and I know he can barely believe what he is hearing either.

'There food there?'

'And beer and fags.'

'I'm coming.'

'So who are you? If you're not the others.'

'Didn't say.'

'So say now.'

'I'm Dazza.'

'But I'm—' The Ape falls silent as the penny finally drops.

'You still there?' asks the Non-Ape.

The Ape's silence bleeds into the carriage.

'Hey!'

'No,' says the Ape, and I can imagine him thinking this is just such a clever thing to say.

'You're not?'

'No. I'm not here.'

'So where are you?' Incredibly enough the Non-Ape might actually be buying this.

'Somewhere else.'

'Not Tesco's?'

'No.'

'Oh.'

'You sure you just found the phone and nothing else?' asks the Ape.

'Nada. Can keep looking though.'

Johnson tightens underneath me. We are both praying that the Ape says the right thing. We both pray in vain.

'Yeah, uh, yeah you do that. Take a look around the train. Don't miss anywhere out,' the Ape says, obviously trying to buy himself time to get out of the supermarket. He might have his new weapon and not be scared of anything, but he clearly doesn't want to meet a better, stronger version of himself. Some primal survival instinct has kicked in. Though it took long enough. 'Take your time,' he says.

144

That's that then. The Ape just signed our death certificate. We are so dead. Killed by ignorance as much as anything the world has thrown at us lately.

'I'll call you back,' says the Non-Ape.

'You can't.'

'How come?'

'It's not my phone.'

'Whose is it?'

'Someone else's.'

'So there's more than just you?'

'I told you that. Can't you listen?'

'I forgot.'

I'm silently begging the Ape to hang up and not say anything else that will get us killed.

'Rev, Billie, Johnson, Moth, that skinny girl and the homo. They were on a train.'

'I hate Johnson,' says the Non-Ape.

I feel Johnson tighten a little at this.

'When I find him I'm going to rip him apart. Fact. Going to tear his arms off, then his legs and then his head.'

I feel Johnson tense at this. Who wouldn't?

'He deserves it for what he did to Billie,' says the Non-Ape.

Johnson nudges me and then gestures towards the door to first class. 'Think we could make it?' he whispers.

The Non-Ape sits down in the row of seats we're hiding behind and the chair squeals loudly in protest at his massive weight. He'll have his back to us and we might just be able to crawl away without him hearing.

'What'd he do to Billie?' asks the Ape.

'You don't know?'

Johnson gestures at Billie to get ready to move.

'I don't like talking about it,' says the Non-Ape, and the heaviness in his heart takes me by surprise.

'Go, Rev,' whispers Johnson, who seems less than keen to hang around and discover what horrors his alter ego might be capable of.

I take a breath and start to edge on all fours as quietly as I can towards the door. It means coming out into the aisle but it's the best chance we've got while the Non-Ape's back is turned.

The Non-Ape shifts in his seat and the springs in the upholstery squeal again. I freeze, not even daring to look back.

'You found anyone on the train yet?' says our Ape.

Thanks a million, Ape, I think as I edge closer to the door, desperate not to be heard.

'I'll look in my own time.' The Non-Ape sounds like he has fallen into a pit of sadness as he thinks of his version of Billie.

I carry on edging slowly forward.

'Listen, there's no point coming back to town,' the Ape says.

'How come?'

'It's all empty.'

'You're there.'

'But I'm not going to be.'

I can feel Johnson crawling behind me. It's taking every ounce of self-control I possess to not just get up and run for it. Because she has waited for us to pass, Billie is going to be last out of the carriage and I can see she is tense and coiled like a cat, ready to move when she can.

The Non-Ape shifts in his seat and again the springs squeal. He's going to turn round any second now, I know it.

'I've got to go, got another call coming through,' says the Ape, obviously tiring of the brainpower this phone call is taking.

I dare to edge faster towards the door connecting the carriages and Johnson is doing the same behind me. I gently reach for the handle and turn it as carefully as I can. The door is slowly opening when it makes the tiniest click.

'Hang on,' says the Non-Ape to the Ape. 'Think I heard something.'

The Non-Ape gets to his feet. Johnson and me are now totally exposed. I look quickly back expecting to see Non-Ape looming over us, but he's still facing away. All he needs to do is turn his head and he'll see us.

I don't know what to do until Johnson touches my ankle. 'Quick,' he mouths.

Johnson and I move as swiftly and as silently as we can behind the last seat in the carriage before the Non-Ape turns. Johnson heaves me back into his lap as the Non-Ape calls out.

'Anyone there?' he bellows.

The Non-Ape waits a few seconds for a response. Billie has clasped her head in her arms – she can't bear to look or listen.

'Tickets please!' He laughs again and I can't believe the joke hasn't grown old. 'You still there?' he says into the phone, but the Ape has hung up on him. It seems like an eternity passes until finally Non-Ape tosses my phone on the nearest seat, then turns and heads for the rear of the carriage where he climbed on board. Johnson is already blowing out a long silent sigh of relief when there's a gentle shunt that stops him mid sigh.

We wait. The train has definitely moved. I dare to sneak a look and see the Non-Ape turn back and frown. There's a clunk from outside, followed by a steamy hiss. GG has uncoupled our carriage and is going to try and escape with Carrie and the Moth. Our carriage starts shuddering as the Non-Ape charges down it, heading for the departing train. He tears through the door and leaps out on to the track.

'Hey! HEY!'

Johnson's phone vibrates with a text. It's from GG. **GO!**

We don't get what he means at first. Another text follows swiftly. This one's from Carrie. **Going to lead him away.**

I understand GG's thinking, but all he's done is enrage the Non-Ape, who lumbers down the track after them. He might be incredibly strong, but thankfully he doesn't change into some sort of speedy animal like Moth Two did. He tries to run and for a second I think he's going to catch the first-class carriage, but GG hits the accelerator and pulls the train out of his reach. The Non-Ape swipes mightily but hits thin air and then goes into an ungainly tumble and crashes to the ground. He bellows after them, his great voice booming down the line.

'Hey! Where you going? Hey! It's me! Dazza!'

The train disappears around a curve in the track with Non-Ape still in hot pursuit and I lean back into Johnson as a wave of relief washes over me. But Johnson is already on his feet and dragging me upright.

'Rev, Billie, move!'

I grab my phone as Johnson reaches for Billie, who is still wrapped in her ball of fear. He takes her hand and speaks gently to her. 'C'mon.' Billie looks up, takes a second to register, and then when she sees Johnson her eyes light up. He gives her a gentle smile. 'We've got to go.'

He takes her hand and together the three of us hurry to the opposite end of the carriage, Johnson all but pushing me on to the tracks before turning and lifting Billie down. We head straight down the steep embankment, slipping and sliding and skidding until we are well out of sight. Ducking into the undergrowth, Johnson holds Billie close as we wait to see if the Non-Ape is following us.

Seconds tick by.

'You OK?'

'What's OK?' I manage to grin.

'Billie?' he says.

'Yeah,' she says, but she's still weak and she's still in a daze. 'Yeah, I'm good.'

We wait in silence until we're sure the Non-Ape didn't see us escape from the carriage. Johnson pulls Billie to her feet and dusts her down. She smiles at him and then whispers something that I can't hear. He nods though and then offers her a cigarette. Billie has never smoked in her life, but Johnson lights one for her in his mouth and then hands it to her. She takes a long drag and turns to me. I thought it was just my imagination before, but this time I know it's real. Her eyes have turned black again.

ANOTHER JOHNSON

As we make our way towards town, careful to keep out of sight of the Non-Ape, Johnson phones our Ape. 'Where are you?'

'Tesco. Can't get out in case Rev Two sees me.'

'Me, Billie and the real Rev are coming to you.'

'Be quick, there's a sale on in the fruit aisle.'

'Will do.'

'That was a joke, Johnson, you're meant to laugh.'

'I am, inside.'

'Is Rev Two still crying?' I ask the Ape.

'Dunno.'

'You must know.'

'Got distracted.'

I shake my head at the Ape and wonder if it's going to be his curse in life to have such an all-consuming fascination for staring at girls' chests.

'We're going to talk to her, but if it turns bad, you've got to be ready,' says Johnson.

'I'm always ready.'

We're sticking to the trees and the undergrowth as best we can but when it gets too thick or overgrown we have to keep edging out onto the trackside, which leaves us visible and vulnerable.

The Non-Ape is still nowhere to be seen as we reach the small train station. Billie, Johnson and I haven't spoken much along the way. The only sound is the vibration of Johnson's phone as he shares texts with GG and then whispers updates to us.

You get away? texted GG.

Yeah. U? Where r u?

Lost Giant Ape. Heading to London. Hope to find people!

Good luck.

U2. We will keep in touch.

We walk up the ramp towards the platform, wary of anything that might spell trouble. The empty town that awaits us feels alien now. Hostile.

'You really think you can talk to her?' I ask Johnson.

'I'm hoping.'

'She might be really aggressive or violent.'

'Or she might be like you,' he says simply.

Billie is finding it hard to keep up and she looks vacant, like a shell of her former self.

'Not far now,' I tell her and try to forget that Johnson just paid me a compliment. At least I think he did.

GG texts Johnson again. **Moth says find the thesis thingy.**

? Johnson texts back.

Rev's dad's science paper.

'Does he think my dad has something to do with this?'

'He's thinking something.'

'I don't want to go back to my flat. We'll have to cross

151

through town. We'll be lucky to get to the supermarket as it is. These things could be anywhere.'

Johnson debates for a second and then texts GG back.

We'll get it.

I think I knew he was going to respond that way even before Johnson did himself. I'm starting to work him out, to see him a lot more clearly. He is all about the go-forward. He isn't going to hesitate, he's going to act. Then, almost as if he's reading my mind he looks at me.

'Today is today,' he says. 'And our choices are limited.'

His ability to stay in the moment is borderline eerie.

'You never read your dad's paper?'

'Never.'

'Was it read by many people?'

'I guess not.'

'Which begs the big one. What's in it that no one was allowed to read?' he says.

I don't get to respond because the Ape phones Johnson.

'She's gone.'

'Rev Two?'

'Duh?'

'Gone where?'

'How would I know?'

'She leave the burned man?'

'That's gone too.'

'You were supposed to be watching her.'

'I was doing stuff.'

I snatch the phone from Johnson. 'What stuff??'

'You know. Stuff.'

My hand tightens around the phone and I wish it was the Ape's neck because I'd squeeze it until he choked.

'So she's out in town?'

'Easy to spot though – she's dragging a burned dead man with her.'

I hand the phone back to Johnson before I burst a blood vessel. Finding Lucas dead, the weird doppelgangers, the missing world population, the Ape's stupidity – it's just not fair to expect a sixteen-year-old to be able to deal with all of that.

'Ape, we need to get to Rev's flat.'

'Cool. I'll show you my new weapon.'

'Can't wait,' I sigh sarcastically.

'And tell you about this woman that phoned me.'

Johnson and I almost freeze solid. Even Billie stirs from her weary trance-like state.

'Say again,' Johnson says.

'This woman. She cut in when I was talking to uh— I can't be sure, right, but I think it was me.'

'A woman?'

'Yeah.'

'What did she say?'

'Johnson,' Billie whispers. He tries to shush her, but she makes him look to where she's pointing. 'I mean it's you. Johnson,' she says, even though she doesn't need to because we've all seen him now. Other-Johnson, sitting in the town square, long lean legs stretched out, black pointed boots up on the bench, a trilby pushed back over his dark curls.

'I can't remember what she said,' offers the Ape. 'Used loads of big words.'

But we're no longer listening, as we duck quickly out of sight behind a builder's skip that's been left beside some scaffolding. What do we do now?

'The Ape spoke to a woman, as in an adult, as in someone else,' whispers Billie not knowing whether to be excited or scared.

I'm trying to take it all in but something else is taking my attention. I touch Johnson's shoulder.

'That Other-Johnson . . .'

'Yeah?'

'I think he's reading my dad's science paper.'

Johnson leans forward, peering at Other-Johnson. He's the second one of us to actually see his own double and it has got him spooked. Even Johnson, the King of Cool, is thrown by this.

'Is that what I look like?' he whispers.

'Yeah,' sighs Billie.

'Thought I was bigger.'

'Bigger?' I ask.

'Bigger built. More muscle.'

I look at Other-Johnson and then at the real Johnson and they are identical apart from the fact that Other-Johnson is wearing a trilby.

'You look great,' I say without thinking. And then find myself blushing. 'I mean, you look, uh, like you normally do.'

Billie raises an eyebrow at me. I pretend not to notice and look away, but clearly she's starting to sense that I like Johnson and in that raised eyebrow there are all sorts of messages being sent my way. One of them is very clear: *Back off, he's mine.*

Johnson doesn't notice any of this because he can't take his eyes from Other-Johnson. 'I don't wear a hat,' is all he says.

'You should. It suits you,' says Billie.

'Why's he reading your dad's work, Rev?' he asks.

'No idea.'

'That's helpful,' says Billie.

'But it's not *my* dad's work though,' I say. 'Or is it? I'm confused.'

Johnson ponders this for a moment. 'I'm not sure it matters. Even if it's not technically your dad, the writing must have the same stuff in it.'

'That's true,' agrees Billie, who suddenly seems to have come alive again now that she's seen me as a threat for Johnson's attention. 'Anyway, Other-Johnson's sitting over there, reading it and we have to find out why. You should also turn your phone to mute, Rev.'

I think of the Non-Ape and how close we were to probable death because of my stupid phone and quickly switch it to vibrate only. A second after I do this it vibrates with a call from the Ape.

'It's the Ape,' I say. 'What do I do?'

'Ignore it,' Johnson says absently.

'But he spoke to a woman. We need to know who she was.'

Johnson seems mesmerised by the sight of Other-Johnson and can't take his eyes off him. 'This is not as cool as it could be.'

I cancel the Ape's call.

'It's not you,' I tell Johnson. 'Not really.'

I'm about to reach for Johnson again – I can't seem to stop myself touching him – when Billie gets there first. 'What if we spoke to him?' she says gently.

Johnson looks at Billie's hand resting on his arm. 'What, just walk out there?'

'He could be dangerous,' I warn.

'But what else are we going to do? We said we needed to speak to one of them,' Billie argues.

'That's crazy, Billie,' I tell her. 'Walking out there? Seriously?'

But Johnson remains transfixed on Other-Johnson. 'I want a hat like that.' I think it's a joke. Johnson finally tears his eyes away from Other-Johnson who seems totally engrossed in my dad's thesis. 'Billie's right. Maybe one of us should go out and talk to him.'

'Billie, it was your idea,' I offer.

Her eyes widen a little. 'Excuse me?'

'To talk to him. You go.'

Her eyes go from wide to narrow in a heartbeat. 'I'm still way too weak.'

'Your colour's coming back,' I say and we start sparring, neither of us saying the real reason we're arguing about who should go out there, but underneath we both know we'd both like to stay hidden with our Johnson.

'Can barely stand,' she says.

'You walked all the way down the track.'

'And it nearly killed me.'

'I'm not going out there.'

'You sort of have to.'

'Since when?'

'Since I got these scars on my face.'

'What difference do they make?'

'He'd ask questions about how I got them.'

'So? You can make something up if you're clever. Which you are. Far cleverer than me.'

'I'm clever academically. You're smart in a street way.'

156

'I'm not going out there, Billie.'

'Someone has to.'

We're at a stalemate and look at Johnson. Maybe he'll go out there.

'He might think something's not quite right if he sees himself sit down beside him.'

Which is a fair point. But that leaves either Billie or me and there's no way it's going to be me.

Billie and I lock eyes. She's not going to budge an inch either.

'Like I said, he'll look at these scars and know that Non-Lucas did them to me. They're from the same place. He'll be able to tell. He'll have seen scars like this before.'

My grip on the world feels like it has just shifted. Like I'm losing my foothold. 'Maybe we should just sneak past him and—' I begin lamely.

'And what?' interrupts Billie. 'He's got the thesis. The same thesis Moth thinks we need.'

'He'll know I'm not the real Rev.'

'But you *are* the real one,' says Billie.

'OK, the . . . fake one then,' I stammer. For a split second I get this image in my head that Johnson and Billie want me out of the way so it's just them. I might just be paranoid but they seem very keen to send me out there to meet Other-Johnson.

'You can do this, Rev. I know you can,' urges Billie.

I look at her. *Oh my God*, I think. *She really wants rid of me.* First she's smoking, then her eyes turn black for a second and now this. I'm starting to wonder about her.

Johnson has been unusually quiet and I know it's because he knows that this is something we have to do. 'I can't go

157

out there, Rev,' he says apologetically. 'If it was one of the others I would, but I can't go meet myself.'

'So let's move on,' I say. 'Stick to the original plan. Go find the Ape, get more supplies and run the hell away from here. It's just Moth's theory. We don't know the paper has anything to do with what's happened.'

'Rev, I can't take much more of whatever this is,' Billie says. 'I'm scared and I want to know that tomorrow it's going to be all right. That we're going to be all back to normal. At the moment this is our only option to try and make sense of this. So get out there and ask him stuff.' She stares at me, almost daring me to say no. I am staggered that my best ever friend could so casually dispose of me, just so she can be alone with Johnson. 'Go out there, get the papers and if you can, find out what he knows.'

'And then what?' I ask. 'I just wander back over here again? Tell him, "Thank you, it was very nice seeing you but I now need to go shopping"?'

'You love shopping. He'll understand.' She gives me a lame smile.

'Would you understand?' I ask Johnson.

Johnson hesitates briefly. 'I'd probably wait for you. Long as you brought me back a hat.' He's trying to reassure me with gentle humour, but it's not working because my fists are clenched so tight my knuckles are white.

They are ganging up on me and because of the crushing weight of disappointment that Johnson would give me up so easily and that my best friend has turned on me, I am ready to give them what they want.

'What if he attacks me?'

'I wouldn't do that to you. Not ever.' Johnson's blazing blue eyes find mine. 'He'll be the same.'

Was that a glimmer of light? Have I got this wrong? Does he like me after all? But if so, why send me out there?

'He looks pretty laid back,' reinforces Billie. I can picture her now offering comfort to Johnson as he mourns my savage death.

I look back out at Other-Johnson and he does indeed look calm and collected. And approachable. It should be any girl's wildest fantasy coming true – not one, but two Johnsons – but my heart is hammering in my chest and the pulse in my neck feels like I've got a scared fish trapped in my throat.

I take a huge breath and force myself to keep calm, my eyes darting from one Johnson to the other. *Can I do this?* I think. *Can I actually go out there?*

'Tell me what to ask him.'

'You're going to do it?' Johnson looks surprised.

I nod my head. 'You're right, we need answers.'

'You sure?' He is genuinely worried.

'No. But tell me what to say anyway.'

'You need to work out what he knows,' says Johnson.

'And if he can tell us where everyone went,' says Billie.

'And grab the science paper.'

'Hang on, I need a notepad,' I say trying to sound calm. 'You might as well send me for coffees while you're at it.'

'Just those three things,' Billie says.

'Where everyone went,' says Johnson.

'Why he's here. Where he's come from,' adds Billie.

'Then grab the papers,' finishes Johnson.

'That's four things,' I say.

'Three is the new four.' he jokes.

I already know I'm going to make a complete mess of this, but I clearly don't have a choice.

My phone vibrates with another call from the Ape. Again I ignore it.

Johnson puts a hand on my wrist. 'Any problems, run.'

'Got it.'

'I'll try and intercept, slow him down, whatever. But if it goes badly you and Billie call the Ape and then go find the others.'

'It won't,' I say. 'It won't go badly. I promise.'

'But be quick.'

'Quick?'

'The other Rev's not in the supermarket any more and we can't have her showing up while you're out there.'

The thought makes my stomach lurch. 'I'd forgotten.'

Billie sees Johnson's hand on my wrist and then pulls me towards her, slipping me out of his grip. She gives me a mighty hug. 'Best friends forever.'

Yeah right, I think before I turn and face the Other-Johnson. He is identical to Johnson and in that lies the blindest hope any fool ever had. I'm trying to make myself believe that he will be just as cool and just as easy-going.

I collect myself and get to my feet. I almost can't move as I try to squash the panic growing through me, and I'm expecting a big comedy shove from Billie as she pushes me out into the square, but when I look at her and Johnson they are as heart-in-mouth scared as I am.

I slide out of my leather jacket and neaten myself up, trying to present myself as appealing and approachable as possible, I step out into the open and walk hesitantly into the

160

cobbled town square. My heart is going like a jackhammer and each step takes at least a minute because my legs are turning to jelly and I don't seem to have any sensation in my arms other than my burns itching like crazy. The tingling in my shoulders is back with a vengeance. This is madness. I realise it now.

I glance back to Johnson and it's like he's realised that too because there's a worry on his face and he's starting to gesture for me to come back. But I'm halfway between Johnson and Other-Johnson now and, even though he hasn't turned or heard me and I still have the opportunity to back out of this, there is something unnaturally compelling about Other-Johnson. It is like a physical force drawing me towards him.

I take another step. He still hasn't heard me. I can still turn back. But somehow my legs are carrying me forward, as if I've been hijacked and I can't maintain control over my body. I'm little more than a few metres from him. I can't even turn back and look at Johnson. Nothing will work like I want it to as I'm drawn closer and closer to Other-Johnson.

'Johnson?' I say before I can stop myself.

Other-Johnson turns his head slowly my way and I watch his grin spread all over his lips.

'Rev!' He gets to his feet and, dropping the thesis, he opens his arms to me.

I look at his wide-open arms and for a moment I can hear the blood rushing in my head. There's a physical force now, like a horizontal gravity that drags me towards him.

'I went to your flat but no one was home. No one's home anywhere,' he says.

As soon as I reach him, his arms wrap around me and I can smell the faint musk of a downright delicious aftershave as he wraps me tighter than tight.

'What's happening?' he whispers.

'I dunno,' I somehow whisper back.

'Waited at your place, found your dad's papers. Remembered you told me he was a scientist so I thought, he was clever, why not have a read? Can't make head nor tail of it though.'

'You went inside my flat?'

'I know where the keys are hidden.'

'Sorry, forgot,' I lie, and raise a smile.

'It was in your room, lying on your bed.'

I'd been reading it? I mean the other me had been. The thought registers but Other-Johnson finds my chin and gently angles my face towards his. I gaze into his eyes and they are alive and brimming with everything Johnson. But there's something else there, something much more magical. He looks at me with love in his eyes. True, honest and pure love. Not like the way Kyle looks at me; that is a watered down version, a pale imitation of Other-Johnson's undeniable passion.

It leaves me giddy and I'm powerless to stop Other-Johnson's lips closing on mine and kissing me. The kiss is mingled with tiny whispers about how he was scared he'd never see me again, how he would have done anything to find me, torn up the fabric of reality if he had to. I don't know how he can speak when he's kissing me and then I realise that his voice is in my head and I go into a panic because if he's a mind reader then I'm dead. And, ohmyGod, I shouldn't even be thinking that, but of course it's too late

162

because the more I think about it the more the Other-Johnson will know anyway. But the kiss goes on and his voice is gentle, reaching inside me and caressing every part of me. His hands run over my back and down to the swell of my hips. It's like he's feeling me all over to make sure I'm real and that I'm actually there.

'Thought I'd lost you,' he whispers, out loud this time.

His lips find mine again and I find myself pulling him tighter because I have never experienced a kiss that I never wanted to end until now. There is nothing in the world like this kiss. The whole awful situation we're in is fading away; everything before now was empty and insignificant.

'Can't believe it's you.' His voice reaches into my head again, but his kiss moves past the physical and touches what can only be my soul. I feel a vibrating between us and I'm imagining it's because my body is starting to shudder. The vibration continues until Johnson's lips finally leave mine and he looks down at the vibrating intruder in my pocket.

'You've got a call,' he says.

I hang there limply not knowing what to do, breathless and exhausted. I don't seem to be able to move but Other-Johnson slips his hand under the hem of my T-shirt and squeezes it down into my front jeans pocket.

'Excuse me,' he whispers with a grin.

The feel of his hand makes my thigh tickle and I have to move slightly so he can get his whole hand into my pocket. I could probably try harder to retrieve the phone for myself, but I want him to do it, I want to feel his hand touching me. He collects the phone and slips it out of my pocket and to my dismay the tingle in my thigh dies away.

'There's actually someone else out there,' he says quietly studying my vibrating phone.

I am already lost to him and I wish that I wasn't. I need to stay focused, to ask my questions and to get answers. I try to clear my head. I've not even considered what the real Johnson is thinking about me. Is he hurt that I'm so easily and readily kissing the Other-Johnson or will he think I'm playing the part perfectly? I know for certain that Billie will be ecstatic now. She'll rest a consoling hand on Johnson and he'll turn to her and she'll whisper something about me being a bit of a slag or something . . . I can't believe I'm thinking so badly of her. Where did that come from? One minute I'm praying she won't die and the next I'm thinking she's my sworn enemy. I'm tired, exhausted and everything is raw and fragile. I keep lurching through the hours and minutes without finding anything solid or concrete to cling on to.

Until, that is, Other-Johnson kissed me.

I wasn't playing along. I loved that kiss and I want him to do it again, to turn us into one lovely moment of the unexpected and the divine all mingled together. I am literally panting as I stare at him.

'Yo.' Other-Johnson answers the phone.

I can hear the Ape's voice even without the speakerphone.

'Who's this?'

'Johnson. That you, Ape?'

'Duh.'

Other-Johnson tenses at the sound of the Ape. 'Uh. Where are you?'

'Around.'

Other-Johnson immediately scans the surrounding area

164

and it's clear he's not keen that the Ape might be somewhere close by. 'And where's around exactly?'

'Around is around. Rev there?'

'Yeah, I just found her.'

'Weren't you already with her?'

I can see it all going horribly wrong and gently take the phone.

'Yowza,' I say, turning my back on Other-Johnson.

'Yowza, you,' responds the Ape.

'What, uh, what you doing?'

'Following you. Well, Rev Two.'

I have to play this right, make sure I don't slip up. But then Other-Johnson slips his arms around my waist and his head comes level with mine as he kisses my cheek and then moves slowly to my neck and it's hard to concentrate.

'OK,' I say.

'What's OK?'

'That, uh . . . That's OK.'

Johnson's lips and warm breath are driving me insane as he slides the neck of my green cotton top to one side so he can leave kisses on my shoulder. 'Don't tell him where we are,' he whispers as he stops kissing me and his lips brush against my ear. 'We should get out of here, go back to yours.'

OhmyGod, I think, *ohmyGod!* Are we doing it? Are Other-Me and Other-Johnson doing IT??

'I'm still following you,' says the Ape again, but his words are tinny and distant as I turn round to face Other-Johnson. It's all I can do not to grab him and race all the way back to my flat.

'We, uh, we can't,' I mumble to Other-Johnson.

He kisses my neck again. 'Yeah we can.'

'W-we-we— No, we can't,' I stammer. Other-Johnson must know what he's doing to me. He's hitting every erogenous zone I possess with his kisses as he moves to my other shoulder kissing the exposed skin. 'I need to know things,' I say.

'Let's go,' he says again.

'I'm scared,' I tell him.

'You don't do scared.'

'But where is everyone?'

'That can wait.'

I can feel his body reacting to mine all over again and then one hand reaches round and travels under the front of my green top and up to my breast. It's all I can do not to gasp.

Other-Johnson ends the call to the Ape, focusing entirely on me now.

'No one's home,' he whispers. 'No one, Rev.'

'Wait.' I place my hand on Johnson's through the thin material of my T-shirt and as much as I don't want to, I force myself to push his hand away.

'You're reading my dad's thesis. You think it might be the answer to what's happened. That's why you're reading it, right?'

'Just picked it up, is all,' he shrugs.

'But you . . . well, you must know what's in it?'

His hand is slipping upwards again and even though I need to concentrate, I don't want to push him away again.

'It was just lying there. Open. Asking to be read,' he says.

'In my flat?'

'Yeah.'

'I didn't see it,' I say with a slow intake of breath.

166

Other-Johnson freezes. 'You went there?'

'Uh, yeah.'

'Can't have. I'd have picked you up,' he says.

'What d'you mean?' I whisper.

'On the airwaves – I checked, even though you told me I was banned from doing that.' He's stopped kissing me and there's a steel in his voice that wasn't there before.

'Airwaves?' I'm not playing this very well and I try my best to pretend that I understand. 'Oh. The *airwaves*. Sorry, I'm pretty much all over the place right now.'

Other-Johnson has grown tense as his hand pulls out from under my top. It's like his eyes are travelling throughout me, checking every inch of me. It takes him a long moment before he says anything. 'Oh, boy,' he says eventually.

I try to smile. 'Oh, boy, what?'

'Just oh, boy.'

And then I feel it, his words inside my head again. *'Who are you?'* he asks, only his lips don't move.

I smile, but it's weak and more of a grimace. 'So, uh . . . where did everyone go?' I ask as calmly as I can manage.

'I went to yours straight after the light appeared, Rev,' he says out loud. 'You remember the light?' he asks. 'I thought you'd be at home, but then I remembered you probably had to buy some hair dye. Shame though, I'm loving the pink look.'

I nod, but I don't know why. I already know that he knows I'm not the Rev he thinks I am so it's no use pretending.

He leans forward and sniffs rather than kisses my neck. I suddenly realise it's totally exposed to him. Goosebumps spring up all over on my flesh.

'Bright light. Then everyone gone,' he says. Then I hear his voice in my head again. *'You are so like her.'*

167

I try desperately to keep up the façade. My eyes glance to where Johnson and Billie are hiding and I hope that they can tell I'm in trouble. 'You were here though. In the square,' I say loudly.

'And?'

'Well, that's when I went to the flat. That's how we didn't see each other.'

'Oh. Yeah. Yeah, of course.' Other-Johnson seems to relax a little. 'I'm sorry.'

'Nothing to be sorry about.' I smile in return, hoping I've got away with it.

But he turns me round and his eyes find mine again, and he looks genuinely sad. 'Really. I am very sorry. How can you be her and not her?' he asks gently. I take another step backward but I realise he has taken hold of both my wrists. Not a grip, just a firm hold. 'How's this possible?' he asks.

'Johnson, what are you talking about?' I'm trying my best but I already know it's hopeless.

I try to slip my wrists out of his hands, but his grip tightens. There is real pain behind Other-Johnson's eyes.

'What did you do with her? My Rev. Where is she?'

'I don't know what you're talking about. I'm Rev. *Your* Rev.'

His mouth opens wide with a smile that isn't really a smile.

'What does it matter? Everyone's disappeared,' I tell him.

'No they haven't.'

'Uh yeah, look around.'

'No one went anywhere, Rev.'

I frown and he traces his finger along the crease in my forehead.

'I love your frown,' he says.

'I need to go.'

'Where are you from?'

'Here. Right here,' I stammer.

'But I'm not sure this is here,' he says. 'Least it's not the here we think it is.'

THIS IS THE THESIS

I'm praying Johnson and Billie can see that I've blown it. Not because I want to look like a miserable failure, but more that they can take the big hint and come rescue me.

'Please help us. We're all in the same situation,' I whisper. I'm hoping to God that Other-Johnson is like the real Johnson, someone who can make up his own mind and not be governed by beliefs or rules or any other such thing. That he'll just go with the flow.

'You said you hadn't seen anyone else,' he says quietly, his lips barely moving.

'Did I?' I try to back away, but there's no way he's going to let go of my wrists.

'Where are they?'

'I dunno.'

'You've got to tell me, Rev.'

'Trade you. Your info for mine.' I can't believe my Johnson hasn't sensed how much I need him to come riding to my rescue. Then I get scared and think that Billie has some-

170

how convinced him that I've screwed up and that she has dragged him away before they're caught too.

'Where I'm from . . .' Other-Johnson begins with a huge regret. 'Where I'm from we're a little different. I can see it inside you – your world looks the same, but it's nothing like mine, not really.'

'Th-this is my world,' I stammer.

'This is nowhere we've ever been before, Rev.'

Other-Johnson takes my wrists in his hands. Tightly.

My eyes fill with panic. 'We kissed,' I tell him.

'Did we ever.' His eyes widen.

I try my best not to glance back to where Johnson and Billie are hidden. I'm wondering if they really have run off and left me. Then I realise I can't think about them because then Other-Johnson will know about them too.

But I'm too late. Way too late.

'That's not Billie,' he says quietly. 'And they didn't run.'

I give a choked reply. 'No?'

'Is that really me hiding behind that skip?'

Christ, he can see everything.

'You should've told him you loved him,' Other-Johnson says.

Which totally stops me in my tracks.

'What? But I don't—'

'It's all too little too late now anyway.'

I look down at Johnson's hands as they grip my wrists and talons like Non-Lucas possessed slip from the tips of his fingers like a cat releasing its claws.

'It doesn't have to be like this,' I say.

'I'm sorry.'

'We can all sit down together. We can. We can talk and

171

share what we know.' I desperately wish I could reach inside him like he did with me.

'I really don't want to do this,' Other-Johnson says. 'Not to you.'

'So don't,' I protest, tears running down my cheeks. I can feel him in my mind, sifting through everything that has happened recently. I try to blank out my thoughts, but he tenses, almost recoiling from me, and I know I've failed.

'You ran a train over the Moth,' he says sadly. 'You shouldn't really do things like that.'

'I was scared, panicked, wanted him to stop chasing us.'

'You think we're not equally as scared?'

'Johnson? That you?' I hear Billie call out and for a moment I think *what the hell is she playing at?* But it's not Billie, it's just a version of her appearing at one corner of the market square. She is identical, minus the scars on her face.

'Hi, Johnson.' Non-Lucas is with her and the sight of him jolts me hard.

'Billie's a healer,' Other-Johnson tells me because he's already reading the images and questions running around my head. 'No one stays dead when she's around. Though I'd better warn you he's going to be a little mad with you and your friends right now. He's ultra sensitive.'

Then I see myself arriving.

Me.

Reva Marsalis.

But she's a puffy-eyed, red-faced version of me and she's carrying the burned man.

The world spins for a moment and for a fleeting second I see Johnson holding my wrists, and my mind is suddenly

172

spinning because I'm in Rev Two's head and I'm looking through her eyes and I don't know how that can be.

Other-Johnson grins. 'I can do so many things. I could take your mind and put it in a dog.'

He wrenches me back again and I can see Rev Two staring at me, trying to take in what she is seeing. Other-Johnson seems crazy-glad to see her and I feel the magic we shared being stolen away as he stares at her. I let out a low moan as the last of him leaves me. Other-Johnson hears this and uses one of his talons to lift my chin up so I'm facing him.

'Rev, you've got to come see this,' he calls to Rev Two.

'I'm seeing plenty,' she calls back, slightly unnerved.

She's got my voice. My *exact* same voice. She walks the same way, she has her hair dyed the same bright colour and she's wearing the same clothes I'm wearing. Our eyes meet and because I have already seen copies of the others, I don't look half as shocked as she does. That thought at least makes me feel a little proud.

'Lucas said there were others. But we'll deal with her later. I think I found my dad,' she tells him, gesturing to the burned man, still tearful. 'Twelve years, Johnson . . . Twelve years.'

'Whoa!' Other-Johnson looks spooked. 'That's your dad?' His eyes widen in disbelief as he looks at the burned carcass in her arms and then looks back to me. 'Is it just me or is that a little weird?' he whispers to me.

'Johnson!' Rev Two calls out.

'Yeah, I hear you. Something wild and weird is happening,' he tells her.

'No, really?' It's so like something I'd say that I think no, you can't do that, you can't be me. *I'm me.* Not you. 'Bring her over.'

I tighten and start trying to pull away from Other-Johnson, but his grip is firm and strong.

Non-Lucas is heading towards me now and he is not at all happy.

'There's more of them,' he tells Other-Johnson.

Another-Billie meets Rev Two and gently they lay the dead burned man down on the cobbles. I don't even warrant another look from Rev Two. I'm insignificant to her. No, I correct myself, not insignificant. I'm history. I'm dead. Was I that cold when we came up against Moth Two? Me? Surely not.

Another-Billie squats beside the dead man and lays her hands on his seared flesh.

'Want to see your dad again?' Other-Johnson asks me.

'That's my dad?' I'm almost too stunned to think straight, but even so the prospect of this man being my dad makes me want to stay and face whatever happens next.

'She doesn't deserve to,' says Non-Lucas, who seems to have all the sporting aggression of our Lucas but none of the gentility or hidden insecurities. 'None of them deserve anything.'

I'm not listening, because I really can't believe that my dad is about to somehow reappear in my life. Only it won't be my father, it'll be hers. Rev Two's.

'Tell your friends to come out.' Other-Johnson speaks so softly I no longer know if his voice is in my head or not.

I turn back in the direction of the skip, praying that Billie and Johnson are long gone by now. But I'm damned if I'm going to do what Other-Johnson wants.

'Run!' I yell. 'Get out of here!'

'Lucas,' Other-Johnson says. 'They're over there.' He points lazily and Non-Lucas gets ready to leap across the courtyard when I hear an angel calling my name.

But it's not really an angel.

It's the Ape.

The one and only Ape.

Our Ape. *My* Ape.

He's in a souped-up four-door saloon and he's going too fast to stop. But stopping isn't on his mind as he ploughs straight into Non-Lucas, knocking him tumbling back into a coffee shop.

The Ape hits the brakes and spins the car round and, as the rubber on the car tyres squeals, he accelerates and aims directly at Rev Two and Another-Billie. Other-Johnson sees what is happening and immediately lets go of me as he turns and tries to yank the Ape's mind out of his body.

At least I think that's what he tries to do because he clutches his temples and strains with all his might to grab the Ape's brain.

But even I know he's wasting his time. The Ape runs on instinct – he doesn't use his brain like anyone else. He's more like an animal who acts without thought or conscience. So Other-Johnson's mind control, if that's what he's attempting, can't affect him, so as much as I hate to see it, the car hits Rev Two and knocks her some ten metres backwards through the air.

Other-Johnson cries out. 'Rev!'

He is stricken as he races for her while the Ape spins the wheel again and roars towards Another-Billie, who is in some sort of trance as she tries to reanimate my father, or whoever he is. She doesn't seem to notice the car coming towards her, until the Ape throws open the driver's door and smashes her with it.

'Rev!' I turn and see my Johnson running towards me.

But Other-Johnson is screaming the very same thing. 'Rev!'

They're both shouting. Both trying to save . . . me.

Non-Lucas is already back on his feet and there is something truly athletic and gorgeous about his rubbery sinewy movement as he leaps through the air and lands on the bonnet of the Ape's car.

But that doesn't stop the Ape. Instead he jumps on the brakes and Non-Lucas's momentum pitches him clear over the roof of the car. I swear I hear the Ape laughing as he roars up beside me and Johnson and brings the car to a halt within centimetres of us.

'Taxi?'

Johnson yanks open the rear door and all but throws me inside.

'Billie's by the skip,' Johnson says to the Ape as he leaps into the passenger seat.

The Ape yanks the wheel hard left and, as he does, we come face to face with Non-Lucas, who leaps back over the car and lands directly in front of us.

'Doesn't he ever stay dead?' The Ape's face scrunches up tight as he reaches a big fat hand into the back seat, and I realise his new weapon is beside me. Only it looks exactly the same as the old weapon to me.

Non-Lucas leaps towards us and crashes through the windscreen, talons glinting, teeth pointed and vicious. But the Ape is fearless.

'Soft spot!' he yells and drives his weapon straight into Non-Lucas's throat. Non-Lucas suddenly goes stiff and then slumps dramatically half in the car and half on the bonnet. The Ape reverses at speed while trying to wrestle his weapon out of Non-Lucas's throat.

Johnson grabs for the weapon. 'I got it,' he says. 'You just watch where we're—'

There's an almighty shunt as the Ape reverses us all the way into the side of the skip. I swear my neck almost snaps as I am hurled violently forward and then back. Johnson would have gone through the windscreen if it wasn't for Non-Lucas blocking the way. The Ape smashes his chest into the steering wheel and probably for the first time in his life he cries out in pain.

I look past Johnson and see Other-Johnson cradling the battered Rev Two. Other-Billie gets to her feet and shaking off the impact with the car door she heads towards them. Other-Johnson's mind momentarily finds me and he talks to me again.

'I'm coming for you, Rev.'

The rear door opens and our Billie clambers in.

'Drive!' Johnson cries.

The Ape has been winded and feels his chest. Johnson tries to cajole him.

'C'mon, Ape, we need you.'

The Ape tries to pull himself together despite the agony he is in. He checks in the rear-view and finds Billie looking back at him.

'Go, Ape, go,' she urges.

The Ape ignores the pain, engages drive and pulls away. Non-Lucas slides off the front of the bonnet and I feel the jarring jolt as the Ape drives right over him.

'Rocky road.' He grimaces as we pull away from the square. I know he is in agony because he does his best to swerve round any potholes or drains in the road. Every time he hits one, though, I notice him wince.

I look back and see Rev Two returning to full health courtesy of Another-Billie who looks pale and weak after her efforts. Then I see Other-Johnson gazing at us and I know we're definitely in a war now and we're up against beings that are not only far superior, but that also don't stay dead for long.

'Rev?' Other-Johnson's voice comes back into my head. This must be the airwave he was talking about.

'Yeah?' I automatically say it out loud. Billie looks at me quizzically.

'We're going to find you.'

'It doesn't have to be like this,' I whisper, 'it really doesn't.'

'We need your Moth,' he says.

I don't understand.

'You killed ours so now we need yours. If anyone can work out what's in your dad's thesis, then he can.'

'He'll know how to get us back home?'

'Not you. Us,' he says, then I hear him sigh. 'I'm really sorry, Rev. But what a kiss, eh?'

Before I can answer, Other-Johnson disappears from my mind and I wonder if it's because we're too far away for him to reach me – we must have driven a mile already at the speed Ape's going. I hope so, otherwise we will never be able to hide. Or plan. Or surprise them. They are holding all the cards and my instinct is to run. But as I look at the big thick hairy neck of the Ape sitting in front of me, and Johnson next to him, I begin to think that with them we might have a chance.

An angel came, I think to myself, *and the angel was called the Ape.*

STOPPED IN MY TRACKS

Billie sits back in her seat, frustrated.

'So, you didn't get the papers,' she says, a little too sharply. I know we're officially in a state of mass panic and desperation but this harshness is something I haven't heard in her before and it's beginning to worry me.

'Hey, I tried my best,' I tell her. 'I was working on him.'

'Guess it was difficult to think when you've got a mouthful of tongue,' she responds.

'Someone do tongue?' asks the Ape.

'I was interrogating Johnson. The other Johnson,' I tell him, but really I'm telling Johnson, who is sitting silently in the front.

'With your tongue?' the Ape says.

'I was playing along with him.'

'You want to interrogate me?' The Ape's eyes find me in the rear-view. 'Ask me anything.'

I don't bother with a response because it seems that every time the Ape does something good he goes and ruins it with his utter crassness.

'So you had your tongue in Other-Johnson's mouth?' says the Ape again and I wish he'd shut up because Johnson is being too quiet.

'I was getting information.' My voice is small and tired.

'And what did you learn from kissing him?' asks Billie. I know that she's sensed Johnson's mood and is subtly trying to make it worse.

'Nothing.'

'Not even when he put his hand under your top?'

Johnson shifts uncomfortably in his seat.

'I don't remember that,' I say quietly.

'He copped a feel? Yowza!'

'He could read my mind, put thoughts in there. I think I was in a trance.' I try my best to explain and wish Johnson would turn around and say something to me. 'It was mind control.'

'But he copped a feel?'

'I don't know.' I'm sure they all know I'm lying because I can feel myself glowing in embarrassment.

'He must have said something.' Finally Johnson speaks, but he is staring ahead, not looking at me.

'Just that he was sorry.'

'For groping you?' asks Billie, just in case anyone forgets.

'No, I think he was sorry about what's about to happen,' I add as solemnly as I can. 'They're going to find us, they're going to take the Moth and they're going to leave the rest of us here – or worse.'

'What does he mean – here? We're from here.'

'I don't think we are,' I say.

'So they want our Moth—' begins Johnson.

'Because we killed their Moth,' I tell him. 'They think

180

he'll know from my dad's writings what's happened. They want him to take them back to wherever they came from.'

'That's OK, isn't it?' Billie seems positive now. 'He does that, they go home, we're safe.'

'But we need him to take us home.'

'This is home!' Billie adds. Vehemently.

'Johnson said it wasn't.'

'I did?"

'I mean Other-Johnson said it.'

'So where are we?' Billie asks.

'I don't know, but they cannot get hold of the Moth – we can't let that happen.'

'No way it can. Not now I've got a new weapon,' boasts the Ape, who winces again. I'm starting to worry that he might have broken some ribs.

'It's the same weapon,' I say.

'This is way different. Old one had two carving knives attached to it but this one – this has three! It's the big three-pointer.'

I'm too frazzled to argue as Johnson finally turns and looks at me. 'So they've got the thesis but we've got the Moth.'

I nod.

Johnson's eyes linger on me as he weighs me up, probably thinking all sorts of negative things about me now. 'We need to find the others, regroup,' he says.

'They were on a train the last—' Billie is about to say more when I cut in.

'Don't say a word! Just don't. Other-Johnson was in my head – he could still be there.'

'That's a big head,' says the Ape.

'If we're going to meet the others then arrange it without me hearing or knowing.'

'We're miles away from him,' Billie says.

'I just want to be safe. I want us all to be safe.'

Johnson weighs this up and then agrees. 'I'll text GG. We'll drive to wherever they are.'

'Better blindfold Rev, then,' says Billie, and there's something about the way she says this that makes it sound like it really appeals to her. 'If he can really get inside Rev so easily, then it's best she doesn't see where we're heading.'

'Or hear it,' adds Johnson.

'Yeah, we'll plug your ears, Rev.'

'Maybe gag her as well,' the Ape suggests.

'Excuse me?' I aim an angry look at the Ape's giant square lump of head.

'Could throw her in the boot.' Billie shrugs. It isn't the fact that she suggests it that upsets me, it's more that she didn't say we could *put* her in the boot, or *lay* her in the boot gently, it was *throw* her in, as if I was a suitcase or something. Our friendship is starting to show some alarming cracks.

'I'm not going in the boot,' I tell her forcefully, then turn and look out of the window and realise we must have already covered over six miles because we're about to enter a long well-lit tunnel that is about a quarter of the way towards the outskirts of London. I like the idea of getting to the city, if only because there are a million places to hide.

We fall silent for a while and I watch the overhead lights built into the tunnel bouncing off the windscreen. They start to hypnotise me and I gently close my eyes. I tell myself that I can rest for a while in the safety of the car.

'Hang on a sec,' says Billie abruptly.

I open my eyes but she stalls a little and won't meet my eyes. 'No, actually, it doesn't matter.'

'What doesn't matter?'

'Nothing.' Billie looks away from me and clearly it does matter.

'Billie?'

'I'm not sure. I had a thought . . . but never mind,' she says and turns away so she doesn't have to look at me. She stares out of the window and then sniffles as if she's trying not to cry.

'Bill,' I say. 'You all right?'

Billie nods her head, but after a moment she shakes her head. 'No . . .'

Johnson looks back at us and he is as confused as I am.

'Billie?' he asks.

She sniffles again, but doesn't answer.

'You're spooking me now,' I say to her.

Finally she turns and I can see that tears are welling in her eyes. 'We can't take you with us.'

I don't get what she means.

'If the other Johnson can jump into your mind then there's no way we can have you around us.' She wipes her eyes and her lower lip is trembling. 'He'll know exactly where we are through you. Won't he? Which means they'll come for the Moth.'

I feel a shiver run up and down my spine as Billie's words sink in. Johnson is starting to understand exactly what Billie means and his face tightens.

I look at him, hoping no one is going to say the words I know are coming. 'Wait. I'll get in the boot, I don't care,' I say desperately.

'But it's when you get out, Rev. That's when he'll know where we are.' Billie is wiping more tears away. Her logic is crippling her. She's back to being my best friend again. At least I hope she is.

I fall silent, imagining that I can think of some brilliant way out of this.

'Christ.' Johnson's voice is gentle.

'No. No, you don't know that,' I tell them. 'You really don't know how far he can see.'

The Ape's eyes loom in his rear-view mirror and I wonder if even his dinosaur-sized brain is spotting a major problem. 'So he's in your head?' he says.

'No. Well yes. Maybe.'

'Does he know your bra size?'

Billie reaches over and pings the Ape's ear, flicking it hard. 'Don't you get how serious this is?'

'Ow.'

'Do you even know what we're saying?!' She is furious with him.

'Yeah, course.' The Ape pauses. 'Other-Johnson can tell bra sizes.'

Billie pings his ear again, totally driven mad by him.

'Ow!'

'Rev, tell us what to do,' she says. 'Tell us if we should keep on going or – or what?'

The question stumps me. I know what I want to say but I also know what I should say.

'We'll risk it,' says Johnson. 'We'll just have to.'

'Risk what?' the Ape asks, but by now he's irritating everyone and together we ignore him.

'Yeah, that's what we'll do.' Johnson's face loses its

184

earlier tightness. 'Yeah.' He smiles back at me as if that's it, discussion over.

'No. We can't do that,' I say as it becomes so clear now that I cannot stay with them. 'We can't risk it,' I say slowly, 'can we?' No one answers and there's a feeling in the car that wasn't there before. It's like they know I'm doomed no matter what anyone says. 'I should get out of the car.'

Billie huddles up on the back seat. 'Why did I go and say anything?' she mumbles. 'Forget I did. Just forget it, Rev. You're staying with us.'

'Can't, can I?' I tell her. 'It'd be crazy.'

'But we're not leaving you, Rev.' She wipes her eyes again.

'No way,' adds Johnson. 'That's not happening.'

'Stop the car, Ape,' I say.

'No.' Johnson tries to be firm with me. 'Conversation over. Ape, keep driving.'

'Stop the car.'

'You need a leak?'

'I'm going to flick your ear right off!' Billie's anguish is almost too much for her to bear.

The Ape keeps driving, but the tunnel seems endless, as if we'll never get out of it. I don't remember it being this long.

'I'll jump out,' I threaten, taking hold of the door handle. 'I will.'

Johnson and Billie share an ominous look.

'It's got to be this way,' I tell them. 'It has to.'

'But they'll find you,' whimpers Billie.

'But more importantly they won't find you or the Moth,' I reply.

'But we still need your dad's papers. We'll have to get

185

them somehow.' Billie is clinging to anything that can provide her with hope.

'You can do that without me. You can sneak up on them, set a trap, whatever, but you can't do any of that while I'm with you.'

Johnson has fallen silent and looks distraught. It takes him a good long moment before he speaks. 'You'd better stop the car, Ape.'

'I'm staying with you,' Billie says to me.

'No,' I respond.

'Course I am. BFF, remember?'

'You're going with the others,' I tell her. 'That's what a real best friend would do. No point in us both . . .' My voice trails off.

'Give Rev your weapon, Ape,' says Johnson.

'No way.'

'Do it.'

'It's my best ever weapon!' the Ape says protectively. He still seems to be on another planet altogether.

'Pull over,' I tell him and he finally starts to slow.

Billie is gripping my hand tight. 'I wasn't thinking. Just talking aloud.'

Johnson looks away from me, clearly not wanting to watch me collapse in on myself. The car slows to a halt in the tunnel. The Ape glances at me again in the rear-view.

'So you've got to get out?'

I nod.

'Cos that other Johnson can see inside you?'

I nod again.

The Ape weighs it up for a moment. 'I'd better stay with you then.' It surprises me as he stares back at me. 'We're a team.'

Inside I'm trembling. 'You can't . . . They need you.'

'We do, Ape. As much as I hate to say it,' says Billie. 'We need you to drive and to be violent.'

'You stay with Johnson and Billie,' I tell him and pat his huge shoulder. 'For me. Can you do that for me?'

'She flicked my ear!'

'Ape, please.'

Eventually he shrugs. 'You can hold my weapon,' he says and then chuckles as he realises he's accidentally said something that amuses him. 'Grip it nice and tight.'

I don't smile, I'm way beyond the Ape's laboured innuendo.

'And go for the throat. Think stab, think throat.'

Johnson turns back to me. *This is it*, I think. *This is goodbye and I never did get to tell him what I feel. But what's the point now?*

'Rev?' For a second it looks as if Johnson's about to say something profound. But then his face clouds over as he backs away from whatever he intended to say and just gives me a lingering look instead, like he's taking a mental snapshot of me, something he can dredge up on a sleepless dark night long after I'm gone. 'Stay on the phone,' he says finally.

I nod, almost too choked to speak. 'I will. Promise.'

Billie throws her arms around me and hugs me tighter then tight. She has more tears in her eyes and I hate myself for ever thinking she was ready to sacrifice me so that she could have Johnson all to herself. 'Dunno what to say.'

'Just get home.' I hug her back and then climb out of the car.

The Ape lowers the electric window and looks out at me.

187

'Bummer,' is all he says. I know he wants to say more, but as usual he can't find the words. 'Big bummer.' But it's in his eyes, the sadness he is feeling, and his simple words somehow mean the world to me.

Johnson is still staring at me through the window, drinking me in, but I step back out of his eyeline. It's too much. This is beyond even Johnson.

The car pulls away and then after it has travelled a few metres the Ape's weapon is tossed out of the driver's window. It clatters to the ground and immediately breaks in half. I watch the car head for the end of the tunnel and as it disappears around a long slow bend Other-Johnson's voice enters my head.

'Almost.'

Surprisingly it doesn't even scare me.

'Thought you might be there,' I say.

'Seriously?'

'Why d'you think I got out of the car?'

'Really thought they were going to talk you into staying with them.'

'I figured that.'

'You're smart. I'm impressed,' he says.

'Is this going to take long?' I ask him.

'We're already on our way,' he tells me, although he doesn't sound that happy about it.

'I'll be waiting.'

He signs off or whatever it is he does and I feel him leave me. He has no need to be inside me any more – they know I'm stuck in an empty tunnel and that the very best I can do is stall them before they head on towards London to track down the others. I'll probably use up all of five seconds of their time.

I start walking and without realising it at first I am heading back towards town. I'm going to meet them head on rather than run. But then again I know there's no point in running when they'll always know where I am.

It's the weirdest feeling knowing you are about to die and that there is nothing you can do about it. I want to break down and cry but there's something about not giving them the satisfaction of seeing me curled up in some pathetic runny-nosed state. I'm going to go with dignity I decide. I will try talking them out of it, but mainly so I can buy the others some time. Then when the moment comes I will not go quietly. I will do everything I can to hurt them.

My phone vibrates in my pocket and I instantly remember Other-Johnson's hand pushing in deep against my thigh. It was electric and if sparks did literally fly then we would have lit up the sky.

I pull it out and answer.

'It's me.'

'Hey, Johnson.'

'We called GG and we're going to meet them. I uh, I can't tell you where obviously, but just wanted you to know that we're still here, so stay on the line,' he says.

'Will do.'

'And listen . . .'

'Yes?'

'I did a callback on the number that phoned the Ape earlier.'

My heart races as a glimmer of hope appears. I'd forgotten about the phone call the Ape had – maybe someone can save us after all. 'And?'

'Was an automated voice offering free calls and texts.'

'Why doesn't that surprise me?' I almost laugh.

'I know.'

'So no one's out there? Just a computer.'

'Looks that way.'

It's official then. No one is coming to save me.

'I heard from him, the Other-Johnson. We were right. He was listening in the whole time,' I tell Johnson.

There's nothing but silence and I can almost see Johnson's face as he tries to process what I've said.

'What did your dad write about, Rev?'

'I don't know, I really and truly don't.'

'The Moth'll figure it out.' Johnson is trying his best to keep my spirits up. 'Somehow.'

I nod, but as I do I think I see movement in the tunnel. I stop, wait for a second and then decide it's just a gust of wind. 'He'd better,' I say. I start walking again, but something darts from one shadow to another. Even with the artificial lighting it's too murky to see clearly. 'Johnson.'

'Yeah?'

I want to tell him, I have to tell him. 'You know if things were different . . .'

There's more movement and I trail off.

'Rev? You still there?'

Non-Lucas appears from the shadows and stands in the middle of the dual carriageway about a hundred metres away. I'm amazed it's just him on his own and already I'm turning back to see where the Ape's smashed weapon is. If I could reach that and somehow use what's left of it then I still have a chance.

'Rev?' Johnson asks.

'I've got company.' GG got overexcited when he said that

yesterday – only yesterday? – but for me it doesn't feel nearly as brilliant or cool.

'This is crazy. We're coming back.'

'What?'

'Turn round, Ape, turn round!'

'No!' I yell.

I hear the car brakes squealing over the phone just as Other-Johnson appears from the shadows. He's as snake-hipped and lithe as ever, calmly coming my way. I may have had a chance with just Non-Lucas, but I doubt I'll have a hope in hell now there are two of them.

'Listen to me, Johnson,' I say into the phone. 'You've got to go. You hear me? You have to stay away. That's the whole point. Just like we did when the Ape was buying us time.'

'Can't do that.'

'Yes. Yes you can! Tell him, Billie! Foot down and go!'

I wait and the moment expands into an eternity as Non-Lucas and Other-Johnson take their sweet time reaching me. Why wouldn't they? There's no hurry.

'Please, Johnson. Please.'

With that I hang up on him and hope to God he gets the message, because I'm already taking off for the broken weapon. I don't care that I don't have a chance. I'm not going to make it easy for them.

Non-Lucas sails clear over my head and lands behind the fallen weapon. He flips it up with his foot and catches it. His every movement is pure physical poetry. 'Looking for this?'

I skid to a halt and know that Other-Johnson is already closing in on me from behind.

'Catch.' Non-Lucas flicks the sharp half of the weapon towards me and I catch it gingerly.

'Got to make it interesting, right?' He grins and again I see the metal in his mouth. His skin ripples and thickens like it did before.

'You want interesting?' I say, gritting my teeth and brandishing what's left of the weapon, turning in a slow semi-circle so both Non-Lucas and Other-Johnson know I mean business.

'I know your weakness,' I tell them.

'Ooooh,' laughs Non-Lucas.

'Thing is, Rev,' calls Other-Johnson. 'We've got Billie, so weaknesses don't count.'

'I'll get you both. Hide your bodies.'

'God loves a dreamer,' smiles Non-Lucas.

They are circling me now, like cats with a cornered mouse.

I look at Non-Lucas and try my best to throw him off balance. 'We got your best pal.'

He stops. I can tell that Other-Johnson hasn't revealed this to him yet. 'That's right,' I continue. 'Show him, Johnson.'

I'm buying time, trying to calculate how far a car can travel in the few extra seconds I'm gaining them. If the Ape put his foot down they could be halfway to London by now. Assuming they haven't done something stupid and turned back for me.

'Johnson!?' Non-Lucas is worried now, needs answers.

'Why'd you go and do that?' Other-Johnson asks. He can see that I've bought myself three times as much pain and misery as before.

'Show me, Johnson,' Non-Lucas demands.

Other-Johnson does exactly that and images are wrenched out of my head and make me cry out in pain. But that's when I take my chance. I push out other images at him too and all of

192

them are of me and him kissing. His eyes filled with love and passion. His desire for me breathtaking. Overwhelming.

'She telling the truth?' asks Non-Lucas.

But Other-Johnson is lost to the images I'm sending him. My body close to his. His arms around me, holding me. His breath on my neck and shoulder. The caress of his lips on my exposed skin.

'Johnson!' snaps Non-Lucas.

Other-Johnson breaks free of the transmission of images and they fade away.

'Yeah,' he says. 'Yeah, she, uh, she got the Moth.'

'We'll go get him after. Take him to Billie.'

'No point,' shrugs Other-Johnson solemnly. He's still looking shaken though.

'No?' Non-Lucas looks genuinely shocked.

Johnson must send an image of the headless Moth Two straight into Non-Lucas because the shock is obvious on his face and for a moment he falters. 'No . . .'

Non-Lucas's breath catches in his throat as he tries to deal with the pain.

'Sorry, wasn't thinking,' Other-Johnson winces. 'I should've broken that to you more gently.'

'I'm OK. I am.' Non-Lucas tries to gather himself, and his skin ripples over and over until it has thickened enough to somehow blot out the shock. His eyes blaze at me unforgivingly. 'But now I'm so going to enjoy this. And even though I'm quick, what I'm about to do to you won't be.'

'We'll see about that.' I raise my half-weapon at them, but Other-Johnson does something to my head that makes my limbs seize up. I can't move. I'm paralysed. He's not even going to let me fight. He slowly walks towards me, then gently takes the weapon out of my hands as I struggle to take a breath. His eyes meet mine and again there's a flash of our kiss. Sadness crosses his face as he loosens his psychic grip on me and I feel control of my body again.

I raise my fists and try not to look too pathetic as I take a step forwards. 'It's rude to hit girls,' I tell them.

Non-Lucas grins darkly with his horribly sharp teeth. 'I guess that makes me ill-mannered,' he smirks.

He leaps towards me and despite my determination to be brave and daring I clamp my eyes shut and await the inevitable.

HEAVENLY

'Am I in heaven?'

  'Could be.'

  'Wow.'

  'Crazy.'

  'It doesn't seem much different.'

  'No.'

  'Weird.'

  'You can open your eyes now.'

  'Not sure I want to.'

  'Open them, Rev.'

My eyes won't open, they refuse to. I'm too scared.

  'Rev.'

  'Is it clouds and stuff?'

  'Not really.'

  'Big lush forest and green grass?'

  'Look for yourself.'

I dare to open one eye. I take a moment to look around. It's dark in places and light in others. It also surprisingly smells of life.

'Well?'

'Uh . . .' is all I can manage.

I open the other eye and everything comes into sharper relief.

'Wait a sec.' I tense.

'I couldn't help myself, Rev. Was a knee jerk reaction.'

Non-Lucas is lying dead with half of the Ape's weapon sticking out of his throat. That's the third time he's been killed in under a day. Ouch.

I turn slowly and Other-Johnson is standing there, leaning back against the walkway in the tunnel. He has the same calm air as always but inside I can sense he's completely confused by what's just happened.

'Not cool, huh?' he says.

'Not cool?'

'What I just did.'

'It works for me.' I straighten. 'Not in heaven then?'

'Not yet.' He smiles. But there's a worry behind his eyes.

'You're going to have to explain,' I tell him.

Other-Johnson falls silent. Maybe he's not sure what happened himself.

My phone rings. I look down and see Johnson's name lit up on my screen.

'He's going to come back,' Other-Johnson tells me. 'I know because I would too.'

'But I told them not to!' I grab for my phone, but Other-Johnson reaches out a lazy hand and stops me.

'I'm not going to hurt them.'

'You're tricky. I know the way you think. This is a ploy. To get them to come here.'

'No.'

196

'You look like Johnson and you're cool like he is but you are also totally, totally devious.'

'I wouldn't do that. Not to you.'

I snatch the phone out of his reach and answer it.

'Stay away!' I yell at Johnson.

'You're OK?' He sounds amazed.

'I'm good. But you've got to stay away.'

'Rev, I'm not lying to you.' Other-Johnson's voice is in my head again. *'I'm as dead as you are when my friends see what I've done to Lucas.'*

His voice caresses me, cloaks me in velvet and I can't fight it. Try as I might I can't seem to escape his hypnotic tones.

'Let them come,' he says.

I shake my head at him, but even as I do this I can hear my voice telling Johnson to come get me. 'Hurry up,' I say to Johnson, despite myself.

'You want us to come get you?' The delight in his voice makes this twice as hard.

Other-Johnson smiles at me because I can't fight his overpowering mental powers. *'It'll be OK,'* his voice says in my head.

'It won't though,' I tell him.

But then out loud I tell Johnson, 'It's safe. Promise you.'

'You beat them?' he asks.

'Uh, yeah.' I can't say what I want to say, Other-Johnson's got me in too much of a mental grip.

'Bet that was my weapon,' I hear the Ape boast. 'My three pointer.'

'We'll be there in minutes.' Johnson hangs up.

'Rev,' says Other-Johnson, out loud this time. 'Think

197

about it. I could've made you call them back before I killed Lucas.'

I hesitate.

'We could've both been waiting to kill your friends right now.'

I can hear the sound of their car echoing down the long tunnel.

I watch Other-Johnson lean back against the walkway again. He moves his hat a little so it's on a different angle, pushed away from his face. He looks more innocent that way, more appealing, if that were possible.

'Rev, I don't even know why I did what I did,' says Other-Johnson. 'But I couldn't let Lucas hurt you. It was instinctive. It was my heart, not my head.' His eyes lower but I don't think it's because he's lying, but more because he's uncomfortable about his feelings for me. They don't embarrass him, but they have knocked him sideways and left him off balance. 'Lucas wasn't a best friend or anything but he was one of my kind.'

The Ape's car appears around the bend in the tunnel. The horn sounds and the noise travels and expands through the empty tunnel. Other-Johnson immediately tenses.

'It's OK,' I tell him. 'I'll explain to them.'

Other-Johnson's eyes widen a little. 'He needs to shut up.'

The Ape sounds his horn again.

'Seriously,' says Other-Johnson, obviously spooked. 'He can't do that.'

Over and over the horn echoes throughout the tunnel.

'Phone them, Rev. Tell him to stop that!'

'What are you talking about?'

'Do it!'

I quickly call Johnson back and the horn is so loud and incessant I have to shout to be heard.

'Tell the Ape to shut up!'

'What?'

'I said—' But there's no need to say any more because coming at a lumbering trot is the Non-Ape. He has heard the car horn and been instantly drawn to it. He must still be roaming around looking for people, or else he somehow followed Non-Lucas and Other-Johnson here.

'It just had to be him, didn't it?' Other-Johnson says. His face has paled at the sight of the Non-Ape.

'Hurry!' I yell into the phone and watch the Ape speed up. But the minute he does, the Non-Ape sees the car and does likewise.

'He uh—' Other-Johnson begins.

'He doesn't like you,' I finish for him.

'You know about that?' he asks and then quickly sifts through my mental history and finds me back on the train while the Non-Ape talks to the Ape over the phone. 'Yeah, I may have upset him. A little,' he offers.

It's now touch and go between who gets to us first. The car or the Non-Ape. Other-Johnson takes my hand and leaps me through the air towards the car, obviously hoping to outrun Non-Ape. But he's not as strong or athletic as Non-Lucas is and I slow him down, so we've still got a way to go before we'll reach the car. Behind us the Non-Ape is lumbering faster and faster and I realise that the tunnel is on an incline and he's coming down it while the car is trying to race up it. The momentum of the Non-Ape's huge body is building with each step. His pace is increasing.

'JOHNSON!' he bellows and it's ten times louder than the Ape's car horn ever was.

199

The Ape sees us and applies the brakes at full speed, trying to do some clumsy handbrake turn that he's probably seen in a film so that at least the car will be facing away from the Non-Ape when he picks us up. But it goes spectacularly wrong – the car starts turning in circles and spins right past me and Other-Johnson.

As it does, I see the Ape at the steering wheel, swearing, and Johnson in the passenger seat holding on tight, but looking astonished at what's happening and also maybe that I am with Other-Johnson. In the back I see Billie being thrown in a heap across the seat. They are heading straight towards the Non-Ape, and Other-Johnson re-grips my hand again, pulling me through the air as he tries to leap us back towards them. The car finally stops but it's now facing the Non-Ape, who is less than forty metres away.

'JOHNSON!' Non-Ape bellows again. The tunnel trembles from the roar.

Incredibly, the Ape starts climbing from the car. 'I got this.'

But I reach him and shove him back into the car, bundling his large body back behind the wheel.

'He destroyed a train, you idiot! You can't fight him!' I scream. I yank open the rear door and make to jump in, when I see Other-Johnson standing looking at me. He doesn't need to enter my head to tell me what he's thinking.

That this is goodbye. Despite everything, he manages a slow lopsided smile at me.

The Non-Ape is thirty metres away and still racing towards us. 'JOHNSON!'

'What did you do to make him that angry?'

Other-Johnson puts on a big fake wince rather than tell me. 'It's complicated.'

'Get in!' Johnson calls. 'Rev, come on!'

I turn and look at the Non-Ape lumbering towards us, his eyes fixed on Other-Johnson, and I can't help myself as I instinctively grab Other-Johnson's hand and drag him into the back of the car with me.

'Back up!' I scream at the Ape.

Other-Johnson and Johnson look totally perplexed and they speak at the same time with the exact same voices. 'What are you doing?'

'I have no idea! But move this car, Ape!'

The Ape engages reverse and the wheels spin then grip and we start reversing away from the Non-Ape.

Only we're not moving fast enough because the Non-Ape is gaining on us and looming ever bigger. We stare in horror through the smashed windscreen as he gets closer and closer. The Ape mashes his big foot down onto the accelerator and we speed up. But the Non-Ape's momentum is building and building, empowered by some deep animal rage.

'JOHNSON!'

'Oh God,' says Billie. 'Oh dear God.'

The engine is screaming in protest as it strains to build speed. I look behind us and see that the opening to the tunnel is close. Bright sunlight beams down onto the empty tarmac carriageway.

'C'mon,' I whisper. 'C'mon, Ape, c'mon.'

The Ape is straining his thick neck round so he can see where he is reversing and glances at Other-Johnson, who is now sitting on my lap while I cling on tightly to him. 'That's weird,' he says as he glances at Johnson. He looks back through the windscreen at the behemoth bearing down on us hollering Johnson's name over and over again. He's definitely gaining on us.

'Turn the car round! We can't keep going backwards!' Billie screeches.

'Going too fast,' says Johnson.

'We'd tip over,' says Other-Johnson at the same time.

'*We?* You're one of us now?' Billie is completely bewildered. 'Last I knew you wanted us dead.'

'People change.' He shrugs lightly.

We break out of the tunnel straight into the daylight and immediately career towards the stone barrier of the central reservation. The Ape is becoming fixated with his other self and forgetting to steer.

'I could take him,' he says.

'No, Ape. No,' I tell him in no uncertain terms.

'Easy,' says the Ape.

'Tell him, Johnson.' I nudge Other-Johnson, but it's our Johnson who speaks.

'You didn't see what he did to the train.'

'I ain't a train,' boasts the Ape.

'You should listen to them,' Other-Johnson tells him. 'That Ape out there is something else.'

'He's giving us advice now?' Billie's voice drips with sarcasm and then as she looks behind us and sees the central reservation looming up she yells out. 'Look where you're going, you idiot!'

The Ape swerves at the last moment and the side of the car scrapes along the concrete dividing the road, banging back and forth against it, sparks flying, until the Ape manages to heave it free of the central reservation.

It has slowed us down though and the Non-Ape is drawing ever closer.

'JOHNSON!'

'You really made him angry,' I whisper breathlessly to Other-Johnson.

'If it's him he wants, then let's throw him out,' shouts Billie.

'Open the door, Rev.' I'm surprised when Johnson says this and my grip on Other-Johnson tightens.

'I can't do that,' I tell him.

'He's in your head again,' says Johnson.

'I'm not,' says Other-Johnson. 'Swear to you.'

'Get out of the car,' says Billie.

'Ape—' begins Johnson.

'Little busy right now,' interrupts the Ape, who's using what brain he has to concentrate on us not crashing.

'I want him out of here!' screams Billie.

'He'll get tired soon,' says Other-Johnson, trying to sound as calm and as pleasant as he can. 'Just keep this pace up.'

'He doesn't look tired to me,' Johnson replies.

The Non-Ape is still coming, but we're now maintaining a distance of about fifteen metres and I'm hoping the Non-Ape can't run any faster.

'He's too fat to keep up,' says Other-Johnson.

'That isn't fat,' says the Ape defensively. 'That's muscle.'

'He'll have to slow down soon.' Other-Johnson sounds confident of this, but I can sense even he's not sure what Non-Ape's levels of stamina are.

The chase continues for half a mile and we don't get any further away and the Non-Ape doesn't get any closer. All he does is bellow Johnson's name over and over.

No one but me is happy that Other-Johnson is in the car with us. I keep glancing at Johnson, who is avoiding looking at me – at us.

'Shall we put the radio on?' says Johnson after the first mile of reversing. It's a joke and I almost laugh.

'Could all sing a song,' suggests Other-Johnson. Which does make me laugh. Billie sees this and rolls her eyes, incredulous that I can find anything funny.

Other-Johnson glances at Billie, again trying to seem kind and considerate. 'What happened to your face?'

'Your Lucas did.'

Other-Johnson takes a moment. 'Oh.'

'Yeah. Nice guy,' she says.

'Yeah,' he says. But I detect a concern in his voice. 'You, uh, you take care of that.'

'Seriously, why is he even in the car?' Billie asks me.

'Yeah, about that,' says Johnson turning in his seat to look at us so he doesn't have to watch the bellowing behemoth bearing down on us for a moment. 'Why *is* he in here with us, Rev?'

It's a question I don't know how to answer with any real clarity. 'He saved me,' I shrug.

'Saved you?'

'I kind of killed Lucas,' Other-Johnson shrugs.

Silence follows for a few seconds.

'I don't get it,' states Billie, who is sitting close enough to touch Other-Johnson, but unlike me seems immune to his charm and looks like she'd rather she was anywhere else right now.

Other-Johnson again turns and looks at her. 'Just happened that way.'

'You saved Rev?'

'I guess.' Other-Johnson is calm, cool and collected just like Johnson is. Maybe even more so.

Johnson can't take his eyes off his doppelganger. He's so spooked, but desperate to look in control. 'What are you?' he asks.

'Could ask you the same,' says Other-Johnson.

'You go first.'

'I'm me.'

'I'm me, too.'

'I'd say there's a few crucial differences,' says Other-Johnson.

'Maybe just a few,' agrees Johnson, with a hard stare.

It's like the conversation between the Apes on the train all over again. Their voices are identical and it's hard to tell who's talking and who's saying what. I still have my arms wrapped tight round Other-Johnson and I can feel the taut muscles of his flat stomach. His breathing is calm and the intoxicating aftershave still makes me giddy.

'We were in detention,' says Other-Johnson.

'Snap,' replies Johnson.

'There was a—'

'—light and—'

'—next thing—'

'—there's no one—'

'—but then I kept meeting the others—'

'—I didn't see anyone until I met Rev—'

'—everyone who was in detention—'

'Even Carrie? That won't turn out well.' Other-Johnson has left my head and I sort of miss it. That connection, that closeness. I have to be careful I tell myself, careful that he's not manipulating me – he might be in my mind and just hiding. But if he isn't inside me right now, making me feel things more strongly, then I'm in trouble. Because that would mean the kiss and the ache I feel for him is very real. Way too real in fact. My Johnson has had an impact on me – I have just about come to accept that now – but Other-Johnson did things to me, unlocked whole layers I never knew were there.

I try and snap back to the real world, watching as the Non-Ape starts to tire. He has been running for over a mile now and has fallen back a little from us, clearly starting to lag. We're going to lose him. Eventually.

The Ape sees this, sounds his horn at him and laughs.

'Who's the Ape, huh? Who's the daddy Ape?'

The horn immediately enrages the Non-Ape and he somehow speeds up again.

'Wouldn't do that,' warns Other-Johnson. 'Irritate him and he'll get stronger.'

'I own you!' shouts the Ape, who then, to everyone's amazement, sounds the horn again, mocking the Non-Ape. 'Come on then!'

Billie lurches forward and pings the Ape's ear again. 'Christ almighty!'

'Ow!'

'Please, just do something sensible at least once in your miserable life!'

The Ape sounds the horn again. Then again, then twice more and the Non-Ape's anger reaches down to his giant thick limbs and they pump even harder, making him go faster.

Billie flicks the Ape's ear over and over. 'IDIOT!'

'Ow!'

Despite himself, Other-Johnson laughs, but more in a total staggering bewilderment at the Ape than actually finding him funny.

206

The volcanic-looking Non-Ape is gaining on us now.

'Ape,' says Johnson, 'leave the horn alone.'

The Ape's hand lingers over the horn – he wants to press it again and it's almost impossible for him to resist.

'Ape,' Johnson says quietly, and finally the Ape eases his hand away from the horn.

The car keeps reversing, but when I look behind us I see we're coming to a large roundabout. It's a major junction with roads leading into North London and also heading east and west.

'Ape . . .' I say.

'I see it,' he says, his eyes moving past mine and out the rear window.

Billie looks behind and takes a short sharp intake of breath. 'Give us a break!' she moans.

Johnson and Other-Johnson have seen it as well and they both look a little grim.

'We're going to have to slow down. We can't take the roundabout going backwards at this speed,' says Johnson.

I look back and realise that we may have made it if the Ape hadn't enraged the Non-Ape and drawn him closer, but there's no chance now.

'Ideas?' Johnson asks.

No one has any.

'This isn't fair! It's not. It's just not fair,' Billie groans. It's a despairing whine that speaks for all of us.

'If we stop, how do we beat him?' Johnson asks Other-Johnson.

'You can't,' says Other-Johnson.

'C'mon, there's always a way,' I say.

'Believe me, I'd tell you if there was.'

'Weak spot?' asks Billie, desperately grasping at anything.

'You'd never get close enough.'

The roundabout is looming up and there's no way we can get round it without crashing. Billie lashes out and pings the Ape's ear again and again. 'Why did you have to make him angry?'

'OK, we stop the car, then run off in different directions,' Johnson says as the car slows. The Ape has no choice or otherwise he'll crash. 'He can't chase all of us down,'

'That's great. It's going to be me, I know it. He's going to catch me.' Billie is dissolving into a whimper now. 'I can't run, I can't do it.'

Other-Johnson looks at the distraught Billie and there's something about her that affects him. His voice comes back into my head.

'This is my problem.'

He shifts in my lap and winds the window down.

'What are you doing?' I ask him as he breaks my grip on his waist.

'Get ready,' he says to the Ape.

'Johnson?' I say. Meaning Other-Johnson, but getting responses from both Johnsons.

'Yeah?' they ask simultaneously.

'I meant . . .' I falter as they both look at me.

'It's OK, Rev.' Other-Johnson's voice is back in my head. *'It's A-OK.'* He hauls himself out of the window and with that other-wordly physical ability he possesses, he clambers swiftly onto the roof of the car.

'Johnson!' I shout.

'Hope you make it home,' he speaks into my mind and it might be the most honest thing I have ever heard. The words tighten around my chest.

'*Johnson,*' I whisper in my head. '*Don't do this.*'

'*That kiss,*' he says one last time. '*Never felt anything like it. Not even with my Rev.*'

The Ape slows as the roundabout looms up. The Non-Ape sees us slowing and even his massively sluggish brain can see what is about to happen. He starts to grin because he can also see Other-Johnson waiting for him on top of the car.

'JOHNSON!' he yells.

Even from inside the car I can sense Other-Johnson coil his muscles and get ready to jump from the roof.

'Johnson!' I shout, but then feel him leap from the car and go to meet the Non-Ape head on.

Non-Ape snaps out a massive paw towards Other-Johnson and catches him by the throat, leaving him dangling in the air.

'No!' I cry.

But the Ape executes another handbrake turn and spins the car in the opposite direction and suddenly I can't see them. It takes precious seconds for me to orient myself as the car turns to face the right way again. I fight the G-forces and try to look back, but when I do all I can see is the Non-Ape's free hand punch Other-Johnson in the stomach, which makes him crease up in agony. Other-Johnson kicks back at the Non-Ape and twists and turns to try and escape the Non-Ape's grip, but nothing in the world could escape that.

The car swerves away and, with Johnson shouting directions, the Ape takes the road towards Central London.

'*Johnson?*' I say in my head. '*Johnson. You there? Johnson, speak to me. Johnson.*'

I strain my head until it aches, but I don't get a reply.

There is no sense of Other-Johnson anywhere. Inside or out.

I slump back, feeling as if someone has ripped something vital from my insides.

'Well that's three of them down,' says Billie as she collapses back in her seat, panting and breathless.

'Yowza,' the Ape says.

I can't find the words to respond.

'Rev?' I look up and Johnson is looking at me.

'Yeah?' I say quietly.

'He left the thesis.' I look down and my dad's paper is lying beside me on the seat. Other-Johnson must have left it for me. Johnson knows it's of little comfort. He can see it in my eyes. 'Thanks to him we've got a way out of this now.'

But right now I don't care. Other-Johnson climbed inside me and with one kiss he gave me life. I was burning so brightly and now it's all been snatched away. I offer Johnson a muted nod, but not even he can find a way through my loss. I watch him turn away and I swear he looks just a little more slumped than usual. I want to reach out to him but I can't find the energy or the strength. The Other-Johnson did something to me. And I don't think I will ever be the same again.

Billie reaches out and puts a hand on Johnson's shoulder. It's the smallest of gestures but Johnson reaches up and pats her hand as a thank you for her kindness.

And suddenly there's a worse thought nagging at the back of my head. Two Johnsons and I don't have either of them.

LOVE IS AN UNKINDNESS

I have never been in a five star hotel before. The best my mum ever managed was a seafront hotel in Brighton. That was our favourite holiday together. Bed and breakfast and days spent on the beach and the promenade. She told me she honeymooned there and it had taken her years before she could bring herself to go back. When my dad left us he took whole chunks of her with him. I don't think she ever fully recovered.

But the hotel I am standing in is like paradise with a marble floor. My mum would love it. I start taking photos of it with my phone, thinking I can show her where I've been. It's such an instinctive reaction, but I'm hanging onto the hope that somehow I'll be seeing her again. If she can see that something incredible took place and that I ended up in a hotel like this then she'd surely understand. Someone has to know that this actually happened.

The hotel is grand and opulent and huge. There are paintings bigger than the Non-Ape hung on the walls of the entrance mezzanine. Fresh flowers sit in giant vases that look like they came from ninth century China.

I stayed silent for most of the drive here. GG kept sending texts to Johnson, telling him he was looking for a place for us to stay. Johnson showed them to us as the Ape drove along a usually packed A41 and down into the heart of London.

We r at Kings X – xx GG.

Walking now (carrie moaning).

Still moaning.

Found hospital. Found wheelchair batteries. Moth mobile again. Phew! Aching arms need rub down from pushing him.

SOMEONE'S STILL MOANING!!!!!!!!

The Ape stopped at a Maida Vale petrol station and let us get out and find a street map because he had no idea where he was going. He said he needed to use the public loos but only because he wouldn't admit to being lost. We grabbed bottles of water and cans of Coke and then I went to the back of the petrol station and took about a dozen toothbrushes and a few tubes of toothpaste. I wondered if it constituted looting but does wanting clean teeth count as a crime?

Carrie riding on back of Wheelchair. (lazy!)

Trotters hurting but in Mayfair now

Have found the ideal hotel. U will love it!!!!

GG thought for the day: If Carrie has a twin version I am leaving the country!

Johnson found the address for the hotel and navigated us through the capital. The evening started to close in and we are all hungry and bone tired. No one spoke much and the only real noise was of the Ape's stubby finger repeatedly pressing the car's radio as he searched for a radio channel that wasn't spurting static.

'Nope. Nope. Nope.'

No one had the strength to yell at him.

I liked that we were driving around an empty London, moving through some of the most famous streets in the world, because it gave me time to think. As we passed Big Ben and the Houses of Parliament, Hyde Park, the London Eye, Big Ben again, went three times around Marble Arch and criss-crossed the quietest Thames in history, I wondered what my mum was thinking. If we were really somewhere else now, then she would be frantic, as would all of our friends and family. There'd be TV reports, missing children notices issued up and down the country, people would suspect everything from a crazed serial killer to an alien abduction. My mum would believe it all, while telling the police not to keep phoning her, that she'd prefer they rang when they had proper news rather than give an update that told her nothing.

We followed the Strand one way then the Ape turned the car and headed back the way we had come. We drifted up into Covent Garden and actually drove through the pedestrianised area usually reserved for street artists. Chinatown came and went as did Piccadilly Circus, and then we were heading back again, past the major theatres where there were no actors and no audiences. London seemed bigger somehow, the empty buildings reaching towards the empty evening sky, casting giant shadows over our non-progress.

The Ape seemed to love driving wherever he fancied, but eventually Johnson pointed out that we really should go to the hotel, that we needed to lie low so that we could work out what to do next. Billie proved an expert map reader and we eventually pulled up outside the hotel where a doorman would usually be, someone to open the car door and wish us a pleasant stay.

Carrie sits behind the concierge's desk spinning slowly on a swivel chair. She is the first person we see when we enter the huge reception area.

'Do you have reservations?' she asks, which surprises me because that's almost like a joke and Carrie doesn't have a sense of humour.

The hairs stand up on my arms and my shoulders tingle as I realise we have walked into a trap. This isn't the real Carrie and I grab the smallest ornate chair I can see and hurl it at her.

'RUN!' I scream.

The chair flies straight at her and even though she ducks, one of the mahogany legs glances off the side of her temple and knocks her clean out of her swivel chair. She crashes down as I grab Billie's good hand and start dragging her away.

'It's not her! It's not Carrie!'

But Billie doesn't budge.

'Billie!' I scream again.

But Johnson isn't moving either and to my amazement even the Ape isn't coming with me, or worse, finding more weapons.

The reason they aren't running becomes painfully clear when the Moth wheels out into the reception area.

'What on earth are you doing?' he asks me, stunned.

I stop as I hear a dazed groan coming from behind the concierge's desk. 'You bitch.'

'It's us,' says the Moth.

I take a moment to realise what I've done as everyone stares at me.

'Carrie doesn't make jokes,' I say quietly, as Johnson and Billie go to her and try and get her to her feet. She is woozy and unsteady after the chair leg hit her but not so much that she can't snarl at me.

'You utter, utter imbecile!' she spits. 'You're so going to pay for that.'

Johnson tries to make things better. 'We're all on edge,' he explains. 'We're just on edge.'

'You want edge?' says Carrie aiming daggers at me. 'I'll give you edge.'

'Easy mistake,' offers Billie.

'You're dead,' Carrie tells me.

I feel totally stupid and totally rotten, but what does anyone expect? Nothing is what it seems any more and I'm on high alert every second. Johnson and Billie sit the dazed Carrie down and the Moth whirrs over towards her to check her wound.

'That's going to bruise,' he says gently.

'She's going to bruise,' snarls Carrie looking my way.

I realise that I'm doomed to never connect on any level with Carrie. Fate is making whatever is going on between us last forever.

Johnson takes a look around the hotel. 'Where's GG?' he asks.

'Oh, he's in his suite,' says the Moth.

'His suite?'

'He took the honeymoon suite. Thirtieth floor.'

Billie flops onto a lush leather sofa in the lobby. 'I'm starving.'

'We found some drinks and food in the kitchen,' says the Moth.

The Ape immediately gets excited. 'Food!!'

My stomach is also rumbling. I can't remember the last time we ate properly, apart from crisps and chocolate from the petrol station. Yesterday at GG's flat probably. 'What is there?'

'Pretty much everything you could ever want.'

Billie looks to the Moth. 'How far is the kitchen?'

'I'll show you.'

'Can't you just bring me something? I can't move,' she moans.

But before she can react the Ape has grabbed her and dragged her to her feet. 'I'll carry you.'

'No! Don't touch me.'

The Ape swings Billie up and around onto his great broad back.

'My arm!' Billie's sling comes loose but the Ape doesn't seem to care.

'You can cook me something.'

'I'm not cooking for you.'

'You'll have to learn sooner or later.' In that moment it seems pretty clear that the Ape is convinced that he could end up married to Billie in this not-so-brave new world. 'That's what girls do. Cook.'

'You're sexist.' Billie is now being piggybacked against her will down the great marble hallway.

The Ape immediately thinks that sexist must also mean sexy. 'Yeah, I know.' He sighs proudly.

Johnson has been watching and can't help smiling as he hands the Moth my dad's paper.

'You said you wanted to read this.'

The Moth accepts the batch of papers with some reservation. 'I'll do what I can, but I can't make any promises.'

'No pressure, but you're the only one likely to understand it,' Johnson tells him, offering a smile of encouragement.

'It's our ticket home,' I add.

The Moth still doesn't get it. 'We *are* home.'

Johnson shakes his head quietly. 'Just read it.' He pats the Moth's shoulder. 'Right now you are the most important person in the world.'

I get worried that Johnson will also tell him that a group of vicious superhumans are probably looking for him right this minute, but Johnson decides that the Moth could probably do without that. He has enough on his plate.

'Me?'

'Yep.'

The Moth's excited eyes drift towards Carrie. 'You hear that?'

Carrie shrugs. 'I can't hear anything over the pounding in my head.' Which is really aimed at me.

'If you can work out what is in this, then we'll have all the answers we need.' Johnson smiles at the Moth, staying gentle, not panicking him.

'I'm going to get myself a drink, find a quiet spot and start reading.' The Moth cranes his neck towards Carrie. 'Can I bring you something back?' he asks her.

'Yeah. My old life would be nice.'

'You got it,' he jokes in response.

Carrie turns away muttering under her breath, but there's less rancour and more amusement in her face now. Has she actually warmed to the Moth?

217

'Wait up.' Carrie has a change of heart and follows the Moth through the magnificent lobby. 'You'd only spill it.'

Johnson heads away and calls the nearest lift. As he watches the lights above the metallic doors he looks slowly back to me. 'Coming?'

'Uh . . .' I say, incoherently. He's taken me by surprise. We've hardly spoken since Other-Johnson jumped from the car.

'It's OK, you don't have to.'

The lift arrives and the doors open. Johnson lingers a fraction of a second and that's all it takes for me to make up my mind. I head into the lift with him.

'Going up,' is all he says as he presses the button for the thirtieth floor.

Johnson and I are both on the verge of falling apart with exhaustion and, because the lift is mirrored wherever we look, we can see each other. There's no escaping our tired faces.

'So London's empty too,' says Johnson. He sounds a little defeated even though this is what he had predicted.

I nod.

'It really is just us,' he adds.

'And them,' I reply.

He nods and his eyes find mine in the endless reflections. 'Rev.'

'Yeah?'

'Has he gone? The other me. From your head I mean.'

I nod and a lump forms in my throat as I think about Other-Johnson. I figure I've had more lumps in my throat lately than most people get in a lifetime.

'So he doesn't know where we are.'

'He wouldn't have told them,' I say.

'Right.' Johnson sounds sceptical.

'He wouldn't have,' I say with absolute certainty. 'He's *you,* remember. You wouldn't do something like that.' I smile at this. It's a tired smile and not quite the smile I want it to be, but even so Johnson reaches across and gently slips his hand into mine. Which surprises me.

'I'll be here for you as well, Rev,' he says and squeezes my hand.

This is a moment that should bring us together. It's been building, subtly I admit, but whatever bond there is between us should become unbreakable. It's how it always works. The quiet moment when the boy I didn't know I liked finally reaches out to me and shows me exactly what I've pretended wasn't there. But the moment isn't going as planned. The bond isn't there. I can touch Johnson but I can't feel him where it matters most. I don't know what Other-Johnson has done to me but since he disappeared I've become numb inside. Hollow.

I try not to let on and we stay with our fingers entwined until we reach the thirtieth floor and then wait for the doors to silently part before us.

I don't know if I should keep hold of Johnson's hand or not, but when we hear singing coming from the honeymoon suite it takes enough of our attention that I slip my hand from his and head quickly for the door.

'He's singing,' I say, stating the obvious.

'I'm gonna wash that man right out of my hair.' GG's voice carries down the hallway, guiding us to his suite.

He has left the key card in the lock and Johnson slides it out and then back in, waits for the little light by the handle

219

to turn from red to green and opens the door. We walk into the most palatial room I have ever seen. It is luxury beyond luxury. A king-sized four-poster bed with three steps leaping up to it dominates the room. But there's also a soft leather sofa, a fully stocked bar, a dining table and a huge basket of fruit still wrapped in cellophane sitting on an ornate coffee table by one of the many windows. A bottle of champagne sits half empty beside it and I accidentally kick the cork as I move around the enormous suite looking for GG.

'I'm gonna wave that man right outa my arms and send him on his way.' GG's voice floats out from the bathroom and I can hear in it a champagne-fuelled disregard for the hopeless situation we have found ourselves in.

Johnson knocks on the bathroom door, but GG is singing so loudly he can't hear us. Johnson pushes the door open and we both peer round it.

Lying in a bath that could easily take eight people is GG. There are soapsuds spilling over the edges of the bath and tumbling down the sides as he sticks a long lean leg in the air and scrubs himself with a bar of luxury soap. Even through the steam from the hot water we can see he is wearing a shower cap.

'GG!' I call out and don't even realise I am running towards him.

'Rev! Johnson!' GG sits up in the bath as he takes me in. 'Jump in. There's room for a football team . . . With any luck, anyway,' he winks.

Seeing GG in a giant bath of foam bubbles seems to make everything go away. At least momentarily. He's laughing, I'm laughing, Johnson's just standing there grinning and for a few seconds at least we're just three teenagers who are really glad to see each other. The glee spills over like the bubbles in the bath and before I know it Johnson has swept me up into his arms and holds me over the bath.

'Shall I?' he teases and before I can answer he drops me into the giant bath. I go straight under and for a second I panic until I explode back up and blow foam away from my lips.

GG reaches over and cuddles me. 'We could live in this bath!' he cries. I'm glad to see he isn't entirely naked and is wearing brightly coloured swimming shorts, though I haven't got the energy to ask him where he got them from.

Johnson takes off his boots and climbs on top of the edge of the bath. He still has all his clothes on, but he removes his T-shirt and I see his taut, tight muscles flex as he whirls it above his head before throwing it across the bathroom. He looks down at me, his curls falling forward and then he brushes them gently out of his eyes. He can't seem to stop looking at me as I watch him towering over us, topless and dynamic. It should be the eighth wonder of my world, but I can't rid myself of Other-Johnson enough to fully appreciate this Johnson. My Johnson. I hate myself for feeling this way and want to scream at the craziness of it.

Johnson takes a step and slips gently into the bath with us. He stretches his lithe arms out along the far edge of the bath and just sits there with a lopsided grin on his lips.

I ease back while my green top and soaking jeans cling to me. *This is what we are*, I think. *Teenagers, just kids, and this is what we should be doing. Stupid things. Fun things.*

GG is still cuddling me and I can feel his slippery skinny body close to mine. 'I'm making a humungous lasagne for dinner,' he says. 'Hope you're hungry.'

But I'm not really listening because all I can see is Johnson's bright-eyed grin rising above the foam. He wants me, I know he does. Before I would have cried out in utter delight, but now I'm hiding from him. On the surface everything probably looks normal to Johnson but underneath, where it really counts, I am no longer the girl he thinks I am.

The way Other-Johnson kissed me . . . the way he touched me. There's no forgetting that.

Maybe not ever.

EATING IN

I must have fallen asleep in the warm bath, because the next thing I know I wake up alone in the tub and the water has turned cold. GG has left a bathrobe for me and a pile of the softest lushest towels I have ever felt. I wrap myself up and pad over to the open bathroom door, looking in to the main room. Johnson is standing at one of the large windows that looks out on to the dark city. The sun is setting, dipping behind the monolithic shapes of the buildings, taking with it the last remaining light. Johnson's in his wet jeans and still topless.

'Anything out there?' I ask as I walk over to him.

'Nothing.'

We both stare out of the window.

'I can't figure any of it out, Rev.'

'The Moth's got the papers now – he can do all that.'

'So did he tell you anything?'

'The other you?'

Johnson nods.

'Just what I said earlier, that here's not actually here,' I tell him.

'So where is it?'

We fall silent again because it's a question neither of us can answer.

'That kiss,' says Johnson.

'Yeah?' I tense a little.

'You were very brave.'

'Brave?'

'To go that far.'

Brave had nothing to do with it, I think.

'He made it happen,' I say, falling back on my old explanation.

'He could actually do that?'

'Oh, he could've made me do just about anything,' I say just a bit too keenly, then quickly try to backtrack. 'Least I think maybe he could have.'

'Weird how he helped you. Killed his friend to save you,' says Johnson.

'He was confused, because I'm like the other Rev or something.' *It sounds so weak*, I think. *Anyone can see through my lies.*

But Johnson either chooses not to see or he really believes me. 'You must have made a big impact on him.'

'First time for everything,' I say with another failed attempt at a smile.

'First time?' says Johnson, looking quietly surprised.

'Think so.'

'What about Kyle?'

I give myself a moment and then look honestly at Johnson. 'That isn't anything.'

'No?'

I shake my head. 'Have barely thought about him since all

of this happened.' I don't mean to sound this harsh but it's the honest truth – apart from right when this all started I haven't considered Kyle once.

Johnson nods then looks back out at the city. 'Part of me likes it like this. Empty.'

'Yeah,' I say. 'Yeah, me too. Though maybe not the near-death experiences.'

Johnson laughs. 'Those I could live without.'

I feel him turn and look at me. 'Want to know something funny?'

'Absolutely,' I tell him.

'I didn't get detention.'

I turn to him, surprised. 'What? How come you were there then?'

Johnson raises an eyebrow. 'You kidding?'

I shrug. I have no idea what he means.

'You really don't know?' He grins and turns to face the starkly empty city. The smile remains on his lips.

'You going to tell me?' I urge him gently.

He turns back to me. 'Because I knew you'd be there.'

My heart has leapt mightily these past few days, but the leap that happens when Johnson says this sets a new world record. It sends a rocket through me, or at least that's what it feels like, as every bit of me comes alive again.

He's broken through the numbness. Just a tiny gap, but Johnson has made contact with me. He takes a breath and is about to say more. *This is it*, I think, *this is what I've been waiting for even though I didn't even know I was waiting for it*. Then the bedroom door opens and Billie walks in. She sees me in my lush towel, looking like some faux Hollywood

225

starlet and then takes in Johnson in his wet jeans and bare torso, and has to take a moment to gather herself.

'Sorry, didn't realise you were . . . busy.'

'It's cool,' says Johnson. He angles himself slightly away from me. It's a small shift, but I sense it.

'Oh. OK,' she responds. 'GG's found something he wants us all to see.'

'What is it?' I ask.

'He didn't say, but he's excited.'

Johnson raises his finger to his temple and gives her that slow one-finger salute he gave me way back in detention. 'We're coming now.'

Billie is eyeing his bare torso a little too keenly. 'You'll need a shirt,' she says.

'I guess,' he replies, but he's looking at me the whole time.

GG MAXES OUT

It is well past nine o'clock in the evening and GG has lined us up as if we're in the army. He inspects each one of us in turn as he moves down the line. He picks a strand of pink hair from my shoulder, he points silently to a dark spot on Johnson's Palma Violets T-shirt and tuts, he reaches for the Ape's grimy Ben Sherman top but the Ape bats his hand away.

'Shocking. There's no other word for it. Yes, you all have your excuses, but to be blunt as a blunter you all look a mess.' He's wearing a plush towelling bathrobe and has taken slippers from the honeymoon suite and on the back of the bathrobe is the words HERS. 'We may be the only people around – well, except for those ghastly others – but that doesn't mean we shouldn't make an effort. I've made us a lovely dinner, and I think that you can at least dress appropriately.' GG elaborately bows and then makes us watch his fluttering fingers as they draw us towards the row of high-class five star boutiques that populate the centre of the huge hotel. 'I'm throwing open the doors to you but if you need advice – Ape, Moth, I'm talking to you specifically – then all you have to do is whisper my name.'

Carrie raises her hand.

'Carrie?' says GG.

'This is ridiculous. We're supposed to be running for our lives.'

'And we're safe now. We're in a city, a massive city, and there are a million places we could be hiding. We are a needle in a concrete haystack.'

I glance at Johnson and he shrugs as if he agrees.

'But the Moth should be reading that thesis. He should be going through every single page until he can tell us what is going on.' Billie turns to the Moth. 'We need the answers more than we need a makeover. You agree, don't you?'

'I do, yes.'

'So get reading.'

'I have been. But it's not easy to grasp.'

'I knew it. I knew you'd be useless.'

'Billie, easy,' I tell her.

'Don't pick on Hawkings.' Carrie squares up to Billie.

'That's all you ever do,' Billie responds.

'I'm allowed to, you're not.'

I can see the Moth enjoying having two girls squabbling in front of him. He has probably never had this much attention in his whole life before.

'Ladies, please,' he says. 'I've started reading but it's not sinking in – I need time to let it settle.'

'I want to be back in a world I know,' counters Billie. 'That's all. And I want that to happen as quickly as it can.'

'Which it will.' GG claps his hands together. 'After some retail therapy.'

'I'll go read,' says the Moth, guiltily.

'Oh no you don't, Timothy. This'll only take five minutes,' says GG. 'I'm already seeing you in a cravat.'

'A what?'

'It's a sort of tie thing,' explains Carrie, who then climbs onto the back of his motorised wheelchair. 'C'mon, Hawkings, I'll show you. You steer, I'll tell you where to go.' Carrie and the Moth motor slowly past me and as she does I can see the bruise turning purple on her head. I'm starting to think I hit her so hard she's had a personality change. Can you do that to people? Beat niceness into them?

The Ape has no idea what he's meant to do because I see him looking down at his clothes and his giant-sized designer rip-off trainers, like he's wondering what exactly is wrong with his 'look'.

GG turns to him. 'I'm seeing Hugo Boss.'

'What's that?' the Ape asks.

'It's you, is what it is. Now let's see what we can find.'

'I ain't going with you.'

'Yes you are.'

'No.'

GG lowers his voice and whispers to the Ape. 'Indulge me.'

The Ape takes an interminable time to process GG's offer. 'Might need fresh boxers I guess.'

To his credit, GG doesn't so much as grimace as they head off together, the oddest of odd couples ever. Which leaves me, Johnson and Billie. She touches her face self-consciously – it seems the scars are bothering her as much as they have ever done.

'I'm going to sit this one out,' she says.

I'm about to respond when Johnson becomes the gentleman you can only ever dream about.

'No you're not.'

Billie looks up and Johnson offers his hand and I know she needs all the comfort she can get.

'I bet you don't even like shopping,' she half smiles.

'I'm open to persuasion.' He grins wryly.

With that Johnson leads Billie into the tiny shopping mall.

I watch them go and don't know if I should follow or not. I'm standing in a bathrobe and all I have to do is slip it off and select some new outfit. But I'd like someone to go with me, to wait outside the changing room while I emerge in a series of increasingly gorgeous dresses. I want to see them captivated by my radiant beauty, like some cheesy movie montage.

I head towards the boutiques and pass a bespoke gentleman's outfitters with cashmere suits in the window modelled by tall lantern-jawed mannequins. The Johnsons would never wear these clothes, they'd always be in T-shirts or a cool top. And they'll wear skinny jeans until the day they die. I'd insist on it. I'd make it part of our wedding vows.

Did I say wedding? I'm becoming delirious. I need to stay focused and remember where we are right now.

I look at the mannequins and for a moment I imagine the people they are supposed to represent. If this truly isn't our world, then whose is it? And where have they gone?

A scream rings out and I jolt, alert again.

'Monster!' A half-dressed Billie charges out of a chic fashion boutique with Johnson following her.

'He didn't see anything, I swear,' Johnson says.

I then see the Ape lumbering out after them.

Johnson raises an eyebrow at me – he looks tired and like

he doesn't need this as he chases after Billie who is still striding away. 'Billie. Wait.'

The Ape stops beside me. 'Who wouldn't try and get a peek? C'mon, Rev. Who wouldn't try and cop a look?'

'Billie's totally fragile, Ape. And people want privacy.'

'So why was Johnson in the cubicle with her?'

The breath catches in my throat.

'He was what?'

'Helping her out of her clothes.' He lumbers away and I'm not sure if I can hold back the shock that's trying to take a hold of me. Johnson was in the cubicle *with* Billie? Were they . . .? Even after what he said to me in GG's hotel room?

The Moth whirrs out of the gent's outfitters with Carrie behind him. He's wearing a cravat around his neck. 'What d'you think, Rev?'

'Yeah. Great.' My words are hollow, numb.

GG comes flouncing. 'Where's that gorilla gone? One minute I'm trying to squeeze him into a long dark overcoat, the next he's disappeared on me. C'mon, Moth, I've seen just the thing for you.' The two head off towards more shops leaving me alone with Carrie.

Carrie turns to me, but another fight with her is the last thing I need so I turn to go.

'Wait,' she says to me.

I don't though and carry on walking.

Carrie trots to catch up with me. 'You not going to choose anything?'

'Not what I'm into right now.'

I want to catch up with Billie and ask her what's going on – it's all I can think of.

'Reva.' Carrie gets in front of me and I'll have to either stop

231

or plough right through her – which is my first choice until she puts a hand on my wrist. 'We've got to do this some time.'

'I don't even know what "this" is,' I say, desperate to get past her.

'I know you want to get to Johnson.'

This surprises me.

'You think a girl wouldn't notice?' she asks. 'Seriously?'

I almost blush. 'You've got that wrong.' But she hasn't, has she? And it seems that I'm the last person to get that I like Johnson.

'I'm glad you're not going to get what you want for once.'

I tighten immediately. It's the same old Carrie.

'You don't know that.'

'You weren't in the cubicle with him. Billie was.'

Her comment lands like a punch.

'But that's good,' Carrie continues. 'You'll understand a lot better now.'

I don't have a clue what she means, and I wish she'd get out of my way.

'You and Kyle,' she says.

'Not sure there is a me and Kyle, considering everyone's disappeared.' I make to walk away but again she gets in front of me.

'I liked him.' Her words are almost inaudible and because she's not sure I heard her she repeats it. 'A lot.'

'Kyle?'

'I saw him now and then, when he had that job in the clothes shop. I used to go in there. He was always nice to me, and I think he pretty much liked me. Something was about to happen, I'm sure it was, and next thing I know I see him with you.'

We fall silent and for the first time ever Carrie looks vulnerable.

'He rejected me, just like Johnson is going to reject you. So now you know what I feel – well *felt* – like. He doesn't know he rejected me, but when do boys ever know anything?'

'You like Kyle?' I repeat.

'Liked.'

'I never knew.'

When she sees that I had no earthly idea about this she hardens a little. 'Don't make fun of me.'

'I didn't know, I promise.'

'You must have seen I was interested in him and jumped in.'

'No.'

Carrie hesitates again. 'He would've said something.'

'You just said he didn't know.'

Carrie looks shocked. 'He didn't even mention me?'

I shake my head.

'Oh,' she says.

'I don't understand. Is that the "this" you wanted to talk about?'

Carrie is starting to look embarrassed.

'That why you hate me so much? I got the boy you wanted?'

Carrie runs a delicate finger over her bruised forehead. 'I thought . . . I thought you knew and you'd be secretly gloating . . . He didn't mention me, not at all, not ever?' She is bewildered.

I remain silent and she slaps a hand on her forehead, forgetting her bruise for a millisecond, and she yelps because she slaps it pretty hard. She staggers back and has to throw out a bony arm and balance herself on a shop window.

'Carrie.'

'I'm OK.'

But her eyes are watering from the pain and it takes her a second or two to gather herself.

'Carrie . . . He, uh, he's not that great.'

'You're just saying that.'

'The others think he's a leprechaun. And he's not that much fun, or even that bright. I liked that he was two years older than me, and that he had a Saturday job that meant he could afford to take me to the cinema. But most of all I liked him because he was the first boy who didn't talk to my chest. Other than that, he isn't as exciting as I'd hoped. You'd have spotted it soon enough.'

'You didn't,' she says bluntly.

'Yeah, but I'm stupid,' I tell her.

'Makes two of us then.'

Our eyes meet at this. 'Two idiots,' I say. 'Except you're not because you've moved on.'

'I have?'

'Duh,' I say, using one of her all-time favourite expressions. 'You'll see. Girls notice things, remember?'

Carrie studies me for a long moment. 'I'm not going to apologise for hating you.'

I can't help the smile that spreads across my lips. 'Wouldn't expect you to.'

'And this doesn't make us best buddies.'

'With you on that.'

'Boys,' she says as she moves away. 'I hate them all. Well, almost all of them.'

234

I know the feeling, I think, because I hate them all too. Until I realise I don't.

We are all sitting at a dining table big enough to seat twenty people and Billie and I have set it with glasses and plates. Carrie offered to help, but I told her to take it easy because the lump on her head doesn't look too healthy. I was going to choose some new clothes just like the others did but instead I trekked back to the honeymoon suite to retrieve my jeans and top. I guess I was avoiding seeing Johnson and Billie shopping together. But when I got up there I found that GG had already laid out a green velvet dress for me. I slipped it on and it fitted perfectly, stopping halfway to my knees. He had even found a pair of black knee length suede boots for me. When we get back home I'm going to go to him for fashion advice.

GG has cooked us all a giant lasagne in the hotel's industrial-sized oven, and we're tucking in. The Ape guzzles the lasagne, forking great mouthfuls into his gullet and washing it down with what we think is probably very expensive wine. It sloshes down his front and he somehow manages to belch even with his mouth full – Carrie immediately pushes her plate away from her.

'Gross.'

'Not want that?' The Ape doesn't even bother to wait for her reply as he grabs her plate and drags it over to him. He's wearing a huge dark overcoat that GG convinced him was the absolute best look for him – so much so that I doubt the Ape will ever take it off again.

'So, what can you tell us, Moth?' asks Johnson.

'Ah,' says the cravat- and leather jacket-wearing Moth,

who lets GG – now wearing a T-shirt and boxers under the HERS dressing gown along with the complimentary slippers and a chef's hat – sprinkle parmesan over his lasagne.

Everyone seems more relaxed after a bit of rest and food. It's probably helping that we're also pretty sure our dopplegangers aren't going to find us. But there is a nagging voice in my head that's telling me they definitely will. Because they *are* us, so if our GG headed straight to the poshest hotel in London then a Non-GG would do exactly the same thing. I'm keeping this thought to myself for now because, as GG explained, London is huge and we're like speck of sand in a concrete jungle. Besides I want us to be normal for a while. To eat and drink and talk. To be who we used to be.

'I haven't read it all,' admits the Moth. 'But I'm getting the gist, I think.'

The Ape belches again. 'Got any more?'

I watch the Ape for a moment – his hugeness seems fitting for a table this size, and he makes me think that he would fit right in at a medieval banquet. He hasn't mentioned his crushed ribs once and I make mental note to ask him about them. I'm sure he's hiding the pain from us.

'Can we stay focused please?' says Billie. She has decked herself out in a simple dress with a ton of jewellery to complement it. She has rings on every finger and wears outrageously expensive bracelets and a necklace. I think it might be to draw attention from her scarred face, but then again maybe Johnson chose them for her.

'Help yourself,' says GG to the Ape, pushing the lasagne dish towards him. 'He won't get it anyway,' he whispers behind his hand to the rest of us,

'Go on, Hawkings,' says Carrie to the Moth.

The Moth realises we are all staring at him now and are about to hang off his every word, and he becomes nervous. 'I'm going to start with the facts. First one being the other versions have come from somewhere not unlike where we're from. They know this world as well as we do, it's just as familiar.'

'I could've told you that,' says Billie, disappointed. She is sitting beside Johnson and there's a closeness to them that I'm trying to ignore. He's found another pair of tight jeans and a crisp white shirt that has the top three buttons undone. I am trying so hard not to look at him.

'But they have evolved in a different way,' continues the Moth.

'They're aliens then?' asks Carrie.

'Aliens, zombies, vampires. Told you,' the Ape says to no one in particular, his mouth crammed with lasagne.

'They're alien to us. But I don't think they're aliens. Which is a big difference.'

'Clones?' asks GG. 'If I saw me I'd want to clone me. Hundreds of times over.' He giggles. 'The world would be such a beautiful place.'

The Ape pours more wine for himself and it glops loudly into his glass. The Moth waits for him to finish before carrying on.

'In the scientific paper he wrote, Rev's dad claims he opened a door in our world and walked through it. He had been working on something called the multiverse theory.' The Ape's slurping and munching is drowning out half of what the Moth is saying.

'Ape,' I say.

He looks over, sees that everyone is looking at him. 'What?'

The Moth starts again, talking a little louder as the Ape ploughs through the lasagne.

'The multiverse theory postulates that hundreds of Earths exist side by side. It's a hypothetical set of infinite parallel universes. Well, it was hypothetical until Rev's dad proved it wasn't.'

'Are we in one now?' Johnson asks.

'I think that, somehow, our original one sort of gave birth to this one.'

'Who's the father?' GG can't help himself, but then gets a dark look from Carrie and falls quiet again.

The Moth continues. 'Your dad opened the gateway and came here, Rev. He wrote down how he did it, and how it's a world with no one in it. A carbon copy of our world, minus the people. A place that runs directly alongside ours from the exact moment you enter it.'

'You lost me on "postulates",' quips GG, already confused.

The Moth clears his throat. 'Maybe I'm not explaining it clearly enough.' He pauses and then starts reading from my dad's pages, as if this will make it easier for all of us to understand. 'In nineteen hundred, a physicist called Max Planck introduced the concept of quantum physics after his study of radiation yielded some unusual findings that contradicted the universally accepted physical laws. His findings suggested that there are other laws at work in the universe, operating on a much deeper and reality-challenging level than the ones we know. Hence the idea of parallel universes where wars may have different outcomes, or species evolve and adapt differently. The worlds are twisted echoes of ours. This was just a theory, but not any more. Because I have found some of them.' The Moth looks up from the page expectantly.

'That's all a load of big words to me, Hawkings. All I want to know is how the hell do we get out of it, this parallel world or whatever?' says Billie.

'And how did we even get in it?' asks Carrie.

'I'm still reading. For now that's all I've got.'

'So your dad did this to us?' Carrie isn't as accusing as she could be but all eyes immediately fall on me as if I'm to blame.

The Moth clears his throat to try and get the attention back on him. 'The main thing though is that everyone else hasn't disappeared. We have.'

A big heavy lead weight of silence descends. I can feel it pressing me down into my chair.

'We're not where we were?' Carrie states.

'I don't think so,' says the Moth, almost apologetically.

'We were moved?' asks Billie, who looks ready to implode and Johnson slips a hand onto her arm for comfort. I immediately look away.

Our moment in the hotel room had started to gently ease the Other-Johnson away from me, but now it looks like whatever happened between us didn't mean what I thought it did . . . Johnson likes Billie and it's becoming more painful by the second.

'So our home world is still there?' GG asks. 'My dad and mum are still alive?' He claps his hands and lets out a whoop. 'Well that's something!'

'But who moved us and why?' asks Johnson.

The Ape is about to refill his glass when Carrie snatches the bottle from him. 'I'm trying to listen!'

'Listen to what?' The Ape couldn't care less. 'We're here, everything's free and we can do what we like. What's the problem?'

239

Carrie takes the bottle and necks the wine straight down, glugging quickly. When she stops she finds us all looking at her. 'What? Who wouldn't need a drink after hearing all that!'

The Moth taps the table, again trying to keep us all focused. 'I have no idea why we're here but it happened after we heard the fire alarm and then there was the white light.'

Johnson takes a moment to compose a thought. 'The fire alarm.'

We wait for more.

'The burned man.' He furrows his brow a little as he processes his thoughts. 'What if they're connected? What if that fire alarm went off because the burned man had tried to come through to our world in the school? That's why everyone was shouting, the hallway was on fire.'

'He wasn't coming through,' says the Moth. 'He was shifting us to here.'

Silence is a strange thing when it happens. You don't realise how much noise is actually going on until there isn't any. Voices and cutlery on plates, the Ape belching, even someone's breathing – when all of that stops, that's when you know what silence really sounds like.

It's eerie and it's jam-packed with fear. Not the fear of anything specific, more the fear of the unknown. The question that no one wants to answer hangs in that silence like a dead man on a gallows. I'm only being ultra descriptive because the silence is expanding and I can't think of anything to say that will break into it. No one can.

'Cool.'

It's the Ape – isn't it always? – who smashes the delicate moment apart.

'I'm liking this guy!'

'Your dad brought us here?' Billie is the first to speak.

'Why would he do that?' Carrie asks/accuses.

'My dad just texts me if he wants to see me,' offers GG.

'I'm not saying that's definitely what happened,' the Moth counters.

'But you're pretty sure it is, aren't you?' Billie says. 'This is Rev's dad's fault, isn't it?' She says this to the rest of the group, as if I'm not there, or worth including. I'm already the enemy in her eyes.

Eyes that turned black I remind myself.

'When did your dad go missing?' Johnson is calm but there's no escaping the shock he's trying to suppress. I can sense it on him.

'Twelve years ago. When she was four.' Billie is answering for me, again behaving as if I'm not present in the room.

'And he could've . . . well, he could've found another world and not been able to come back.'

'I—' That's all I get to to say because Billie cuts right across me.

'So finally he does find his way back, but in coming through, he makes a mess of things and we get shifted to here. Moth? What d'you think? Is that possible?'

The Moth takes a moment, wants desperately to give the right answer. But it's also an impossible answer to give. 'I haven't read enough yet,' he says quietly.

'So read more.' Billie is much more assertive than I have ever seen her.

Johnson takes her in and I know for certain that he likes this tougher persona.

'So why didn't we get shifted again when he did finally

come through outside Tesco's?' Carrie asks, and for once I'm glad of her. Because I know they're all thinking it, that I have somehow been the catalyst for this nightmare. And what's worse is, I'm thinking it as well.

I can't feel anything, apart from a massive and sudden migraine as my head throbs. 'That can't be,' I say barely audibly. 'It can't.' Tears are welling in my eyes and I try and hold them back as my throat swells. 'No. Not possible. He's long gone. Why would he want to find me? Why now? No. That can't be.' My teary eyes find Johnson's again. 'Can it?'

Johnson keeps it gentle. 'We're just thinking aloud, Rev, making connections. Everything has connections, right?'

'It's *her* dad, Rev Two. W-we all know that,' I stammer.

'We don't really know anything,' offers the Moth. 'And none of this explains why the other versions of us are here as well, but I'll keep reading,' he declares with as much care as he can. 'I'll work it all out, and once I do, we can go home.' They are brave and proud words and I know the Moth is trying to keep us all sane, but I'm still too numb to really take it in. Someone who could be my dad has been looking for me? For twelve years? He didn't run away without a word, he literally disappeared into thin air and he's been tramping through the multiverse trying to find a way back ever since. *All those worlds*, I think, *and he kept going because he wanted to see me and Mum again*. I have no idea how he'll explain any of this to her, but that isn't really the point. He's trying to come home and that's all that matters.

'Just get us back, Moth.' Billie has leaned back into Johnson so that he is half forced to prop her up.

'Yeah, take us home, Hawkings. Be my hero.' The slightly drunk Carrie pats the Moth's arm in encouragement.

Johnson shifts in his seat and to Billie's annoyance he gently sits her up straighter. 'But how can we leave without Rev's dad?'

'*If* it's her dad. The other Rev thought it was *her* dad, so she can take him home.' Billie is again talking without looking at me.

'But what if it isn't?' Johnson looks directly at me – into me. 'We can't leave without him, not after he's this close.'

Johnson is so spectacularly right and I want to go over and hug him. I'm not leaving without my dad, though from the looks on everyone else's faces they don't seem to agree.

'He was burned to a crisp, I don't think he'll be going anywhere,' says Billie and again there's harshness in her tone.

I catch her eye and she must see she's overstepped the mark because she quickly tries to compensate.

'OK, OK. How about this? We'll come back for him,' she adds. 'Once the Moth has figured out how it all works, Rev can zip back here, with an ambulance crew if necessary.'

I can't believe Billie just said that. An ambulance crew? Was that a joke? *This is my father*, I want to yell at her. But is it even *her*? I need to get her alone, to tell her about her eyes turning black, to warn her that something is happening to her and she isn't the Billie I know.

'D'you think they could shift an ambulance?' Billie continues, but no one is listening – they're all too focused on the awkwardness of her joke. If it is a joke.

Another round of silence pins us all to our seats and the only person who is unaffected by it is the Ape who shoves his empty plate away from him and looks to GG. 'Got any ice cream?'

GG gives him a wide-eyed excited look. 'So glad you asked. I made a pavlova.'

'What's that?'

'You'll see.'

GG pads off to the kitchen.

'Why don't you come and sit here with me?' the Ape suggests to Billie.

'You're actually talking to me?' Billie asks.

'Later you can see the room I chose.'

Billie gives him a dark piercing look. 'Guess what. It's a no thanks.'

'You're just saying that.'

Billie seems to be making damn sure Johnson knows that there is nothing between her and the Ape. I wonder if she is haunted by the Non-Ape and Another-Billie's apparent 'relationship'.

'I'm just saying what every girl you've ever asked out says to you.'

The Ape shrugs. 'I do very good with the ladies.'

'You do nothing. And you know why? Because you're stupid, fat and disgusting.'

'Billie,' I say, trying to keep her calm.

But Billie isn't finished yet. 'Don't defend him! I was in a changing room and he pulled the curtain back to take a peek. Perv!'

'And you weren't alone,' I say, almost too quickly.

'So?' Billie is shouting now. 'That's not the point.'

'If Johnson was allowed in then how come I wasn't?' asks the Ape.

'Because some things are private, you oaf!'

I'm not sure I want to hear any more.

'She wanted help with a zip,' Johnson says to everyone, but his eyes stay on me – but I don't believe him.

'So why close the curtain?' The Ape is making it all the more painful for me without realising it.

'Because,' says Billie.

The whole table wants to hear why now. That is, everyone except me. I remain staring down at my plate.

'Because what?' Carrie just has to know.

'Because I . . .' Billie falters. 'Because maybe I . . .'

I can feel her looking over at me and she must be wondering why I'm not looking at her.

'Maybe I pulled the curtain across, OK?' Which is all she needs to reveal, because everyone is getting the picture now. I lift my head a little to see Johnson looking straight at me. So Billie called him into the cubicle and then pulled the curtain closed behind them – no need to ask what she was planning.

The Ape belches again. 'That's what I think of that,' he tells Billie.

Billie looks like she's about to lose it completely. Clearly she was going to try something with Johnson, and the Ape loomed up and ruined it for her.

And there it is again, just a millisecond, but her eyes flicker to blackness. Like a lizard's blink but even quicker. They flick again, blazing blue then black then blazing Irish blue again.

'I've had it with you,' she screams at the Ape. 'I'm done being around you. And you know why, *Ape*? Because you're hideous. You're ugly and a slob. There's no one in this world, or our world, or any other world come to that, who would want anything to do with you.'

'Billie, enough,' I warn.

Billie gets to her feet and looms over the Ape who has fallen silent in the face of her onslaught. 'Get the message. We don't want you here. No one does. You're not one of us. You should find somewhere else, another universe, because *we* do not want anything to do with *you*!'

Her eyes flicker once more and in the darkness is another darkness. Something from a deeply unsettled soul.

'You need to understand that there is no room for you anywhere. Even in an empty world there is just no room for an Ape. So why don't you take your simian self up to your room, lock the door behind you and never come out again. We'll leave you here. You said you liked this world right, so here's your big chance. When I get back I'll go round to your mum's and tell her you won't be coming back, like ever. I'll take a bottle of champagne and we'll celebrate together.'

The Ape looks down at his empty plate and opens his mouth, looks set to say something, but then stops and closes his mouth again.

'Ape.' Johnson can see he is hurt.

The Ape doesn't respond.

'Billie didn't mean that, we're all just on edge,' I say.

The Ape slowly gets to his feet. He is still looking down at his plate as if it holds all the answers. 'I got this,' he says very quietly.

'Ape, c'mon, sit down,' says Carrie. 'Pudding's coming.' Even she seems to be surprised by Billie's harshness.

'I'm good,' he mumbles.

'Ape, sit back down,' encourages Johnson. 'Tell him, Billie, tell him you didn't mean that.'

246

'Every word,' she says straight to the Ape. 'I meant every single word.'

'In the car you said you needed me,' the Ape says, before stopping to compile the rest of his thoughts. Billie has turned completely away from him, so he has to speak to the back of her head. 'That's what you said. Driving and doing violence. You needed me for that.'

'We needed you then. We don't now.'

With that the Ape nods his great head. 'OK,' he says, and then with a self-conscious rub of his bruised chest he lumbers slowly away from the dinner table. I glance at Billie, who is unremitting in her rage and hatred.

'You didn't need to say that,' I tell her.

'C'mon, Rev, you find him just as annoying as the rest of us do.'

'Go after him,' I say.

'You go after him.'

I turn and see the Ape hovering at the door, possibly hoping for some nice words from Billie that will make everything all right again. But when none come he turns and slopes humbly away. I get to my feet to go after him.

'I just said what you're all thinking,' she says defiantly. Her horrendous attack has confirmed that I don't think this is any Billie I've ever known.

'No, you're not. *I'm* not thinking that. He saved us.'

'Twice,' adds Johnson.

'All he did was commit gross violence. It just so happened we got some benefit from it.' Billie folds her arms in front of her.

'I'm going to go see him,' I say, despite her. I have no idea where my best friend has gone.

'Uh, there was one more thing,' says the Moth, his nasally voice echoing through the empty dining hall.

I want to go after the Ape, but Johnson stretches out a leg and pushes my chair out for me so I can sit back down. It's a simple movement but it's one that tells me he wants me here, where he can see me. 'Be quick, Moth,' I tell him.

'It's just a thought, but if this other Billie can heal people like you say, then if she brings the burned man back to life then he could feasibly take us home. And that's all of us, the other usses as well.'

'Usses? Is that even a word?' says Billie in that hard tone. 'And I'm not going back through any flames, because it seems to me that Rev's dad doesn't actually know what he's doing, considering he's been wandering around lost for so many years, and then when he does find what he's looking for he goes and gets himself burned to death. C'mon, the man's seriously not the answer here. If he was, the other usses wouldn't need the Moth, would they?'

The man is my father, I think, and Billie's basically calling him an idiot. *Who are you, Billie? What the hell have you become?*

The Moth stalls but then tries to get back on track. 'But maybe with his theories and me helping, then maybe there's a way.'

'I'm not spending the next twelve years on a maybe.'

'Nice try, Hawkings,' says Carrie slurping the last of the red wine. But it's said with a smile and the Moth smiles back. Yeah, there's definitely something building between them.

GG waltzes back through with his pavlova. 'Ta da!' He then looks around and sees that the Ape has gone. 'Where's the gorilla?'

No one answers because we're all still a little embarrassed by Billie's attack on him.

'Hello?' GG says in his sing-song voice. 'Anyone want pavlova? I spent ages on this.'

GG starts cutting up the pavlova and dishing it out. He's fussing around us, trying to be maternal and paternal all rolled into one. He's no longer wearing his chef's hat – it must have fallen off in the kitchen.

Carrie finds the sight of the rich creamy pavlova too much for her alcohol fuelled stomach and pushes away from the table. She gets unsteadily to her feet, her face looking a little green. 'I've drunk too much. Need some air.'

'Be very careful if you go outside,' says the Moth.

'I will.'

'Don't stray too far,' he adds – their eyes meet and I know Kyle is already a distant memory for Carrie.

'If you see the Ape—' I begin.

'I'll drag him back.' She looks at me and it seems finally we have found a moment's peace between us. The war's over. She senses it too as she nods to me and then heads for the door before stopping and, just like the Ape did a few minutes ago, turning back to the table. 'I really want to go home.' She looks at the Moth though and there's a kindness there, a sense of care and warmth for him. 'So take me home, Hawkings. Promise me.'

The Moth nods, sits up taller and tries to look convincing. 'Course I will.'

'Thank you,' she whispers before turning and leaving the room.

We watch her and her footsteps are faint and delicate and it's as if she can barely make an impression she is so light.

'Pavlova?' asks GG, trying to cut through the ugly thick atmosphere. 'Anyone? Mm?'

He's not going to get an answer, which is just as well because he isn't really expecting one.

'Maybe someone should make sure she doesn't wander off too far,' I say.

'I'm on it.' GG hurries off after Carrie. 'I'll guard her with my life,' he says dramatically and is out of the door in an instant.

The Moth engages reverse on his wheelchair. 'I should finish reading.'

'How much more is there?' Johnson asks the Moth. 'Only I don't like that we're sitting ducks. Assuming they find us.'

'They'll never do that.' Billie is convinced of this. 'We could barely find you. Mind you the Ape was driving.' She hiccups. 'What a waste of time and space he is.'

'I'll get on it,' promises the Moth.

But as he heads for the great dining-room doors a long piercing scream stops him dead.

It echoes shrilly throughout the vast hotel – a scream of great pain and anguish. And as we turn to the restaurant door GG staggers back in, eyes bulging in holy terror.

'He's here.'

'Who?'

'Me. I'm here. I've found us.' He holds up his hands which are covered in blood. Not his blood though.

'Carrie's,' he says simply.

PRESS BUTTON MARKED HELL

We race past the stunned GG and find Carrie lying in the marble-floored reception area. She is bleeding from wounds that have punctured her all over. Even before we reach her, I know she is dead.

'Carrie?' Johnson gets to her first, turns her over. 'Carrie?'

Carrie's red-wine lips have already turned grey. Her eyes are open and staring and a halo of blood spreads behind her head.

The Moth whirrs up to get a better look and lets out an anguished cry. GG is shaking behind us, a trembling mess.

'What happened?' I say to him.

He has fallen mute and can't seem to answer.

'GG!' I urge him.

'GG, say something.' Billie joins me.

GG eventually looks at us and can barely find his voice. 'It was me. I did it.'

'No,' I tell him. 'It was the other GG.'

'Evil-GG,' adds Billie, as I turn back to Johnson who reaches over Carrie and closes her eyes. The Moth isn't crying, but he looks totally and utterly bereft as he stares at Carrie's body.

'Where is he?' I ask GG. 'Where's the other you?'

'Was me,' says GG, still shaking.

'GG, please. Where did he go? You saw him, right? If the others are nearby then we need to make a plan, and fast.'

GG falls silent, seemingly unable to answer, and I look all around for any sign of Evil-GG.

'We need the Ape,' I say to him, and then glance accusingly at Billie.

'Don't,' she says. 'Don't you dare make out this is my fault.'

Johnson is still scanning the huge expanse of marble lobby stretching out in all directions around us.

'GG, where did the other you go?' I ask again.

GG opens and closes his mouth but no words come. He's just staring at the dead Carrie and then looks down to his bloodied hands.

'Where did he go?' repeats the Moth, who whirrs over to us. We have formed a human circle, all of us facing one corner of the reception area.

'What?' GG looks lost, totally blank.

'Where the hell is he?' shouts Billie.

'I dunno,' he says. 'Was too fast. I think he went outside. I think that's what he did.'

We fall silent and I can tell the Moth is heartbroken just from the way he can't take his eyes off Carrie. There's a vicious creature in the hotel and all he can do is stare forlornly at the lifeless bony shape on the floor.

'Moth,' I say, but he doesn't respond. 'Moth. Come on.'

GG is backing towards the lifts with Billie. 'We should take the lift up to another floor,' he suggests.

'No way,' I tell him.

'We go up, find a room, lock it, make a plan. There's hundreds of rooms in this hotel. He won't be able to find us.' GG is starting to sound more sensible than at any time I have ever known him. He's not nearly the flake he pretends he is.

I look to Johnson to see what he thinks.

Johnson weighs it up. 'GG's right – we're too vulnerable out here.'

'So let's go,' urges GG. 'Before he comes back.'

I look back to the main entrance to the hotel lobby and I hate to think what might be out there waiting for us.

'He was so fast,' says GG, seeing my hesitation. 'We wouldn't even know he was here before he attacks.'

Johnson looks to the Moth. 'Moth, move.'

The Moth is reluctant. 'What's the point? What can we do? They will get us anyway.'

'I'll phone the Ape. Get him to come back. He'll fight them off,' I tell him.

'We're dead,' says the Moth despondently. 'We're all dead. If he's found us, the others won't be far behind. Including that Non-Ape. Why won't they leave us alone?'

Johnson and I share a reluctant look. The Moth sees it.

'What? What is it?'

'Nothing,' says Johnson.

'Forget it,' I add.

'So it is something, because if it was nothing I wouldn't have anything to forget, would I.'

The Moth is too intuitive for his own good. He holds my look. 'Tell me.'

I look to Johnson and he smiles ruefully. 'It's you. They want you. They haven't got their Moth so they want our one.'

'You're the only one who seems to knows anything,' I add. 'The only one they think will be able to get them home.'

The Moth allows this to settle for a moment. Then he sucks in a deep breath and gives me one of the bravest looks I've ever seen.

'Let me go to them.'

'What? No!'

'I'm who they want. They'll leave you alone then.'

'We do that and we're stuck here forever.' Johnson is clear on this.

'If it's a coin flip between being here and being dead, I know which one I'd take,' offers the Moth, his eyes unable to leave Carrie

We don't have time for this. I know that Moth is hurting, but the others could be here any minute and I don't want to be sitting in the lobby when they arrive. Not wanting any more discussion, I start wheeling the Moth back towards the lifts.

'Leave me alone!' he yells and tries to jab the brakes on.

I ignore him and together with GG we back towards the four lifts. Johnson stabs all of the buttons and we wait for the first one to arrive.

'Rev, I don't want this any more,' says the Moth. 'Look at me, what good am I?'

'You're the most important person in the world,' I tell him, echoing Johnson. 'And I'm going to protect you at all costs.'

I keep scanning the lobby while the lifts take forever to return to the ground floor.

GG is still trembling. 'He's coming. I can feel it.'

My shoulders are tingling like crazy. The inbuilt spider sense is screaming at me. Evil-GG is close, I know he is. The elevator pings behind us and I almost jump out of my skin. The reflective metallic doors take an eternity to open and I half expect Evil-GG to be inside waiting for us. But the elevator is empty and we bundle in, despite the Moth's protests.

'We can't just leave Carrie lying there,' the Moth says.

'She's gone,' Johnson tells him as the elevator doors slowly close. 'I'm sorry but she has, Moth.' He hits the button for the penthouse floor.

The mirrors in the elevator reveal our scared faces many times over and we all look washed out, and way too near the end of our own personal lines. Johnson's eyes find mine. 'We're going to have to make weapons,' he says.

'We going to make a stand?'

'And we're going to beat them.'

GG is wiping his bloodied hands on the front of his jeans. 'Got to get rid of this,' he says. 'It's icky.'

I smile through my fear. The same old GG, despite everything.

'Red is so not my colour.'

I lean back against the bank of buttons, trying to take stock. What sort of weapons does Johnson expect to find in the penthouse?

'You OK, Moth?' GG asks.

'Oh yeah, I've never been better.' The Moth is fighting back his tears.

'Good Moth, keep it up.' GG somehow ekes out a reassuring smile.

255

As he does I catch sight of something in the never-ending reflections that are all around us.

As GG smiles he reveals a glint of metal in his mouth.

Just like Non-Lucas did.

My heart freezes.

This isn't our GG.

'Ca-can you still feel him?' I ask him. 'The other GG?"

He stops trying to wipe the blood away and takes a moment to try and sense Evil-GG, or at least pretend to. 'No,' he says.

'Good,' I say. 'Good.' I add a smile that I know is fractured at best.

I turn to Johnson as the elevator keeps rising. 'This is taking ages.'

'Forty floors,' he says.

'Forty,' I repeat and then try to open my eyes wider so he can see I'm trying to get a message to him. But he doesn't understand and looks away. I glance back at Evil-GG. This must be delighting him no end. I bet he can barely stand to keep up the pretence before blowing his brilliant ruse.

If he's anything like the real GG he'll do it in the medium of song.

'What weapons?' I say nervously. 'What you got in mind?' I'm trying desperately to get Johnson's attention again. 'What weapons, Johnson?'

Billie gives me a nervous look. 'Rev.'

'Yeah?'

'You're babbling.'

'Am I?' I ask Johnson, thinking *Please look at me.* 'Am I babbling, Johnson?'

Johnson turns to me and again I try and widen my eyes

so he can sense that I'm really trying to tell him something else.

Then a thought hits me, a fragment of memory. 'GG?' I ask.

'Yeah?'

'You said you got detention for flirting with the games teacher.'

Evil-GG falls silent, which is probably unusual for any GG in any world. He cocks his head to one side as he scrutinises me. For a second I think he's going to attack me, but then he grins, full of himself.

'It was more the other way round. And who can blame him?'

I'm hoping Johnson is cottoning on now.

He frowns when he catches sight of my wide-open eyes again. Then it dawns on him. Our GG was warned for flirting with the *maths* teacher.

The lift keeps rising. Slowly, almost painfully so, I make a point of moving my eyes slowly in the direction of Evil-GG.

Johnson follows my lead and flicks his eyes towards Evil-GG. I'm praying that Evil-GG doesn't see us doing this in the reflection from the mirrors in the lift.

Johnson waits for more and I gently lift my right index finger and pretend to rub my bottom lip with it. But what I'm trying to say is *Look at the mouth. Look at the metal in Evil-GG's mouth*.

Johnson gives nothing away. He studies me as the lift keeps ascending through the floors. But then, after a moment, he gives me the tiniest of nods. It's barely more than a gentle rock of his head.

I look to Billie and the Moth and they remain oblivious. The Moth has retreated into his grief and shock, and given his outburst earlier I wonder if he might welcome having Evil-GG riding in the lift with us. He's already lost two people he cared about and I'm not far behind him in his despair, but the thought of what this murderous Evil GG just did to Carrie hardens my resolve. She may have been a colossal bitch, but she was *our* colossal bitch. I grit my teeth and feel my muscles tightening. I'm not sure what he did with our GG or when he made the switch, but I'm guessing that he's lying dead in the kitchen way below us. I should have sensed something when he made the switch – how could we not have noticed?

But it's too late now. We're locked in our own ready-made coffin. The lift reaches floor twenty and I have no idea what we're going to do when it reaches the top floor.

'Wonder where the Ape is,' I say, racking my brains for something positive to hang on to. 'Think he went out of the hotel?'

'Doubt it,' says Johnson who is trying his best not to look too closely at Evil-GG in case he gives the game away.

'You think he might be close by?' I ask. It's so clumsy what I'm trying to do. 'Maybe waiting for us when the doors open.'

'He will be. Knowing the Ape,' says Johnson.

'He knows how to kill them.' My voice is cracking and I can't help it. 'He's lethal.'

'Yeah.'

Billie looks from me to Johnson and back again. 'Why are you both talking like that?'

'Like what?'

'Like robots.'

'We're just chatting,' says Johnson.

'Chatting?' The Moth stirs from his deep despondency. 'Chatting? After what just happened to Carrie! What is wrong with you two?'

'We all have different ways of coping,' I say weakly, silently begging them both to just shut up.

I feel Evil-GG slowly shift his stance beside me.

'I don't even want to be in this lift,' says the Moth.

'Who does?' I say and then hope to God I haven't given myself away.

Evil-GG shifts again. It's the tiniest movement, but he has fallen too quiet now. The real GG doesn't do quiet. Not ever.

We hit floor thirty and continue rising.

I look around the sleek mirrored interior and there is nothing that remotely resembles anything that we could turn into a weapon.

Evil-GG's breathing slows, his fake hysteria of before has all but left him.

Johnson stretches his arms and when I catch his eye he immediately looks down to his feet. I follow his gaze. Half hidden in a small recess behind his skinny calves is a mini fire extinguisher.

'You're quiet,' Billie tells Evil-GG.

'Wouldn't you be?' he responds. But the lightness of his voice has gone.

'Yeah, sorry. It's just we've seen so much,' she says. 'I'm becoming immune. Is that the right word? Immune? Is it? Moth? What's the word I'm thinking of?'

But the Moth has fallen silent as well and his eyes are fixed on a spot about a metre away from his eye level.

259

I follow his stricken gaze and realise that he has spotted Evil-GG's talons sliding out.

'Moth?' presses Billie. 'Is it immune?'

The Moth's eyes leave the talons and rise the length of Evil-GG's body until they meet Evil-GG's. The moment plays out in a thousand reflections as Evil-GG straightens a little, and I instinctively take a step away from him, which isn't easy in a confined space.

'Oh, no,' moans the Moth.

'Oh, yessy yes,' says Evil-GG.

Johnson is tensing as Evil-GG shakes off the last of his fake panic and horror with a little wave of his taloned fingers.

'Guess who?'

Billie realises a second later than the Moth does. 'Oh my God.'

'I should be an actor. That was Oscar-winning,' boasts Evil-GG.

The lift soars past floor thirty-six.

'So glad I've got you all gathered here,' says Evil-GG who suddenly slams the STOP button and the lift lurches to a shuddering halt.

'How? I mean – how?' Billie backs away until she is pressed up against one of the mirrors.

'I knew my clone would come here. It's exactly where I'd go. Isn't it lush?'

We're all backing away from Evil-GG now. But in the small space of the lift, there's no real place to back away to.

'Five stars! Did you read the brochure? They clean your room three times a day.'

I look to Johnson as we fan apart as best we can from Evil-GG. We have no weapons, no Ape, nothing.

'Three times a day, Moth. In they come, in they clean, in they come again. What's not to love?'

Billie is already folding in on herself, sinking to her knees. 'I can't do this any more. I can't,' she whimpers.

Evil-GG looks at her with a gentle pity. 'Imagine being locked in this little cell with me. And I'm the worst of the lot,' he tells her. 'I am. I'm just plain wicked.'

The Moth reverses his wheelchair and inadvertently runs over my foot. 'Moth!'

The movement takes Evil-GG's attention and Johnson makes his move. He grabs up the mini fire extinguisher and swings it as hard as he can at Evil-GG.

Evil-GG isn't expecting it and the blow sends him crashing to the floor.

'Out! Out now!' Johnson screams and I jab the OPEN button and the lift jolts upwards towards the next floor.

Evil-GG is already shaking off the blow as Johnson hits him again, harder than before.

The lift glides to a stop at floor thirty-eight and the doors start to open. Evil-GG springs to his feet and we see his talons unsheathe fully from his fingers. These look more deadly than the others. Sharper, honed to the finest sharpest points. He waggles them at us.

'I spend hours on my nails.' He moves and positions himself between us and the corridor outside the lift. 'I think this is your stop,' he grins as he rises to his full height. 'Well, in a manner of speaking.'

Johnson swings again with the fire extinguisher, but Evil-GG is ready this time and with unbelievable speed he catches the fire extinguisher and rips it out of Johnson's hand. He tosses it behind his shoulder and it bounces down

261

the landing. 'And I thought we were all becoming such friends.' Evil-GG licks his lips. 'Now who wants to die first and who wants to watch? Shall we have a vote? Shall we? Hands up who wants to die first?'

Out of the corner of my eye I see the Moth slam his wheel-chair into drive and whirr forward. It's not fast, but he doesn't have far to go as he barrels straight into Evil-GG. 'How about you?' he screams.

Evil-GG is so busy lording it over us that he isn't prepared for the Moth's attack. He sticks out a hand, but the Moth rams him, ploughing him straight out of the lift.

'GO!' the Moth screams and it takes me half a second to process what he means. I slam the DOWN button and the doors start to close.

Evil-GG swipes the Moth clean out of his wheelchair, sending him cartwheeling down the hallway. 'Oops,' Evil-GG says, realising that he's meant to be kidnapping and not killing the Moth. 'Got a little carried away, but you just wait there, oh Mothman of mine.'

Evil-GG turns and sees the doors closing and leaps faster than anything I have ever seen. But like Moth Two with the train, he arrives a microsecond too late and the doors close before he can reach us.

We start descending and I'm already trying to calculate how long it will take to reach the bottom floor.

'Do they go down quicker than they come up?' I ask Johnson. 'They should, right?' I say trying to keep the panic out of my voice. 'Should be easier and therefore faster, yeah?'

'What does it matter – did you see how fast he moved?' Billie is still on the floor with her knees drawn up. 'He'll be down those stairs in seconds. He'll be there when the doors open. Then what are we going to do? Go all the way back up again. Then down again. Then up again. That the plan? Up and down, up and down till he's all worn out?'

I squat down in front of Billie and take her hands in mine. 'The plan is to survive.'

'And we're doing great with that.'

I glance at Johnson.

'I want to go home,' she says. 'That's all. I just want to go back home.' All trace of her earlier, darker side has fled from her. It's as if her fear has overpowered her alien – well, to me anyway – traits.

'And that's going to happen,' Johnson tells her. 'Promise you. But we've got to get through this first.'

I glance at the lights moving down through the floor numbers then stand up and hit the button for the thirteenth floor.

'Rev?' Johnson senses I'm planning something.

I hit the button for the ninth floor and then the fifth. The lift is already slowing as it reaches the thirteenth floor.

'OK,' I whisper, imagining that Evil-GG has amazing hearing as well. 'We all get out on different floors.'

'Are you kidding me!?' Billie wails.

'Listen to me. If we split up, maybe one or two of us can grab the Moth and escape with him.'

'No. No way, Rev,' she says.

The lift stops at floor thirteen.

'Billie, he's going to get one of us, but he's *not* going to get all three,' I tell her.

Johnson watches the doors silently open. 'Whoever gets out of here, contact the Ape and then make sure you grab the Moth and get home.'

263

'While he's hunting us down, one of us has to go back up and get Hawkings?' Billie looks panicked.

'I'm going to make some noise, see if that distracts him. I'll keep him occupied as long as I can,' I tell her.

Johnson looks at me as the doors start to close. I snake out a foot and stop them. 'Rev,' he says quietly.

'Yeah?'

'Don't get caught.'

'Don't intend to.' But of course I do expect to be hunted down, and we all know that, but it's the only way some of us will get home.

Johnson grabs me and hugs me as tight as he can and the feeling behind the hug melts whatever indifference I was feeling away completely. Other-Johnson finally evaporates from my insides and I feel Johnson so acutely it takes all of my willpower to let him go. He looks into my eyes and I think our first kiss is finally coming when he bends down and gives Billie a similar hug. This is life or death now – there's just no time for a kiss.

'Stay safe,' he says and then darts out of the lift.

'I'm going to call all the lifts,' he says. 'Evil-GG might think we've switched, jumped in one of the other ones.' The doors slide closed and I feel a huge wrench as he disappears from sight.

The lift drops further, heading for the ninth floor.

'I'm not going out there,' whimpers Billie. 'I'm not.'

'You've got to, Billie.'

The lift stops at floor nine.

She gulps and I help pull her to her feet as the doors open. 'Be quiet. Be careful. If you get through to the Ape tell him you're sorry.'

'Why do you even care about that beast?'

'Dunno. But I do,' I tell her.

We hug and then after making sure she can't see Evil-GG lurking, Billie slips gingerly out onto the ninth floor landing.

The doors close and I stand in silence as I head for floor five. I'm hoping my plan works, that Evil-GG will go straight down to the lobby and not think for a second we'll try and outwit him. He'll be standing there probably filing his nails, maybe whistling or doing a little Irish jig, because he is so full of his own wonder and self-adoration.

The lift comes to a gentle halt.

Floor five.

I brace myself. There's no way Evil-GG will be expecting this, I tell myself. But I should be close enough for him to be able to hear me.

The doors open.

I wait, listening for the faintest sound. There's nothing. I peer out of the lift. The floor is empty. I take a step. Then another.

There's a wooden plaque on the wall directing people to the stairwell in an emergency. Whoever put it there probably didn't have this in mind when they were contemplating emergencies. I strain hard to see if I can hear Evil-GG.

Again there's silence.

The closest I've ever been to a hotel like this is watching *Gossip Girl* and I try to rack my brains. Do the staff have their own lifts? Isn't there a laundry chute? Or am I just imagining that these things would exist? Whatever, I need to drag this chase out as long as I can.

I tiptoe away from the direction of the stairwell. I have to be smart about this, to make it look as close as I can to someone trying desperately not to be heard. But I tiptoe heavily, if there is such a thing.

I walk quickly; the thick plush carpet under my feet gives little away and I'm not so sure I will be heard. I round a corner and stop. Did I hear something? I look down the landing but all I can see are a series of evenly spaced doors leading to rooms that are furnished in ways me and my mum could only ever dream of at home.

I carry on, slower this time, trying to make it seem like I'm being as quiet as I can. There's no hiding place anywhere, so I need Evil-GG to come looking for one, giggling to himself about how hopeless I am. It may even slow him down as he savours the hunt.

Something creaks above my head and I instinctively look up. There's another creak and I realise that someone is on the floor above me.

It could be Johnson or Billie.

Or it could be Evil-GG deciding to check out every floor.

I'm imagining that he reached the lobby and was met by an empty lift. That wouldn't have pleased him and he'd then work out that we got out on another floor.

There's another creak above me.

It can't be him, I think. I'm not being logical. He'd start off on the first floor and work his way up. He can't already be above me because I'd have seen him.

I move away, breaking into a light-footed trot. But again, just heavy enough to give myself away.

There has to be some other way out of this hotel. A fire escape or something. Anything that will lead him out into the streets while Johnson and/or Billie grab the Moth.

Whoever's above me is matching their footsteps to my own.

It has to be Billie. She must have moved quickly to a different floor.

I speed up because I'm pretty sure that Evil-GG will be systematically checking every floor now. From the ground up. He has to be below me.

The footsteps overhead carry on down the hall as I crouch down and try to listen through the carpet. I have to put my ear to the floor, but when I do I immediately hear movement. Something is moving incredibly fast along the fourth-floor hallway.

Evil-GG is coming at speed and he's coming my way.

THE EVIL THAT GGS DO

I start trying the doors of the rooms on the floor, but it's pointless because all of them are locked. Even if I was to somehow miraculously force one open, Evil-GG would spot the damage and be on me in a heartbeat. But that would make it too quick anyway. He'd tear me apart in seconds and I've got to make this last minutes.

He bounds at speed until I hear the door to the stairwell crash open below me. He's moving up to my floor.

I break into a sprint and run as hard as I can. It's futile I know, and I should really be saving all my strength for when he catches up with me.

I charge round another corner, but all I find are more rooms and more locked doors.

I am sure Evil-GG will be on my floor by now.

I keep going and round another bend.

More locked doors.

I keep on telling myself over and over that somewhere there's going to be a laundry chute that I can throw myself down. All hotels in the movies have them. It's got to be somewhere. He'll hear it and follow.

'Someone's a little heavy on their feet – should've gone to ballet classes.' Evil-GG's sing-song voice is shrill and darts through the air, curdling my heart. 'I've got a tutu you can borrow. Oh wait – too late.'

I turn another corner and crash through a set of fire doors and find that I have quite brilliantly run into a dead end. All I can see are more closed doors, more rooms and then a wall at the far end of the hallway. There's a large window that looks out on to the building next door, but that's it. This is as far as I can go.

'Hold that pose,' I hear Evil-GG call out and I realise he must have sensed me come to a stop. Whoever was running on the floor above me has stopped too, or more hopefully found an exit. I scan the hallway and then start trying the locked doors. It's completely futile because even with the best will in the world I'm not really going to last more than a second when Evil-GG comes for me. Even if I got a door open and then barricaded it he'd slash through it all in no time.

I look back and even though Evil-GG isn't here yet, I know he has only slowed down because he is just so cocky and in control.

I back up towards the window and as I do I spy a rolled up fire hose built into a recess of the wall. I glance at it, dismiss it as being utterly useless, then stop and rethink. It's amazing the thoughts that can suddenly spring into your head when you're being chased by an evil version of one of your friends, and before I know it I have smashed open the casing for the fire hose and start tying it round my waist. I've seen

269

this work in films and the reality I am in right now feels more like a film than anything, so what the hell. I tie the hose as tightly as I can and then brace myself.

'You can do this,' I say out loud. 'You can.'

'You *so* can't,' says Evil-GG as he pushes open the fire doors with the tips on his talons. When he sees me with the fire hose wrapped around me, he sniggers. 'Nice belt. Not sure it really goes with the rest of your look, though.' He laughs and takes a step forward.

I back away, hoping I can engage him in conversation, buying every valuable second I can.

'We could all just go home and forget this ever happened,' I tell him.

'Yes. Yes let's do that.' Evil-GG claps his hands. 'Yes, yes, yes! Spiffing idea.'

His irony is as sharp as his talons.

'Let's have a party first, get to know each other, swap numbers.'

'Let's do that. Why not?' I am barely keeping my voice steady.

'Actually, second thoughts, the only person we'll be inviting is your Moth. Because he's all we need.'

'So why are you down here chasing me?'

'Because I'm like that. I like to hunt. Usually it's for bargains in boutiques but this is fun too.'

I have to keep him talking, I just have to. 'What if I get the better of you?'

Evil-GG laughs and does a robotic voice. 'Does not compute. Reload information. No. Still does not compute.'

'I took your Moth down, so I'm going to take you down too.'

Evil-GG is revelling in what he thinks is my total stupidity. 'Honey, you couldn't take a picture down from a wall.'

'You are one big bitch,' I tell him.

'You noticed?' He laughs. 'Well for that you get a prize. You get these.' Evil-GG flashes his talons at their fully extended length. 'All to yourself.'

I can easily imagine them cutting into me and take a step back. I have no idea how long I've detained him but I've got one last chance at making this as hard as I can for him.

'Are your friends coming?' I ask for no particular reason other than using up time.

'They sent me on ahead. They knew I'd find my other self, because most of the time I'm horrendously predictable.'

'But they're all coming here?' I'm now fishing for information, trying to picture how Johnson and Billie will ever escape with the Moth. If they're going to do it, they'd better do it now. 'So what's it like in your world?' I ask. 'What sort of things do you guys get up to?' It's so lame but my brain is starting to wind down. I didn't realise I was so tired until now. It's like someone's flicked a switch and turned me to off. I've run out of conversation.

Evil-GG can sense something about me now. I must have given everything away because he has stiffened slightly.

'Oh, I see,' he says, metal glinting in his mouth. He wags a talon at me like a teacher telling a child off. 'You're trying to keep me talking. You've got a plan.'

'No.'

'Yeah.'

'No.'

'Now what would that plan entail? I wonder. Could it be you're diverting me from my true purpose? Ooh. D'you like

271

that? "True purpose." Must write that down. GG's true purpose. Yeah, that's catchy.' He turns serious in a heartbeat, snarling, nasty. 'I'm too fast,' he roars. 'They'll never get away. Never!'

He's about to come for me. He's coiling and he's angry that I've played him for a fool.

'You thought you could outsmart the great GG? Silly, silly girl.'

I tighten the hose one last time round my waist then look behind Evil-GG. 'Johnson!' I call.

Evil-GG spins and in the time it takes him to figure out that there is no Johnson and I have just conned him with the oldest trick in the book, I am already hurtling towards the window at the far end of the hallway.

I leap at the glass, curling forward and burying my face and head in my arms as best I can, hoping that the fire hose is long enough to reach the ground floor, and then I crash into the window.

And bounce straight back into the hallway.

I have no idea what the glass is made of, but from the way I bounced off it, I doubt a sledgehammer would make a dent in it. It must be triple-thick safety glass designed to stop idiots like me throwing themselves through it.

I land hard and feel the carpet burn my already raw skin as I skid to a halt.

Evil-GG has found my pathetic attempt at escape so hysterical that he has to bend over, he is laughing so much. He has tears in his eyes. 'My God. Oh man. I'm going to wet myself. Oh my God.'

So much for making it difficult for him. I get to my feet and quickly untie the hose. There's a brass metal attachment for aiming the water at the end of the hose and when I feel it in my hand I realise it has a weight and solidity to it.

Evil-GG leans back against the door of one of the rooms and giggles at me. 'Do it again! Go on. Pleeeeeeaaaasss-seeeee! Wait, let me get my phone out so I can video you.' He retracts his talons and slips his hand into the pocket of his dressing gown. He flips the phone open and clicks the camera on. 'Let me just focus. OK. Take two. Reva tries to escape from little GG. You ready?'

But when he looks up all he sees is the brass attachment flying straight at his head. I've hurled it as hard as I can and it hits him right in the throat as something finally goes my way. He immediately starts choking, unable to catch his breath.

'Film that!' I say in a pitiable attempt at being movie cool.

Evil-GG paws at his throat as he drops his phone and coughs and splutters. He sinks to the floor and bends over. He looks like he is dry-puking as he fights the damage his caved-in throat is doing to him.

I want to stay and watch him die, to make sure he's not going to recover and come after me, but I know I need to find the others and get us as far away as possible. I burst through the fire doors, leaving Evil-GG gagging for air and charge down the endless hallways until I find the arrow that points to the stairwell. I crash through more fire doors and find the stairs.

'Johnson! Billie! I got him!' My voice carries up and down the richly carpeted stairwell. 'Johnson? Billie?' I listen hard. 'I got the other GG!'

I don't know whether to go up or down, and decide that down would be best when I hear footsteps hurtling down the stairs, taking two at a time.

273

Johnson appears above me and my heart leaps so hard in my chest I swear it hits my ribs.

'I got him,' I say as Johnson sweeps me up into his arms and holds me tight again.

'You OK? Did he hurt you?'

'No. I got lucky.'

Johnson steps back, taking me in, checking me over, making extra sure. That warmth of feeling I felt earlier comes back as his protective instinct for me takes over.

'Where's Billie?' he asks.

'Getting the Moth, I hope.'

'You really beat him?' Johnson looks seriously impressed.

'I beat him,' I smile.

His eyes find my lips and I know this is it, this is the moment. I move closer to him.

'Johnson . . .' I say.

'Way ahead of you, Rev,' he replies and our mouths close towards each other.

'Is it safe?' Billie's voice echoes up the stairs.

No, I think, *don't interrupt now. Not when we're so close . . .*

But Johnson is already drawing away from me. 'Billie?' he calls down the stairs.

No! I scream inside my head.

'How'd you get down there?' Johnson yells out.

'Service lift.'

'There's a service lift?' I say to Johnson, with a certain amount of disbelief. 'How come I didn't see it?'

'What about the Moth?' Johnson calls.

'I thought you were getting him?' Billie calls back.

'I thought you were.'

274

Yet again the Moth has been left behind. What a plan.

'Wait,' says Billie, 'I'll go back up. You sure it's safe?'

Johnson looks to me and I try to nod but I don't really think anywhere is safe. 'We need to do this quickly,' I tell him.

Johnson calls down the stairway again. 'Be quick, Billie.'

Johnson looks at me and I know that yet again our moment has been snatched away. He seems to know it as well. 'One day,' he says to me and brushes the hair from my forehead. 'One day, Rev.'

He starts downstairs towards the lobby and I follow, feeling just that little bit deflated despite having saved our lives. It's crazy the way one feeling can be stronger than everything else. We're lurching from danger to danger, and yet the way I feel about Johnson keeps taking over. Something that has no tangible state at all, but when your heart tells you to feel something, there's absolutely nothing that will stand in the way of it. Not even an Evil-GG with his murderous nails.

GROUND FLOOR ZERO

It takes all of three minutes for Billie to collect the Moth, return to the lobby and collapse into my arms.

'We're still alive,' she breathes rather than speaks.

Johnson joins us and we do this spontaneous three-man hug in silence. Until the Moth tries to get in on the act by driving his wheelchair in between us all.

'You always forget me. What is it with you guys?' he says in his nasally tone.

'Sorry.' I move away from Johnson to let the Moth through and we stay in an awkward huddle for a long moment.

'The others are on their way,' I eventually tell them. 'The other usses.'

Billie looks exhausted, flat out on her feet. 'Really?'

'We have to hide out somewhere else,' I tell them.

But as we huddle, the Moth again sees Carrie lying on the lobby floor. He turns pale and his mouth dries.

'Carrie.' He sighs. 'Why would he do that?'

'Moth, we need to leave,' I tell him.

But he is already whirring towards her fallen body.

'Carrie?' he says, as if she's going to wake up and answer him.

Johnson heads over to him. 'We didn't know it was him, no one knew.'

'Carrie, get up.' The Moth has walked into one shock too many and he is losing it now. 'Carrie, I'm taking you home, remember. I promised you.'

Tears are gathering behind my eyes now. I glance at Billie and she looks as devastated as I do.

'I'm going to work it all out and we'll uh . . . We'll . . .' The Moth stops talking, then hunches over and I watch as his shoulders shake. He's crying silently into his chest.

Johnson stands behind him, respectfully letting the Moth run out of tears. Probably two minutes pass before the Moth gathers himself as best he can.

'I think she liked me,' he offers quietly. 'I think I had a chance with her.'

He takes one last look at Carrie and then wheels his chair round. The last time I saw that much despair in one person was in my mum when she eventually gave up waiting for my dad to come home. That moment she realised he was never coming home again.

'She liked you. A lot,' Johnson says.

'What about GG?' the Moth asks. 'Is he . . .?'

'Oh God,' I say quietly. I'd forgotten that Evil-GG must have been waiting in the kitchen for GG. He did what he had to do and then changed into GG's lush bathrobe before he brought out the pavlova.

'I'll go,' Johnson tells us, knowing that finding GG

isn't going to be pretty. 'Meet you at the entrance,' he says quietly.

Billie takes a moment to wipe her eyes. 'We're losing everyone, aren't we?' she says.

'No,' I tell her. 'That will not happen.'

'The others'll be on their way and we'll need more blankets to cover people up.' Billie touches her scarred face and winces. 'God that stings.'

More blankets, I think to myself. *I hope we don't need any more blankets. Ever.*

I step gingerly past Carrie on my way to the reception desk and start looking for keys to a store cupboard or even a room where I can find a blanket or sheet to cover her with. I accidentally knock one of the computer monitors behind the reception desk and it slips from sleep mode to operational and I realise it shows a series of collected images from a bank of CCTV monitors, all of them aimed outside the hotel. I scan them all just in case there are more of the other versions of us out there. But nothing moves. The city is dead, devoid of life.

I find a set of keys in a drawer that have a tag attached which has *Storeroom* written on it. There's a colour-coded plan of the hotel on the desk too, so I use it to try and find out where the storeroom might be located. As I do, I sense movement out of the corner of my eye. I turn to look at the CCTV images and although there's nothing there now, I'm sure something – or someone – just sped in and out of the camera shot. I look at the touchscreen and am trying to work out how to press rewind when Johnson walks back out into the lobby, carrying GG in his arms.

'Well look at me!' GG flutters his fingers at me.

I am staggered as GG clings on around Johnson's neck. He doesn't have a scratch on him.

'You won't believe what that beast did to me.'

'Can I put you down now?' asks Johnson.

'Give me another minute, I'm still very woozy.'

'What happened?' I am already heading towards GG and Johnson.

'He was so quick. And so rough,' says GG.

'Found him tied up and gagged,' Johnson tells her.

GG shudders. 'Poor GG suffered.'

'He didn't kill you though.'

'I don't like to boast, but he said he'd save the best till last.' GG buries his head in Johnson's shoulder and continues playing up to us. 'Being gorgeous is all that saved me.'

Johnson lets GG down out of his arms. 'I think I prefer the other one,' he says with a wry smile.

GG makes a big show of not being able to stand without staggering and sort of half shuffles, half flounces to a big leather armchair that sits under one of the huge paintings.

'Any chance of a gin and tonic?' asks GG, and I am so glad he's still with us that I forget what I was doing at the CCTV screen.

'Evil-GG was so vain he couldn't bring himself to kill you?' I ask.

'I know,' says GG. 'Can you imagine anyone being that self-obsessed?' He raises a knowing eyebrow and I bend to him and give him a big kiss on his forehead.

'It's out of this world,' I say, thinking it's quite a clever comment, all things considered. Billie and the Moth have joined us and we're ready to leave.

'We need to go,' says Johnson. 'Like right now. It's dark out and we might get lucky and not be seen.'

'What about the Ape?' I ask.

'Call him. We'll need a car.'

I fumble for my phone but as I do, one of the lifts just off from the lobby dings.

We freeze, listening to the lift doors open. The bank of lifts are out of view from where we are standing, but we are all here. Johnson, Billie, GG, the Moth and me. All present and correct. So unless the Ape has come back, there's only one person left for it to be.

The footsteps on the marble floor are laboured but still it only takes a few seconds for Evil-GG to appear in the lobby.

He isn't as cocky or all-powerful-looking as before, but his talons are out and he looks as dangerous as ever.

'Uh, Rev?' queries Billie. 'You said you got him.'

'Never look a window of opportunity in the mouth,' says Evil-GG, his voice deep and hoarse now. His throat is bruised and sore-looking, but with every step he takes towards us he seems to regain some of his swagger. 'Not sure I like the new voice though.'

'REV!?' shouts Billie, who clearly now thinks I'm the go-to girl in dealing with these creatures. But it's Johnson who acts first. He grabs the chair I threw at Carrie earlier and breaks the legs off it. They come off, leaving rough but sharp wooden points. He tosses one to me.

'The throat,' he whispers.

I nod.

Evil-GG tenses when he sees what we are planning to do.

'Think you're quick enough?' he asks in his new husky

280

voice. Evil-GG then waves his hand at me and, before I can move, his nails have shot from his fingers and are hurtling towards me. His other hand twists towards Johnson and he sends another set of nails straight towards him.

I drop to the floor and feel the whoosh of the nails soaring over my head.

Johnson does the same, but we quickly realise the nails are just a way of occupying us, because Evil-GG leaps with unbelievable speed straight at GG. He lands upright on his lap and, looming all over him, he stretches his fingers and more nails appear to replace the ones he fired at us.

'So gorgeous. So sorry,' says Evil-GG as he raises his hand and drives the talons straight at the helpless defence-less GG. But they don't reach because Billie has somehow roused herself and charged at Evil-GG, with what's left of the chair Johnson broke the legs from.

Evil-GG is knocked from his perch on GG's lap but twists gracefully in the air and lands on his feet. He giggles hoarsely and turns towards Billie. 'I'm loving what you're doing with your face. Those scars are divine. Want some more?' He leaps at her and she swings the chair with all of her might.

I'm already running for Evil-GG, with the leg of the chair gripped tightly. But he must possess some sixth sense, because without even turning around he raises his leg and catches me full in the stomach with his foot. It knocks the wind clean out of me and I slump to the floor, finding myself landing in Carrie's blood.

'Like I said, I'm the worst of the worst.' He chuckles.

Evil-GG swipes the chair from Billie's hands and then grabs her throat. He moves so fast I don't actually see what he has done. One second Billie has a chair in her hands and the next she is being lifted into the air by her neck.

Right about now the Ape should be arriving, I think.

Right about now, Ape!

That's what you do, Ape, you save the day!

But this time he doesn't come. My angel of violence just doesn't show.

Evil-GG brings Billie closer to him and he takes a moment to sniff her. He then giggles again.

'Ah poor Billie-clone.' With that, he gives a flick of his wrist and sends Billie flying through the reception area, where she crashes into a wall before slumping to the floor. As soon as she lands she starts having some sort of fit. It is ugly and violent and her body arches so high I'm scared she'll snap her spine. I go to her as Johnson snatches up the sharp talons that Evil-GG fired at him and, gripping one in each hand, calls to Evil-GG.

'Hey!'

Evil-GG turns to him and grins. His teeth are as sharp as his talons. 'Now I like that macho pose, Johnny Johnson. Let me get a photo. Say cheesey wheeze.' He leaps onto the wall and, with his talons digging in, he starts running horizontally along the flock wallpaper towards Johnson. 'Gravity's such a drag.' He grins.

Billie's fit leaves her as suddenly as it began but her eyes have turned black again, and worse, they have stayed black. But Evil-GG is homing in on Johnson, who readies himself, eyes zeroing in on Evil-GG's bruised neck.

Evil-GG leaps from the wall and is almost upon Johnson when he suddenly clutches his head in agony and crashes down onto the hard marble floor, letting out a high-pitched scream.

'Rev?' Other-Johnson's voice slams into my head.

I turn quickly and see a battered and bruised Other-Johnson, barely able to stand, in the doorway to the hotel. He is hunched over, holding his head.

'I've got his mind,' he pants, and then does something that makes him cry out in agony.

I have no idea what he's done but he collapses from the strain.

Evil-GG's body doesn't move. It lies there still and lifeless. I can't figure it out.

Johnson is as confused as I am until GG screams.

We turn and see Carrie – as in dead, battered Carrie – getting to her feet. Her eyes spring open and she laughs.

'Hi-de-hi.' She flutters her fingers and I realise Other-Johnson has grabbed Evil-GG's mind and thrown it straight into Carrie's body.

We watch her stumbling forward as Evil-GG tries to get used to Carrie's body. She/he frowns.

'What the hell?' Her/his eyes have settled on Evil-GG's body and this rocks her/him to a sudden halt. 'Are you kidding me?'

Carrie/Evil-GG takes a good long moment to try and take in what she/he is seeing. She/he looks down at her/his skinny wrists and then touches her/his bloodstained blonde hair.

'Mother always said I should've been born a girl.' She/he lurches towards us.

'No,' I say under my breath. 'No, there can't be another one.'

The Moth whirrs forward when he sees what he thinks is Carrie standing there. He shoots from despair to delight in a millisecond. 'Carrie!' He slams his wheelchair into full throttle and speeds towards her, when Johnson gets in his way.

'Whoa, Moth, wait.'

'Carrie!' I see true love in the Moth's eyes as he swerves past Johnson and barrels forward.

Carrie/Evil-GG looks at the Moth coming towards her/him and pulls the biggest, most disgusted face of all time. 'No. Now you stop right there. Oh, no. I'm sure you're really sweet but seriously, the wheels, the glasses, the acne.'

For the third time in my life, after Moth Two and Evil-GG, I try and inflict irreparable damage on another being. I grab the fallen chair and without hesitating I smash it into the back of Carrie/Evil GG's head, knocking her/him to their knees, whereupon I hit her/him again until she/he pitches forward into an unconscious heap. She/he falls still instantly, like someone's thrown a switch and turned her off.

The Moth slams on his brakes and stops dead, wide-eyed and frozen with shock. 'What the hell, Rev?'

'That isn't Carrie,' explains Johnson.

'Yeah, it is,' says the Moth, confusion obvious on his face.

'No,' I tell him. 'No.'

'You just killed her!'

'She's not dead,' I say. 'And it's not Carrie. You know it's not! You're in shock, but you saw Carrie earlier. Remember?'

'How can you hate someone that much?' he asks bewildered. 'Hitting her with a chair. Not once but twice.'

I look to Johnson for help and he gets in front of the Moth again. 'It was Evil-GG. He's inside her somehow.'

The Moth doesn't listen and just stares with absolute hatred at me. 'You bitch. You horrible, hateful bitch!'

GG tries to keep the Moth sane by explaining a complete insanity to him. 'Calm down, Moth. You see, what happened was the other me was getting pretty violent, then this other Johnson shows up, and he does some blacky-magicky mind thing and then Carrie is back on her feet. You listening? Mothy? You following this? So she's back up, but it's not her. No. It's not. It's him . . . Me. The other me. And he's shocked. He doesn't get it. Mothy, stay with me. Then he sees himself lying there and it's all just kind of very weird. Not something you want to particularly remember. It's his mind, but Carrie's body. Confusing, I know, but that's the way things are going right now. It's all just – well – it's not the way my days usually pan out. So anyway Rev whacks her, or is it him, with a chair and everything's all right again. Amen.'

The hotel lobby looks like the aftermath of a war zone. Carrie remains dead, but I'm presuming whatever might be left of her mind is now in Evil-GG's body, which is still sprawled on the floor. Evil-GG is hopefully trapped forever in Carrie's body, which lies close by. The Moth looks battered and bruised, but more mentally than physically, and I hope to God he's going to stay sane enough to read my dad's work and then get us home. Right now he's just whimpering as he tries to match what he's just seen with GG's less than clear explanation.

Other-Johnson is slumped in the doorway, but he's stirring as he gradually comes round. He gets to his hands and knees and starts coughing up that same black liquid we saw oozing from Moth Two on the tracks.

His voice enters my head. *'I had to play dead,'* he tells me even before I ask the question. *'Had to pretend till the Ape got tired of throwing me around.'*

Having him back lifts me and I climb to my feet and go to him.

285

'How badly did he hurt you?' I ask him.

'Scale of one to ten?'

I nod.

'Twenty.' He tries to laugh, but winces. I kneel down beside him and am about to put my arm around him when I remember that my Johnson is in the lobby too and because of what's happening between us I'm struggling once again to work out who means what to me.

'C'mon,' I whisper. 'I'll help you up.'

'I'm fine.'

'You don't look it.'

'Hey.' He taps my wrist. 'Aren't you going to ask?'

'Ask what?'

'Why I'm here.'

'OK,' I say. 'Why are you here?'

'I came back for you, Rev,' he whispers and reaches for my hand. I sneak a look at my Johnson; he's with Billie. She looks shattered and is smoking again. I hope he hasn't heard what Other-Johnson just said. I'm not sure I know how to respond right now.

Other-Johnson squeezes my hand tight. 'I'm crazy about you, Rev. Can't get you out of me.'

And just like that I can feel him rushing back inside me, pouring his feelings deep into me like I'm an empty vessel that needs all the love it can get. I've never been wanted so much. Thoughts about my dad abandoning me when I was so young swirl around me. I know now why I wanted to be with Kyle. I told him I had a huge gap in my life and he immediately said he would do his best to fill it. His crass attempt at profundity swept me off my feet. All along I've been a sitting duck to any boy with the right key.

286

'Where are the others?' Johnson calls over to us.

'We were about to leave,' I tell Other-Johnson.

'They won't find you here,' he assures me. 'I could, because of what I can do, but they sent GG on a train. He told them he'd bring the Moth back.'

GG comes over to us. 'I'm going to lock all the doors.' He turns to the Moth who is as pale as a ghost now. 'Want to give me a lift?'

I know GG is trying to draw the Moth away from all the carnage. Away from Carrie. He hops on the back of the wheelchair and leans past the Moth to steer the motorised wheelchair across the marble floor.

Johnson turns and I can feel him watching me gripping Other-Johnson's hand.

'Billie's out of it. We need to move her into a room or something,' he says and heads for the concierge's desk. There's a tall luggage trolley behind the desk that he pulls out and wheels towards the unconscious Billie.

'Rev?' he calls out, indicating he needs my help, but also that he wants me away from Other-Johnson.

I start to move, but Other-Johnson grips my hand tighter and all but pulls me back. 'I mean it,' he whispers. 'I'm lost to you.'

I try to ignore the violent flip my heart makes and ease my hand from his.

'How do I know?' I ask him silently. *'Maybe these feelings are the feelings you have for your Rev. You're just confused. I make you think of her.'*

'You make me think of you,' he tells me in no uncertain terms. *'I wish you didn't, but you do.'*

He doesn't take his eyes off me as I help to put Billie gently on the luggage trolley.

'We should get a key card, find a room and put her in it,' Johnson says, his eyes avoiding mine.

'Uh, hang on.' I head back behind the reception and glance at the CCTV screen. The only movement is GG and the Moth locking the rear entrance. They have found an electronically operated grille that slides slowly down. It should make me feel safe and reassured, but I'm not convinced. The hotel feels more like a prison now.

But as I see the grille coming down I remember that the Ape is still outside and we really can't lock him out with whatever else is out there. As soon as I think of him my phone vibrates. It's like he has a sixth sense, because when I answer the Ape's voice booms out, almost deafening me.

'I'm not coming back.'

'Ape!' I'm so relieved to hear his voice.

'EVER,' he shouts. 'NOT EVER.'

'Why are you shouting?'

'Why shouldn't I?'

'Where are you?'

'Like you care.'

'Course I do.'

'Didn't come after me.'

'Ape, I wanted to—'

'It's not Ape, it's Dazza.'

'Dazza, please.'

'I don't care that you all hate me.'

'We don't. You're a part of the gang.'

'Don't care. The gang's dead to me.'

'Well I care that you don't care,' I say, then regret it because it might confuse him. 'Come back.'

'Nope.'

'We're a team, you and me. Remember?'

'No we're not.'

'I need you. We got attacked, Carrie got . . . She didn't make it.'

The Ape falls silent.

'And she was attacked because she went out to find you. She was going to try and get you to come back. Because you're one of us, that was what she said. Her last thought was worrying about you.'

'You're only saying that.'

'I was on my way to get you as well. Because I'm the same. I care too.'

The Ape takes a few seconds to formulate a response. 'How much?'

I laugh to myself. 'This much.' I hold my hands apart. Not that he can see me do it.

But he takes this on board and I'm hoping I've made some headway.

'Billie was just stressed,' I tell him. 'And there's something not right about her. She's, I dunno, she's changing.' Saying it out loud seems to make it all the more real and I lose my way for a moment.

The Ape tightens up at the mention of Billie. I can hear it in his voice. 'I liked her.'

'I know.'

'We clicked.'

'You two, you were like a house on fire.' I know he's delusional to think he had a chance with Billie but I need to lure him back to the hotel. 'Ape, c'mon. Come back.'

'Thing is, Rev, I got some thoughts together. And you know what?'

'What?'

'I like it here. Even if I don't know where here is.'

I take a moment, imagining there's more. 'OK,' I say eventually.

'I'm staying.'

He trails off again. I wait. He doesn't speak again for a good thirty seconds. When he does, he lowers his voice and I wonder if he's hiding some feeling of upset. 'You lot can go back home. I'll be all right on my own.'

'You'd get bored. No one to beat up.'

'I'll get a boat, sail somewhere.'

'There's no one else anywhere. It's empty.'

'You've got something to go back to. I haven't.'

'You've got plenty.'

'Like what?'

I rack my brains, wishing I could think of something.

We both fall silent as Johnson comes over. 'You found a key card yet?' he asks me.

'It's the Ape,' I tell him.

'Dazza,' corrects the Ape.

'Dazza,' I repeat.

Johnson nods and takes the phone from me. 'We need you back here,' he says to the Ape before handing it back to me and looking for a room key.

'We're locking the hotel up so you need to come back now,' I tell the Ape.

Johnson finds a drawer with key cards scattered inside it. He grabs a handful and heads back to help Billie.

'Dazza? You still there? You don't want to be locked on the outside.'

'I'm on the outside even if I'm inside.' Which is a way

more insightful thought than I would ever give the Ape credit for. 'So name me one thing I should come back for,' he adds.

I rack my brains wondering how I can get through to his big thick brain. Then it hits me. 'For the fight,' I tell him eventually.

Again he falls silent. The moment expands and for a second I get scared that he's hung up. But then I hear him clear his throat.

'I'll get you home, Rev,' he says. 'But after that I'm staying here.'

My heart sinks. I really can't leave him here, not the Ape. I silently vow to find a way to persuade him before it's too late.

'That mean you're coming back to the hotel?'

'I guess.'

I breathe a huge sigh of relief. 'Good, because I know Carrie's dead but I really don't want anyone else to die.'

'Stick insect isn't dead.'

'Uh, yeah, she is. I told you, remember?'

'I just saw her.'

My eyes immediately go to Other-Johnson. He's obviously been listening in as he is back in my head in an instant.

'*Did she see him?*' he asks me.

'Did she see you?' I ask the Ape.

'Dunno.'

'*Did he speak to her?*'

'Did you talk to her?'

'I'm not talking to no one. Well. I'm talking now, to you, but right then I wasn't talking to anyone.'

'Where is she now?' I ask the Ape.

291

'Dunno.'

'Tell him to go really careful.'

'That's not the real Carrie, so listen, OK? *Listen.* You mustn't let her see you. And you can't talk to her and, please, don't go and pick a fight with her either.'

'He's got to be silent,' whispers Other-Johnson in my head. *'Totally silent.'*

'Silently as you can.' I lower my voice so much, I doubt the Ape can hear me.

'I got it. I'm not stupid.'

'Did I say you were?'

I wait for a response and when none comes I try again. 'Don't go anywhere near her.'

The phone call ends abruptly. I look at my phone and it just tells me how long I have been speaking for. I press redial but it goes straight to answerphone. The Ape's message is accompanied by 'Eye of the Tiger'. *'Yowza to the yowza. Leave your skinny words and the Dazman will pump you right back.'*

'Ape? Where did you go? Ape?' I say into the machine.

I hang up and stare at my phone, willing it to vibrate with a call from the Ape. I walk back towards the doorway that Other-Johnson is still slumped in.

'Are the others out there?' I ask him.

He shrugs. 'I can't tell.'

'Thought you could see into people?'

'I'm kind of struggling with that right now. Doing what I did to GG wiped me out.'

'You just talked to me in my head.'

'You're close.' He thinks for a second. 'And you're also you. We've got a . . . bond.'

'What about the other Rev? Your Rev? You have a bond with her, right?'

'I think you broke it.'

My phone vibrates and I immediately answer. 'Ape?'

'Told you, it's Dazza.'

'Where'd you go?'

'Had to stay quiet, like you said.'

'You see Carrie again?'

'Nah. But I saw me.'

'You?'

'Yeah.'

I look to the Other-Johnson and take in his battered body. 'Get here quick,' I tell the Ape.

The Ape ends the call and I go to the CCTV screens and study each one of them in turn. There's no sign of the Non-Ape or Carrie Two. GG and the Moth have closed a side entrance now. More metal grilles guard against entry. I briefly wonder if that's like putting out a big sign saying 'WE'RE IN HERE!' but it's done now and all we can do is wait this out.

Other-Johnson tries to get to his feet but he's too weak and sinks back down to the floor again.

'Will Billie do it?' I ask him. 'Bring my dad – or the other Rev's dad – back to life?'

'She'll do enough to get him jump-started,' he says. 'But it won't be enough to bring your – *or Rev's* – father back to full life. They still need the Moth to make that happen. They can get him fixed up properly back home. Billie'll be worn out from putting Lucas back together for a second time.'

'If they've found him.'

'Good point. Let's hope they haven't, considering what I did to him.'

I get a scary thought. 'Wouldn't that mean you can't go back with them?'

His eyes meet mine full on. 'Who said I was planning to?'

The searing intensity of his words make me take a metaphorical step back.

He can't stop looking at me and I can't stop looking at him.

'But you have to.'

'Why?' There's a daring look in his eye. 'Who says?'

I am lost for words. He's basically telling me he's going to cross a universe to be with me. At least I think he is.

Johnson returns and walks over to us. 'Billie's in room seven,' he says and bends to help get Other-Johnson to his feet. 'Seems like you could do with a rest too. Want me to show you to a room?'

'I'd be delighted.' Other-Johnson manages a smile at his double. Or is it Johnson's double? I can't figure it out any more.

'Word of warning.' Other-Johnson looks back at me. 'If you thought GG was bad, you haven't seen what Carrie can do. And the worst thing is, you won't even know she's done it till it's too late.'

'Does she hate me? Like in my world?'

Other-Johnson avoids my look and doesn't want to say, but that's an answer in itself. *That's great*, I think – *that's really just the icing on a miserable cake.*

I watch them pass the reception desk and it dawns on me that I really need to move Carrie and Evil-GG's bodies. But I don't know if I can bring myself to touch them. Blankets will have to do. The unconscious Evil-GG isn't really going to pose much of a threat now that he's trapped inside Carrie's brittle, bloodless body. She/he hasn't moved since I hit her/ him with the chair and I can only presume the body he's inside is completely dead now.

The thought doesn't fill me with much in the way of self-esteem. Battering someone who was already dead is the lowest of the low.

A movement on the CCTV screen grabs my attention. The Ape is lumbering towards the front of the hotel and I go quickly to meet him.

He walks in, more subdued than usual, but I need him at his best.

'We've got stuff to do. The others are out there and we need to make sure we're safe,' I say, trying to rally him.

'Let's get it done.' He winces and I wonder if his ribs still hurt.

'You OK?'

'You calling me a wuss?'

The Ape helps me close the last entrance grille and we stand together, watching it slowly lower to the floor.

'Fort Knox,' I say.

'What's that?'

'A big bank. Lots of gold.'

'I want to go there.'

The Moth and GG arrive back in the lobby after sealing every door and window they could find. GG is trailing two large duvets and he stops by his doppelganger before laying a duvet over him. The Moth wheels over towards Carrie's body and he almost can't bring himself to lay a duvet over her. GG joins him and attempts a prayer.

'Dear God, please take Carrie and make sure she eats something up there. Despite what she was like and how she sometimes came across as a total bitch, she was one of us, God, so take care of her.'

'That's not Carrie,' I say meekly. 'What I mean is, she's not in that body any more.'

'Oh, I'm hopeless. You're right. Moth, this way,' GG says and strides back to Evil-GG. He points emphatically. 'That's her.'

The bewildered Moth whirrs round to face Evil-GG's body. He looks ready to implode with bewilderment. 'But that's her.' He points back to Carrie's body. 'Isn't it?'

Even his brilliant brain is continuing its struggle to cope and he looks cruelly lost.

'Wait,' says GG weighing it up. 'Let's do eenie meenie.'

The Moth howls and GG is quick to try and placate him.

'Joking! *This* is definitely Carrie.' GG points to Evil-GG's body.

'Definitely?'

'Definitely.'

'OK.' The Moth tries to brace himself. 'That's her. Right. Got it.' He wipes his red-rimmed eyes as he gathers himself and adds to GG's earlier prayer. 'I liked her, God. I hope you like her too.'

I fight that now familiar swelling lump in my throat as GG stands beside the Moth's motorised wheelchair in a deeply respectful silence.

I check on the Ape to see if he's holding up but he's not even watching.

'Ape.' I nudge him quietly.

'Listen,' he says.

I fall silent, but can't hear anything.

'Another great thing about me is my hearing,' says the Ape.

I listen hard, but there's still nothing.

'What is it?' I ask.

GG and the Moth have stopped because they have now heard something too.

'He's outside,' whispers the Ape.

'Non-Ape?'

He nods.

And now I hear it. Lumbering footsteps passing right outside.

GG and the Moth don't move a hair as we stand stock-still, waiting for the Non-Ape to walk all the way past the front of the hotel.

One footstep after the other, plodding but thunderous. And then they stop, right outside the entrance grille.

Silence descends.

Then the grille is shaken.

GG can't help it and a sharp intake of breath squeaks out of him.

The grille immediately stops shaking.

The Ape clamps a giant sweaty paw over GG's mouth.

'Anyone?' the Non-Ape calls out, just like he did on the train.

No one says a word. No one breathes.

'Anyone?" he calls again.

The grille rattles and we can see it bowing inwards through the tall glass doors.

'Oh God,' the Moth whispers, but immediately gets the Ape's other meaty paw slapped down over his face. The Ape holds GG and the Moth like a plumber trying to block several leaks all at once.

We wait.

297

Stubby fingers slide under the grille.

The grille starts to lift.

It shouldn't do that, and certainly not this easily. The Non-Ape is powerful beyond belief.

The grille screeches in metallic protest but it's coming up whether it likes it or not.

'Move,' I mouth.

The Ape releases GG and the Moth and the only place I think we can reach in time is the concierge's desk. I point to it and GG tiptoes towards it, as light as a ballerina. The Ape tips the Moth back in his wheelchair so that only the rear wheels are touching the marble floor and he pushes him as quick as he dares. I want to go with them but then I remember the bodies under the blankets. I go for Carrie who isn't Carrie and start tugging her out of sight.

But the grille is rising too quickly and I can already see the lower half of the Non-Ape's body. A quick glance assures me that the others are now out of sight behind the concierge's desk. I'm caught, trapped between trying to move bodies or trying to run to safety.

I'm too late though. The screeching pierce of the grille stops and the Non-Ape is starting to hunker down to take a look inside the hotel.

There is nothing for it but to slide under the blanket with Carrie who really and truly isn't Carrie, and in so many ways now.

I pull the blanket over me as I stretch out along Carrie's body. My face presses close to hers and when I look I realise her dead eyes are staring straight back at me.

'Anyone?'

The Non-Ape could walk clean through the glass doors if he so desired. As easy as walking through air.

The only thing I have in my favour is that the Non-Ape might actually be stupider than my Ape. He may look at the blankets stretched out on the lobby floor and think that's pretty normal for a hotel.

He may even think the pools of blood are a feature.

'HEY!' His voice booms out.

I realise I am shaking now, trembling all over.

But then Carrie's eyes blink.

And I realise it's not me that's shaking, it's Evil-GG. He has heard the Non-Ape and he is trying to reanimate Carrie's desperately lifeless body.

He blinks again and I can feel myself moving, rising upwards.

'I heard someone,' the Non-Ape bellows.

I almost have a spasm. He's going to come in here!

Evil-GG blinks again. A smile turns up the corner of Carrie's lips. He's doing everything he can to move her body. I can feel the vibration through my own body. I push down as hard as I can on him.

The entrance doors are flung open as the grille is dropped behind the Non-Ape. He is coming into the lobby.

The marble floor soaks up the heavy impact of his giant feet. Evil-GG is doing his utmost to move Carrie's body and it's all I can do to keep him as still as I can. But he's getting stronger and any second now I won't be able to contain him.

The Non-Ape stops.

He must have seen the struggle I'm having with Evil-GG – there's no way he can't have.

I can hear his laboured breathing.

'Anyone?' His inability to think of something new to say

would be funny if I wasn't rising up underneath the blanket. Evil-GG is giving it everything he's got to try and get the Non-Ape's attention.

A little of me wonders how he thinks he's going to explain with any chance of success to the Non-Ape that's he's inside a girl's body now. I strain every silent sinew as I shove down hard again, pushing Evil-GG back down, using the whole of my body to keep him still.

The Non-Ape rings the bell on the reception desk. 'Got any rooms?' he laughs. No one I've ever met laughs at his jokes as much as the Non-Ape does.

Evil-GG is pushing as hard as he can against me. Carrie's body is weak and frail though and I hold him down as best as I can.

The reception bell rings again.

'I want a double room with a nice view.' He laughs again.

Evil-GG is reanimating Carrie with all he's got now and again I feel myself rising. I get cramp in my wrists as I struggle to hold him still. His/her mouth opens and closes – he's trying to talk, to call out.

I'm losing the battle. I can feel my strength dwindling and there's a creeping numbness in my hands. I'm going to be exposed . . .

The entrance doors crash open again, the screeching protesting whine of the grille attacks my ears and then it clangs down mightily – I realise the Non-Ape is leaving. I slump on top of Carrie's body, not caring if her blood and cold skin is touching me.

Within seconds the blanket is whipped off me and the Ape pulls me to my feet.

'Is he gone?' I ask stupidly.

300

'Yep. They didn't have any rooms available,' quips GG.

The Ape sees Evil-GG make Carrie's body twitch again.

'He was trying to throw me off, get the Non-Ape's attention,' I pant.

The Ape bends down and punches Carrie in the face. 'Won't be doing that again.'

Carrie's body stops twitching as we hear the Moth wail. 'For God's sakes! Stop hitting her! Why do you keep doing that? I know you didn't like her but that is just not fair!!'

TOP OF THE WORLD, MA

After finally moving Carrie and Evil-GG out of the lobby, washing the floor and double checking that all of the grilles were locked in place I go to check on Other-Johnson, who is propped up in a double bed. The first thing he does is ask me to kiss him.

'I can't,' I tell him.

'It's the only thing that kept me going. Thinking we could kiss again,' he says.

Lying there, bruised but still gorgeous, he tries to get into my mind and manipulate my limbs. But the beating from the Non-Ape and effort of moving Evil-GG's mind mean he's too weak.

'You should've gone back to your Billie,' I tell him. 'She could help you get better.'

'Mm . . .' he says and avoids my look.

I sense he's hiding something from me. 'Mm?' I ask him.

'She uh, she's not too happy with me.'

'You going to tell me why?'

'It's in the past.'

'It's not that far in the past, assuming your Ape wants to kill you because of what you did.'

'It was a misunderstanding. On Billie's part. Not mine.'

I wait for more.

'Do I have to give details?'

I nod. Other-Johnson searches for the right words.

'Rev and I – we were on a break.'

'How long have you been together?'

'A year or so.'

A whole year of Other-Johnson, I think. *Three hundred and sixty-five days of him. There can't be many better ways of spending your time.* Then I try and shake those thoughts because he'll be able to read them and I'll be completely lost to him all over again. But this time we'll be alone, in a hotel room, with a double bed.

'But you had a break during the year.'

'Yeah. Rev's a little hot-headed, got the worst temper in the world. Shortest fuse you ever saw.'

So she's not *that* like me. Which makes me a little happier.

'We had our first big fight and I went away to cool off.'

'With Billie.'

Other-Johnson hesitates. I can see him thinking, *Should I lie, or should I tell the truth?* He likes and respects me enough to go with the honest facts.

'Billie was there almost immediately. Offering comfort and understanding and doing all that Rev's-amazing-but-she-can-be-difficult stuff. I was a little down and we sort of . . .' Other-Johnson stops.

'You kissed.'

He nods and I feel the heat rising within me. Another Billie kissed him behind her best friend's back. It makes me

303

so angry I could scream. Didn't he see what she was doing? How she was manipulating him?

'The Ape really has a thing for Billie and when I tried to tell her the kiss was stupid and silly she got mad. Told him that I'd come on strong to her.'

Bitch, I think. I can see her scheming little mind thinking she can get Other-Johnson beaten up and she can then heal him while Rev Two gets forgotten in all the kerfuffle.

'I went to detention because Rev wasn't really talking to me and I wanted to explain to her about the kiss. Wasn't expecting to see the Ape there, but he couldn't do much to me in school, apart from tell me what he was going to do to me after school.'

'So you and your Rev are unresolved,' I state.

'That's the thing, I'm wondering if there is a me and my Rev any more.' He reaches out and holds on tightly to my hand. 'Not when there's someone like you.'

Again he invades me, but this time he doesn't need to use his powers. He gets inside me because I can't resist him. It's driving me crazy the way I'm lurching from one Johnson to the other.

'Know what would make me feel a lot better?' he says, his eyes alive with desire.

'I'm sure I can guess.'

'Lie down with me.'

'No.'

I don't know how I manage to squeeze that word out because I am desperate to snuggle up close to Other-Johnson. I want to feel his body reacting to mine again.

'I've got a boyfriend,' I tease him. 'I'm promised to someone else.'

304

'There is no one else,' he says. But it's not cocky or arrogant, it's just a simple straightforward truth.

I try to think of Johnson, my Johnson, the *real* Johnson, but I'm starting to lose sight of him again and with a huge effort I get to my feet. 'No,' I say. 'No.'

'Rev.'

'You've got a Rev,' I tell him, backing towards the door of the hotel room.

'You're different,' he says softly.

'Yeah, but you and her, you should be together.'

'Wait.' He looks at me again and I am powerless to stop him entering my head. *'I came here for you. I all but crawled on my hands and knees to find you.'*

'How can I be that different from her?' I ask him.

Other-Johnson's eyes soften as they gaze into me. He's lulling me again, compelling me, pulling me back to him. *But he's weak*, I think, and it's me who's actually going towards him. It's me who is letting myself draw closer and closer to him.

'In a million ways you are her and in one way you're not. The one way that counts.'

'Which is?' I whisper.

'You love me with all your heart.'

I am already by his bedside again and his hand reaches up and he trails a finger down the inside of my arm.

'Don't you?' His finger trails slowly back up my arm. 'I saw it all, Rev. Your heart is full of me.'

'And yours?' I say in a hushed voice.

'You really need to ask?'

His hand closes round my wrist and he pulls me gently towards him. I look at his mouth, his lips and I'm thinking, *I can't let this happen again.*

305

'We can't.'

'I didn't crawl here for any other reason.'

We're drawing closer and closer. 'And you're still hurt. Weak.'

Our faces are inches apart and I want his kiss. I need it. It'll be better than the first one and the one after will be even better than that. He's going to do things to me that I'll never come back from and even though I'm scared to death I know there's no stopping it.

'God, Rev,' he sighs.

'I know.'

Our lips are millimetres apart and his eyes find mine. The time for words is over.

There's a loud thump outside the bedroom door.

'Ouch! Sorry, people.' It's the Moth. 'Lost control of this stupid chair. Anyway, can I come in?'

My eyes flick to Other-Johnson's and he puts a finger to my lips.

'Rev?' The Moth raps on the door.

We wait in hushed silence. But the Moth isn't going away. He raps harder on the door.

'I finished the book, Rev! I know how to get us home!'

It's GG's idea to go to the roof. I wanted Other-Johnson to come with us – he did save us, and he feels like he's one of us now, but he gave me a gentle smile and told me he was still a little too bruised and battered. I promised I'd come back to his room as soon as I knew anything. But in that promise lies a horrible fear. If the Moth can get us home then Other-Johnson can't come with us, *with me*. I try and shove it to the back of my mind, as far away as possible because then maybe it'll somehow resolve itself. Yeah, that's some hope, Rev.

Midnight has arrived with alarming haste and GG has packed a supper for us. The rooftop is chilly, but he has brought enough blankets and duvets to keep an army warm.

The Moth didn't want to come up because he said he doesn't like heights, but we persuaded him. If we're going to hear news about the book, then at least we can do it in nice surroundings with food and alcohol. Billie is asleep in her room and we decided it was best to leave her there. I think it was me that made that pronouncement, and then tried to tell myself it was because she needed the rest. It had nothing whatsoever to do with not quite being able to confront her about the black eyes and the way she is changing. I don't want to believe it but I think she's been infected, or some genetic material from their Lucas has got into her bloodstream.

GG, wearing his clothes freshly laundered under his *WAR(M)* jacket, is setting up a midnight picnic beside the Moth. 'I've been thinking. How come there's static on the TV and radio but we can still get a phone signal?'

'I think, and I'm only guessing, but the signal came with us. It's trapped just like we are – it was taken as well. One of us must've been using our phone at the exact same time the light appeared.'

'That's a hundred lines for someone,' tuts GG.

Johnson opens a bottle of wine and fills five glasses. We pick at slices of brie and salami that GG found in the hotel kitchen. I try to swallow an olive even though I hate them, because Johnson says he loves them and I want him to think I'm just like him.

307

The moment I've just shared with Other-Johnson is still at the forefront of my mind, but being near my Johnson again means he's squeezing back into my thoughts too. It's like I'm two-timing the same person.

As we were riding the elevator to the top floor I caught him studying me in the mirrored interior.

'You're amazing,' he'd said, so quietly that at first I hadn't realised he was talking to me. When I did I immediately blushed. That's all he said. He hadn't even made a move towards me. Just one simple sentence, no huge romantic sentiments like the Other-Johnson, but it's everything.

GG has spread out the blankets and duvets and we are sitting on them while we stare out across London. Up here it's like we're kings of everything we survey. The city is all ours. Even the Moth has managed to counter his fear of heights.

'How did you even know you had that fear?' asks GG. 'You know, what with being sat down all the time.'

'I've been up high before.'

'Where?'

'Went in a glider once. Two-man. I was at the front while this man piloted it from the seat behind me.'

'A glider,' echoes GG wistfully. 'Would love to be in one right now.'

'I threw up in my lap,' admits the Moth, and it sets us off laughing. The wine helps loosen all the tensions. I feel Johnson's foot touching mine and quietly leave mine there. 'I was never asked back.'

I laugh some more, falling back and looking up at the sky as the moon rises high into the night. The stars twinkle and I plan to count them, but for no reason other than thinking that if I angle my head in a certain way Johnson will see my poised and profound profile and be unable to resist. The wine is wrapping my brain in a warm fuzzy feeling and while my foot touches Johnson's I feel totally relaxed.

'So you read it all,' says Johnson to the Moth finally.

'Every word. I did it for Carrie. I made her a promise which I can't keep now, but I said I'd find a way.' The Moth says this with an awkward sadness.

'Is that a person?' says the Ape, who is way too close to the edge of the roof, peering down into the darkness.

I rise up a little, but my movements are sluggish now, impaired by the wine.

'A person?' asks Johnson.

'Hang on . . . It's a lamp post,' says the Ape.

I silently curse him and look back at the Moth. 'So how do we get home?' I ask, getting everything back on track.

'Well,' replies the Moth, 'we need to go back, back to the classroom I mean.'

'Well that's good, isn't it? That we know what we have to do?' I say.

'Yeah. It should be,' he says, but there's no excitement in his voice.

'But?' Johnson's foot moves away from me and we lose our precious contact as he sits up.

'Well Rev's dad wrote the paper, OK? Which means he got back in order to do that. Where he went after he disappeared, I don't know. But there's a rule we need to obey. A simple straightforward rule. We have a forty-eight hour window from the point that we were first shifted, and we *have* to be exactly where we were when we were sent here. A fracture in time and space will open up and we'll be swept through it. But if we don't get back within the forty-eight hours then we don't go back. Ever. Or at least not unless we want to try what Rev's dad tried and get all burned up.'

'Forty-eight hours means we've still got time. Not loads, but enough,' Johnson responds.

'But we can't go back,' the Moth says.

'What d'you mean? We can't stay here!'

'Think about it, Johnson. How do we take Carrie back? She's in that other body. Dead. How do we explain that? Because time will not have passed in our world and Mr Allwell will walk back in after the fire alarm has been switched off and he might just notice there are now two GGs and no Carries.'

'I'll get the other Johnson to put her back into her own body,' I tell him.

'And then we'll have Evil GG reanimated and coming after us.' The Moth looks hopelessly troubled and I go to him and try my best for him.

'Then we have no choice. We'll have to leave her behind.'

'I'm not prepared to do that, Rev. I promised I'd get her home, she might be . . . gone, but I don't want to break my promise.' The Moth's words linger in the air for a good minute while we try to accept what he's saying.

Johnson is the first to break the silence. 'I don't have an answer to that, Moth, but what I don't understand is how come the other versions of us weren't at the school just after the flash? They were doing the same detention that we were. Shouldn't we have all shifted, or whatever, to the same spot?'

'I don't know,' says the Moth. 'Is it even important?'

'I've just got this feeling that more is going on than you'll ever find in that paper.'

'I own this city!' The Ape is still dangerously close to the edge of the roof as he gazes out across London. 'How many people can say that and it's actually true?'

No one is really listening to him.

'We'll go first thing in the morning,' says Johnson. 'We've got till four o'clock tomorrow afternoon. We'll go as soon as it's light, make sure we're not seen and GG can drive us back on the train. With any luck we'll do all that while the other usses are searching London for us. We have an advantage now – we know there's a time limit and we know what to do and we know where to be.'

The Moth looks hurt by this. I know he's still thinking about Carrie and how we'll have to leave her here.

GG senses it as well and tries to console him. 'What else can we do, Mothy? Seriously. We have no choice.'

'I own this city,' says the Ape again.

'We're trying to talk,' I snap.

'I need a leak.'

'C'mon, Moth, we can go home. You've got to see that, right?' says Johnson.

'As long as we get the timing right.'

I hear the Ape belch and laugh as he unzips his trousers. 'Look – it's raining.'

'But only if we make it to the classroom before the others,' warns the Moth. 'Because if they do somehow figure it out, or see us and chase us down, then we'll have to hold our ground against them.'

'We will,' says Johnson in a way that sends a thrill shooting through me. I tingle all over as the strength and determination in his words lift my spirits. He just keeps believing and I'm going to stand right alongside him. I can't not, no one can.

'Yeah,' I say, backing Johnson up. 'We'll get there and we'll hold it if we have to. We'll hold that classroom.'

GG claps his hands excitedly. 'This is our very own Braveheart moment.' He then adopts a thick Scottish brogue. 'We will hold! We will hold the classroom!'

My heart is racing. We have a plan, an escape route. *We can do this*, I think. I can feel a swell of optimism breaking out around us.

I glance over at the Ape and if there's anyone who can hold a classroom then it'll be him.

Though right now he is too busy peeing over the edge of the hotel.

'Ape!?'

'Shh, I'm trying to hit that man,' he laughs.

Everyone is on high alert when he says this.

'What man?' asks the Moth.

'Him down there.'

'What are ye talking aboot mon?' says GG, still doing his Scottish brogue.

GG, Johnson and I head quickly over to the rooftop. I don't get too close because I don't really want to see the Ape's penis as it sprays a torrent of urine down onto what is most definitely a person.

'That's not a man,' says GG.

'Looks like one, but it isn't,' says Johnson. 'It's a girl.'

The person is showered in the Ape's urine and when it looks up I know immediately who it is.

'It's Carrie,' says GG.

The Moth hears this and speeds over. 'Did you say it was Carrie?'

'Not our Carrie,' I say, turning to him.

But his forward gear sticks again and I realise he is coming right for the edge.

'Stupid thing!' The Moth hammers at the control.

'Moth!' I yell.

Johnson and GG turn and the Moth is now three metres from the edge and he can't get his wheelchair to stop.

'Back up! Back up!' I scream.

'I can't!' yells the Moth as he sails past me. I grab on to the back of his chair and dig my feet in.

'Grab him!' I shout to the others.

The Ape turns and finally catches on to what is happening. 'Hawkings?'

Johnson and GG grab the Moth and heave him out of the wheelchair while the wheels fight against my grip. As soon as they've pulled him clear I let the chair go and we watch as it powers straight over the edge of the roof. I hurry after it in the undying certainty that there's only one place that wheelchair can possibly land.

My gut instinct is totally correct because when I peer over the edge I see Carrie Two sniffing her hand and then recoiling as she realises she has just been urinated on from a great height. She shrieks and turns to look up but all she sees is a heavy motorised wheelchair blotting out the sky as it crashes down on top of her.

It seems that no matter how many different worlds there are, and how many hundreds of me and Carrie there might be, I will always, always do something to ruin her life.

The solidly built wheelchair, complete with its heavy battery attached, flattens her, smashing her otherworldly body into a mass of pulp and black oily blood. I can barely take it in as Johnson looks down at her misshapen outline lying hundreds of feet below us.

'You're lethal,' he says quietly.

'Earlier I was amazing.'

'That hasn't changed.'

The Ape zips up behind me and then ruffles my hair with his urine-smelling hand. 'Teamwork. I set them up, you flatten them.'

'That's divine intervention,' says GG. 'And oh so divine at that. Someone wants us to find our way home. I don't even need to tap my heels together.'

The Moth reaches for a glass of wine and takes a sip before raising his glass. 'Here's to you, Carrie.'

He is about to take another sip when the glass is knocked clean out of his hand by a thunderous shunt to the hotel.

'What was that?' GG's eyes widen.

I try and look over the edge but Johnson pulls me back. 'Careful.'

There's another great shunt and the hotel seems to move.

I stagger and then regain my balance.

'Earthquake?' asks Johnson.

I tread carefully back to the edge of the roof.

'Rev!'

'I need to see.'

I creep ever closer to the edge.

There's another tremor and this one sends me tripping towards the edge. I reach out, my arms flailing, and as my loss of balance drives me towards oblivion Johnson catches my ankle and drags me back. I land hard on the shale covering the roof, but at least I get a great view of what's down below us.

Standing with splattered Carrie Two at his feet is the Non-Ape.

A Non-Ape that is flooding with rage. He's finally found someone in this horribly empty world. But thanks to me she's smeared across the pavement before he can even say hello.

He lets out an almighty roar that can be heard all across London.

This cannot possibly be good news.

LONDON FALLING

The Non-Ape takes aim at the side of the hotel again and punches it.

The whole building shakes.

'He's trying to knock it down!' I scream. 'He's actually trying to knock a hotel down!'

GG grabs the Moth by the arms and starts dragging him backwards through the shale towards the door that leads off the rooftop. Which is when we feel the first major structural rumble as another of the Non-Ape's rage induced punches hit home.

Boom!

That's what it sounds like. A great big boom. It's quickly followed by another.

Boom!

This one is harder and the roof trembles like it's just been hit by a small earth tremor. The bottle of wine breaks and something called Pinot Noir spreads out, ruining our picnic blanket.

'He's lost it,' says Johnson, who reaches for my hand and

pulls me to my feet. He holds on tight as we make our way to the door.

'He's gone loco,' wails GG.

Boom!

The roof quakes again and knocks us clean off our feet.

'No one's that strong,' screams GG. 'No one!'

'He gets angry,' I tell him as I climb back to my feet.

'Very angry,' adds Johnson.

GG's face sags and he looks totally forlorn and desolate. 'We were beating them,' he says. 'We had them.'

Boom!

The Moth flails and skids across the tottering roof. GG grabs him again as another punch opens a huge rift in the roof. The Ape reaches the doorway to the roof first and kicks it open, almost taking it straight off its hinges. It was unlocked but he can't help himself.

Boom!

Johnson helps GG drag the Moth through the door, then takes my hand again and drags me inside.

Boom!

There are six steps to get the Moth down before we reach a fire door that leads to the top floor.

Boom!

The tremor shakes me off my feet again and I start to go over the banister when Johnson grabs me and hauls me back. Twice in twenty seconds he's saved me. The Ape reaches out to the wall as if he can somehow brace it and stop the hotel from shuddering under the impact. But the next punch rocks the hotel so much that flakes of cement and dust come loose and shower us.

We barely make it through the fire doors, trying to time our movements between impacts.

317

The Non-Ape is working his way steadily around the building, punching it over and over, his anger seeming to grow with every punch.

We carry the Moth down the next flight of stairs and reach the top-floor landing only to feel an almighty shudder ripple through the entire building.

'This is a five star hotel,' babbles GG. 'It should be holding.'

Boom!

'He's destroying an entire hotel!' The Moth turns pale with astonishment. 'Doesn't he realise it'll fall on him as well.'

'But it won't hurt him,' I say. 'I don't think anything can.'

Boom!

The punches are growing in strength and the last one sends all of us careering towards one wall. GG cracks his forehead and howls in agony.

With no one holding on to him, the Moth is forced to ride the next tremor alone and the shockwave sends him tumbling down the hallway. He slews to a stop outside one of the lifts. 'Down,' he says. 'We have to go down.'

'I'm not taking the lift,' says Johnson.

Boom!

We are thrown across the hall as the Moth pulls himself up to a near-sitting position, jabs out a hand and calls the lift. It's the same one we used to come up to the roof, so the doors open immediately for him.

'Moth, don't!' I call out. 'It's too dangerous.'

He glances back at us and a brief sadness flickers across his face. 'You can't carry me the whole way down those stairs.' He heaves himself into the lift.

'Moth!'

The doors close silently behind him.

Boom!

The elevator starts down.

GG clutches his aching forehead. 'This hotel is supposed to be luxury upon luxury!' he tries to joke as we ride the next tremor and are flung towards the stairwell at the far end of the hallway. We have forty flights to try and get down before the hotel collapses. The Non-Ape's punches are coming every five or so seconds and ugly cracks are starting to appear in the walls. His monumental strength is staggering.

Boom!

'See what happens when you don't make a reservation,' says GG, who is obviously going to go down quipping.

The Ape is leading the way towards the fire doors and kicks them open. Every now and then he glances back to make sure I'm close by.

Boom!

The hotel lurches again and we are thrown into a mass of tangled limbs as we flail along the landing. The Ape is first to his feet and he crashes through another set of fire doors and finds the stairs.

'Rev!' Other-Johnson enters my head.

'Can't you stop him?' I call telepathically to him as we clamber to our feet and start running down the stairs.

'It's the Ape,' he responds.

'No kidding.'

Boom!

Again the hotel lurches and we hang on to the banister as best we can while the floor literally shifts several feet to the left.

'Get in his head, swipe his brain, whatever it is you do.'

'Don't you think I'm trying?'

'So try harder!'

'But it's the Ape! He barely has a brain.'

Boom!

We hit the thirty-seventh floor and watch a crack appear down one wall and then run all along the landing. More cement crashes down and this time there are whole chunks of it.

'This is taking too long! We have to take the lift,' says Johnson.

'We can't,' I say. 'We'll get trapped.'

'We'll be trapped anyway.'

'Where's a parachute when you need one?' asks a breathless GG.

The Ape stands waiting for the next impact – even he is a little bewildered by the inhuman power of the Non-Ape.

'I could still take him,' he tells me. 'I could.'

Boom!

Part of the floor and stairwell slips away and crashes down onto the floor below.

'Stop him, Johnson!' I scream in my head at Other-Johnson.

'I'm trying!' he yells back.

My Johnson grabs my wrist and we head through another set of doors and back into a hallway lined with rooms. We trip and stagger towards the lift situated in the midpoint of the hallway.

'We've got to go quick,' he tells me.

'I don't want to die trapped in a lift,' I reply, fear obvious in my eyes.

'I don't want to die period,' says GG.

Boom!

The ceiling above us erupts into a mass of cracks and then starts to come apart. Johnson calls a lift as we watch the ceiling breaking up.

The Ape yanks me close to him and puts his great hairy arms around me, sheltering me as best he can.

'I got this.' And I hope to God he has.

Boom!

The ceiling gives way above us and GG screams, but Johnson is already pushing us into the opening doors of the lift. The Ape smothers me completely as chunks of hotel rain down on us.

'Yeah, I got this!' He barrels me into the lift a half-second before the entire ceiling collapses behind us.

The lift starts down without the doors closing and for a second I think that this is going to be OK – it's going fast, we've got a chance.

But it's moving far too fast and the truth is we're now in free-fall. The lift has been shaken from its mechanisms and whatever holds it up, and is now plummeting straight towards the ground.

Johnson looks both confused and shaken. He has made the first bad call of his entire life and he can't understand what's happening. This is not how it should end.

But GG is babbling behind me. 'They've got brakes,' he says. 'They have, these fancy lifts have got special brakes, they'll kick in, they will. They've got brakes. God? You listening? They've got special brakes. Do your magic!'

But if there is a God, he's obviously not listening right now, because if anything the lift seems to be gaining more speed and GG whimpers.

The Ape is still half wrapped around me and his bear-like arms seem intent on keeping me from harm as they tighten. 'I got this, I got this,' he says over and over. Quietly. Gently. Soothingly. It's the first time he has seemed afraid, or even aware of what is actually going on. He and Johnson are having a mutual epiphany, but at the wrong time and for all the wrong reasons.

'It'll slow down,' says Johnson.

'Yeah,' I say from under the Ape's smother.

The lights on the console have been damaged in the free-fall, so we have no way of knowing what floor we're at now, but it can't be long till we hit the ground floor at what feels like a thousand miles an hour. Suddenly a weird fact pops into my head. I think I read somewhere that just before the moment of impact you should jump up in the air and that when you land you'll be all right. You just need to time it right. It seems like such a stupid thing to try, and there's no way gravity and the G-forces are going to allow that anyway.

Boom!

We are rocked again and Other-Johnson's voice comes into my head. He is distressed but not for himself. *'I've got Billie.'* He tells me. *'We're getting out.'*

'The Moth?'

'Haven't seen him. But, Rev . . .'

'Yeah?'

'If not in this one, I'll find you in another world.'

These are the last words we share because the elevator hits and, despite the brakes kicking in like GG said they would, they don't do quite enough to avert the impact.

Boom!

Only this time, the boom is not a punch from the Non-Ape,

it's us hitting the ground floor hard and fast. The Ape does his best to protect me, but it's not enough. The last thing I see before everything goes black is Johnson crying out and clutching his head.

As I tumble headlong into unconsciousness I wonder how come my big violent angel didn't manage to save me this time.

LIFE LIVES

'How's your head?' a voice says.

    'I've still got a head?'

    'Just about.'

    'Anything else?'

    'Like?'

    'A body. Arms. Legs.'

    'Let me count. Yep. You've got all of them.'

    'Can't feel them.'

    'No?'

    'Nope.'

    'Wiggle your toes,' the voice instructs.

    'I've still got toes?'

    'If you've got legs, chances are you've still got toes.'

I try and wiggle my toes but feel nothing.

    'Well?' I ask.

    'Try again.'

I have another go.

    'Mmmm,' the voice says.

    'Mmmm? That doesn't sound good.'

'Again.'

'OK. But I don't think . . .'

There's clapping and another voice joins the first one. 'There they go, wiggle wiggle.'

'That you, GG?'

'Haven't got amnesia then?'

'What's that?'

'Ho ho ho. She can even make jokes.'

I'm not sure where I am, but I can sense that I'm moving, or being moved. At pace.

'My head hurts,' I say.

'We all hurt,' says the first voice.

'Johnson?'

'Hey you.'

'Stop!' a deep voice calls out. It's the Ape, I'm sure of it. I feel myself come to an abrupt halt.

'What is it?'

'It's the other me again,' he whispers now. But it's a bit late I think, shouting one second and then whispering the next. Typical Ape.

'Can you drive a taxi?' whispers GG to the Ape.

'If it's an automatic,' comes the reply.

'There's one over there, so fingers crossed.'

I imagine GG is pointing and then I feel myself being turned through one hundred and eighty degrees. My stomach lurches with the speed of it.

'Yes, that's an automatic! First lucky break in two days.'

'We need to get to King's Cross station,' says Johnson.

'No need, I'll drive us all the way home.'

'But what if we meet that other Ape again?'

The Ape's brain takes another age to formulate an answer. 'I can take him.'

'Let's stick to the King's Cross plan.'

'More trains,' says GG with undisguised glee.

'More trains,' agrees Johnson.

I try to open my eyes, but my head is so sore and everything seems to hurt so much that I can barely lift my eyelids without a blinding pain.

'The Moth?' I ask.

'Shhh,' says GG.

'Yeah, keep it down,' orders the Ape.

'Billie?'

'We think they got away. Her and the other me,' says Johnson.

I can taste cement in the back of my mouth. When I touch my arm it feels like dry dust is clinging to my skin, but I still can't open my eyes to check on how I am. I hear a car door open and I'm lifted from the trolley I'm on – it must be from the hotel, a luggage trolley – and placed gently along the back seat. The car slumps down at the front as someone – I'm assuming the Ape – gets in behind the wheel.

I hear the seats behind the driver's cubicle flip down and GG and Johnson take one each. One of them stretches a seatbelt around me.

'We can't go without Billie.'

The taxi starts up and pulls away.

'Wait, we have to get her! And the Moth!' *And Other-Johnson* I want to add, but I don't because I know Johnson wouldn't appreciate it. I also can't feel Other-Johnson in my mind and I start to fear the worst for him.

'You there?' I ask silently. *'Hey.'*

I wait, but nothing comes back.

'We're going to the school,' says Johnson.

'But Billie won't know we're doing that. She wasn't on the roof. Didn't hear the plan.'

'Rev . . .' says GG. But stops because he can't say what he wants to.

'What? What is it!?' I all but scream. But I already know.

I have the biggest migraine I have ever felt and when I finally open my eyes the moonlight is sharp enough to force me to squint. I look over at Johnson and GG. In the low interior car light Johnson has a pale dust-covered face and he is holding his arm awkwardly. GG is wiping his face free of the same dust and shaking it out of his hair. He looks remarkably unscathed but not unshaken.

'We looked for them,' Johnson says eventually. 'We did, I swear.' He won't meet my eyes.

I blink as rapidly as I dare considering it sends bolts of pain through my temples.

'How long have I been unconscious?'

'Couple of hours. But, Rev, listen—'

'You said you thought they got away? That's what you said, Johnson.'

Johnson looks extremely awkward now, shifts in his seat.

'What happened at the hotel?' I demand.

'There is no hotel,' says Johnson with a grim realism.

'It's rubble,' says GG quietly. 'Five star rubble. And it came crashing down on – on everyone.'

'We barely got out ourselves,' says Johnson quietly. 'I'm sorry, Rev.'

I close my eyes again. Tight.

'God, no.'

'I'm sorry.'

'Not Billie, please, not her.'

There are some things that are just too difficult to accept. The loss of my best friend alone is enough to break me, but coupled with the loss of Other-Johnson too, somehow it brings a numbness that leaves me without the capacity to think or feel. It floods through me, closing everything down before I can even cry one tear. I don't know how long it has been since we were in detention. My biggest worry up till then was being held behind after school, but it's like a lifetime of wonder and dread has been crammed into the short time since I slumped down in detention. I've reached a breaking point, but I've been fighting so hard for my life that I can't break. At least not now. *When I get home I'll do my crying*, I tell myself. *That's when I'll become the girl I used to be. I'll collapse into my mum's arms and weep for a year.*

The taxi rounds a bend and the Ape is actually driving sensibly for once because we don't go up on two wheels. The journey is so remarkably gentle that eventually the motion of the car lulls me back to sleep. But it's not a real sleep, it's just an escape because I'm scared and can't face what has happened, and if I close my eyes I'll not have to think about any of it. I can feel the monotonous drone of car tyre on tarmac, and sense the street lights rolling by. No one is speaking but I can hear Johnson and GG breathing and I wonder if they're as lost as I am. It's a stupid question, though. Of course they're lost – it's the first time ever in his life that GG has been silent.

'Rev? Hey. Rev.'

I stir and open my eyes. They don't hurt as much as they

did earlier and I realise we have stopped. Johnson is half crouched over me.

'What d'you want to eat?'

'Eat?'

'The Ape's going shopping.'

The Ape's giant head looms into the open taxi window and looks down at me. 'Chicken?'

'Uh, yeah. Chicken's good.'

'Crisps?'

'Sounds great.'

The Ape looks down at me and I feel his eyes settle on me. But this time it's like he's checking I'm all right. Not ogling me.

'Yeah, chicken, crisps and beer.' He says it like he's a doctor giving out a prescription. He then heads away with GG.

'I think he cares about you,' says Johnson. 'You're probably the only person he's ever liked.'

'Good. Because if I had to choose anyone to get us through this, it'd be the Ape every time,' I say.

Our eyes meet at this.

'And I'd also choose you,' I add quietly, as I reach up a hand and touch the bruise under his eye.

I remember what Other-Johnson told me. That I loved Johnson. Was he saying it because he thought I'd have to tell Johnson how I felt? Learning we weren't already together must have surprised him. But that's where they're so different. Other-Johnson is full on, out and out, I-would-die-and-kill-for-you, but this Johnson is much more guarded.

It's about three in the morning and he's wide awake, looking at me but not looking at me.

'What is it?' I ask him.

'Nothing. Just thinking.' He seems awkward though, not himself.

There's something behind his eyes, a deep sadness, but if I so much as attempt to explore it I know I'll fold into myself and maybe never come out again. When we get back, *if* we get back, I'm not sure how it will be between us. I know how it should be but what if it ends up that all we do is remind each other of the people we lost. Chances are we would never talk again.

The smell of chicken and cheese and onion crisps fills the cab. I sit up with some difficulty and Johnson is winding down a window as the Ape speaks with his mouth full.

'I could become a cabbie.'

'You wouldn't get any fares,' says GG who is riding up front with the Ape now, feeding him chicken as he drives.

'But I wouldn't need any. Because I wouldn't need money.'

'So why bother being a cabbie?'

'Cos I'm a good driver and I know my way round London.'

'You still haven't found King's Cross.'

'It's around. Somewhere.'

GG is tense and lets the Ape know it. 'The clock is ticking, c'mon, how hard can it be to find one of the biggest train stations in the country.'

I listen to them for a moment before turning to Johnson. He pulls a trilby onto his head.

'What d'you think?' he asks, modelling it. 'GG saw it in a shop window and went and got it for me.'

The trilby hat is not unlike the one Other-Johnson was wearing before his one-sided fight with the Non-Ape.

Johnson waits for my response and, as he does, all the memories of Other-Johnson come rushing back to me. They come so hard and so fast I double over and almost tip onto the floor of the cab.

'Rev!' Johnson grabs me.

'Don't feel too good,' I mumble, hoping Johnson will think it's my injuries that are doing this to me. He slips an arm round me and lifts me gently back onto the seat.

'I got you,' he says softly.

I glance up and he still has the trilby on his head and I want to yell at him to take it off. But all I manage is a groan, because it's now becoming so obvious that I can't rid myself of Other-Johnson no matter how much I want to. Every time I tell myself he's gone, the feeling comes back and knocks me off my feet.

Tears are streaming down my cheeks and, even though I promised myself I wouldn't cry, I'm suddenly opening up and bawling my eyes out. And it's not just about the Other-John-son, it's Billie and the Moth, Lucas and even Carrie. They're all wrapped up in my tears too. I can't believe I won't be seeing any of them again.

I only stop crying when, through some minor miracle, we finally reach King's Cross station. I'm probably a total mess with red eyes, a runny red nose and my pink dust-cov-ered hair stuck to my forehead. Johnson's still wearing the trilby and it takes a monumental effort not to grab it and throw it away.

The concourse of King's Cross looms before us as the Ape decides to mount the pavement and drive all the way onto it. The suburban line platforms are positioned at the far end of the vast open area and the Ape stops a few feet from the automatic ticket barriers.

'We'll need weapons,' says the Ape climbing from the cab. 'If we're going to hold the classroom.'

'It might not come to that,' says Johnson.

'It will,' responds the Ape simply.

There's a train at two of the platforms now and I'm presuming one was driven down by Evil-GG. We head towards it but Johnson stops us.

'Just say one of them is waiting on that train, like in a back-up plan, in case GG fails.'

'Evil-GG,' GG reminds him.

'Yeah, sorry, Evil-GG.'

We stop to take in the train standing silent and apparently empty, waiting for any sign of movement.

King's Cross is probably one of the busiest train stations in the world but when it's empty like this it means there are no hiding places, no disappearing into a crowd or losing yourself on one of twenty trains. It's a vulnerable open space.

'Let's stick with what we know,' GG declares and heads for the train he brought the Moth and Carrie to London in, all two carriages that are left of it. 'Let's imagine that they don't second-guess us and aren't actually hiding on this battered old thing.'

We're almost running to the train now, and every step makes my body feel like acute migraines are exploding all over my body.

'Wait, it's facing the wrong way,' says the Ape.

GG starts to explain to him that train engines are designed to pull or push, but gives up when he sees that the Ape isn't even listening. 'Just trust me, you big daft simian.'

The fact that GG is talking again, babbling like usual, is a positive sign that he's clawing his way back to his normal self, and I take a moment to marvel at how tough this effeminate fey boy really is. He jumps aboard and starts the train. We're all very aware of the noise it makes but, for now, nothing is stirring on Evil-GG's train.

The doors ping open and before we set off I take one last look along the empty concourse. A small part of me is hoping that Other-Johnson, Billie and the Moth are going to somehow arrive in the nick of time with Carrie miraculously reanimated. Maybe I could make friends with Another Billie and get her to come to the hotel and heal them all. *That's an idea*, I think. *We'll talk to her, she'll talk to Non-Ape and he'll dig his way through the rubble to them*. But as Johnson offers his hand to pull me onto the train carriage all I can see is a vast empty darkness, which leaves me feeling more hollow than ever.

'We looked as best we could,' he tells me, seeing me scanning the approaching dawn. 'But the Non-Ape was lurking and . . . Well . . .'

'But he told me, the other you that is, he told me that he had grabbed Billie and they were leaving.'

'I guess,' Johnson says with a regretful look, 'I guess they didn't make it.'

The thought hits me hard all over again and I have to take a few deep breaths.

'What do I tell Billie's dad?'

Johnson stops and looks like he hasn't got an answer for the first time since this began.

'I can't even tell him where she is.'

'We should go, Rev.'

'I know we should,' I tell him. 'But that doesn't mean I will. I can't go home without them. I can't do that. The Moth and Carrie, I don't even know where they live or who their parents are. Where would I start?'

Johnson laces his fingers with mine. 'What about your mum?' he asks quietly. 'What would staying here do to her?'

He gets me right where I wish he couldn't. And it hurts. I'm stuck in some no-man's-land now. Of course I have to go back, but how can I explain any of it to anyone?

'We'll think of something,' he tells me. 'I promise. It won't be adequate or remotely easy but we'll get home and somehow or other make some pathetic attempt at dealing with it and we'll do it together.'

GG sounds the train horn.

'We've got to go back, Rev.'

I know that Johnson is right but I know that not all of me will be going back. Half of me will be forever trapped here with Billie and Other-Johnson.

GG leans out of the driver's window and calls to us. 'All aboard!'

The sun breaks through the last of the night and starts its slow ascent. With luck and a huge amount of good fortune it'll be the last dawn we'll see in this world. But if things don't go our way, well, it'll also be the last dawn we see in this world, but for all the wrong reasons.

A SHORT DAY'S JOURNEY INTO NIGHTMARES

I wish we were in first class again as I sit with the Ape and Johnson at a small table with nowhere near enough leg and elbow room for all of us. The Ape is beside me and his bulk squashes me up against the window.

Johnson sits opposite me and has gently laid his foot on top of mine, a small, secret act that seems to bond us.

'How did we get out of the hotel?' I ask Johnson.

'We went down to the basement.'

'There was a basement?'

'Underground car park.'

'GG was right about the automatic brakes – they kicked in, but they sort of also ripped up the lift.'

'You went first,' says the Ape. 'Led the way.'

I look at him in confusion.

'By falling through the floor of the lift,' explains Johnson.

'There was a hole in the lift floor?' I have no recollection of that at all.

'Half of it fell away.'

'I thought the Ape was protecting me?'

'He was.'

'But I let go,' the Ape says without apology.

'Yeah, you sort of fell straight down to the car park,' says Johnson.

'Ouch,' I wince.

'We had to climb down after you.'

'But I slipped,' says the Ape.

'No,' I say, because I know what's coming.

'Afraid so, Rev.'

'He fell on you.' Johnson shudders. 'You were looking all right till then.'

As the train judders towards my home town I feel more and more bruises making themselves known to me. My teeth ache too, and I wonder if some of them have been loosened from the impact of the Ape landing on me.

I try to replay the past few days minute by minute. Things that I hadn't really questioned start to surface now that I have a moment's peace to think. The heat in the lorry and around the bus. The voice I heard that no one else seemed to hear. A voice that I swear was calling my name. If Rev Two's dad came through from the lorry, is it feasible to think that my dad was trying to come through on that bus? Is he lying burned to death inside and I never knew? It stands to reason that if one dad came through, then wouldn't another one do the same thing? Or am I just plucking irrelevant thoughts out of thin air because all that really matters is going home? There may well be answers here, but I don't think I'll ever find them.

The train starts to slow and it makes all three of us tense up. I can feel the Ape sit a little taller in his seat as he drains

336

the last of his lager. Johnson's foot slips away from mine as he moves towards the window, checking what's out there when our town comes into view.

Everything looks familiar, just like it always did. It's our world I think, and yet it's a million miles away. The bridge that passes over the bottom of a posh road my mum always dreamed of living in. The small park with the ultra-modern children's play area – all safety first and soft landings.

The train passes a silent hill of coal, one that has grass and weeds growing out of it. I used to wonder if all hills were made of coal. Modern flats loom as close as they dare to the rail track with satellite dishes attached and angled towards the sky.

'*Ding ding.*' GG's voice comes over the tannoy. But it isn't as high-pitched or thrilled as usual. 'We're home.'

The train glides slowly to a stop. Platform number one waits to welcome us.

We get up slowly as the doors open with a quiet hiss. Johnson steps onto the platform first, with me close behind.

But already there's movement on the opposite platform. Johnson sees it first.

'Whoa,' he says.

I turn and look to where his eyes are trained.

I haven't seen the man standing on the platform for twelve years and even though he looks older and has slightly receding hair it's definitely him.

My father.

He's wearing a dark, lightly pinstriped suit, like the one I saw in the window of the shop in the shopping arcade. He's also wearing shiny brogues and an open-necked white shirt. He's more handsome than I remember, but then again I was

337

only four back then and I'm not sure I could tell what hand-some was.

'He looks like you,' says Johnson quietly, knowing exactly who the man is.

I don't know what to say. Or do. I can only stare at the man.

He stares back at me and a smile breaks out along his lips.

'Oh, God,' I finally manage to squeeze out. 'Oh, God.'

The Ape's head leans past mine as he takes in my father. 'Who's the suit?'

'Time for school, children,' GG says as he walks down the platform towards us. He obviously hasn't noticed my dad yet. But when no one responds he looks past us and sees the man in the pinstripe suit. A sharp intake of breath follows.

'They did it, they made your dad all better,' says GG, scared. 'I mean that is him, yeah?'

I nod, too dry-mouthed to find words.

'So they'll know. The other Billie and you. They'll know where to go, where to be. That isn't going to be good.'

'Dad?' I whisper. Suddenly an impulse takes over me and I break into a run.

'Rev, no, wait!' Johnson calls after me, but I sidestep GG and start running along the length of the train.

'Rev!' GG is coming after me. 'Don't do this.'

But I don't care as I reach the end of the second carriage and then climb down onto the track. For some stupid, inbuilt reason I stop and make sure there isn't another train coming my way. Which of course there isn't, because the whole world has disappeared. But it gives GG time to catch up to me.

'You need to come with us. We've got to get to the class-room before the usses do,' he pleads.

'That's my dad.'

'You know it's not,' he tells me. 'You absolutely know that.'

I look back down the track and see that my father has turned to me. He's still smiling.

'Rev, you can't go to him.'

'But why's he there? Why's he waiting for me? He knew I was coming.' I look back to my dad who is now walking down the platform towards me. He's not in any hurry and the hard leather of his brogues echo around the station.

Johnson and the Ape catch up with us and Johnson offers me his hand. 'C'mon, climb back up here.'

'Smiley man's coming,' says the Ape.

'It's not your dad, Rev,' Johnson echoes GG.

'You don't know that,' I tell him.

I turn back and my handsome father is drawing level with us. The width of two railway lines is all that separates us. His smile remains fixed in place.

'He's one of them, not one of us,' says Johnson.

'Hey, smiley!' the Ape calls out to my father. 'Hey!'

But my dad doesn't react. Just carries on smiling.

Johnson again offers me his hand. 'C'mon, climb up.'

My father's smile is etching itself into my brain, so much so that it's all I can see. I know I should reach up for Johnson's hand, but this is someone I haven't seen in years, someone I thought I hated, but now that he's here, all I can do is go to him. *I love him*, I think. I love him like any daughter loves her dad. I don't even care that my shoulder is tingling, that my personal alarm bell is ringing. I have to go to him.

'Rev!' Johnson cries out.

I stumble and almost lose my footing but I reach the opposite platform and look up. 'Dad?'

He squats down and I can smell aftershave on him. It's the same brand he always wore and I can remember it so clearly. I used to love it when he'd come into my room and kiss me goodnight just after he'd got in from work. I'd fall asleep with that same scent on my pyjamas. By morning it had always worn off but I knew it'd be back later.

I just didn't think it would take over twelve years. But it's back now.

'It is you. Isn't it?' I say, almost afraid to ask.

My father reaches out and places a hand on my cheek. 'You shouldn't be here,' he tells me. His voice is not quite how I remember it. 'This isn't a good place.'

'I know, I'm leaving,' I tell him. 'We've got a plan – we read your paper, I mean the Moth did.'

Johnson is already clambering over the track to be with me.

'You need to be quick,' my dad tells me.

'I will.'

'Rev . . .' Johnson puts a protective hand on my shoulder.

'I should've left well alone. The things I've opened up.' My dad's smile stops as he takes a moment to struggle with something that is trapped deep inside of him.

'Come with us,' I say.

'Rev!' Johnson is starting to pull me away but I stand my ground.

'Listen to me, Rev.' My dad's eyes find mine. 'Listen carefully.'

340

I lean closer because my dad's voice is soft and the approaching wind is whisking it away.

'*Run!*' he says.

I open my eyes with a start. I'm still on the train. I look out of the window to see the familiar town station coming into view. Dawn is well and truly here and I realise that GG has driven very slowly, creeping along the track because the rising sun has probably revealed our progress. He wanted to make sure we weren't heard. Despite the flaky pretence, GG really does step up and get it together when he has to.

'Did you see my dad?' I ask Johnson feeling slightly dazed.

'Your dad? No.'

I try to calm a little. 'No?'

He tenses, checks around. 'You see someone, Rev?'

'I uh, I must've been dreaming.'

'You didn't look like you were asleep.'

'Oh.' I attempt to collect myself. The dream was so vivid that it has left me breathless. And I'm assuming it was a dream and not some sort of visitation from my dad, or something that happened on another plane of existence perhaps. He came to find me, and as soon as he does he tells me to run. That just doesn't seem to make sense. It had to be a dream. I sit up straighter and look at Johnson and the Ape, fixing them with an earnest look.

'Let's get going.'

'We'll have to go through town to get to the school,' says Johnson. He knows what this means.

'OK,' I say quietly. 'I guess it's game on.' But my attempt

341

at hero dialogue gets caught way back in my throat and my voice is barely a squeak.

The Ape gets to his feet and approaches the train doors, his great head scanning for danger as the train slows to a gentle stop. GG's voice comes over the tannoy again.

'This is it, the end of the line. Choo my choo.'

The alarm sounds and the doors open. The Ape looks out, scrutinising the area.

'Anyone out there?' Johnson asks him.

The Ape is about to shake his head when he stops. 'Yeah. There is,' he says.

'Who?' I clamber to my feet and quickly join him in the doorway. Maybe my dad is really here.

'Dunno,' says the Ape, 'but they're out there. Somewhere.'

I take in the world around us. A place I have never really bothered to pay too much attention to. It's just another town. Streets, houses, cars, shops. I must have walked a million steps east, west, north and south and not noticed any of it. Yet now it looks like a place I will never forget. There's something in the air, something that's got the Ape's innate sense for danger on high alert. My shoulders start tingling and I know that if we're going to get to the school we're going to have to fight our way there.

The other versions of myself and Billie are somewhere in the town, I know they are, I can feel it just like the Ape can feel it, and even though they don't know what we've got planned, when they see we made it this far, they'll want to know where their friends are. They'll demand answers, they'll come to conclusions, and they'll act.

I know Billie is a healer but Rev Two could be anything. She could be powerful beyond belief, and that power, whatever it is, will go into overdrive the second she realises that her beloved Johnson, whether they're on a break or not, is dead. She will come at us with all the blind rage and broken-hearted fury of any sixteen-year-old girl who has lost the boy of her dreams. She'll come at us exactly like I would, which could well make her the scariest of them all.

Johnson and the Ape step down onto the platform as GG joins us from the driver's cabin. He has a look of apprehension but is trying to keep it light. 'We've made it this far,' he says. But that's also all he says.

I join them and the Ape steps closer, at my side again and ready for anything. He glances at me. 'I'm still staying behind, Rev.'

'Let's just get there first,' I tell him.

We start walking, leaving the station platform without saying a word to one another. Johnson looks as brave and determined as ever. He's wearing the trilby and I'm relieved I can at last look at him and not double over with pain.

We walk in silence and even the Ape doesn't speak. He just grips his latest weapon a little tighter. It's a four pointer now.

Before we know it we're back in the town square. The last time we were here Another-Billie was trying to reanimate my – or is it Rev Two's – dad. But right now it's silent and empty.

Johnson stops to scan the area.

'Why are we stopping?' asks GG.

'I think this is as far as we go,' Johnson replies.

The tingling in my shoulders is back. 'They're here,' I say softly. 'Aren't they?'

'I don't see nothing,' says the Ape but he re-grips his weapon.

343

'Let's keep moving,' I tell them.

But Johnson is holding back as if he senses something we don't. 'Wait a sec.'

'I like Rev's plan better,' says GG looking all around.

Johnson takes a long moment before turning to me. 'We're going to have to be so clever.'

I can sense GG and the Ape tensing up beside me as they scan the empty square.

'Clever?' I ask.

'Just bear with me, OK? Whatever you do, don't give anything away.'

'Uh-oh.' GG's voice takes my attention as Rev Two and Another-Billie appear.

The Ape raises his weapon.

'My dad's not with them,' I say, hope rising within me. 'That must mean they didn't manage to revive him. They won't know about the classroom! We'll talk our way out of this, we will.'

'I've got an idea,' says Johnson to the Ape, eyeing Rev Two as she and Another-Billie stand silently waiting for us.

He waves, and I immediately understand what he's doing. He's trying to make them believe he's the other Johnson. 'Hey, Rev,' he says.

'Hey, Johnson,' Rev Two answers. She seems very calm, almost unnaturally so. 'Got yourself some new friends?' She says this in a way that makes us all know we are definitely not friends. 'Where are the others?' Rev Two asks as she and Another-Billie start towards us.

The Ape watches them warily.

'Wish me luck,' Johnson whispers to me as he goes to meet Rev Two and Another-Billie. 'I found us a way home.'

'I asked where the others were,' Rev Two says, a little more sharply than I ever would.

'They didn't make it. There was an accident. A hotel fell on them.'

'A hotel?' Another-Billie is quietly stunned.

'The Ape,' explains Johnson, hoping they are going to buy every word.

'So how come those three are still alive?' Rev Two looks at us with a sneer on her face.

'Forget them. We can go home,' Johnson tells Rev Two.

GG steps alongside me. 'What's he *doing*?' he hisses in my ear.

I can't answer – I'm too scared that I already know, that he's going to lead them away.

'Rev?' GG whispers louder. But I can't find a way to respond.

'Let's go get them,' says Another-Billie. 'I can bring them back.'

'The Moth read the pages,' says Johnson. 'We don't have the time. We need to get moving. To the supermarket. To where your dad came through.'

'He's still burned,' says Rev Two, who is openly staring at me now. It's obvious she hates the sight of me. 'Billie's been trying her best but we need to take him home.'

Even though he isn't my real dad, that simple statement hits hard. I want to meet him, to see him and talk to him. I don't care what we talk about, I just want to hear his voice again.

Rev Two seems so much more matter-of-fact than I am. She isn't choked any more, she isn't standing there wondering what her dad will look like or what he'll tell her. She cried earlier, but now he's lying somewhere else, on his own, abandoned, while she comes out to deal with us. I think I can see now why Other-Johnson likes – *liked* – me more. I have a bigger heart.

'It's the way home,' Johnson continues, his voice calm and with no hint of fear. 'We can do it, but we have to be quick. As in, we have to go now. Go get your dad, Rev.'

He's trying to keep them focused on anything but us. But I'm starting to panic now. I've lost one Johnson, I can't lose another. I'll die before that happens.

'Ape,' I whisper.

'Yeah?'

'Get ready.'

The Ape straightens and stands as tall as he ever has. His long black coat adds a whole new dimension of danger and foreboding to him.

'What about me?' whispers GG. 'I'm ready too, Rev.'

I glance at GG and the look on his face tells me that he means it.

'Hey!' I call out to Rev Two. 'We're the ones who are going home.'

Johnson turns to me and he can't believe it. 'What are you doing?'

'I can't let you do this, Johnson.'

'I'm saving you, Rev.'

'We go together or not at all,' I tell him.

'I'm doing this for you!' he replies. 'You'd never make it home otherwise.'

'Johnson, that's exactly where we're going. All of us.'

GG looks at me with a deep-furrowed frown. 'Who are you talking to?'

'Johnson,' I tell him, looking at him like he's mad.

'But, Rev. He hasn't said anything.'

'Thanks a million, GG,' Johnson sighs. And it's only then that I realise his lips haven't moved, and suddenly everything becomes horribly clear.

'I had to do it,' Other-Johnson's voice says, and now I know for sure that it's in my head. *'Had to make sure you'd be safe.'*

I don't understand what's happening. It feels like I've just been punched by the Non-Ape. *'But how is this even possible? You said you were leaving with Billie . . . Johnson was with us the whole time . . .'* I say silently to him as my mind tries to catch up with what's happening. I feel sick. *'Wait . . . You swapped? You're inside my Johnson?'*

'The hotel doors were locked, the security grilles wouldn't open in time.'

I stare at him.

'I couldn't not be with you, Rev.'

My heart snaps in two. It folds in on itself and keeps folding until it dies and takes me with it. Other-Johnson looks pleadingly to me, his blue eyes seemingly brighter than ever. But they're not his blue eyes, I tell myself, they're Johnson's, *my* Johnson from *my* world, and he's stolen them.

'I did it before I even realised what I was doing,' he tells me, desperate that I'll believe him.

'Rev?' GG has detected that something terrible is happening.

'It's not him,' I say quietly.

'It's not Johnson?' GG eyes widen.

Rev Two has grown tired of Other-Johnson staring at me. She might not be able to hear what we're saying by thought alone, but she's not stupid, she knows what Other-Johnson can do.

'What are you saying to her?' she asks Other-Johnson.

'Goodbye,' he lies.

'Why would you do that?' Her voice is brittle and harsh.

The one thing boys will never understand is how girls can sense so much about each other, and we don't even have to be mind-readers to know what we're all thinking. We can tap into the invisible and the unspoken as easily as opening a book. Especially when it involves the boy we love.

'Goodbye sounds good to me. There's only one Reva Marsalis,' she tells him. 'And I don't want you thinking any different.'

Other-Johnson's eyes find mine and his voice enters my head again. *'But I do, Rev, I do think different.'*

That's all it takes. Rev Two turns and leaps straight for me.

'Ape,' I say, straightening.

'Yeah?'

'It's your moment.'

I needn't have bothered to say anything because he was already lining Rev Two up and she runs smack into his powerful swing.

'I got this,' he cries, as his blow sends her toppling backwards. A normal person would either be dead or unconscious, but these are not normal people, so the best we can hope is that she is at least dazed enough to give us a fighting chance to escape.

'Run!' I tell GG and the Ape, and we set off across the square.

I SHOULD'VE LISTENED TO DAD

But we can't run fast enough.

Rev Two is beside herself with rage. She is the Amazon woman I always wanted to be, or maybe it's more the Amazonian I need to be right now. She gets up from the ground and leaps through the air, sailing over our heads to land face to face in front of me.

'One touch is enough.' She opens her right hand and it changes colour as if she's switching on some strange power. It's become ice-blue.

'Me first then.' And with that I hit her as hard as I can. My punch hits her flush on the jaw and she staggers back, surprised. But, just like Non-Lucas, she cracks her neck and shakes off the blow.

'One out of ten for effort,' she snarls.

She raises her hand and reaches for me when GG leaps on her arm and grabs it tightly between his arms.

'Not on your best day!' he yells at her.

But Rev Two is far too strong for GG. She grabs him by the hair with her left hand and yanks him off her arm, holding him a foot off the ground. Her right hand is now a throbbing sky blue and she makes as if to touch GG, when the Ape wades in and cracks her on the back of her head with his four pointer. She drops GG, and as she turns, the four pointer is rammed straight at her throat.

But she's too quick and sidesteps the Ape's lunge, bringing her knee up as his momentum pitches him forward and hitting him straight in his gut. He lets out a low groan, winded, doubling over, and Rev Two slams down on his back with a mighty blow from her elbow. The Ape doesn't go down, he never will, but he does trip forward, staggering, meaty hand gripped round his four pointer for balance.

'So wish it was the real one,' Rev Two says in delight. 'You unloved maggot.'

Rev Two yanks the Ape's head back, all but snapping his neck. GG goes again for her, this time just throwing his entire body at her to knock her off balance.

'Get off him!'

Rev Two loses her footing, and her grip on the Ape. He straightens, and for a fleeting second I can see that tears have sprung up in his eyes, not from fear, but from the pain. He whirls, angry now, and smashes Rev Two with the four pointer.

'Shouldn't have done that.'

He drives her back, lost to his violent rage. He is going all out and for a moment I know we're going to win, that he's going to win, because that is what the Ape does. He doesn't know it, but he's a born winner. Back she staggers, fending off blow after blow, but always on the retreat. She doesn't possess Non-Lucas's physicality, nor his hardening skin. The blows wind her, they hurt, and even though she's still faster and stronger than all of us put together, the Ape will not let that get in his way.

'Go!' he yells.

And we're right back at the fight he had with Non-Lucas. He's buying us time.

I look at GG and he says the words before I can even think them. 'We're not leaving him.' I nod and we are about to go and help the Ape when a voice stops us.

'I wouldn't.'

Another-Billie is already upon us, blocking our way. 'I'm way stronger than you.'

GG eyes her carefully, weighing her up. 'But you're no fighter. I mean look at your hands, soft as silk. So why don't we just talk instead.'

Another-Billie freezes. I turn to Johnson/Other-Johnson and despite GG's bravery I know he has done some mind thing on her, and frozen her like he froze me.

GG is full of himself though. 'See that, Rev? See? I am a force to be reckoned with!'

I step nonchalantly past her. 'Ape!' I yell. 'Let's go.'

The Ape turns from knocking Rev Two clear over a bench. 'It's Dazza.'

But in turning he takes his eye off Rev Two and she rises, decides that she isn't going to beat the Ape and instead springs over his head and lands in front of me.

Her eyes lock on to mine.

'He's mine. You got that? Johnson is mine.'

Her bare hand, glowing royal-blue now, is spearing for me before I can move.

'Rev!'

Other-Johnson launches himself at Rev Two. But he isn't

351

in his old body and he hasn't got the spring or the sinewy strength he usually has, which slows him down. Rev Two reacts without thought and swipes her glowing hand at him just as he reaches her.

Her skin touches his and Other-Johnson cries out and slumps hard to the ground with a loud smack. Rev Two looks down, unable to believe what she has done.

'Johnson?'

Johnson/Other-Johnson has turned a horrible grey, lifeless colour and for a moment she doesn't know whether to look at her hand or him.

'Johnson!' she screams.

But I'm screaming as well. 'Johnson!'

'God that hurts . . .' Other-Johnson's voice enters my head. It's weak and faint and he is already drifting away from me. *'I told you, I had to go back with you, just didn't quite get there . . . I'm so sorry.'*

His voice disappears from my head and I see him slump, lifeless, eyes open and staring. Not seeing, just staring . . .

'C'mon!' The Ape has grabbed me and drags me away.

'We're going!' GG urges.

I try to fight the Ape off, kicking and writhing in his grip. 'I'm not leaving him!'

'Billie!' Rev Two screams at Another-Billie. 'Help him!'

'Put me down, Ape! Put me down!' I yell.

'He's gone,' the Ape says.

'No! No, he hasn't. He hasn't gone.'

But I know it's true. There's no Other-Johnson in my head any more. There's no sense of him anywhere, not even the slightest residue. *Not both Johnsons.*

I stare at him lying on the ground, not moving, not breath-

352

ing. Another-Billie is touching him, trying to revive him, but she looks at the stricken Rev Two.

'It's not working!' she says, looking hopelessly at Rev Two.

Rev Two howls and I howl with her.

'We've got to go.' The Ape grips me tighter, drags me clean off my feet.

'NO!'

'Ape's right,' says GG.

I kick again, writhing and twisting as hard as I can. 'LET ME GO!'

'GG!' barks the Ape, who can barely hold me, I'm fighting so hard. I look up and GG is looking totally apologetic.

'Forgive me, Rev.'

GG's hand bunches and flies at me and, for a boy that everyone believes is a fairy and a lightweight, he packs a mean punch. I slide out of consciousness and a small part of me welcomes it, because I know the agony that is coming my way, and I don't think I'm going to be strong enough to cope.

I come round in the school classroom. It smells of the same stale mustiness that it did when we were stuck in here all of two days ago. My first instinct is to get out, to head for the town square.

The side of my mouth aches from where GG hit me and he's immediately apologetic.

'That was the worst thing I have ever ever done. Ever!' he says.

I ignore him and look for the door because there's no way I'm staying here. But the Ape is blocking the doorway.

'Please,' I say, finding my feet.

GG tries to calm me. 'Rev. You can't do anything.'

'Maybe I don't want to,' I cry. 'Maybe I don't even want to go home. I'll stay here because there's nothing, nothing for me. And you know that feeling, Ape, you do, you said you weren't going to go home. So let's not go home together.'

'Can't do that now.'

'Why not? I've got nothing.'

The Ape looks like he feels sorry for me but he won't budge. 'You still got us.'

'Please,' I beg him, 'I don't want to be anywhere. Here or there. D'you understand that?'

The Ape thinks for a moment then responds. 'No.'

I wail at him. 'You have no right to keep me here.'

'They'll kill you, Rev,' says GG.

'I'm dead anyway.' Tears are running down my cheeks now. 'I'm nothing. There's no reason for me to exist, don't you get that? Surely you can see that.'

The Ape studies me for another long moment and speaks so quietly I can bárely hear him. 'But you're my friend.'

It takes a while to register what he has just said and the weight of the emotion behind his words is like a force of nature.

'So there. That's your reason. That's why I'm going home with you,' he says equally quietly and then bows his head.

But it's too late for arguments because my tingling shoulders tell me that something is happening, That it's starting and now is not the time for turning back.

I don't have to see the white light to know it has filled the hallway outside.

HI MUM, I'M BACK

We're back in our seats. The three of us. Me, GG and the Ape. It happens in the blink of an eye and then the door opens and Mr Allwell walks back in. The fire alarm has stopped and everything is quiet again. Quiet and unbelievably normal.

'That was strange. There was this flash of heat and we thought for a second the school was on fire—' He stops when he realises only three of us are sitting there. 'Where'd the others go? And where's your uniform, Reva? '

I stare emptily at him, devoid of everything that went into making me. I'm sitting there in the present but in reality I'm history. I died with both of the Johnsons. I can't bear the agony of their loss and I'm already thinking that all it'll take is a handful of tablets and then I'm gone for good. I don't think I can handle one heartbreak, let alone two. And Billie . . . I can't even think about her, because I know I will just disintegrate completely.

'Hello?' Allwell tries to get our attention, but he'll never reach any of us.

* * *

Outside, the Ape wants to walk me home. GG does as well but he's looking shell-shocked as everything is starting to hit him hard and it sinks in that five of us didn't make it back.

'What do we tell people?' he asks.

'I dunno,' I say simply. 'Who would believe it?'

'Billie's dad,' he says. 'He'll want to know, he'll ask us . . . And the Moth and Lucas's parents and Carrie's and . . . and . . .' GG knows better than to bring up Johnson's name. 'Well, they'll want to know and I have no idea what to tell them.'

My head is spinning. I can barely think straight.

'I need to go home,' I tell them.

'I'll come with you,' says the Ape.

'No. I need some time. I'll call you. Both of you.'

'Promise?' asks GG, as if he can sense I'm planning on not calling anyone ever again.

'Yeah. Cross my heart.'

GG gives me a warm and tight hug and I can feel his quiet tears on my cheeks. 'I haven't even got a joke right now.'

He pulls away and I turn to the Ape. He is awkward and unsure. Intimacy doesn't sit well with him but I grab him and hug him regardless. 'You big Ape,' I whisper.

'It's Dazza,' he says, and slopes away.

GG goes with him and I watch until they have disappeared over the top of a rise.

I don't know how I get home. I am hunched over, huddling into myself and staring at the ground. I look at my feet, watching them carrying me along, but that's all I see. I can sense people around me, coming my way, then passing, but I don't look up. I'll never look up again in fact. I know it. I just won't ever, not ever, do anything but bow my head and try not to cry for the rest of my life.

When I open the door to my flat I can hear the bath taps running. Mum is home.

I check my look in the hall mirror but I don't see anyone I recognise. I've changed inside and out, done and felt things that no sixteen-year-old should ever have to deal with. *But I'm not dealing with them*, I remind myself. *I'm just not that strong.*

I take a seat and slip my phone out of my pocket. Unsurprisingly it's out of battery charge. I can't believe it's lasted this long. In fact, I don't even know when it died. I find the plug for it and out of habit switch it back on again.

It takes over a minute to boot up and in that minute a lifetime passes through me. I was meant to end up back here with at least one Johnson, that's how stories always pan out. The guy gets the girl or the girl gets the guy.

My phone powers on and immediately buzzes with a text. It's from Kyle. **Hey you coming? xx**

He is still at his parents' waiting for me. But he's going to spend the rest of his life waiting because there's no way I'm going round to see him.

The bathroom door opens and my mother emerges. She is wrapped in a towel and has pinned her hair up.

'Mum!' I shout and throw my arms around her.

'Steady,' she says, returning my hug. I feel her kiss the top of my head. 'You OK? What's happened?'

I don't respond. I just hold her as tightly as I can.

'Well it's good to see you, too.' She eases out of my hug and takes a long look at me.

'Have you been crying?'

'A little,' I say choking back my despair.

My mum remembers that the bath tap is still running and darts back into the bathroom. 'Wait there, don't want to flood the place.'

Another text comes through from Kyle. **Rev? I'm waiting!!**

I text back and relish it. **Go away.**

I lay my phone down and walk into the kitchen, crossing to the window and gazing out. Outside, there is a life and a world I just can't face. I hope that GG will understand and then he can spend the rest of his life explaining it to the Ape.

'Rev?' my mum calls, and I head back out into the cramped hallway.

'Yeah?'

My phone beeps with more texts but I ignore them.

'I know you're upset so how about you take your mind off things and help me with these.' My mum opens her hand and shows me her nails.

Only they aren't nails. They're talons.

I look up into my mum's eyes and she is as warm and friendly and scatty as she ever was.

'They need filing and you know how I come over all funny when I have to do it.'

I back away – it's an instinctive knee-jerk reaction.

'Rev?'

'No,' I say. 'No.'

My phone beeps again and I turn and grab it. There are a cluster of texts all sent hours ago, when I was in the other world, and because my phone was out of battery I didn't know they were in my inbox.

They're from Johnson.

Where r u?

I'm with Billie and Moth. We got out of the hotel.

We're going to try and get to the school.

Try and drive a car if I can.

Rev??

Pls tell me u r ok.

I am choked with amazement. They're still alive.

My non-mum advances on me.

'Rev, nails?'

'Uh, yeah, uh, can you give me a minute?'

My non-mum smiles and a familiar glint of metal sparkles in her mouth. 'You sure you're OK?'

I walk as casually as I can into my bedroom and make a phone call with what little charge the phone has taken.

The Ape picks up on the second ring.

'Missing me already?' he says.

'It's the wrong world,' I hiss. 'We're in theirs.'

'Whose world?'

'*Theirs*. The others. The ones we were fighting!' Doesn't he get anything?

'Didn't you notice?'

'Wait one.'

I listen in and hear a front door opening in the Ape's flat. There's a long, long silence which becomes excruciating.

Then the Ape finally comes back on the line. 'You're right. My front door was locked, this one's open.'

'What took you so long?'

'Nothing.' He sounds too innocent.

'What did you just do?'

'Didn't have to do anything. My mum's fast asleep drunk, just like always.' He's so matter-of-fact I almost

359

think I'm dreaming. 'But she's also turned some weird green colour.'

I have to take a moment to stay calm. 'We need to get GG and go back,' I tell him.

'Second that.'

'Johnson, *our* Johnson, and the others are still alive. He sent me texts when my phone was dead. They got out of the hotel.'

I turn round and to my shock my non-mum is standing there watching and listening with a growing sense of curiosity.

My eyes meet hers. 'Oh, and we, uh, we might need to fight our way back there,' I tell the Ape.

'Yowza.'

I hang up and turn to my non-mum. She is already sensing that something is different about me.

'Are those burn marks on your arms?'

'I've got to go out,' I tell her.

'Why didn't Billie make them better?' she asks.

My phone beeps with another text.

'Have you two fallen out?' my non-mum pushes.

'I left something back at the school,' I tell her, hoping she'll let me pass. I make to move, but she steps in my way and eyes me with a coldness my real mum would never possess.

'I hope it's your school uniform,' she says, taking in a green dress she never knew I owned.

I remain silent, thinking, *Let me pass, please, just let me pass*.

Non-mum's hand closes round my wrist. 'Reva. Talk to me.'

I still don't answer her. Instead I glance down at my phone and see that the text is from the Ape.

And it makes everything I'm planning seem possible.

I got this. ☺

ACKNOWLEDGEMENTS

Things aren't always achievable on your own, so my gratitude goes to my amazing editor Jane Griffiths for all the clever suggestions that worked an absolute treat. And the book wouldn't have been seen by anyone if it wasn't for Valerie Hoskins and Rebecca Watson doing the hard yards. Sara Moore gets name checked because she so got the book.

Ingrid Selberg, Elv Moody, Kathryn McKenna and Elisa Offord are now my favourite ever people in publishing.

My brother Tim said the book sounded like a good idea and my sister Mandy agreed.

Jenni and Niamh Stewart read an early draft and they agreed that it *was* indeed a good idea.

And for anyone who loves Johnson, a boy by the name of Tom Wiggins was the template.